Flirting in Cars

ALSO BY ALISA KWITNEY

Sex as a Second Language

On the Couch

Does She or Doesn't She?

The Dominant Blonde

Till the Fat Lady Sings

Flirting in Cars

A Novel

ALISA KWITNEY

WASHINGTON SQUARE PRESS

New York London Toronto Sydney

Washington Square Press
A Division of Simon & Schuster, Inc.
1230 Avenue of the Americas
New York, NY 10020

First Washington Square Press trade paperback edition August 2007

WASHINGTON SQUARE PRESS and colophon are registered
trademarks of Simon & Schuster, Inc.

For information about special discounts for bulk purchases,
please contact Simon & Schuster Special Sales at 1-800-456-6798
or business@simonandschuster.com.

Manufactured in the United States of America

10 9 8 7 6 5 4 3 2 1

Library of Congress Cataloging-in-Publication Data

Kwitney, Alisa, date.
  Flirting in cars / Alisa Kwitney. — 1st Atria Books hardcover ed.
     p. cm.
  1. Mothers and daughters—Fiction. 2. Relocation (Housing)—Fiction.
3. Cities and towns—Fiction. 4. New York (State)—Fiction. I. Title.

PS3611.W58F55 2007
813'.6—dc22   2007001665

ISBN-13: 978-0-7432-6897-4
ISBN-10:   0-7432-6897-0

This book is for Joanna Novins,
my critique partner, for emotional support,
practical advice, and the occasional brilliant insight

Part One

Zoë Goren

New York City: The Center of the Universe

There was a time when Texas decided to secede from the Union. Oh, nobody wants to talk about that now, not with the President going back to his ranch every chance he gets to remind us how gosh-darn-grassroots American he is. But for a brief moment in our nation's history, Texas put its cowboy boot down and, citing the "imbecility of the Federal government," decided to go its own way. Now, I have to differ with Texas's reasons for seceding (as strict interpreters of the Constitution, they didn't like radical left-wingers like Lincoln trying to rewrite the slavery laws) but I kind of like the precedent they set. Like many New Yorkers, I've been getting more than a little fed up with the federal government's barefaced lying and sneaky manipulations. So why not consider a divorce? Let's face it, we don't really feel like we have much in common with the rest of this country, anyhow. We don't even feel like we have much in common with the rest of the state. Hell, we're not all that sure about Staten Island, but as long as they don't get too obstreperous about where we put our garbage, they're invited to join.

New York Chronicle **Op-Ed**

One

Zoë woke up feeling chilled and groggy, like a bear roused too early from hibernation. She blinked myopically at the light filtering in through the shades, trying to figure out why she was suddenly conscious. Over the background hum of the air conditioner, she became aware of another noise, the clanking, hydraulic wheeze of a garbage truck from ten flights below. Rolling over, she fumbled for her glasses on the bedside table and peered at the clock. Seven fifty-five.

Zoë shuddered and turned off the air conditioner. This wasn't fair. It was Saturday and Maya had spent the night at a preteen slumber party, which meant that Zoë could sleep in as late as she wanted. And since the real estate agent had said he wanted to hold an open house on Sunday, this was probably her last moment of peace before everything imploded. Flopping back onto her stomach, Zoë closed her eyes, trying to imagine herself lying in a still, green valley.

The garbage truck made a series of piercing beeps, which sounded twice as loud without the air conditioner rumbling in the background. *Try to ignore it.*

Last night Zoë had been up till three AM finishing an article on the evolving relationship between the United States and the European Union. In every love affair, she'd written, there comes a point where the balance of power shifts, and the more dominant partner has to cede some control or risk a separation.

This had certainly been true for Zoë, whose last love affair had ended ten months earlier. Glad to have found an attractive man who could make intelligent dinner conversation, she'd put up with Jeremy's plaid shirts, his history professor beard, and his nocturnal blanket hogging. And then, on Halloween, Jeremy had told Zoë that he disapproved of Maya's Disney Cinderella costume, as it branded her as belonging to a vast, patriarchal conglomerate. In that moment, Zoë had realized that life was too short to spend with someone who not only lacked a sense of humor, but also a sense of the absurd. The first was regrettable, the second, unacceptable.

The only thing she missed now was the sex, which had been surprisingly good. No telling when good sex might reenter the picture, either, since Zoë was now intent on holding out for a man who understood the distinction between being politically savvy and being politically correct.

Don't think about that now. Sleep.

Down on Riverside Drive, the garbage truck made a noise halfway between a crunch and a crash, and then there was silence. Zoë groaned, trying to will herself back to drowsiness. No use. Behind her closed lids, the list of everything that remained to be done unscrolled itself. Clean the apartment, contact the bank, hire movers. You're supposed to leave some furniture in place so as not to look desperate, but what if she didn't find a buyer before the end of the month? Rubbing her eyes, Zoë gave a low, humorless laugh. Christ, it was ironic, worrying about not selling her home fast enough, when the thought of losing it still made her feel like rending her garments and throwing ashes on her head. She'd been so touched when she'd inherited this place ten years earlier from Mrs. Erenfeldt, an elderly widow who had rented her a room and then wound up becoming a kind of surrogate mother. Zoë was still amazed that the co-op board had agreed to let her keep the apartment, given her unreliable freelance income and lack of assets. Possibly the fact that she'd been six months pregnant and overcome with grief at the time of her interview had affected their decision.

Oh, God, maybe there was still some way to avoid giving up the place completely. Except that the current co-op board was intent on cracking down on subletters, large dogs, and therapists who worked from home.

Zoë dragged her fingers through her hair. I need to get up, she thought.

No, what she needed now was sleep. Zoë curled onto her left side and her stomach gave an empty gurgle. Or maybe she needed a cup of coffee and a bagel with cream cheese, and then sleep.

Zoë imagined someone bringing her the coffee; a man, telling her he thought she needed this. She could picture him sitting down next to her on the bed, the mattress dipping under his weight. Stroking the tangled hair away from her forehead with one big hand. Pulling the covers over her head, Zoë had the fantasy man place the coffee up on the side table and join her in the bed.

Just as she was about to get kissed, the doorbell rang.

* * *

Zoë opened her front door and automatically said, "Houdini isn't here." But the woman standing on her straw doormat wasn't Nora from 9C, searching for her escaped Siamese. This woman was slender and blond and elegant in her complicated blouse and boutique jeans, the perfect outfit for an autumn day that still felt like summer. She had accessorized with a sleek red sports stroller and a cherubically bald baby, who was wearing a miniature version of the mother's outfit. Zoë didn't recognize either of them at first glance, but since she met so many people, she wasn't sure if she was supposed to know who they were. She decided to play it safe. "Hello?"

"I'm here for the open house."

Zoë felt a stab of panic. *Was* there supposed to be an open house here this morning? No, the agent had definitely said Sunday. Today was her day to get things ready. "I'm sorry, but I think you have the wrong apartment."

The blond woman appeared unconvinced. "But this is sixteen D?"

"It is, but there's no open house today."

"Oh, crap. Did I get the date wrong?"

"I'm afraid so." Zoë kept standing behind her front door, acutely conscious of the fact that all she was wearing was an oversized Kiss My Bush T-shirt that barely reached the top of her thighs.

"This is so irritating." The blond woman flicked open her cell phone. "Hello, Ayelet? It's Susan. I'm standing here at Three Hundred Riverside Drive, and it seems that there is no open house today." Desperate for a cup of coffee, Zoë contemplated closing the door and walking away. The baby looked up at Zoë as if it knew what she was thinking.

"You're shitting me!" Susan caught Zoë's gaze and held up a finger, signaling that she needed another minute. The imperturbable infant continued to gaze at Zoë with what appeared to be rapt fascination. Well, fine, Zoë decided, no point in alienating a potential buyer. And even with financial assistance, paying tuition for the Mackinley School meant that money was going to be extremely tight. Her six-article contract with *Vanity Fair* might earn her some respect at Sebastian Junger's bar, but she still had to shop for the supermarket's daily specials.

"All right, fine, Ayelet, we'll talk later." Snapping her cell phone shut, Susan turned back to Zoë. "Listen, is there any way I can take a quick look around? I'm leaving for Paris tomorrow."

"Then why don't you make an appointment to see it when you get back?"

"You'll probably have sold it by then." Susan sounded forlorn.

Zoë sighed and thought about it for a moment. Was she really up to watching a stranger take a tour of her home? After all, she'd lived here for over a decade. This was the first place she hadn't shared with a roommate. All her memories of Maya as a newborn were bound up with these rooms, this light, this view. "I'm sure you'll find something else that suits you," she said, making up her mind.

"But I can already tell how much I'm going to love your place. Can't I take a quick peek? That's really all I need to decide whether or not I like something. I swear, I won't even take Maya out of her stroller."

Zoë glanced at the infant, who was chewing on her sleeve. "Oh, how funny. That's my daughter's name." Of course, Zoë thought, it wasn't really funny. It was deflating. Eight years earlier, the name "Maya" had sounded unusual to her ear, yet not unwieldy or pretentious. She'd liked the fact that it was easy to pronounce in at least ten different languages. Now it had become another ubiquitous urban fad, like Victorian mourning jewelry or thick, black, nerd-chic spectacles. Both of which Zoë happened to wear.

Oblivious to Zoë's reaction, Susan smiled as if she'd scored a point. "See? It's fate. You have to let us see your place."

Despite herself, Zoë found herself relenting. Chutzpah, she felt, was underrated as a virtue. Maya's school was forever stressing the importance of character traits such as empathy and diligence and industriousness, but she always warned her daughter that without a little boldness and misplaced confidence, these other qualities pretty much ensured a lifetime of grunt work.

"All right," she conceded. "A quick look."

"You're a doll," Susan said, steering her stroller through the foyer and into the living room, which still had *Le Monde* spread over the coffee table, along with a copy of the *Guardian* that the cat had begun to shred. Zoë resisted the urge to apologize for the untidiness.

"Oh, hey, that's interesting." Susan paused by the sectional sixties-style couch, looking up at Zoë's framed Shag print of Polyphemus and Grace.

Zoë walked over to the picture, which depicted a weeping Cyclops in a cave, looking yearningly at the mod brunette perched on his lap. "Isn't it funny? I picked it up in this quirky little art gallery in Melbourne. They call it hipster pop surrealism."

"Uh-huh. Actually, I was wondering whether this wall was structural, or if you could break through it to make an archway."

"Sorry, but I don't have the architectural blueprints handy."

"Oh, that's all right." Susan pointed to a thin crack in the ceiling. "Was there a leak there?"

"Nope, there were a lot of days like this." Zoë ran a hand through her wildly frizzing hair, always an accurate barometer of the humidity. "Listen, I'm going to get some clothes on while you take a quick look at the kitchen." She pitched it halfway between a statement and a suggestion, which turned out to be a little too subtle for her uninvited guest. Before Zoë had done up her brassiere, there was a knock on her bedroom door. "Is it okay if we take a look back here?"

"Let me just get my jeans on," Zoë said, wrestling with the zipper.

"Don't feel you have to get dressed on my account!"

"Gee, thanks," Zoë answered, tempted to open the door in her underwear. But the truth was, she felt exposed enough just inviting this upscale yummy mummy into her bedroom. Besides, when you were five-foot-eleven and built like one of Robert Crumb's zaftig hippie cartoons, the line between casual and slatternly was a fine one.

"Did you say come in?"

"No, but don't let that stop you." When she turned around, the woman was already wheeling her stroller into the room.

"Oh, gosh, what a great space. The last apartment we saw didn't even have a master bedroom. But I won't look outside of this neighborhood." The baby made a sound, and Susan rummaged around in her Prada diaper bag. "Here, Maya, chew on this. You know, my husband wanted to live on the East Side, but I said, no, the East Side is too chilly and tense and fashion-conscious."

Privately, Zoë thought that sounded like a good fit. Out loud, she said, "I've always loved the Upper West Side," then used the old reporter's trick of cutting herself off to signal that an interview was at an end. "Listen, I hate to rush you, but I have an appointment in about half an hour."

"Of course, I'll just peer out your window for one sec and then I'll go." Susan wheeled the stroller through Zoë's bedroom and pulled up the shade. "Wow, what an incredible view of the park." Susan looked back over her shoulder. "What's it like when the trees start changing color?"

"It's lovely," said Zoë, wondering how to speed things up. "Listen, the time . . ."

"Of course." Susan lowered the shade back down. "You do have such great light in here."

Zoë mumbled something in agreement. The truth was, she almost never remembered to look out her window. This was the place where she worked late and then fell asleep in exhaustion. Light was basically the enemy.

"And you're so close to the Museum of Natural History . . ." Susan paused, then turned from the window as if suddenly making up her mind about something. "Mind if I ask what's making you want to leave?"

Zoë paused, a little startled by the other woman's directness. She wasn't used to people asking *her* so many questions; usually, she was the one digging for information. "We're moving because of my daughter's school."

Susan frowned. "They have bad public schools in this district?"

"Actually, there are a couple of good ones."

"And does your daughter attend one?"

"No, until recently she's been going to West Side International."

Susan raised her perfectly arched eyebrows at the mention of the private school's name. "Oh, I've heard they have a good reputation. Did you have a bad experience there?"

Zoë hesitated, choosing her words with care. The truth was, West Side International was a fine school, particularly if you wanted your first-grader exposed to Russian and Chinese as well as Spanish, and felt that the accomplishments of the early Islamic era were not sufficiently stressed in the standard elementary curricula. It was the kind of school that attracted artistic and academic families, and for the four years Maya had been a student, Zoë had felt part of a warm, nurturing community of teachers and parents. Best of all, the school had a sliding scale of tuition, and made allowances for single parents with fluctuating incomes.

Which made it all the harder to accept how badly the school had failed her daughter.

"I don't mean to make you uncomfortable," said Susan, "but we've heard that if you don't start doing your research now, you can find your child stuck in a school that doesn't really address their needs."

Tell me about it, thought Zoë. "It's not that West Side International was a bad school. In fact Maya loved it there, but we felt she needed a different academic environment for the fourth grade."

Susan lifted her head, instantly alert. "Different how? More challenging? Less permissive? Are you moving to relocate to a different public school district?"

I should have gone with my first impulse and shut the door in her face, thought Zoë. Then an unpleasant thought occurred: Did *she* make people feel like this when she was interviewing them? Of course, she was far less confrontational in her approach, but still, she did ask intrusive questions. It was her job.

"Actually," Zoë said, "we're moving out of the city." As if in response, a car from ten flights below gave a loud honk of its horn.

"Westchester? I have a girlfriend who just moved to Pound Ridge."

"A bit farther than that. My daughter's just been accepted to a wonderful school in Dutchess County."

"Ah." Susan looked blank. "Where is that?"

"Two hours from the city."

"What's the name of the town?"

"Arcadia."

"I've never heard of it. So, let me get this straight. You're moving out of Manhattan just to send your daughter to school in a small town?"

Zoë sighed. Clearly the woman was concerned that there might be some new educational trend she should know about. "There's one school in particular," she said. "It's one of the best places in the country for students with dyslexia. And since I didn't realize that Maya required specialized teaching until the academic year had already started, it was the only place that had room for her right away."

"Oh," Susan said, visibly discomfited. "I see. Well, it sounds like you're doing the right thing. Personally, I could never leave the city. I'd just go insane out in the boondocks."

Zoë, who feared that very outcome, tried to look unfazed. "Well, in our case, it's just for a year, so that Maya can get caught up." The head of admissions had said a year at Mackinley would make a huge difference in Maya's reading and writing, and had shown Zoë the marked improvements that other students had made in just a few months. Of course, there were no guarantees, but Zoë figured that Maya's dyslexia was mild enough that all she needed was a little extra assistance to get her back on track.

Susan looked puzzled. "I don't want to shoot myself in the foot here, but why are you selling your apartment if you're only making a short-term move?"

Zoë felt herself flush. "Our co-op board is extremely strict about subletting." She left out the fact that the current president of the board was a high-powered lawyer who was slowly replacing all the old, middle-income tenants with other rich lawyers and Wall Street types.

It didn't matter, really. Some people said the real estate market was peaking, and that it was better to sell now and buy later.

"So, let me get this straight," Susan began, when something seemed to catch her eye. "Hey, um, what's all that smoke out there?"

Zoë looked out the window in the direction Susan was pointing. "Oh, that's the chimney of the apartment building next to us."

"Does it do that a lot?"

"Only when they're running the incinerator. As long as the smoke's white, it's okay, but when it burns black we call the local fire station and they send someone over to yell at the other building's super."

Susan looked appalled. "How long has this been going on?"

Zoë shrugged. "As long as I've lived here."

"It shouldn't be. You should complain to the Environmental Protection Agency. I mean, that stuff probably contains all kinds of toxins."

"That's the downside to living in the city, I guess."

"I'd just worry about an infant breathing that in all day. You know, at this stage, babies are very sensitive to chemicals." At that moment, the baby began to fuss, kicking her soft legs and squirming against her restraints. "Hush, honey, we're going to go right now."

The baby's face contorted, and she began to cry.

"Listen," Zoë said, "if you have any more questions . . ."

"Oh, no, I've taken up enough of your time." There was a definite chill in her voice.

Zoë followed them out of her bedroom. She felt like saying "That smoke was not the cause of my daughter's dyslexia," but she restrained herself. After all, she'd been in this woman's shoes once. When you had an infant, the weight of all that new responsibility gave you the mistaken impression that every single choice you made had a profound impact. So you fretted over the mobile you hung over the crib, the television shows you did or didn't turn on, the bedtime stories you read aloud each night, the organic foods you prepared. You deluded yourself that if you did everything correctly, made the best choices, timed it so you hit each developmental phase just right, then your baby would rise to her fullest potential.

At this stage of the game, nobody wanted to accept that so much of your child's destiny remained beyond your control.

The other woman's Maya was red-faced and screaming now, jerking her knees up to her belly. Zoë opened the front door for them. "You might just try taking her out of there," she said.

"Thank you, I think I know how to handle my child."

Just throw up your hands and back away, Zoë instructed herself as she went into the kitchen to help herself to some long overdue coffee. Claudius, her massive Maine coon cat, was curled up around the warm pot.

"Come on, fatso, move it over." Claudius blinked his green eyes at her, his pupils narrowing to vertical slits in the sunlight. Zoë scratched him under his chin and then counted out scoops of ground roast, trying to ignore the baby's hiccuping sobs. God, these walls were thin. Through the back door, Zoë could hear the woman yelling at someone, presumably on her cell phone. "No, absolutely not. I looked out the window and saw a chimney belching smoke."

Zoë took the milk out of the refrigerator, wishing that both the elevator and the coffee machine would hurry up. Even though she already had a pretty good idea of what Susan thought of her apartment, she had no desire to hear it spelled out.

"Yes, there was good light and a lot of space, but the place is basically a wreck. It would need at least six months' work to be even close to livable."

Why was the woman speaking so loudly? Did she *want* Zoë to hear what she was saying? A sudden, unpleasant thought occurred: Was she as audible to people in the hall as they were to her?

In the back of her mind, she'd always been dimly aware of the acoustics of her place, but still, there were times she'd forgotten to be quiet. Like the other week, when she'd had a screaming match over the phone with her mother. And that weekend last spring, when she and Jeremy had found themselves alone in the house and had gone a little wild with the chocolate syrup. How was it that she'd never let herself realize how exposed she was?

Outside in the hall, Susan had not finished complaining. "And I'm also sure there was some kind of a leak in the—oh, crud. I forgot Maya's diaper bag in there."

Zoë went back to her bedroom, retrieved the bag, and handed it out the door just as Susan rang her bell.

"Oh! Aren't you a mind reader," Susan said, overdoing the charm a bit. "I was just going to ask you for that."

Zoë smiled thinly as she shut the door. These were the mental accommodations you make in order to live in the city, she thought. A little selective deafness in the kitchen, a touch of polite amnesia in the elevator, the pretense that the people living next to you and above you and beneath you aren't privy to your secrets. Without at least the illusion of privacy, how could hundreds of strangers co-exist stacked one on top of the other?

That was one of the side effects of leaving a place: you got to see it from a different perspective.

Two

*O*kay," said Mack, using his most reasonable, patient, first-responder voice. "Let's slow down and figure this out." He put his palms out, as if he were approaching a belligerent drunk at the scene of an accident. Jessica said, "Fuck you," and threw another egg at his head. It cracked on his bare chest; Jess had always been a lousy pitcher, even in high school.

"Come on, Jess," he said, looking at his girlfriend's flushed, tear-streaked face. "What's this all about?" He gestured at the mess of flour and egg on the kitchen counter. "You want to make me pancakes, go ahead. I'm not stopping you."

She shook her head, looking exasperated. "Jesus, Mack, even you can't be that stupid."

"Are you kidding? Of course I can." And he must have been stupid, because he couldn't get what had set Jess off. He'd let it slip that today was his thirty-first birthday, and she'd said she'd make him pancakes. He'd said he wasn't really that hungry yet, and then she'd gone off on a tear about why hadn't he said anything, she felt so bad she hadn't bought him a gift like a sweater or a watch, and then she'd gotten upset because she had to work tonight. And he'd said that was okay with him, he didn't need a sweater, his old watch worked fine, and he figured birthdays were for kids.

That was when Jess had thrown the egg at him.

"Jessica," he said, grabbing a kitchen towel and wiping the egg off his chest, "just tell me what it is I've done wrong."

She looked at him as if she'd just discovered he'd been hiding an extra head. "What the hell am I to you? A pal? Someone to hang out with? Someone to fuck?"

Going by the tone of her voice, the correct answer was no, but Mack couldn't for the life of him understand why. What was better than an old pal to hang out with, unless it was a pal you wanted to fuck? "You're more than that," he offered.

"Am I? Do you love me? Can you honestly say that you love me?"

"Sure, I do," said Mack, meaning it.

Jess ran her hands over her face. "Oh, please. Admit it. I'm just convenient." She took a deep breath and lifted her head, and Mack was struck again by how pretty she was. Unlike him, she looked almost exactly the same as when they'd graduated Amimi High fourteen years earlier. It wasn't just that she was still slender and blond, it was something in her face that was still girlish, something expectant and hungry. He was damn lucky to have caught her right after her divorce from Jed Miller, before someone else snatched her up.

"I do love you," he said, stepping in closer, putting his hand on her shoulder.

She looked up at him, blue eyes brimming with more tears. "But you never say it."

Mack shrugged. "I'm a guy." He smiled, trying to make a joke of it.

"Okay, fine, but you don't act like you love me. You don't tell me it's your birthday. You don't want me to give you anything."

"I don't need anything."

"What, are you joking? You don't have anything in your closet except jeans and black T-shirts. You own exactly one pair of hiking boots that look like they belonged to your grandfather. And I know for a fact that the one sheet you own did belong to your grandmother, because it has these seventies-style pink flowers on it. Jesus Christ, Mack, you don't even own a CD player."

Mack shrugged, which made his jeans slip down past his hip bones: without the structure of army life, he'd been losing weight again. "I don't care about any of that. I have all the really important stuff." He had his own apartment over his sister's horse barn. He had a secondhand '95 black Ford pickup truck as reliable as a bloodhound. He had a job in town as a driving instructor, which didn't pay much, but it also didn't take up too much time. He had his part-time work as a volunteer firefighter and EMT, which made him feel like he wasn't just taking up space. He had all his limbs. He had Jess.

Out loud, he said, "I have you."

"You have me. That sounds good, but what does it really mean? We never make plans to go anywhere. You call me when I'm about to get off work, like it's only just occurred to you that you might want to see me. You never ask me anything about anything that's happened to me since I graduated high school, and you never want to know about what I want in the future."

"Aw, Jess," he said, and tried to put his arms around her. She batted his hands away.

"Oh, no, no, no. I am not going to fall for that. For three months I've taken whatever you've been willing to give, but that's my limit. It can't just be hanging out and sex." Jess looked up at him, her eyes bright but clear, as if she'd cried herself out. "I want to know if you see a future for us." Shit, thought Mack, how had they gotten into this?

He and Jess had started seeing each other in May, after running into each other at the Stewart's shop a few times. He'd noticed her right away, even standing behind the counter, wearing the convenience store uniform, a shapeless maroon polyester shirt and matching baseball cap. He read her name off her shirt, pretending he remembered it. She told him she'd moved back home recently, and that she'd gotten divorced. He started buying more milk and ice cream when he was gassing up the truck. Like him, Jess was having trouble figuring out what to do at night. Everyone in their old crowd was married and had kids and farms and struggling businesses to keep them busy. He hadn't known Jess that well in high school—she'd been in the band, and he'd spent all his spare time working in Mickey's auto repair shop—but it turned out she'd had a crush. On their first date, he got diarrhea of the mouth and started telling her all about the army, how he joined to get advanced mechanical training, but had somehow gotten placed in the infantry, which turned out all right, because he was good at being a soldier, not that it took a lot in those days to be considered good. God, he'd even boasted about qualifying for Special Forces training at Fort Bragg, liking how Jess's eyes got wide when he told her about the Survival, Evasion, Resistance, and Escape course.

And it had worked—she'd had sex with him that first night, in the back of the car, both of them knowing how silly it was to be acting like they were still in high school. At least Mack had known it was silly. On second thought, he wasn't really sure what Jess had thought, since she'd looked surprised when he showed up at her folks' house two days later. She didn't talk much about her failed marriage, but Mack suspected that she had her own war to get over.

"Jessie, I don't know what you want me to say." She looked pale and strangely blank, and for one bad moment, Mack saw what she would look like dead. Medic vision, Adam had called it.

"Well, I guess that answers my question." Shit, there had been a question? Mack tried to recall what it was as Jess sank down into a chair, her head in her hands. Her long, bare legs distracted him for a moment, but then he got his focus back. This was turning into a breakup argument, and he didn't want to break up with Jess.

"I don't want us to break up," he said, in case it helped anything.

She frowned at him. "So what's your plan? We just carry on like this forever?"

Mack rubbed his neck. "Jeez, I don't know. I can barely figure out next week, and you're asking me about forever." He thought about his sister's husband, Bill, who had first appeared to be a big, gruff, gentle man, but now radiated a constant, low-level hum of irritation. The way Mack saw it, he'd already signed away a good chunk of his life to the army, and it had taken him some places he hadn't wanted to go. He wasn't about to commit himself to anything else that had the potential to turn nasty.

Jess leaned forward, giving him her compassionate, concerned nursey look. "Is this because of the war?"

Now, that was a good out. Yes, he could say, looking all haunted. She'd buy that. He could probably even get away with acting like a total asshole from time to time. Except that in a way it was true, and if he used it like that, it would be like holding out a stump and saying, Look, look, I was wounded in the war, here's my excuse for being a bum.

Mack looked out the window and saw that the old maple was already beginning to change color. He realized it was going to be deer season soon, and wondered if he'd go hunting this year. He tried to imagine carrying a gun again, wearing camouflage. It didn't fill him with joy.

He heard Jess come up behind him. She put her arms around his waist and rested her head on his back. "I'd love to know what's going through your mind right this minute."

"Nothing." She'd serve him his ass if he admitted that his mind had wandered to hunting.

"It can't be nothing."

Mack stepped out of Jess's embrace, wondering if there was some way to get out of this whole conversation. He noticed that the coffeepot was full. "Hey, is that fresh?"

Jess walked over to the counter, ignoring the congealing pancake batter, and poured him a cup of coffee. "I wish you'd take a chance on opening up to me." She handed him the cup. "You know, it's something I'm good at. Listening."

Mack took the cup from her. "I guess I'm just not much of a talker." Unlike Adam, who'd turned everything into a stand-up routine. He took a sip of coffee. It tasted burned and bitter.

"I'm not asking you to entertain me. I want to know what you went through."

"I don't know how to tell it, Jess. When I talk about it, it sounds fake." Mack kept his voice neutral, but knew damn well what she really wanted. She wanted *the story,* something big and personal and awful and tragic. But Mack didn't have a story, he had a bunch of fucked-up memories, and a few funny ones. Sometimes he wasn't even sure which were which. And it wasn't like talking about Iraq was going to make any kind of sense to Jess, anyway.

Mack walked over to the sink with his cup and poured the coffee down the drain, then stood for a moment looking out the window. A wasp buzzed, caught between two panes of glass. There was an old cobweb there, too, with a couple of ladybugs caught in it, but no sign of the spider.

"Jesus, Mack, what do you want me to do? Never ask you anything at all?"

Mack rubbed his head. His scalp felt tight, which meant he had a headache coming. What he wanted, really wanted, was to get back into bed with Jess, naked, and climb inside her body. Even if it made his head hurt worse. There was a bad kind of tension in him, and he couldn't think of another way to get rid of it.

He looked out the window, imagining it. He imagined the pancakes, too. Suddenly he wanted them. He wanted that fake maple syrup, too, the kind he'd had as a kid, that tasted twice as sweet as the real stuff.

"Are you even listening to me, Mack?"

He focused on Jess. "Sure I am."

"Then what was I saying?"

"That I don't really listen," he said, hazarding a guess. "And that I don't open up." But she was already on to a new criticism.

"It's like you still think you're seventeen and you've got all the time in the world to figure things out. But you're not a kid anymore, Mack, and neither am I. I'm thirty and I can't just hang out with you like we're still in high school."

That was so wrong it made him laugh. "I don't think I'm seventeen." Jesus Christ, at seventeen, his biggest fear had been getting stuck in some boring job fixing engines down on Church Street. But that was never going to happen to him, because he was moving to Charlotte, North Carolina, to race stock cars. At seventeen, he'd worried about not getting the right opportunities, but he'd never spent a single moment wondering if he might not be up to the challenge. Oh, no, he'd known that when the shit hit the fan, he'd be brave and decisive and quick to act. And he'd never doubted for one single second that he was basically a nice guy. A nice, normal guy.

"Okay, fine, you're all grown up," Jess was saying, her arms folded together over her chest like a pissed-off schoolteacher. "So why aren't you making any effort to get your life together?"

For a moment, Mack stood there, suddenly feeling stupid standing there with his shirt off, conscious of his army tattoos, the clumsy eagle and flag on his chest, the Special Forces dagger on his arm, like an old uniform he could never take off even though it didn't fit him anymore. Why wasn't he getting his life together? He tried to think of something to say in his own defense, but all he could think of was that wasn't the right question. He didn't know what the right question was, but he did know that wasn't it.

Just then Mack's pager went off at the same time as the siren from the firehouse. He pressed the first number in his cell phone's memory. "Dutchess 911, this is Arcadia 5627 responding."

"Arcadia, you are responding ten ten for an automotive accident between Route Eighty-two and Wildwind Road. One occupant, male Caucasian, possible head trauma."

"On my way." Mack felt the familiar kick of adrenaline and ran out to his truck, where he kept his EMT and firefighter gear. Jamming his left arm into the sleeve of his blue coverall, he pictured the curve between 82 and Wildwind, and figured he'd better take the rescue truck in case they needed to do an extraction. Shoving his bare feet into his work boots, Mack wondered if either of the other EMTs would be responding. Cory was a police officer, so he might be working on a Sunday.

"So that's it? You're not even going to say good-bye?"

Mack turned to see Jess standing on the grass in her bare feet. She'd wrapped her arms around herself, as if to keep warm. Incongruously, a bird warbled happily in the background.

"What do you want me to do? I have to go," he said, sliding into the driver's seat. "We'll talk later."

Her arms still folded, Jess shook her head slowly, no, they wouldn't. But he was out of time, so he ran to the car and started the ignition without bothering to buckle himself in.

When he got back, two hours later, the kitchen was still a mess and Jessica was gone. She'd left him a note, but his head was hurting, so he didn't bother to read it. The accident victim, a high school senior, had died on the way to the hospital.

Mack went out to the hammock that hung between the two Norwegian pines and laid down in it. It was only noon or so, but he felt exhausted. The day had turned oppressively hot and he stripped off his shirt, now stained with blood, and stared at the sky through the tops of the tall trees, rocking himself with one foot on the ground. He wanted to sleep but wound up thinking about the dead teenager, the story the skid marks told, the way most problems usually boiled down to not having enough reaction time to correct a mistake.

Three

On her last day as a New Yorker, Zoë took Maya to Harry's Shoes to buy new school shoes appropriate for stomping through muddy fields. As usual, the store was swarming with determined older women in search of serious German walking shoes, frazzled middle-aged women in pursuit of something that looked like a stiletto but felt like a sneaker, and anxious young girls trying to convince their mothers that the miniature cowboy boot really was comfortable enough for everyday wear. Looking trapped and miserable, the men, boys, and toddlers roamed the aisles, tripping over outstretched feet and unattended strollers. They may not have liked it, but they accepted the necessity of being there. With its two large parks, wide sidewalks, and gently sloping hills, the Upper West Side of Manhattan was a walker's paradise, and walkers require good shoes.

Maya looked at the crowd and groaned. "This is going to take forever. Why can't we get new shoes in the country, Mom?"

Zoë pushed her glasses higher up her nose as she made a quick journalist's assessment of the number of people in the store. "Because I have no idea where to go there. From what I remember of Arcadia, the town consisted of a small general store, a video shop, and five real estate agents."

"But I hate this place."

"So quit growing so fast." Zoë led them to a pair of seats filled with shoe boxes, which she promptly placed on the floor.

As she sat down, Maya pulled a face that Zoë recognized as the English Dowager.

"Pardon me, madame," she said in a haughty, upper-class British accent, "but are you saying that I have large feet?"

"Growing feet, milady, not large." Out of the corner of her eye, Zoë saw an elderly woman give her a sharp look, clearly irritated that her shoes had been ousted from their chair. She left in a huff, complaining loudly to the salesman.

"Remember," Maya drawled, still in character. "Large feet are common."

"Absolutely. Hey, wait a minute, I have large feet!"

"Indeed," Maya sniffed, raising her eyebrows. "Pray do not speak of it." Then, switching back to her regular voice, she said, "I wish we could just come back later."

Zoë looked into her daughter's face, struck as always by the strange dance of genetics that had given her this petite, slender, delicately beautiful child with straight blond hair. Strangers sometimes assumed that Maya was adopted, and Zoë didn't always correct them. The real story—that she'd had a fling with a man who'd left his unborn child with his phenotype and nothing more—she shared only with intimates. "The problem is, it's not going to be as easy to get around in the country."

Maya frowned. "Don't they have buses and cabs?"

"They do, but not as many as in the city, and everything's much farther apart."

"Are we going to get a car? Because my vote is for a pink Cadillac convertible. With real leather seats," she intoned silkily, rolling her *r*'s. "And, of course, a bike rack. And a kayak rack. Can we have a kayak, too?"

Zoë laughed. "You know who you remind me of? Carole Lombard."

"Who's she?"

"She was one of the great comediennes of the 1930s. She was a sort of strange and wonderful combination of glamour-puss"— Zoë made a gesture that encompassed her daughter's pink sequined top, embroidered jeans, and silver sneakers—"antic goofball, and natural athlete."

Maya looked pleased with this description. "Can we watch one of her movies? She sounds cool."

"Absolutely. And have I mentioned today that you, my child, are also very cool?" That her daughter should be so was as big a surprise as Maya's fair coloring. Unlike Zoë herself, who had shuffled through childhood as a clumsy, frumpy bookworm, Maya was never teased by the other children. Teachers, who had always given Zoë report cards that contained high grades with caveats such as "stubborn" and "opinionated," called Maya "a joy to have in the classroom." Maya did not, of course, receive the high grades, but Zoë did not expect her child to be a carbon copy of herself. Other mothers boasted about their children's similarities to themselves; Zoë boasted of her child's differences.

"So, Mom," said Maya, bouncing a little in her seat, "are we getting a car? Do I get to help choose?"

"You would if we were, but we're not."

"Why not?"

"Because I don't drive, honey."

"How come?"

"I don't know. I just never learned."

Maya frowned. "So how are we going to get places?"

"We'll manage." The truth was, Zoë hadn't quite figured out the logistics of life in the country yet. Ever since the car accident that had nearly ended her life at sixteen, she'd had a bit of a phobia about cars. For the first few years, she hadn't even been able to bring herself to sit in the front passenger seat. After some intensive work with an excellent therapist, she'd gotten to the point where she could ride in the front without hyperventilating, and these days she seldom even thought about crashing and dying, unless the driver was particularly young or inept. Learning to drive herself, however, was not an option she'd ever considered seriously. They didn't make passengers with flying phobias learn to operate airplanes, did they? Zoë had told the real estate agent to make sure that the house she was renting was a short walk from the village. She had a vague idea that she would ride a bike in the good weather, like an English lady, and put her groceries in a basket. Once a week she would take a taxi or hire a neighbor with a car to make a larger shopping trip, and on weekends, they'd take the train back into Manhattan.

Zoë turned back to her daughter and saw that she was suddenly looking forlorn. "Are you okay, honey? What's the matter?"

"I just don't feel like shopping today." Her face had lost its usual animation, and Zoë was forcibly reminded that they'd just sold the only home Maya had ever known. Up until now, her daughter had revealed nothing but uncomplicated excitement at the prospect of going to a new school, and Zoë had felt as if she were the only one experiencing the stress of the change.

She put her arm around her daughter's shoulders as shoppers babbled and pushed and test-walked new shoes in the aisles all around them. Leaning in to press her lips to the top of her daughter's head, she caught the scent of strawberry shampoo and sun-warmed hair. "What are you feeling right now, Bunny? A little overwhelmed?"

"A little."

"Me, too. But I know this is the hardest part, when you know everything's about to change but it still hasn't happened yet. Hey, I have an idea. How about we go to Constanza's for pizza after we finish here?"

Maya brightened. "Is this a special occasion? Can I rot my teeth with a Coke?"

"It's a deal. Hang on, I think I see a salesman. Over here! We're next!" Zoë raised her hand and flagged down a burly man with a white handlebar mustache. The man paused, looking at their feet the way the damned in hell might look at a pitchfork. "What do you want?"

"I need a good school shoe for my daughter that can handle mud and, I don't know, maybe snow as well. And can you check my daughter's size?"

Just then, someone else called out for assistance, and the salesman gave a dyspeptic grunt and lowered himself down to measure Maya's feet. Zoë glanced up to see who'd been trying to poach their help and saw her daughter's best friend Polly. At first glance Polly looked as if she could be Maya's sister, but their personalities were very different. While Maya was more socially adept and easygoing, Polly was academically and athletically driven. Zoë wasn't sure how much of this was nurture, or the lack thereof; Polly's mother, Celia, was high-strung and intensely focused, and made Zoë look like a laid-back, bohemian earth mama by comparison. If their daughters hadn't thrown them together, Zoë wouldn't have spent more than five minutes in the other woman's company. But in Manhattan, affinity sometimes counts for less than proximity, and Celia lived less than two blocks from Zoë. In addition, she was a freelance graphic designer, with a similar schedule.

As a result, Celia and Zoë had spent a great deal of time in each other's houses, gone out to lunch together, and had even spent an entire Sunday ice skating, but always attended by their daughters. Although Zoë had told Celia all about her failed relationship with Jeremy the history professor, and Celia had confided to Zoë that she fantasized about having an affair with her computer repairman, their friendship still belonged to a category that Zoë termed "child-provisional," meaning that the adult relationship was entirely contingent on the children's. This was due, in large part, to the fact that Celia's achievement-oriented parenting style always left Zoë feeling both irritated and inadequate.

"Hey, Maya," said Polly, clomping over strollers and shoe boxes with the same determination she showed on the soccer field. "What are you getting?"

Maya put her left foot down for the salesman to measure. "School shoes. What about you?"

"Cowboy boots."

"Awesome." Maya turned to her mother. "Mom, can I have cowboy boots, too?"

"Sorry, pardner, not today."

"Hello, Zoë," said Celia, who was casually dressed in khaki slacks, loafers, and a patterned blouse that was undoubtedly part of some designer's latest collection. "Mind if we join you?"

"Not at all." Zoë moved her bags over to make space. "How's life?"

"Oh, just crazy. I can't keep up with Polly's schedule anymore. Fencing, horseback riding, piano—and we've just had her retested to see if she qualifies for Hunter."

"But didn't you test her last year?" Zoë wasn't sure why she was bothering to ask. Many of the parents in her social circle had their children's intelligence tested year after year, certain that the right tester administering the exam on the right day would result in a near-genius score, qualifying a child for a free, accelerated, enriched education. This, in turn, gave the child a head start on admissions to Harvard, provided the kid didn't have a nervous breakdown at the age of eleven.

"Last year was a mistake," said Celia. "I knew Polly was coming down with something, but it's so hard to get a testing date with Marina Skulnik, and she's considered the best at getting the best out of the child. So I just went along with it, and can you believe it, Polly was just three points away from a qualifying score. Three points!"

"You know, Hunter isn't for everyone," said Zoë, who'd graduated from the school back in '82, when the competition for admission had admittedly been a tad less frenzied. She had liked the school, but recalled that the rapid pace and heavy workload had taken its toll on some of her friends.

"But I do think Hunter would be right for Polly. I just don't feel that West Side is challenging her enough. I mean, she's reading Camus's *The Stranger.*"

"Existentialism at age eight? That seems a little premature."

"That's what I said, but she insisted. She's such an advanced reader, she seeks out these books that are really for teenagers or adults." Celia sighed. "Sometimes I just don't know what to do."

Zoë never knew what to make of comments like these. Even though Celia wasn't aware that Maya had been diagnosed with dyslexia, the woman clearly knew that Maya was not reading on Polly's level. When she talked as though both girls were equally proficient, was Celia slyly pointing out her own daughter's superiority, or was she making a misguided attempt at making Zoë feel better? Zoë was pretty sure it was the former.

Resisting the urge to counterattack with some thinly disguised boast about Maya's emotional maturity, Zoë tried to think of an appropriate response. "Still, Celia, you have to admit, worrying that your kid is too gifted for her school is kind of a baroque problem."

Celia lifted her chin. "Do you think so? I think it's a very real concern when a child isn't being sufficiently challenged."

Zoë smiled, thinking, Oh, I'll bet having you as a mother is pretty damn challenging. On her right, she overheard Maya ask Polly, "Where do you ride horses?"

"At Claremont Stables on Eighty-ninth Street."

"At my new school they have horseback riding every day."

"God, you are so lucky. English or Western?"

"I don't know."

As Polly rattled off the relative merits of each, Celia tapped Zoë on the shoulder. "Hey," said Celia, "are you changing schools?"

"Yes," said Zoë, suddenly making up her mind to forestall any repeats of her last conversation about dyslexia. "It's all about the horses for us. We really don't feel the city stables are challenging enough, particularly if you're interested in either fox hunting or barrel racing."

"Ah," said Celia, sounding impressed. "But the schools . . ."

"The way I see it, a decent elementary school education isn't really that hard to get. But a solid foundation in equitation, at a stage where Olympic-level performance is still a distinct possibility?" Zoë looked the other woman straight in the eye. "We really want to focus on the horses."

"You know, I told my husband we were making a mistake, having Polly participate in so many different activities. How will she ever really excel unless she picks one and really buckles down?"

Zoë was saved from having to reply to this by her cell phone, which started ringing the opening bars to the original *Star Trek* theme song. "Hey, Bronwyn."

"Zoë, you can't leave me. I'm sorry, but I can't permit it."

"Too late, I've already enlisted."

There was a deafening wail, and Zoë held her phone away from her ear. "You'll just have to visit me in the wilderness."

"Oh, don't be ridiculous. You know I'll never be able to escape. I can barely convince Brian to let me have the odd evening off." Unlike Celia, Bronwyn was a close friend, and had been since they'd met freshman year at Georgetown University. Married since the early nineties, Bronwyn had put off having children till last year, and was now the forty-one-year-old mother of twin boys. She'd given up practicing law to look after them, while her husband, a financial analyst on Wall Street, was compensating by working eighteen-hour days. Their marriage had known happier times.

"So bring the boys and visit."

"Yeah, sure, maybe in a decade or so, when they stop trying to impale themselves on every available sharp object. Oh, please don't leave me, Zoë. You know you're going to hate it there. You're going to be lonely and bored and miserable and you're going to miss me like hell. And they won't have any decent take-out."

"Don't sugarcoat it," said Zoë, "tell me what you really think."

"Well, if you really want to know, I think you're crazy to be doing this just because of your daughter. I mean, it can't all be about her, can it?"

"Okay, I take it back. I can't really listen to what you think."

"But I'm so depressed. Know what I'm doing now? I'm looking at a website for fostering animals. Oh, look, there's a picture of an adorable miniature dachshund, only he can't be housebroken and needs a diaper."

Zoë was relieved to see the salesman approaching, his arms full of shoe boxes. "Bronwyn, the last thing you need is another diaper to change. Listen, I plan on coming back into the city at least once a week, sometimes more. I won't see you any less than I do now."

Celia snorted as Zoë put her cell phone back in her purse. "It's not going to happen," she said.

"Excuse me?"

"The going back all the time." Celia took a shoe box from the salesman. "That's what my girlfriend Stacey said before her family moved to Westchester, and they never come back in. Even though she's only half an hour away, I haven't seen her in over a year. She might as well be living on a different planet." Celia slipped her foot into a handsome, short, square-toed boot. "What do you think of this style?"

For a moment, Zoë felt sorry for Celia, who clearly didn't understand what a child-provisional friendship was. "You know, you can also visit us," she offered.

"Oh, I wish we could," said Celia, putting on the second boot. "But between school and riding lessons and dance classes, we'll never find the free time. I almost envy you, getting a chance to slow down and stay at home. You'll probably get a ton of work done, but all that quiet would just drive me crazy." She stood up and walked down the aisle in the Italian boots. "I really like these," she said. "Do you?"

"Enough to want them for myself," Zoë admitted.

Celia made a sympathetic face. "But wouldn't waterproof be better for the country?"

"I'll wear them when I come into Manhattan," said Zoë firmly, gesturing to the salesman. "I'd like to see those in size nine and a half, please."

They said good-bye on Broadway, Maya and Polly crying, Celia and Zoë half-hugging each other, their shopping bags banging into each other's legs. Celia didn't ask for Zoë's new address and phone number and Zoë didn't offer them. When they arrived at Maya's favorite pizza shop, six blocks from the shoe store, they discovered that it had closed down. Carpenters were working inside, rearranging the layout.

Maya was understandably upset. "But what happened, Mom? It was always full."

Zoë hugged her daughter, not knowing what to say. This was the downside to life in Manhattan: restaurants and friendships had a high turnover rate.

Four

*a*ll right, Jeanine," said Mack, "let's start with the basics. You're going to put your hands at the nine and three o'clock positions on the steering wheel."

"Nine?" Seventeen-year-old Jeanine DiMatteo turned to him, her face so soft and milky-pale that she could have been a custard. "My dad said ten and two." Even though all she'd done was sit down in the 2002 Honda Civic, the girl's blue eyes were wide with anxiety and her silver-ringed fingers were trembling on the wheel.

"They've shifted people's hands down because of the air bags. If they go off and your hands are too far up the wheel, you can wind up smacking yourself in the nose."

"Oh," said Jeanine, sounding terrified. Mack would've bet his honorable discharge that Jeanine had already stalled out someone's engine or braked hard enough to make the air bags pop.

Which was pretty typical of the students he got at Moroney's Driving School. In the country, most folks learned to drive from friends and relatives, first in a big parking lot, then on quiet back roads. Nobody actually paid for driving lessons unless they had some form of emotional, psychological, or physical disability, or a note from a judge saying that nobody was giving Grandpa his license back unless the alcoholic ninety-five-year-old's road skills were evaluated by a professional.

Although Mack was not at all sure that working for Jim Moroney really qualified him as a professional. Anyone desiring to risk whiplash and ulcers in order to make a whopping $8.50 an hour could realize that dream by becoming a genuine New York State driving instructor. All you needed was a high school education or GED, and to pass a multiple-question test that was not exactly written for MENSA members. If you knew that "leaving the correct distance between you and the vehicle in front of you" meant not jamming the nose of your car up the other guy's rear, then you were a prime prospect; if you were also courteous, respectful, and, above all, patient, then buddy, you were in.

At least for a little while. In the six months that Mack had been working for Moroney, he'd seen three different instructors leave, one for a better-paying job in retail, one to prison for breaking and entering, and one to get his commercial driver's license so he could become a trucker.

That left just Mack and old Pete Grell, who could barely hear through the mass of crusty white hair sticking out of his ears. Pete tended to get the older drivers who had their licenses suspended for some infraction or other, and his main mission in life seemed to be to build up the confidence of folks who had good reason to be nervous on the roads.

Personally, Mack preferred to teach teenagers like this one, who had a good sixty or seventy years of driving ahead of them. If he did his job right, then she would be able to keep herself, her passengers, and the other people on the road safer than if she hadn't been behind the wheel. And it was a damn sight easier to train a person the right way than to retrain them after they'd gotten used to driving one-handed while eating a burger, fiddling with the radio, and cursing at the stupidity of the car in front of them.

Which is what Mack told the girl as he moved her hands into the correct position on the steering wheel. "There you are. Now, you'll probably see a lot of folks driving with one hand, or both hands on top," he told her. "They'll tell you this is just for beginners. But guess what? They're wrong. You want to keep both hands on the wheel, even when you're a hotshot twenty-one-year-old cruising down to Florida for spring break."

That got a smile out of the girl. She looked down, fingering the small gold cross around her neck, and Mack wondered if she was praying to Jesus to get her to Miami or to protect her from it. He figured the kid had probably never been farther south than Poughkeepsie: folks in Arcadia tended to stay close to home. Hell, until he'd shipped out to Iraq, he'd been to Manhattan only twice, and that was only a hundred miles away. The city's dangerous, his mom always told him. Mack turned back to the girl, who was saying something under her breath. He listened carefully. "Okay, step on brake, put car in drive, check rearview mirror." She glanced over at him. "Right?"

Mack nodded, forcing himself not to laugh. "You might want to turn the key in the ignition first. But before we do that, I always like to check something first. How do you feel right now?"

"Nervous."

"So you've got to pay attention to that, same as you'd pay attention to changing weather conditions. How you feel affects how you drive. So if you feel nervous, you're going to drive nervous, and that's no good."

"But I can't stop being nervous."

"Sure you can. What we're going to do is, we're going to get that nervous right out of your body. Take a big, deep breath. There you go. Now, take another. Excellent. Shake out your shoulders. Go on, don't be embarrassed, I'll do it, too." Mack shook his shoulders out like a prizefighter about to go into the ring, and the girl laughed. "Come on, let's shake together." He went a little wilder now, going for zombie with palsy, and now the girl was laughing a little easier, not so tight and frightened. "That's better," he said.

"My dad kept telling me to take driving dead seriously, because you can take a trip to the grocery store and wind up dead. Or killing someone." Mack could see the girl tensing up again, just remembering. "He called it a fatal instrumentality."

That explained it: Dad was either a cop or a lawyer. "Well, that's true. But you could also kill yourself trying to change a lightbulb in the kitchen, or blow-drying your hair in the bathroom, or just plugging in an old space heater and keeping your bedroom door and windows shut tight. And yet you manage to change lightbulbs and blow-dry your hair, right?"

"I do my hair," the girl allowed. She had streaked blond hair, cut in a lot of layers that stuck out from her head. "But I don't see how that makes me qualified to drive a car. I can't even ride a bike!"

"How about I fill you in on a little secret?" Mack pointed out the window. "You see that tree there?"

"The tall one or the scruffy one?"

"Either. See, you just passed my first and only requirement for a student—you're not blind. You see, a car goes where your eyes go, which is why I don't teach the blind. I'll teach the old and the young and the one-legged and the one-armed, I'll teach the hearing impaired and the extremely short, and I'll even teach you if you got just one eye, but I do not teach the blind."

Jeanine cocked her head to one side. "How do you teach the one-armed?"

"We got modifications for the car." At least, Moroney bragged that there were, and that he had personally taught a cripple them other schools said couldn't do it, although nobody one-armed had actually shown up since Mack had started working. "Now, if I can teach a guy that's only got one arm, what are you so damn worried about?"

"As a matter of fact, I'm not feeling as jumpy as I was. And look, my hands are on nine and three."

"All right then. Let's go for a drive."

* * *

Forty-five minutes later, Jeanine pulled back into the parking lot behind the driving school, her cheeks flushed. "That was great!"

"You did fine, Jeanine. Next week, what do you say we take a cruise on by the high school?"

A worried frown creased Jeanine's baby face. "On the main road?"

"You call Route 199 a main road? I could take a nap near the traffic light at rush hour."

Jeanine laughed, and she gave him a happy wave as she got into her parents' car. Mack was feeling pretty good about the lesson when he walked into the office, but Jim Moroney looked up from the *Hudson River News*, tapping his watch. "That was an hour, Mack. The father only paid for forty-five minutes."

"You don't need to pay me overtime."

"That's not the point." Moroney leaned back in his chair, which made his shirt buttons strain against the taut, almost muscular hump of his belly. "People value what they pay for. You give away your time for free, people figure it ain't worth much."

Mack helped himself to a doughnut from the box on Moroney's desk. "So how come my students always come back?"

Moroney gave a snort of laughter. "Why do you think? All those little girls like having a big old Special Forces guy teaching them how to parallel park. And the boys probably figure you'll show them how to kill someone with your bare hands."

Mack felt a rush of anger that left him light-headed. He made himself swallow the bite of doughnut in his mouth. "That wasn't in my job description."

The chair creaked as Moroney swiveled back to his desk. "Yeah, I know that, but all the kids around here know you were over there with the Rangers, so they figure you're some kind of hero."

"That's bullshit."

Moroney looked up, his expression almost kind. "Listen, Mack, you take it from me. There's no shame in deriving some fringe benefit from having served your country in uniform. Some people want to think you're a hero, you let them, 'cause there's other people who're going to think you're a killer."

"I was a medic in Iraq."

"You were a soldier. Like me."

Mack stared down at his boss, who still wore his graying brown hair in a regulation crew cut and always talked about the time he'd spent in the army, even though Mack knew damn well he'd spent his four years practicing missile launches that never went anywhere, eating bratwurst and striking out with all the cute antimilitary Fräuleins. Mack thought about saying some of this, but then he'd be stuck working at Stewart's shop next to his ex-girlfriend. Or worse, he might be forced to find work in Kingston.

Like most of the folks in Arcadia, Moroney had more than one job, only in Moroney's case, he moonlighted as town assemblyman, which meant he was the most influential member of the town planning board. For a town like Arcadia, which had no zoning, this meant that Moroney had the authority to approve, disapprove, or modify site plans and subdivisions, and could use his own discretion to hand out permits to build in sensitive wetland areas. And it didn't hurt matters that his mother, Mabel, was also on the town board, ready to second all his motions.

Shaking his head in disgust, Mack walked out the door, throwing what was left of the doughnut into the bushes.

"Mackenna." Old Pete Grell, skinny as Scrooge and dry as yesterday's toast, was standing by the Honda. Pete refused to use nicknames, and Mack refused to answer to "John," so they'd settled on Pete's calling Mack by his last name.

"What is it, Pete?"

"You left something in the school car." Bundled up against the sixty-five-degree October day in a plaid wool jacket, fleece-lined baseball hat, and gloves, Pete handed Mack an army satchel.

"That ain't mine," said Mack, inspecting it. There was a peace sign embroidered on the front, and a button with a no-smoking sign. Inside he found a spiral-bound notebook, a pack of cigarettes, and the *Ardsley Anthology of Poetry.* "Must belong to that girl I just taught."

"You're supposed to check the car before your student leaves it," said Pete.

"Guess it slipped my mind."

"You can't be sloppy in this line of work. Forget to check the car this week, might forget to teach about checking the rearview mirror next."

"I'll try to remember not to forget that."

Pete glared at him, as if trying to ascertain by sight whether or not Mack was being sarcastic. Mack smiled, not offering any clues. "You go on and make sure Jim gets that book bag."

"What, you think I'm going to steal the girl's biology homework? Maybe sell this poetry book on eBay?"

Pete scowled at him, clearly not knowing what eBay was. "Just do it," he said, stalking off as if the few leaves scattered on the ground were roadblocks in an obstacle course.

Pissed off, Mack slid into his pickup truck and slung the book bag on the passenger seat. He'd had enough of Moroney for the day: easier to just find the girl's address and drop off her school things. Glancing in her notebook, he discovered that Jeanine was taking chorus and art history, and that she had a crush on a boy named Travis. No address. He checked the inside cover of the poetry book, just in case she'd written something in there, and his eye caught on the word "virginity." Mack read the lines again, struck by the description of a dead woman as a tightly budded flower, nocturnal and inviolate. The image made sense, a funny kind of sense, like an old Bob Dylan song. Mack rubbed his chin and read the next bit, which compared the corpse bride to long hair and fallen rain. Okay, he was lost now. Which irritated him. He felt like he'd glimpsed something in that first section, something that had reminded him oddly of the army and Iraq. But why a poem about a girl who either was or wasn't a virgin should remind him of the war, he couldn't say. His eyes slipped to the next line, and with a little chill of recognition, he got it.

She was already root.

It was a poem about death. Mack had no idea how he knew it, but he did. And something in this poem reminded him of the way it felt to be back in his hometown, touched by death and by some strangeness he didn't know how to describe, that made him feel cold and quiet and balled up inside himself. Like a new virginity, except not at all like it, either, since he'd had no problems having sex with Jess. Just with everything else.

Mack flipped to the beginning of the poem, which was called "Orpheus, Eurydice, Hermes," and read the introduction.

This is a poem by Rainer Maria Rilke, who wrote in German in the beginning of the twentieth century. This poem takes its title from the Greek myth about Orpheus, a musician whose young bride, Eurydice, dies shortly after their wedding. Orpheus descends into the underworld and plays a song so beautiful that Hades permits him to lead Eurydice back to the land of the living—so long as Orpheus does not turn around until they reach the sunlit earth. But Orpheus does turn around, and Eurydice is lost to him forever.

So it really was about death. He'd gotten it right. How come he'd never learned this stuff in school? Or maybe he had, and it just hadn't penetrated. He read to the end of the poem, then went back to the very beginning, before the bit he'd already read, and started over again. And then Mack started the engine and drove through town and out the other side, making his way along the pretty country roads, Rilke's phrases trailing like Eurydice's graveclothes through his mind.

Five

The short, dark, and handsome Israeli driver, who hadn't been in the States long enough to stop calling himself Dudu, was lost.

Of course, Dudu wasn't admitting this to Zoë, but they had been driving for almost two and a half hours and were still on the Taconic, and the real estate agent had said the entire trip should take them no longer than two hours, door to door. Zoë hadn't said anything, but Dudu had finally stopped enumerating the reasons why the Golani brigade was superior to the paratroopers, and was paying some attention to the road signs. Unfortunately, there weren't many of them, and they all said things like "Rip Van Winkle Bridge" and "Bull's Head Road." For long stretches, there were no signs at all, just the narrow, winding road, which seemed much too small to be a highway, and the autumnal trees on either side of them. It reminded her a little of Ireland.

Dudu accelerated to pass a tractor that was chugging along at twenty miles an hour and got back in his lane scant moments before a pick-up truck hammered along in the opposite direction. Zoë shot him a look. "Don't do that."

"What? It was fine. Relax."

"I can't relax if you're going to cross into oncoming traffic."

"You're a nervous passenger."

"Fine. I'm nervous. Drive carefully or I'll throw up on you."

Dudu laughed. "Just look out the window and let me drive." The car, which had probably been somebody's pride and joy back in 1976, navigated a corner with all the grace of a stampeding bison and a view appeared to their left: mountains, fields, a postcard-pretty view of orange and red and gold.

Oh shit, Zoë thought, I'm really going to live here. She felt sick to her stomach.

Dudu accelerated again, switching lanes to overtake a vintage 1950s convertible. "Wow," he said. "What is that?" He watched the convertible in his rearview mirror until Zoë cleared her throat.

"Eyes front, please."

"Where did you say this town was again?"

Zoë glanced at the directions. "The real estate agent said we take the Millbrook exit."

"But what number is this? In America, the exits have numbers, right? What's the number?"

Zoë checked the directions again. "It doesn't say."

"But you were there, right?" Dudu flipped down the sun visor and removed a pack of cigarettes. "You been to this place before, yes?"

"Not to the house. I was in the town last month." She and Maya had visited the Mackinley School in late September, two weeks after the West Side International School's new reading specialist had concluded that Maya had a learning disability.

"So you should know how to get to the town, yes?" Dudu gave her a steady look as he stuck a cigarette in his mouth.

"Well, not exactly. By the way, you can't smoke that in the car."

"Why not?"

"Because I don't want my daughter breathing secondhand smoke."

"No, I mean, why don't you know where you are going to live, when you just visited there a short time ago?"

"I'm not too good with directions." Which was the understatement of the year. Zoë had once read that the section of the brain that deals with location and geography was markedly more developed in British cabdrivers. The same section of her brain, she suspected, was either stunted, deformed, or just plain missing.

"Besides," she added, "last time Maya and I took the train, and the head of admissions at Maya's new school picked us up at the station."

Dudu raised his eyebrows, the unlit cigarette still dangling out the side of his mouth. "Why didn't you drive?"

Zoë shrugged. "I don't know how."

Dudu's eyes widened. "And you're moving out here? What are you, meshuga?" He reached for the car's cigarette lighter.

"Excuse me, but I think I'm paying you to get me to my destination, not to give me your opinion on my plans. And as I just told you, you can't smoke in here."

Dudu unrolled his window, took one defiant drag of his lit cigarette, and then threw it out the window, muttering in Hebrew about how Zoë wasn't paying him enough to make him put up with her for this long. He then added a more prurient comment about what Zoë needed to set her right.

"You do know that I speak Hebrew," she said in that language, keeping her tone neutral.

"Are you Israeli?"

Zoë shook her head.

In Arabic, Dudu told her that she might have fucking mentioned that earlier.

"I understood that, too," she said, in Arabic.

Dudu gave her a respectful nod. "Wallah, with a good accent. You speak something else?"

"A little Spanish, some basic Russian."

"How about German?"

"Not really."

Dudu let out an impressive stream of German curse words.

Zoë narrowed her eyes. "You know, instead of blaming me for not knowing the way, you might want to call your friends in the moving van and see if they know where we are."

"You said you didn't speak German!"

"I was being modest." As Dudu punched the numbers into his cell phone, Zoë looked out the window, berating herself for hiring Dudu's euphemistically named Elite limousine service. The movers —also Israelis, of course, but reliable—had recommended him, but all that meant was that one of them knew Dudu from the army. She should have known better than to hire a driver from a company that sounded like an escort service.

"Mommy."

Zoë turned to look at Maya, who had been sitting quietly in the backseat for over an hour and a half, listening to an audio version of the latest Harry Potter book on her CD player. Zoë waved her fingers. "How are you doing, honey?"

"I'm okay, but there seems to be something wrong with the back of the car. I think it's on fire."

* * *

Dudu, swearing in Hebrew, Arabic, and German, steered the ancient Cadillac into a gas station, trailing a thick, foul-smelling plume of gray smoke in his wake. The smell had penetrated the interior of the car, too: so much for Zoë's concerns about second-hand smoke. As if all that weren't enough, the cat had clearly passed the limits of his endurance and was voicing a steady protest at being confined in a pet carrier. The moment the car stopped, Claudius was silent for a moment, and then started up yowling again.

Maya unbuckled her seat belt. "Mom, where are we?"

"Somewhere near Arcadia, I think."

Dudu got out of the car, slamming the door behind him.

Maya looked out the window, watching as Dudu walked around the back of the car. "Is the car broken, Mom?"

"I'm not sure, honey."

Maya looked down at the cat, who was still bleating, and clawing at the bars of his pet carrier. "Can I let Claudius out?"

"I don't think that's such a good idea, honey. How about we go into the store for a moment? Do you need to go to the bathroom?"

"Actually, I do."

Zoë and Maya got out of the car. There were two other vehicles at the pumps, both pickup trucks. One was empty and had a bumper sticker that read: IF YOU CAN READ THIS, BACK THE F**K OFF. The other had a sign taped to its back: FRESH VENISON FOR SALE. There were four large, bloody brown paper packages in the truck bed, and Zoë clutched her stomach, revolted. The owner of this truck, a burly man with a baseball cap and a huge, bushy beard, winked at Zoë as he tapped the last drop of gasoline from the nozzle of the pump.

She approached Dudu, who had moved around to the front of the car and was leaning over the engine. Whatever he saw in there wasn't making him happy. "Hey," she said, "do you want something to eat or drink?"

Dudu straightened up. "What I want," he said, "is a mechanic."

Zoë took a deep breath. "It's that bad?"

"I don't know, but I can't drive like this. I tried to call Mukki and the others on my cell phone, but I don't get reception here."

"Shit."

Maya held out her hand. "That's a dollar, Mommy, remember?"

Zoë handed her daughter a dollar bill as they walked into the gas station shop. "Hello," she said to the middle-aged Pakistani woman behind the counter, who was incongruously wearing a black turtleneck under her red cotton sari. "Can my daughter use your restroom? And do you happen to have an auto mechanic around?"

"The ladies' is just there," said the woman, "but a mechanic I don't know. Ibrahim!" She called out in Pakistani, which Zoë didn't understand at all. Ibrahim emerged from a back room, revealing himself as a young man in Levi's and a Green Day T-shirt. As the two discussed mechanics, Zoë looked around the store. It had a surprisingly large selection of items, from tampons and disposable diapers to cans of Chunky beef and barley soup. There were rows upon rows of cookies and doughnuts, a few ancient used children's Christmas videos, as well as miscellaneous items such as baseball hats, lottery tickets, and an entire stack of folded neon orange rain ponchos. If you wanted to chew on a bit of jerky, there was an entire revolving rack to choose from, not to mention the jar of Slim Jims by the cashier's register.

She glanced at the newspaper rack, which contained the *New York Post,* the *Poughkeepsie Journal,* and a small paper called the *Hudson River News.* Clearly, this was the local rag, since its headline proclaimed the breaking news that "Pleasant Hill Second Graders Win Regional Science Fair," which also merited a color photo of a blond-headed child holding up what appeared to be a cotton ball. The article underneath contained an actual hint of controversy: it seemed that Arcadia's town board was considering a proposal to develop the empty lot behind the post office, and not everyone was in agreement. The pull quote was "I'm just not sure the town needs to have two pharmacies," and was attributed to Clovis Peabody, the town undertaker.

Okay, thought Zoë, at least now I know that we're in the right general area. I also know that spending a year here may liquefy my brain.

"I'm sorry, miss," said a male, Pakistani-accented voice, and Zoë looked up to see a plump middle-aged man in a crisp blue shirt. "The only mechanic shop I know is maybe fifteen miles from here. Can you drive there, or do you want me to call them and see if they can send someone over?"

"I think we'd better call them," said Zoë, and despite the fact that she was used to all the potential hazards of driving through rural areas from Egypt to Mexico, she felt a sudden rush of anxiety. When would they ever reach the damn house? Where was the moving van with all her stuff? How much was all this going to cost in overtime? Zoë took her glasses off and rubbed the bridge of her nose. "Oh, shit, shit, shit, shit."

"That's four dollars," said Maya, emerging from the ladies' room.

"Well, maybe you ought to cut your momma some slack, now."

Zoë pushed her glasses back into place. The owner of that wry, laconic voice was a good-looking young man in faded jeans and a plaid flannel shirt worn over a black tee. He had the kind of straight-backed posture that suggested some time in the armed forces, and shaggy blond hair that said he wasn't intending to head back there in a hurry. I remember when all the guys my age looked like this, thought Zoë, before they went bald and their bodies began to resemble papayas. Maya smiled at the stranger, dimpling, and Zoë caught a glimpse of the teenager her daughter would someday be. "I guess you're right," she said, averting her gaze.

"No, a deal's a deal," Zoë said, putting her hand on Maya's shoulder. "You get your money."

"Overheard you're having some car trouble, ma'am," said the young man, meeting her eyes.

Ma'am? When the hell had she turned into a ma'am? "Yes, I

don't suppose you know anything about cars and what makes them start smoking all over the place?"

"I could take a look."

"Oh, I'd be so grateful. My name is Zoë Goren, and we're actually moving from the city, there's a van filled with our furniture on its way, and this is just making everything incredibly complicated."

The young man smiled at her, and Zoë shut up. "I'm Mack," he said, shaking her hand with an endearing formality. "So where's this bad car of yours?"

"Just out here," Zoë said, watching with amusement as Maya followed him with a slightly star-struck expression on her face. Hell, thought Zoë, if I were ten years younger, I'd probably be looking at him like that, too, even if he probably thinks Bush is a great president and Andrew Lloyd Webber musicals are high culture.

Zoë hung back, watching Mack walk up to Dudu and ask him what was wrong, his whole body language quiet and observant. She had half-expected to see some sort of macho posturing on Dudu's part, but he was already showing Mack something under the hood, gesticulating his confusion. Mack said something that made the Israeli laugh, and then he bent over the hood.

"Do you think he can fix it, Mommy?"

Zoë looked down at her daughter's smooth-skinned face. "I have a hunch he can," she said, looking back at the two men, silhouetted against the almost painful brightness of the October sky. "I think folks in the country know about cars."

And sure enough, ten minutes later Mack walked up to her. "I jerry-rigged it so it'll take you to Arcadia now," he said. "I gave Dave there instructions."

"Dave?"

Mack smiled, crinkling his eyes. "Man can't go around calling himself Dudu." Mack knelt down to Maya's level. "You all ready for your new home?"

"My room is going to be huge!"

"That's great." He straightened up.

"I can't thank you enough." Zoë fished around in her purse, unsure what to offer him. "Listen, is forty enough? Because if you hadn't helped us, God knows how long we'd have been stuck here."

The young man shook his head. "It was my pleasure."

"I wish you'd let me repay you."

"Tell you what. When this little miss gets old enough for driving lessons, you send her on over to me at Moroney's. That'll make us even." Mack shook Maya's hand and she nodded enthusiastically. "That sound okay to you? You come on by when you're sixteen."

"I don't think we're going to be here that long," said Zoë. "We're really just planning on staying for a year."

Mack shrugged, then waved to Dudu and walked toward a black pickup truck. "Well," she said as she got back into the Cadillac, "wasn't he nice."

"He was in the Army Rangers," said the driver formerly known as Dudu, as if that explained everything. "Almost as good as Golani."

Following Mack's directions, it took them twenty minutes to reach their destination.

Six

*M*ack shoveled another heap of manure onto the wheelbar-
row. "That's all of it," he told his sister. "Where do you
want this?"

Moira slid the saddle off the horse's back. "Just leave it by the
door, I'll lay it over the garden later."

Mack wheeled the horseshit to the big sliding door at the back of
the barn, pausing for a moment to admire the way Amimi Mountain looked silhouetted against the blue October sky. They looked
completely alone out here, even though Mack knew that there were
other small houses dotted here and there around the base of the
mountain, mostly weekenders, but also a few reclusive types, hip-
pies and rednecks and the kind of people who devote their lives to
studying some rare kind of turtle that pretty much looked like
every other kind of turtle, only with a yellow spot on its head. He
used to feel sorry for their kids, trapped so far from town that they
couldn't walk or bike to Stewart's shop for an ice cream. Growing
up, he'd always been pleased that their farm was close enough to the
mountain to give him a chance to see bear and coyote and bald
eagles, but near enough to town so that he didn't have to ask someone to drive him to a friend's house. Glancing back at the mountain, he realized how long it had been since he'd hiked out there.

Maybe he'd take a turn around Starling Pond later. In the marshy wetlands around the base of the mountain, you didn't get the bright, splashy colors of dogwoods and maples, but if you were lucky you might spot an osprey or an egret among the bright yellow swamp rose leaves, and if you could bear with all the little stinging insects, you'd get to hear the raucous sound of all the late-migrating birds settling into the cattails.

Mack returned to the barn with the small wagon, which someone had already stacked with bales of hay. "Just give everybody one?"

Moira reached one arm around the horse's neck and removed the horse's bridle. "If you don't mind. Don't forget to break it up, though."

"Jeez, Moira, it's not as though I never did this before."

Moira pulled the halter over the horse's head. "Don't get me wrong, but as far as I can recall, the last time you did this was 1989."

Inside Wild Epiphany's stall, Mack shredded the hay. "Let me tell you, it hasn't changed much."

Moira made a noise halfway between a cough and a snort. "Not as much fun as driving around with teenagers all day?"

Mack closed the stall door behind him. "That's not fun. That's a public service."

"Well, God knows we could use a few less crappy drivers. You hear about that boy from Eastville? Wrapped his car around a tree last Saturday night, killing himself and leaving his sister paralyzed from the waist down."

Mack sat down on a bale of straw, then stood up abruptly when something sharp poked him in the ass. "Yeah, I heard," he said. "I didn't take the call, but I heard it was bad."

Moira paused. "I don't know how you do it," she said. Unspoken between them were the circumstances of their own parents' death, a commonplace country-road collision between the exhausted and the incompetent.

"And I don't know how you get up on those things," said Mack, indicating the horse. "Scares the crap out of me."

"Unlike some souped-up Ferrari that goes three hundred miles an hour."

"You don't soup up Ferraris, woman." Moira didn't respond right away, and Mack inhaled the familiar sweet, musty odors of horse and hay, watching his sister working on the glossy Thoroughbred's coat. Under her hands, the stiff rubber curry comb made economical circular motions that spoke of practiced ease and competence.

The minutes ticked by, the only sound in the barn the clucking and squabbling of the little gray guinea fowl up on the rafters. Mack reached over and patted the horse's nose. "She's a nice one," he offered, in case his sister was ticked off about that Ferrari comment. The mare sniffed at him, then nibbled at his hair, making Moira laugh.

She stroked the mare's long brown nose. "You're right, you know. Fandango is one nice horse, and it drives me crazy knowing her owner is just going to wind up breaking her leg on a foxhunt. She's too much horse for some midlife crisis Wall Street type." Moira came around and worked out a knot in the horse's mane. "Not that I should be talking about somebody else's midlife crisis. Bill keeps saying we need a new truck but I have half a mind to take your advice and get me a little red sports car. Isn't that what you do with a midlife crisis? Buy a fast car and move someplace warm so you can drive around with the top down?"

"If you're serious, the Mazda MX-5 is affordable," Mack said, "and they haven't screwed it up yet, even if they did get rid of the pop-up headlights in ninety-eight. But don't you have to be middle-aged to have a midlife crisis?"

Moira snorted. "And what do you think I am, a teenager? I'm about to turn forty, little brother."

Shit. His sister, forty. She still wore her dark blond hair in a long braid down her back, but it was going gray at the temples, and her arms had begun to look scrawny rather than slender. "Well," he said awkwardly, "that kind of blows my mind."

Moira bent to pick up the mare's right hoof, resting it on her knee. "You and me both. Sometimes I think about the fact that if Bill and I ever wanted a child, we'd have to do something about it right away. And even then it might be too late." She took the small metal hoof pick and dug out a large clump of something black and foul-smelling.

Mack stared at his sister, unsure what to say. "You want a kid?" They never talked about stuff like this. Personally, Mack couldn't imagine a worse candidate for fatherhood than Bill, who got grouchy every time the wind blew. But hell, who was he to judge?

"Nah, probably not." Moira looked uncomfortable, and Mack wondered if he should pry a little. But then his sister grinned lop-sidedly and added, "I suppose raising one ornery brother was enough for me."

With a start, Mack realized that she had just turned nineteen the week before their parents died. Shoot, at nineteen he hadn't known how to take care of himself, let alone anyone else. Which was why he'd joined the army—why most guys joined, if they were honest. It wasn't for the money or the training or the adventure or patriotism. You joined the army because you had no fucking idea what to do with yourself, and you were hoping somebody else had a clue.

But at nineteen, his sister had been grown up enough to take charge of him and set up a horse training and boarding business. He wondered if her jokes about midlife crisis meant something, whether she was regretting not having more of a wild youth. "Well," he said awkwardly, "you don't look middle-aged."

"I feel it, though," she said, making a face as she straightened up. "I can't say I'm looking forward to winter this year. Twelve horses is a lot to take care of on a morning that starts at nine below zero."

"Not much you can do about the weather. Unless you want to move south."

Moira didn't say anything for a moment as she walked around to work on the mare's back feet. "Mack, reason why I asked you about your plans . . . I got an offer on the farm."

"Yeah? Who is it this time?" From time to time, wealthy city folks came by, offering Moira ridiculously low sums for the whole operation. Like the fact that the main house was run-down and the fences needed mending meant that they didn't read the real estate ads, same as anyone. Like they were too ignorant to know how property values had risen in Dutchess County.

"A million and a half."

Mack whistled. "Who was it?"

Moira came back around the stall. "Some group called Emerald Acres. I heard from Deanna down at the diner that they want to buy up all the land behind the post office." She unhooked the horse's cross ties and took hold of the lead rope. "Can you open that stall there?"

Mack held the door open as his sister led the horse inside. "You interested?"

Moira patted the horse's neck. "I'm not sure. It's a lot of money." She closed the stall door. "So you're not opposed to the idea of selling?"

"I don't know. Worth considering, at any rate. You know what they want with all that land?"

Moira shrugged. "Another horse farm, maybe. A big one. Or maybe they're wanting to subdivide, build a bunch of houses."

"Maybe. And you heard they want to buy up all the land?"

His sister looked at him. "You thinking they might be willing to pay even more?"

"Hell, I don't know. But it is a lot of land." Behind the post office, there was a large, empty tract of land, some of it farmers' fields used for grazing beef cattle, some of it empty. There was a side road that had some small houses on it, and the town beach and lake, which had been closed last summer because of pollution from the recent onslaught of Canada geese. Tourists liked to go there to take pictures of Amimi Mountain, which loomed up behind the post office and over the town lake. Teenagers liked to hike up the mountain, them climb up the fire tower and carve their names in the window frame. Carving your name meant you'd done it, of course. Mack's name was up there, along with Tara Healey's, summer of '92. His first time, right before he joined up.

Of course, Amimi Mountain was also a prime location for doing drugs and jumping to your death. His classmate Jason Lane had done both, also in '92.

Mack ran his hand over his jaw. "So, what would you do if you sold the place, Moira? Train horses for somebody else?" He tried not to think about what he would do. Rent a room in somebody else's house. Buy a double-wide.

Moira picked up a bridle from a hook and ran her fingers over the bit. "Maybe move on down to Virginia, get something small there. Or try Saratoga. Make a change." She turned to him. "You'd get a share, too, you know."

Mack shook his head. "This place ain't mine. You've done all the work."

"Still. They were your parents, too."

"Well"—Mack looked at his sister—"it's your call."

"Guess so." She gave him a rueful smile. "Know what? I was half hoping you'd tell me I was crazy, that it was wrong to even think about selling."

"Okay, if it makes you feel better." He gave his sister's arm a friendly squeeze. "You're crazy."

* * *

That night, in bed, Mack read another poem from the book he still hadn't returned to his driving student. This one was by T. S. Eliot, and it contained a phrase that made him put the book down and stare at the ceiling.

What did it mean, "what is kept must be adulterated"? He knew what "adulterated" meant with regards to gasoline: It meant someone had diluted the purity of the grade by adding something like diesel. "What is kept"—that must mean passion, the passion that isn't lost, watered down, corrupted. Mack thought about how he used to love cars—taking them apart, putting them together, figuring out how to get just the right amount of oversteer so the back of the car gives a satisfactory, cop-chase-style fishtail.

Before his sister had gotten him thinking about sports cars, he hadn't thought much about cars lately. They were just a means to an end, a way of getting from point A to point B. It hadn't occurred to him to head on over to Lakeville to see who was racing at Lime Rock. Hell, he hadn't even dropped by the old garage where he'd spent the better part of his adolescence.

Why didn't he love cars anymore? Moira still loved horses. The boys he'd hung out with, now men, still followed NASCAR like it was a religion. Why was he different? Had he changed in the army? Changed in some fundamental way, not the usual change of getting older and just caring less about everything?

Mack folded his arms behind his head and it came to him what Adam would have said: Man, stop thinking about it. You don't want to wind up some potbellied wannabe, farting around in an old muscle car for two months in the summer at five miles an hour so as not to screw up the vintage engine.

Which, now that he thought about it, was what the poem seemed to be saying. What is kept must be adulterated. Mack skipped to the end of the page: "Tenants of the house, thoughts of a dry brain in a dry season." He closed his eyes, wondering who the poet was talking to.

Mack fell asleep with the lights on, and for the first time in six months he had a dream about Adam. They were both wearing civilian clothes, and they were standing in a club with a disco ball that might have been a high school auditorium. And Adam was being goofy, screwing around with some dumb dance, and all the kids were watching him like he was crazy. Mack was clapping, laughing so hard he thought he'd bust a gut. Then Adam came up to him, looking exactly like Adam, big and barrel-chested with a full head of dark curly hair, more Italian- than Jewish-looking. In the dream, he held out his arms. "So, how about it?"

Mack shrugged. "Yeah, why not?" There was a sappy song playing in the background, and he joined Adam in a mock tango, goofing, first Adam leading, then him having a go, both swooping each other around, the expressions of outrage all around them hilarious to see. Despite the disco ball and the multicolored lights, the mood had been more silly than romantic, but even so, waking up, Mack felt guilty at how happy he'd been, dancing in his dead friend's arms.

Seven

*I*t was somebody else's wet dream of a country house: a lovely little gray Colonial with a pleasingly laid-out garden, complete with three sweetly gnarled apple trees and a breathtaking view of a mountain. Inside, the house had wide, wood-planked floors, open fireplaces, and low, beamed ceilings. Okay, so there was a bit of seventies linoleum on the kitchen floor, and some really horrible floral curtains in the living room. Remove those, and you had the kind of house that children's book artists drew, along with happy badgers in calico dresses and bonnets.

Zoë hated it. And it didn't take her long to realize that she hated it. By the time the Israeli movers arrived (they'd gotten lost on the unmarked side roads) she suspected that she disliked her new home. The head of the crew, a wiry redhead, scratched his chin when he saw the place. "You're really going to live here? There's no town." Zoë realized that there was no word in Hebrew for the country. There were words for town and village, and for various kinds of farms, and there were words for nature and forest and desert, but there was not one word that expressed that you were living in the middle of nowhere, with nothing to look at but trees.

"Americans," said Dudu. "They like a lot of space." When the movers left for the city, two hours later, they looked relieved. Zoë felt like asking them to take her back with them. Still, she thought, the house was pretty. The whole area was pretty. She and Maya spent half an hour watching the sun set behind the big mountain to their west, the clouds turning an improbable cotton-candy pink, then a watercolor violet before sliding artfully into darkness. Maybe, Zoë thought, she'd grow to love it here. And it was only a year's rental, and a year wasn't so long, unless you were under the age of twelve or incarcerated.

By the middle of her first week, however, Zoë could categorically say that she hated her new home.

She hated the fact that there was so much of it, that she and her daughter could be in the same house and not be able to hear each other. She hated the fact there were no neighbors visible, in case some Manson-style gang decided to drop by for some ritual slaughter. And didn't that kind of thing always happen in quaint little towns with charming cottages and deceptively friendly villagers?

Zoë had never considered herself the superstitious sort, but something about the country made her uneasy. The house was over one hundred and fifty years old, and there were peculiar cold drafts that seemed to waft in out of nowhere. The washing machine and dryer were located in a basement that looked like a medieval dungeon, complete with dank stone walls and an uneven dirt floor. Zoë wondered if someone might be buried under the mound beside the boiler. When the house was quiet, she could hear odd creakings and rattlings coming from rooms she knew were unoccupied. There were things scurrying around inside the walls.

These, Zoë assumed, had a prosaic explanation—she must have an infestation of mice or squirrels. This did not make her feel any better. She wondered if the fact that she had a cat would convince the local rodent population to move out. Probably not: there were scarier things than fat Claudius out there.

Once Maya went to sleep, Zoë felt trapped and utterly alone. Nobody had come to install the satellite yet so they didn't have television, and logging on to the internet with the old phone lines took so long that both Zoë and her computer kept falling asleep. More upsetting still, Zoë hadn't read a newspaper for four days. She had no idea what was happening in the wider world, her world had shrunk to this house and this moment in time, and when she sat down to work on her article, "Behind the Veil," she found herself writing, "Like the women of Saudi Arabia, I find myself isolated, stuck at home, unable to drive to a shop without assistance."

Of course, Zoë added mentally, the women of the Arabian Peninsula are the victims of a repressive regime, while I am just a prisoner of my own incompetence. So actually, not such a great comparison.

Shutting down her laptop, Zoë looked out her bedroom window, the darkness outside so complete that all she could see was the reflection of her own pale, unhappy face, and wondered how she would make it through the winter. Even though she knew she was only two hours from Manhattan, it felt as though she had moved to Alaska, or the far side of the moon.

And now she was resorting to clichés. She wasn't even being witty with the self-pity.

Maya, on the other hand, seemed to be adjusting well to the change. She was still trying to decide between the small bedroom with the view of the mountain or the larger bedroom, which looked out over the forest behind the house. Even though she had only been there two days, Maya already said that she liked her new teacher. She was a little worried about making friends, but she loved the fact that the school had horseback riding as a required after-school activity in the fall and spring.

Zoë knew she should be happy that her daughter was enjoying

school. And she *was* happy for Maya. It had been worth all the stress and discomfort of dislocation just to see Maya bouncing off the school bus that first day. "The teacher asked if anyone hadn't understood what she'd just explained, Mom, and everyone, I mean every single kid, raised their hand!"

For the first time in years, Maya did not feel that there was something wrong with her, and she spoke about school with an enthusiasm that made Zoë's eyes sting with tears. But after the morning rush of finding clothes and fixing breakfast and making sure that Maya had her backpack before she got on the yellow school bus, Zoë found that the big house rang with silence, and that her happiness was tinged with something flat and sad. It was pathetic. She'd never had a problem with Maya's going off to school in the city, but then, in the city, Maya hadn't been gone from seven in the morning to five-thirty in the afternoon.

Of course, back in Manhattan, it wouldn't have been quite so awful to have Maya go off to school for more than ten hours a day. In the city, Zoë had possessed a circle of friends, the comfortable background presence of like-minded strangers, and a choice selection of foreign films and documentaries, as well as a host of unusual little museums and boutiques, all a short subway ride away. Not that she'd even needed to try that hard to entertain herself: in Manhattan, just walking around the corner to pick up some Greek yogurt and Afghani flat bread could be an adventure.

And this was the thing Zoë hated most about the country: there was nowhere to walk. The lying bitch of a real estate agent had claimed that the rental property was within walking or biking distance of the village, and theoretically, this was true. But what the woman had neglected to say was that the five-mile walk would have to take place along Route 82. Granted, there wasn't much traffic on Route 82, but when a car did go by, it was going ninety miles an hour.

Which meant that Zoë didn't just *feel* as though she were stranded in the middle of nowhere. She actually was stranded. And rapidly running out of her city-bought supplies.

As Zoë contemplated the last of the Zabar's goat cheese tortellini, her phone rang. Bronwyn, she thought happily. "I was just going to call you," she said.

"For the new year? That's nice," said her mother, "but it's better if you wait for me to call you."

Oh, God, Zoë had forgotten about the High Holy Days. "*Shana Tova,* Ema."

"You know that tomorrow is Yom Kippur, right?"

"Of course." Zoë glanced at the Mackinley School calendar and realized that there was no mention of the holiest day of the Jewish year. That must have been why it had slipped her mind. In Manhattan, all the schools closed on the important Jewish holidays. Should I keep Maya home, Zoë wondered. She's already missed a month of classes.

Her mother gave a long sigh. "Of course you know it's Yom Kippur. I don't suppose there's a synagogue out there in the wilderness?"

"I'm sure there's one around somewhere."

"But you're fasting?"

"I may have to," said Zoë. She still hadn't worked out exactly how to get to the little town supermarket. On Monday, she'd left four messages with Betty's Friendly Taxi Service, but Betty, who sounded extremely old on her answering machine, had yet to return her calls. Zoë knew there was some sort of loop bus that took migrant workers to their jobs, but she hadn't figured out how to access its schedule. It was ridiculous that she, who did research for a profession, couldn't figure out how to get into town to shop. The problem was, she usually started out by canvassing people on the street, and here there weren't any.

"Listen," her mother said, "your father's coming back soon, so I don't have long. How's Maya? She's happy in this new school? Are there Jews there?"

Zoë gritted her teeth, not sure what pissed her off more: that her father's concept of religion meant that he still wouldn't acknowledge her out-of-wedlock child, or that her mother visited Maya on the sly, instead of confronting her husband and saying, You're in the wrong here, not me. "There are Jews everywhere," said Zoë.

Her mother made an impatient noise. "I mean our kind of Jews."

"I have no idea, Ema." For Zoë's parents, born in Iraq and raised in Israel, their kind of Jews were fellow members of the Bene Naharayim synagogue, who lived in houses that looked like theirs, both inside and out, listened to the same Middle Eastern singers, and vacationed in the same Miami hotels. When they visited their extended families in Israel, the Gorens would run into their Queens neighbors at the corner store, and laugh at the coincidence.

Before the shame of her daughter conceiving out of wedlock, Rivka Goren had spent most of her time worrying that her eldest child would marry a Jew whose family came from Eastern Europe. Zoë's mother concluded her ritual litany of regrets with what she considered her first mistake: allowing Zehava to attend Hunter instead of the religious girls' yeshiva.

"Ema," said Zoë now, interrupting, "even if I'd gone to the yeshiva, I wasn't going to marry a nice Iraqi boy. And can you really tell me you'd want me to be like Aviva? She won't even eat in your house anymore." Zoë's younger sister, Aviva, had married an Israeli whose parents also came from Iraq, and the two of them had moved to Jerusalem and become deeply religious. Zoë wasn't completely surprised. Her little sister had always been extremely nervous in any situation that did not have clearly defined rules, and

Judaism, which was rife with commandments and injunctions, was the ideal refuge for an obsessive-compulsive.

"I'm very proud of the life Aviva's made for herself."

Zoë remembered how her old landlady had boasted to all her friends that she had an internationally renowned journalist living in her spare bedroom. "Ema, I know you're incredibly proud that your younger daughter sits at home all day with six kids, but does it mean anything to you that I'm a working journalist? People pay me to read my analysis of what's going on in the news." Oh, God, thought Zoë, two minutes of talking with my mother and I start making petty comparisons with Aviva. What am I, thirteen? She started to apologize, but before she could begin, her mother heaved a deep sigh.

"What do you want me to say, Zehava? That I'm proud of you, too?" Her mother paused. "You're a very intelligent girl, but to be living on your own with a child, having to support yourself . . . it's not what I would choose for a child of mine."

"Well, it's what I've chosen for myself."

Her mother clucked her tongue in disapproval. "So you're happy out there in the wilderness?"

"Yes," said Zoë, because to say anything else would be to admit defeat.

"Then what can I do? I wish you a happy and a healthy new year."

"Thank you, Ema."

"There's your father," her mother said in a very different tone of voice, and then the connection went dead. Zoë imagined her father, tired from a long day of engraving Hebrew inscriptions, sad-eyed kittens, and images of Jerusalem's Western Wall on glass and crystal awards, windows, and plaques. Benjamin would glance at Rivka, knowing that his wife had gone against his wishes and called their fallen daughter, but pretending ignorance. Zoë supposed it was a form of acceptance, a minor act of kindness.

But he had barred his home to her, as if Maya were a contagious disease and not his own grandchild, and for that Zoë would never forgive him. And while her parents might have thought she'd abandoned her religion when she changed her name and left Queens, it was only after Maya's birth that she'd stopped going to synagogue.

Zoë slammed the phone down in its cradle, her heart pounding. She was damn well going to find a way to go shopping today, if only to ensure that while guilty Jews the world over refrained from taking food or water, she'd be washing down a bacon sandwich with a glass of milk.

Eight

*T*here are days, Mack thought, when a man is better off not getting out of bed. But there he was, standing in the doorway of the town diner, and now he had to walk in and sit himself down, even though his ex-girlfriend was sitting at a booth with Jim fucking Moroney. He made his way to the back of the diner the way he'd been taught to move through potentially hostile crowds in Iraq; relaxed arms, steady eyes, the barest trace of a smile and a nod.

"Hello, Jim," he said as he passed his boss. "Jess." Moroney had the grace to look a little uncomfortable, his fleshy face brightening over his plaid shirt collar. Jess, on the other hand, gave him a strange little smile, as if she were enjoying his discomfort. Hell, maybe she was; Mack sure as shit couldn't imagine why else a woman would be attracted to Jim Moroney. Not that the man was bad-looking, but his jaw was so flabby it looked like it was melting, and he had to be at least fifty, he'd been married at least twice before, and he had grown daughters, one of them the same age as Jess.

At the counter, Deanna gave him a sympathetic smile as she poured him a cup of coffee. She'd been a friend of his sister's, plump even in junior high, but fifteen years of serving all-you-can-eat Thursday-night buffets had turned Deanna borderline obese. She wasn't self-conscious about her weight, though—she simply dressed her big body the way she decorated the diner, with cheerful bad taste. Today, she was wearing a long black-and-orange shirt under her apron, and her earrings were plastic orange jack-o'-lanterns. "Need a menu, Mack?"

"Nah, I got it memorized."

"Wish I could say the same for the new short-order cook. Hang on a sec, will you? I'll be right back to take your order." Deanna lifted the hinged section of the counter and turned sideways to maneuver herself through, setting her earrings to swinging wildly. "Jeez, I think this was wider yesterday."

With Deanna gone, Mack sat on his stool, his back itching from self-consciousness. Behind him, he could hear snippets of their conversation:

Jess: So there's definitely going to be a reassessment?

Moroney: That's the way it looks, I'm afraid.

Jess: Aw, jeez, Jim, it's getting so no one local can afford to live around here.

Moroney: Well, now, don't you worry. There's some good money going to be coming in to Arcadia. We got some developers interested in building up a little shopping mall back of the post office—a restaurant, a gourmet market, even some clothing stores. There could be some nice job opportunities.

* * *

Well, Mack thought, that explains all the interest in Moira's horse farm. The conversation wasn't what you'd call flirty, and Mack's shoulders loosened a little. Maybe all Jess wanted was some tax advice from the town supervisor. The town diner wasn't exactly a romantic setting, but it was the place where all the real political decisions got made. Moroney and his band of merry crooks might attend the monthly meetings at the town hall, but everyone knew they'd already voted in private, over Deanna's early-bird special of meatloaf or pork chops, $6.99.

Hell, they probably paid for the damn food out of the town budget.

Deanna came around the counter, her cheeks flushed from hurrying from the back of the restaurant.

"What can I get you?" She refilled his cup, then took a deep breath, pressing one hand to her chest as if she were a little winded.

"I'll have the corned beef and eggs." Without thinking, he reached out and took Deanna's fleshy wrist in his hand.

"Hey, what's all this about?"

Mack smiled up at Deanna, his two fingers pressed to her pulse. "Making Jess jealous," he said, glancing over at the wall clock.

"You ask me, that girl's an idiot if she's choosing him over you."

Mack paused, calculating Deanna's blood pressure. "Maybe I need *my* value reassessed." He noticed that her wedding ring was cutting into her finger, and that her flesh was still white where he'd pressed into it. "How're you doing these days?"

"Busy. No time to be holding hands with a customer, even one as cute as you."

"Any chest pains? Pains in your left arm?"

"No, Mack. Stop worrying, I'm not having a heart attack, I'm just a little out of shape."

"Look, it's probably nothing, but you should know that women don't always feel pain before a heart attack. Sometimes they just have some swelling in the feet and ankles, or dizziness and shortness of breath."

"Aw, terrific. Thanks for sharing that with me. No, you're right, I guess I should get checked out."

Deanna cocked her head to one side, her jack-o'-lantern earrings swinging. "You know, I never would have expected you to become a medic. I thought you were all about machines."

"The body's kind of a machine. Besides," he admitted, "it was more of a rush. Blood and guts, fight the clock to get somebody stable enough to move." Not the only reason he'd chosen the course, but one of them.

"Okay, speedy boy, you about done now? I got customers waiting."

Mack pressed his hand closed over hers, keeping her with him. Her skin was clammy. "So you think it's more than business?" He tilted his head to the side, indicating the booth where Jess and Moroney were sitting.

Deanna took another deep breath, and this time, he could feel her pulse slow. "Oh, I don't know, Mack. Probably not. I mean, look at them, they don't exactly look like a couple, now, do they?"

Maybe not, but in Mack's experience, the less you liked an explanation, the likelier it was to be correct. "Just in case," he said, "could you act like I just said something really charming and funny, and you find me incredibly attractive?"

Deanna gave his hand a squeeze before sliding her fingers from his. "I'll do that, right after I bring you your corned beef." She disappeared off into the kitchen, and Mack took a sip of his coffee. On the wall was a mounted display of old Matchbox cars. He remembered that ambulance, a back loader with doors that really opened, and the little yellow Corvette. He wondered if he still had them somewhere, in a box, and where all his old childhood stuff would go if Moira sold the house.

Behind him, Mack heard Jess laugh.

Jess: Oh you do, do you?

Moroney: Not as much as I used to.

Jess: Well, would you do it with me?

No way, thought Mack as he kept his eyes glued to the Matchbox cars on the wall. It's just too obvious. She knows I'm listening, so she's making it sound all suggestive, but really they're talking about measuring her driveway or checking her property borders.

He heard them standing up, both of them laughing now. Moroney had an irritating, nasal little laugh. "Bye, Deanna," said Jess. "Mack."

He gave her a wave. Moroney came up behind him. "Hope this sits all right with you, Mack," he said, lowering his voice. "You know me, I'm not a man to stab a friend in the back."

Well, shit. If it was an act, it sure had Moroney fooled. "I'm relieved to hear that. I'll tell Pete, too, in case he starts worrying you might be after his girl. Course she's pushing eighty, but what's age but a number?"

Moroney sighed. "Come on. It's not like I snuck around and stole her from you."

"It's not like you could," Mack muttered into his coffee cup.

"Mack, don't be an asshole about this. If you're an asshole, I'm not going to be able to keep you on the payroll."

Mack swiveled around on his stool so he was facing his boss. "Gee, thanks for spelling that out, Jim. Now I can really weigh my options—poor asshole or brownnoser with a job."

"For Christ's sake, I'm trying to be adult about this."

Mack laughed, and it sounded unpleasant, even to himself. "Oh, I get it. You're trying to be adult, and Jess can be the little girl?"

The punch took him by surprise, which was stupid, really. He flew off the stool. His head hit the side of the counter going down, and for a moment, Mack saw a few spangly lights, just like in the cartoons. Who could have guessed the chubby bastard had it in him?

"What the hell is going on here?" Deanna came out of the kitchen, carrying his corned beef and eggs. She looked at Mack, then over at Moroney. "Christ almighty, Jim, what did you go and do that for?"

Moroney set his jaw. "He was asking for it."

"You sound like one of my kids. And you, Mack! What the hell do you think you're doing, picking fights in here?"

Mack struggled to sit up. "I'm all right, nobody rush to my side or anything. I'm fine." He touched the side of his head. "A little bloody, maybe, but fine."

Jessica walked over to him and knelt down. He liked the way her hair looked today, all silky and smooth, but that bright blue sweater she had on really brought out the unfriendliness in her eyes.

"I suppose you think I should be flattered by this."

"I'd settle for sympathetic. Or just disgusted by your current choice of boyfriend." He touched the side of his head and winced. "Are you actually dating him, Jess? As in, removing clothing and getting sweaty?"

She didn't blink. "Remember when I said you were acting like you were seventeen, Mack?"

"I think I recall it."

"This is what I'm talking about." Jess stood up and walked over to Moroney.

"Hey, I don't know if you were watching, but he hit me."

Moroney turned to Jess. "I am genuinely sorry this had to play out like this. You know it was not my intention."

Jess put her hand on Moroney's beefy shoulder. "I know."

Mack, who had finally gotten to his feet, made a disgusted noise. "By the way," he said, raising his voice so it carried to the other side of the diner where Moroney and Jess were standing. "Just in case there's any confusion about the matter, I quit."

"Fine with me," said Moroney. "That way, I don't have to pay you any unemployment."

"In that case, I don't quit. I'm fired."

Moroney shook his head. "I wanted to cut you some slack, seeing as how we're both army vets, but you just crossed the line, son."

"Both of us vets," Mack began, the burn of anger back in his chest, like something he'd swallowed but couldn't force down. But Deanna came up behind him before he could find out what he was going to say next, slapping an ice pack on the side of his face. "Ow," he said. "What was that for?"

"You want to pick another fight? Take it outside."

Mack dropped the ice pack on the counter. "What do you say, Moroney?"

Moroney shook his head. "I don't want to hurt you, Mack, but if you try to take this further, I will call the cops." While Mack was digesting the unfairness of this threat, the older man opened the door for Jess. She turned and looked back over her shoulder.

"Don't expect me to feel sorry for you. You did this to yourself."

"That may be so, but at least I'm through kissing up to Jim Moroney."

Jess made an exasperated sound and flounced out. Moroney followed her, sending Mack a last, pitying look. "You just shot your own self in the foot, Mack."

Asshole. Mack sat back down on his stool as the door slammed shut behind them, the bell giving an incongruously cheery little jingle. He inspected the gash over his right eye in the mirrored surface of the napkin dispenser. It was probably going to leave a small scar, but he didn't feel like the long drive to the emergency room to get stitches. Man, he could just imagine the ribbing he'd get.

He glanced over at Deanna, who looked both pissed-off and worried. It seemed to Mack that he'd seen that expression on his sister's face a few times. "You feel dizzy? Sick?"

He shook his head, then wished he hadn't. Ouch.

"Well, you should. You realize you're out of a job, right?"

"I did notice that, yes."

Deanna sighed. "And was it worth it? Just to get your two cents in? It's not like you scored any points with Jess." She paused. "Mack? Hello? You're not even listening to me, are you?"

He looked up. "Sure I am."

"Well, fine, then." She poured him a fresh cup of coffee.

Mack took the coffee cup in his hands. "You know what burns me, Deanna? All this 'we're both war vets' shit. Guys that talk like that? They've never seen any real action." Mack dropped his voice an octave. "'Yes, Mack, I was a manly man in the army, with other manly men.' But you know what? Mortar comes down, it flattens the manly and the not so manly, and you can't really tell which guts belonged to the brave infantry guy and which slipped out of the pretty-boy reporter. And you know what? Maybe you wind up flat on your ass from the blast, and the soldier who drags you to safety is a little eighteen-year-old farm girl from the Midwest."

Deanna made an exasperated sound. "That's enough of that, Mack." She pointed at a table with three little blue-haired ladies. "Do you really think they need to hear all this?"

Mack felt his face heat up. "Sorry about that, ladies."

"That's all right, son," said the blue hair on the left. "This is the most interesting breakfast we've had since Nancy here announced that her grandchild was black and that we had to get used to it."

"I still don't think it's right, girls fighting in the army and getting themselves killed," said the little old lady with tight white curls.

The smallest little old lady banged her fist on the table. "Well, then, I'm not sure it's right for boys, either."

Deanna looked sideways at Mack. "If they get to breaking things," she said, "I'm putting it on your bill."

Nine

*a*fter making one last call to Betsy's Friendly Taxi Service and learning that Betsy had just gone into a nursing home, it took Zoë over an hour to find a cab that would take her into town. The first two companies were based forty minutes away in the city of Poughkeepsie, and the third in the equally distant city of Kingston, and were booked all day. The fourth car service was located in the nearby town of Rhinebeck, but the driver said he was heading into the city to do an airport run. He suggested planning her trips to town at least twenty-four hours ahead.

Zoë turned to Claudius, who was howling for more food. He'd only recently emerged from beneath her bed, and now he clearly wanted to make up for lost meals.

"Don't worry," she said, opening the last tin of cat food. "I'm not giving up."

By the time Zoë reached Rudy of Rudy's Taxi and Limousine Service, she was on the verge of tears. "You're a little bit off my usual route," said Rudy.

"Oh, please," said Zoë. "I'm desperate. I've just moved out here and I didn't realize how far out from the town I am."

"I heard that before," said Rudy. "One lady I know, she moves out here, buys a Mercedes, and paves this big, long driveway. Only she can't drive, see, the car's just for the help."

"That's not really an option for me."

Rudy laughed, a dry, wheezing sound. "Tell me about it. Okay, lady, how about this. I have to charge you for the trip from me to you, that's going to be at least eleven to Arcadia plus five for the first mile out of town to get to your house. After that, it's two dollars for each additional mile, and then I have to charge you for waiting while you shop. I hate to do it, but it's not like I can get another fare in Arcadia."

"I'll do it," said Zoë, not even trying to add up the numbers.

"See you in an hour," said Rudy. He arrived nearly two hours later, with no explanation and no apology. He just pulled up in her driveway, stuck his cheery, bald, mustached face out the car window and yelled, "You ready?"

Zoë came down from the front porch where she'd been waiting. "Yes," she said, sliding into the backseat. "I've been ready for over an hour."

Rudy, busy fiddling with the car radio, grunted in reply. "Yeah," he said, "it took me a little extra time to get here, on account of I had to drop my wife's mother off at the doctor." Zoë didn't say anything. The back of Rudy's sunburned neck was the same shade as his handlebar mustache. He was wearing a camouflage shirt and his car smelled like a wet dog. Was there a single cliché the man had not embraced? "Ah," he said, "here's a good station."

Rudy pulled out into the road as a country singer sang about growing too old to win bar fights. Zoë leaned her head back on the seat, longing for Manhattan with an exile's fervent passion. Outside her window, there was nothing to look at but trees, cows, and the occasional house. "So," Rudy called from the front seat, "you moved out here full-time, huh?"

"Yes." Zoë continued gazing out at the countryside. Some people, she noticed, had a couple of goats or pigs in their backyard, or a scrawny horse. Others appeared to have vast, neatly fenced-in farms filled with fields of glossy Thoroughbreds.

"Bet it's a lot different than what you're used to." He tried to catch her eye in the rearview mirror.

"That it is," she said, looking out the window again. God, she was too tired to make generic conversation with a stranger.

"What was it made you move?"

"The schools."

"Oh, yes," said Rudy, sounding pleased. "The schools here got to be lots better than what you find in the city. Course, my wife teaches our kids at home. She says, I don't need anybody telling my kids that the Bible's got it all wrong. I mean, why should our kids learn some human being's guess instead of God's own truth?"

Zoë forced herself to count to five before speaking. "The theory of evolution isn't a guess."

Rudy scratched his ear. "Sure it is. Just some scientists guessing."

"No, it's a theory. A guess is when you have no way of knowing something, and you venture an opinion anyway. A theory is when you try to make sense of things by putting together a bunch of clues and coming up with the simplest explanation that makes sense."

"But it's not a fact," said Rudy, looking over his shoulder at her. "None of them scientists can say for sure we came from apes."

"We didn't come from apes," said Zoë, knowing it was a mistake but somehow unable to stop herself. "We *are* apes. A group of naked, bipedal, highly evolved, tool-using apes."

The corners of Rudy's long mustache twitched. "You aren't Christian, are you?"

Zoë just shook her head. No way was she admitting to being Jewish.

"Well, then, I'll just pray for you, lady." The rest of the trip was conducted in silence, until Rudy said, "Here we are," as he pulled up in front of a small supermarket. Zoë got out of the car and looked around her. Across the street was a small video shop, an antiques store, and a real estate agent's office. Ahead of her was Arcadia's sole traffic light, the bank, and an old-fashioned pharmacy. Beside the bank, there was a little green area with a gazebo, and a building that looked like a saloon straight out of a Western.

It was charming, if you didn't mind the fact that your neighbors were still holding out against newfangled heretical notions like evolution. Or that there was absolutely nobody on the streets. "I won't be long," she told Rudy.

"Take your time," he said in a good-natured voice. "You're paying for it."

"How Christian of you," Zoë said under her breath. Inside the supermarket, there were a surprising number of living, breathing human beings. In the cheese aisle, two plump young women with babies sitting in their shopping carts were discussing breast-feeding, while two men in camouflage vests were waiting their turn at the meat counter, which made Zoë wonder at how good their hunting skills were. Over in frozen foods, two old women were complaining about the price of prescription medication.

It was almost like being back in civilization. The choice of food was also surprisingly eclectic. "I wasn't expecting to find organic goat Gouda," she said to a small, blue-haired old lady who was reaching for a stick of cheddar.

"That's weekender food," the old lady said, not unkindly. "The city folk like it. As for me, I grew up with goats, and there is no way I am going to eat anything made from the milk of an animal that would happily eat a shoe."

The store seemed equally divided between what Zoë assumed were weekender tastes (organic mesclun, tiny free-range chickens, pomegranates) and what she figured must be local favorites (containers of macaroni salad; pallid, fleshy, prepacked chicken breasts; local Red Delicious apples). When she asked the butcher if he had any all-natural ground beef, he told her to come back on Friday, when he always took delivery of specialty meats.

And then Zoë discovered yet another thing to dislike about the country. There were no pre-prepared foods. In the freezer section, there was a small selection of waffles, pizzas, and chicken pot pies, but the small market did not have a selection of rotisserie chickens or cooked casseroles or gourmet pasta sauces. And it wasn't as if there were any take-out. In fact, as far as Zoë could tell, there weren't even any restaurants in town, just a small fifties-style diner that resembled a railroad car.

How do the young men around here eat, wondered Zoë, who knew how to order food in six different languages, but had never learned to roast a chicken. She figured her best bet would be to take the train into the city on Saturday and stock up on ready-made foods there.

The check-out girl was a plumpish blond teenager who appeared to be studying a driver's manual as she punched in the amounts of Zoë's purchases. She paused as she reached the pomegranate, which she held up with one silver-beringed hand. "Hey, Nina, what's this?"

"I don't know," said an older woman at another register. "Let me look it up."

"It's a pomegranate," said Zoë, glancing up from the local newspaper, which boasted the headline "Raccoon Rampage."

"Huh," said the girl. "How do you eat it?"

"Break it open, and eat the seeds. They're small and red and very juicy."

The girl made a face at her fellow cashier and rang it up without further comment. Imitating her fellow shoppers, Zoë wheeled her shopping cart out the door, instead of carrying the bags as she would have done in Manhattan. But when she went to look for Rudy's car, it was gone.

"Rudy?" She pressed her glasses up on her nose, suddenly realizing that she'd forgotten what the car looked like. She paused, trying to remember. Beige. Station wagon. He must have parked a little farther from the supermarket doors. But as Zoë walked around, peering into the windows of all the tan sedans, she realized that the car simply wasn't there.

"I don't believe it," she said. "I don't fucking believe it."

The little old blue-haired lady from the cheese counter gave her a sharp look as she got into her car.

"Sorry." Zoë spun around in a circle. There were only three other cars left in the parking lot, and none of them resembled the one that had brought her here. "Oh, Jesus, Rudy, where the hell are you?"

"He had to go get his mother-in-law," said a male voice from behind her. Zoë spun around, and there was the good-looking mechanic from the gas station, his dirty blond hair now pulled back in a ponytail to reveal a butterfly bandage over his right eye. Zoë prided herself on being able to recall visual details, and she was fairly certain that he was wearing the same black T-shirt, flannel shirt, jeans, and hiking boots as last time.

"Hello again," she said. "You here to rescue me for a second time?"

The mechanic gave her a lopsided grin. "Yeah."

Zoë shook her head, trying to clear it. "Okay, so let me understand this. Rudy, who runs a taxi service, arrives at my house an hour late because he has to take his grandmother to the doctor."

"Mother-in-law."

"Whatever. And then, when I go to do my shopping, he just deserts me because he had to pick her up again."

"It was an emergency. His wife was going to pick her mother up, but she got stuck behind an accident on Route Nine in Pough-keepsie."

"So what exactly am I supposed to do here? Wait a few hours? Ride the shopping cart home? Hitch?"

The mechanic laughed low in the chest, and Zoë tried to remember his name. "Calm down, you're not stranded. Rudy asked me to take you home."

Zoë paused, considering. "That's nice of you," she said. "Is this a typical occurrence in the country? Do taxis regularly just take off and leave their passengers to hitch rides with friends?"

The mechanic appeared to consider this. "I guess you wouldn't call it typical," he said. "Most people drive their own cars. Come on, I'll get you home." He began walking away from her.

Zoë hesitated. "No offense, but I don't really know you and you're a little banged up."

"Don't worry," he said, motioning that she should follow him across the parking lot. "It's not from a driving accident and I don't have a concussion."

"That's good," she said, absently admiring the lean, muscled view of him from the back as she walked behind him. "And you would know this because . . ."

"I'm an EMT." He led her over to a black pickup truck, then lifted a bag of groceries out of her cart. There were three large canvas bags in there already, one stamped with the medical insignia of winged staff and coiled serpents. He unzipped it to reveal a medical kit, complete with stethoscope and bandages.

Zoë raised her eyebrows. "An EMT who fixes cars?"

"I'm multitalented."

Distracted, Zoë watched him as he started to lift another bag before she realized what he was doing.

"You don't need to do that. I can get it." She picked up another bag, aware that the multitalented mechanic was watching her with a little smile on his face. "What?"

"Don't meet many women who ask me not to help them with groceries."

Zoë lifted the last bag and deposited it in the back. "Not a lot of feminists around here?"

"Guess not."

"Well, there aren't many left in Manhattan, either. It's gone out of fashion, along with in-depth news reporting and spiral perms." Zoë straightened. She had the feeling he'd been looking at her rear when she'd bent over. It was a fairly large rear, and the only men who usually checked it out in the city were from certain ethnic minorities. "Listen, I'm sorry about this, but I can't remember your name from the other day."

"John Mackenna. Everyone calls me Mack." He held out his hand. "To be honest, I can't recall yours, either."

"Zoë Goren." They shook hands, Zoë looking into the mechanic's amused blue eyes and thinking, This man is a redneck who would probably vote Bush in for a third term if he could. But he was physically attractive, there was no getting around it.

"Well, Zoë Goren, hop on up."

Zoë climbed up into the passenger's seat. "Did Rudy tell you where I live?"

"He did. He also told me that you were a nice lady who had the misfortune not to have found Jesus."

Zoë stared at Mack. "Is this a problem?"

"Not for me. I'm a godless atheist myself. But if you don't mind, don't let Rudy know, or he'll start quoting me scripture and trying to save me."

Mack drove quietly through the town, waving at one other car through his rolled-down window. It took Zoë a moment to realize he'd been giving her some advice about dealing with Rudy and his ilk. I know better than to wind up the local populace, thought Zoë, suddenly disgusted with herself. Why am I forgetting everything I know here?

Because she wasn't a journalist living in a suburb of Paris or Barcelona or Jerusalem and trying to blend in. She was in her own country, supposedly a melting pot of races and cultures and beliefs. No. That wasn't right. Her country was Manhattan. Arcadia wasn't melting anything more exotic than processed cheese spread in its pot.

So think of this as an alien culture, she thought. All I have to do is treat it like an overseas assignment, and I'll be all right.

She watched Mack out of the corner of one eye. Unlike Rudy, he didn't try to fill every moment with small talk, and his silence was the comfortable kind. Sitting high up in the front of the pickup, she also noticed that Mack drove a lot faster than his friend. He kept his window rolled down, letting in the smell of woodsmoke from someone's bonfire.

"Hey," she said, alarmed, as she noticed a crow sitting in the middle of the road just ahead of them, pecking at something dead. Mack swerved around it so smoothly that the bird was back to its meal in the space of a second.

Mack turned to her. "Hey, what?"

And just like that, she made up her mind, the way she did in foreign cities when she needed to choose a guide. "Let me ask you something. If I wanted to hire you to drive me places, would you be interested in an arrangement like that?"

Mack glanced at her, one eyebrow raised. "You want me to drive you places?"

Ridiculously, Zoë felt her cheeks heat with embarrassment. She chose to ignore it. "Yes, I mean, if I want to do some shopping, or visit my daughter's school, or get to the train station. We could plan it out week by week. Would you be interested?"

Mack turned his attention back to the road. "You know, it might make more sense for me to teach you how to drive." He paused. "I'm a certified driving instructor. It's what I do."

"When you're not patching up cars and people?"

He smiled, opening the gash over his right eye a little. "Cars is just a hobby. Patching up people is a volunteer position. Most of the EMTs and firefighters around here have day jobs." He pulled up into her driveway before she even realized they'd reached her house.

"Wow. That was quick." Zoë fumbled in her purse. "How much do I owe you?"

"No charge." In response to her questioning look, he added, "I think Rudy felt bad about everything."

Something about the way he said the other man's name made Zoë think the free ride wasn't really Rudy's idea. "Well. Thank you." She jumped down from the seat and found Mack already unloading the bags of groceries.

She took the remaining bag and followed him up to her front porch. "So," she said, "how about it? Do you want to consider being my driver?"

Mack stood there for a moment, hands stuffed into his back pockets. The sun was behind him, and Zoë couldn't see his expression clearly. "How would it work? You call me whenever you want a ride? Sometimes I'm in the back of the ambulance. I can't always be available right when you want me."

"We could set something up ahead of time."

"Woman like you doesn't want to be waiting on some man. You said you're a feminist, right? So how come you don't want to learn to drive yourself?"

"It's not that I don't want to. It's just that I don't think I can."

"Why not? You think you're not as smart as Rudy? Driving a car's not exactly rocket science."

"It requires a different kind of intelligence," said Zoë. "A different kind of brain. Also, I have no sense of direction. And frankly, the whole idea intimidates me."

"But you trust me to drive you? Even though you don't know me? You trust Rudy? How do you know I'm not a reckless, risk-taking idiot who makes bad choices?"

Zoë folded her arms over her chest. "And this is supposed to convince me to sign up for lessons?"

"I just can't stand for anyone to accept being helpless," said Mack.

"I'm the farthest thing from helpless! I'll have you know that I've lived and worked in some of the roughest areas in the world. I've gone into brothels in Thailand and the slums of Brazil. I spent a week on the Gaza Strip."

"Around here, you can't drive, you're totally dependent on other people."

They stared at each other. "I am not going to be bullied into learning to drive," Zoë said at last.

"Fine. Just explain where you got the idea that you have the wrong kind of brain for driving."

Zoë gave a deep sigh. "Look, I was in a car accident when I was sixteen, all right? The driver had a seizure and I nearly died." She rolled up her sleeve and showed him the long, thin scar that went up the back of her left arm. "It goes up my scalp and into my hairline, and half my teeth are caps. But the girl I switched seats with at the last minute? She's a vegetable." She waited for it to come: the apology, the admission that now he understood, she had a valid lifetime pass from driver's ed.

Instead Mack frowned, looking bewildered. "So you were in a car crash as a passenger. Why would that make you scared to learn? I'd think you'd be scared to have other people drive you."

Exasperated, Zoë ran her fingers through her hair. "I'm not saying it's logical. My mind agrees with you completely. But my body has a different reaction."

"You tried getting behind the wheel?"

"Once. With my father. I had a complete panic attack and passed out."

Mack nodded, as if she were confirming something he'd suspected. "You get on well with your dad otherwise? He good at teaching you other stuff?"

Reluctantly, Zoë shook her head.

"All right, then. How about this. If you're willing to work around my EMT schedule, then you pay me fifteen dollars an hour, which is my fee for teaching students to drive. And you let me keep trying to change your mind."

"Fair enough." They shook hands, and Zoë felt the tug of physical attraction again. His hands were rough, calloused. She hadn't touched a man's work-toughened hands in more years than she could recall.

Mack, however, seemed unaffected. "You want me to come by tomorrow?"

"Sure," said Zoë, not knowing exactly where she wanted to go, but certain that she wanted a way out of the house. "Can you come pick me up at noon?"

"You got it. In the meantime, how about you take a look at this." He pulled a booklet out of his back pocket.

Zoë took it. It was a driver's road instruction manual.

"I think you're jumping the gun a bit," she said, alarmed. "I said you could try to convince me, but only because you don't stand a chance."

"I wasn't talking about starting this minute," said Mack, already walking away. "I still need to order the passenger-side brakes and install them before we begin."

"In your truck?"

"No, in a car. Of course in a car," said Mack with a little laugh, getting into his truck before she could say anything else. Back inside the house, she looked down at the booklet in her hands as Claudius rubbed his large orange face against her ankles. "Dear Friend," said a letter from the Commissioner of Motor Vehicles on the first page, "Whether you are a new driver or an experienced driver reintroducing yourself to New York State's traffic rules and regulations, this manual will provide the basic information you need to be a knowledgeable, safe motor vehicle operator."

The second page suggested that the new driver consider enrolling in the New York State Organ and Tissue Registry, presumably in the event that he or she turned out to be something less than a knowledgeable or safe motor vehicle operator.

Claudius yowled and leaped onto the counter. Zoë rubbed his whiskered cheek and looked out the window. "I know, puss," she said, picking him up. "I want to go back to Manhattan, too."

But Claudius didn't want to go home. He wanted to go out, which he demonstrated by leaping out of her arms and onto the screen, where he hung by his claws, gazing fixedly at the brave new world beyond the front door.

Part Two

Zoë Goren

My Car, My Self: A Gas Guzzler's Manifesto

Everyone agrees that it would be nice not to be so dependent on those durn Middle Eastern oil-producing countries, what with their strange headgear and their peculiar notions about religion and such. And yeah, it sure would be swell if we could find something else to make our cars run, like vegetable oil or batteries. But notice that no one ever suggests that Americans try something radical, like taking the bus or the train, or, God forbid, riding a bicycle. Because while effete Europeans may opt for these sissified options, Americans tend to talk about their cars the way cowboys in the Old West used to talk about their horses.

It's my baby. My pal. My buddy. It's not a means of transportation, it's my independence, testimony to my taste and skill and wealth, the symbol of my freedom to wander at will, the proof that I am old enough to take charge, but still young enough to ride fast and live free.

Plus, who wants to be dependent on somebody else's schedule, or have to sit next to strangers? Americans, not content to idealize car culture, have made damn sure that it's nigh unto impossible to live without a set of wheels. We build our houses and our towns and even our cities sprawled out so that it would take a Lance Armstrong to bicycle from home to shops. We build those shops in giant malls at the edge of huge four-lane highways, and then spend next to nothing on our public transportation.

With the notable exception of New York City, there are few places in this country where not having a car is not a handicap. In most of Europe, on the other hand, cars are a luxury, not a necessity.

Which means that while we cling to a symbol of independence, Europeans have a shot at the real thing.

New York Chronicle **Op-Ed**

Ten

"Hello, Redneck," said Skeeter Davis, with an amused glance at Mack's flatbed Ford. "I knew you'd show up one of these days."

In the army, Mack had gotten used to being called a Damn Yankee. He'd forgotten that Skeeter liked to rag on him for liking dirt-track racing and driving a pickup. "Yeah, well, sorry it took me so long."

"Guess you must have got lost without your GPS."

Mack gave a polite chuckle, glancing around the garage where he'd spent most of his adolescence and trying to come up with a good excuse for why it had taken him six months to pay his old friend a visit. He couldn't think of any reason other than the real one: he wasn't the same gearhead kid obsessed with building stock cars and smashing them up in dirt-track races. And as far as he could tell, Skeeter hadn't changed at all. He even looked the same, from the long, lank ponytail hanging down his black Ford racing T-shirt to the intricate tattoos on his bony arms.

Well, maybe there were a few more tats, and a bit less hair under the NASCAR baseball cap, but the slightly crazed light in Skeeter's husky-pale eyes was undimmed by the years.

"Shop looks good," Mack offered, passing by a poster of Jessica Simpson orgasming on the hood of the General Lee. He stopped to inspect the cop car in the corner. "Hey, is that a dough mixer in the trunk?"

"Cool, huh?" Skeeter picked up a welder's helmet and indicated the conveyer belt running through the body of the car. "The whole car is like a doughnut maker. I copied it from a segment on *Monster Garage.*"

"Does it work?"

"I'm out of dough, but yeah, course it works." Skeeter turned the ignition key and the conveyer belt began to move. "But you want to check out my new project, man." Skeeter led him to the back of the garage, to a 1972 Ford Town and Country complete with fake wood paneling and most of its underside cut away. "I'm going to make it a pro street station wagon," said Skeeter proudly. "See the sketch?" He held up a rough thumbnail of the car suspended on enormous tires. It was like looking at a picture of the Brady Bunch dad wearing a massive gold chain and droopy-ass trousers. "The bitch of it is getting all the curved bits right."

Mack whistled. "That's a lot of cutting and welding." To be honest, he didn't see the point. The only thing you could do with a car like that was haul it off to some drag race where you slammed on the gas and then hit the brakes, or take it to a car show, where you'd sit your ass in a lawn chair and talk for a weekend. Back in the day, Mack had liked the adrenaline rush of dirt-track racing, where you might lose your car or you might lose your teeth, but at least it was always exciting.

Still, he didn't want to be rude, and if Skeet was still into beefing up muscle cars, the least he could do was act interested. Mack bent over and inspected the stripped door frame. "Nice work," he said. "Very smooth."

"Except for that bit." Skeeter put on a welder's helmet and

picked up a blowtorch, shearing away a slight metal protrusion. "How's that?"

"Better than I could've done."

Skeeter lifted the face mask. "Hey, you want to help me? I could use an extra pair of hands to get the new hinges in place, and the high school kid who comes here just up and joined the damn army." Skeeter's pale eyes glinted with mischief. "What an asshole, right?"

And it struck Mack that Skeeter was right, he had been an asshole, because that was all his old friend was ever going to say on the subject of Iraq, unless Mack himself brought it up.

"Sure," he said, "if you don't mind my being out of practice."

"Shit, man, you were never that good to start with," said Skeeter, still examining the old Ford's underbelly.

"No, I guess not," said Mack, surprised at how easy it was to fit back into their old, easy banter. "Hey, think you can get me a deal on something like a Honda Accord?"

"An Accord?" Skeeter straightened up as if he'd just been insulted. "No way, man. That's for pussies who think they're car guys because they can slap a spoiler on the trunk and change the rims. Plus, you don't want to drive around with some wet fart muffler making that damn blurp blurp Honda sound."

"I don't want to turn a hatchback into a hot rod," said Mack. "I just need a basic car. Well, actually, I need a shit car I can turn into something basic." He stuck his hands into the back pockets of his jeans, a little embarrassed now to say what he was planning out loud. "I'm, uh, going to start my own driving school. But I don't have much cash right now."

Skeeter looked appalled. "What's the point?"

"I know, it sounds kind of lame," said Mack, rocking back on his heels. He looked out the open doors of the garage and saw a young boy furiously pedaling his tricycle down a long driveway. Another future NASCAR fan. "It's just I was working for Jim Moroney, and I was kind of half decent at it, but I got sick of answering to that son of a bitch." Mack checked to make sure the kid was staying well away from the street. Yeah, he was being careful.

"I didn't mean what's the point of teaching folks to drive," said Skeeter, sounding amused. "I meant, what's the point of teaching them to drive slow? Everyone's safe at thirty miles an hour. You want to slip in something torquey, make sure they're really roadworthy."

Mack grinned. "So you're not against the idea?"

But Skeeter was already thumbing through the back of the *Hudson River Gazette.* "Seems to me I saw something back here . . . there it is: 1968 Mustang, motivated seller."

"Notice how it doesn't say the thing actually runs. I need something practical, Skeet."

"Nineteen seventy-six Corvette, original paint job."

"Because nothing says Responsible Driving School like an ancient muscle car."

Skeeter looked up. "Listen, Mack. I don't know if you recall, but this here is the Big Dog Garage. Remember what it was we specialized in?"

"Fucking up perfectly good station wagons in a doomed attempt to turn them into speed demons?"

"Exactly. You want a rice burner? Go on down to Church Street and Sal and his crew will be more than happy to oblige."

Mack laughed out loud, then realized Skeeter was serious. "Well, shit," he said. "I don't have the damn money for Church Street. And you're my friend." Even though we haven't spoken in more than a dozen years, he concluded silently.

"Yeah, well, friends don't let friends drive Hondas."

"And most of my friends don't quote bumper stickers."

Skeeter raised his chin, eyes glittering like ice. "You read the news lately? General Motors and Ford are going up in flames."

"So what are we saying here? That you'll only help me if it's American and if it turns you on?"

Skeeter didn't respond, and they stared at each other for a moment. Mack was the first to fold. "Okay," he said, "but it can't be some stick-shift lowrider. My students need to be able to see over the front windshield."

"So no to the Corvette. Any other sissy girl requirements?"

Mack thought about it. "Dual side air bags?"

Skeeter shook his head. "I can't believe you'd fall for that shit, man. I mean, driver's side, yeah, so you don't get the steering wheel implanted in your ribs. But what's the passenger-side air bag for?"

"Not going through the windshield?"

Skeeter nodded, but he didn't look happy. "Okay, it limits us, but we can put in dual air bags. But it has to be an American make."

"Fine. But don't go crazy on me. This can't be some wild project where we restore a sixty-six Mustang from a steering wheel and half the front seat. We need to meet federal safety regulations, so nothing older than the mid-nineties."

Skeeter rubbed his chin. "I guess I can live with that." He indicated the vintage station wagon with his thumb. "And you come by and help me get the tubing in."

Mack stuck out his hand. "You got a deal, man."

And just like that, they were in business.

* * *

The New York City woman was standing on the porch of her house, looking as if someone had rammed a pole up her butt. And it was quite some butt, Mack had to admit, particularly in those blue jeans. It might wind up crushing a man, but he'd sure as hell die happy.

"I thought we agreed on noon," she began, hoisting an enormous leather sack onto her shoulder and marching down the steps like she meant to hurt him some.

"Around noon," he corrected her, jamming his hands into his back pockets. Don't get smart with her, don't get into an argument. Can't afford to lose two jobs in as many days.

"No, we said noon," she insisted, pushing her dark glasses up farther on her nose. She was wearing her thick, black, curly hair down today, and he noticed a few strands of white at the temple. Premature, he decided. She didn't look that old to him. She was actually quite attractive, in an exotic way. He particularly liked her generous mouth. "I have to tell you, this isn't going to work if you're not able to arrive here on time. Do you realize that it's already twelve-thirty," she added, showing him her watch.

On the other hand, there was such a thing as too much mouth. "So, how bad is that? We about to miss some important conference? There a sale that ends at one?"

"No," said Zoë, walking past him and opening the passenger-side door to his truck. "But I was hoping to see my daughter during her lunch period, which is almost over."

Okay, so that shut him up. "You should have said so," he said, jumping into his seat and turning on the ignition. "Maybe we can still make it."

And maybe they could have, except that Zoë didn't have the faintest idea where the McKinley School was, except to say that it was on Chestnut Drive, near a lake, and surrounded by two old weeping willows. He had to explain that no, just the address wasn't enough, there were all kinds of unnamed roads around here.

"So how does anybody find anything? Do you want me to call the school and get directions?"

Why did women never understand that asking directions was tantamount to saying I am an idiot, incapable of finding my way out of a paper bag?

Mack swallowed. Ignoring the urge to tell Zoë that he'd once navigated himself out of a sandstorm and back to his platoon using nothing more than the stars and a compass, he forced himself to say yes, by all means, let's get those directions.

"Shit," she said, as her cell phone dropped the call twice in a row. "Damn it, it's not working."

"You want to try from inside the house?"

She paused, and Mack saw that underneath her irritation, she looked almost ready to burst into tears. Holy Jesus, he thought, I really don't want that to happen.

"I am sorry about getting the time wrong," he said abruptly, and she seemed to shake off whatever was riding her.

"That's all right. Okay. You know what? Since we're already probably too late to visit Maya today, how about you take me on a little tour of the area, help me get my bearings? And then maybe we could stop by a drugstore, a hardware store, and a liquor store on the way back."

Mack decided to take her on a scenic route, so he drove her up Skunk's Misery Road, past the goat farm and the crazy publishing lady with the pet donkeys, and over Mountain View to the new horse farm with the helicopter pad. "That belongs to some rich Wall Street fellow," he said. "Been there about six months. I give it another six before he sells up—these rich finance guys don't seem to hold on to it for long."

"Has it always been horse farms around here?"

Mack glanced over at Zoë. "Not until about ten, no, fifteen years ago. Folks started buying up the old dairy farms around here right around the time I left for the army." The minute the word "army" was out of his mouth, Mack felt his whole body go rigid. Great work, asshole, he thought. Now she's going to say, What did you do in the army, and where did you go, and for how long. She's going to feel entitled to the whole fucking story of my life, and because she's a paying customer, I can't just tell her, Sorry, not going to go there.

Mack stared out at the road ahead, waiting for it.

"Has it changed much?"

He turned to see that Zoë was looking out the window, taking in the landscape of open fields and white fences, the countryside formed by dairy farms and preserved by wealthy horse folk. "Not so much," he admitted. "In some ways, it's prettier now. Cows trample up the ground more."

"You don't resent city folk coming in?"

He snuck a glance at her, saw she wasn't teasing. "I guess I might if I wanted to farm. On the other hand, my sister actually runs a Thoroughbred training stable, so she makes her living off horsy weekenders." There was a young deer standing at the edge of a field and Mack slowed down in case it decided to jump out in front of him. "But she might be selling out. She's had a good offer."

"Another rich Wall Street type?"

"Nah, actually, there's some developers wanting to subdivide and put in some commercial stuff." Mack swerved as the deer finally made his move, and Zoë slammed her hand onto the glove compartment.

"Oh my God, you nearly hit him!"

Mack looked at her white face, surprised. "You kidding? I missed him by a mile. Hang on a sec." A doe followed the other deer, leaping spasmodically across the road. "They tend to go in pairs this time of year. Sometimes you can even get five or six of them."

"And you expect me to learn how to drive with deer leaping out at me?"

"I thought you said you weren't afraid of a little danger."

"When did I ever say I wasn't afraid of danger? Fear is a perfectly appropriate response to danger. I think I might have said something about having faced danger, which is something else entirely. But whenever possible, I like to avoid taking unnecessary risks, including playing dodge 'em with rampaging deer. Why are there so many of them, anyway?"

"No natural predators left. Can you believe that some of the city folks think we shouldn't go hunting them?" Mack shook his head. "We've already had about five deer-related accidents this fall. If folks didn't shoot some, we'd have deer crashing into cars every damn hour of the day."

Zoë raised her eyebrows. "So you have a huge number of deer wandering around bumping into cars, and you think the most humane solution is to blast away at them with shotguns?"

"Well, yeah," said Mac, turning up a side road. "Bow and arrow is okay in theory, but too many people don't really have the skill to make a clean kill."

Zoë gave him a cold, sidelong look. Her glasses had a funny way of reflecting the light, almost making it look as if she had a second face. "In my opinion," she said in a prissy voice, "there are more humane and environmentally sound ways to control surplus animal populations. The problem is that some people think they have a macho prerogative to get out and destroy wildlife."

Mack had never heard anyone speak in such complete sentences before. "You rehearse all that," he asked, "or was it just off the cuff?"

She drew herself up. "How could I rehearse it?"

Great, he'd pissed her off. Again. Mack turned onto a side road, past an old Revolutionary graveyard with smooth gray and white stones tilted in different directions. "In high school, I had a friend on the debate team," he said, thinking that maybe if he explained himself better she'd stop curling her lip at him. "Chris said you sort of prepare arguments ahead of time, like football plays."

"I didn't rehearse it."

This was really not going well. "Hey, there's a great view here," said Mack in an artificially bright tone of voice. He pointed to a field of tall corn. "This is all part of the Havers farm. You might want to take your daughter here this weekend, they're going to have a corn maze there, and a pumpkin catapult and hay rides and some local band playing."

"That sounds nice," she said in a very measured way, and Mack remembered that she had no means of getting there, other than himself. *She probably thinks I'm just trying to drum up more business.* Stupidly, he felt stung by this thought. I was just trying to be a good tour guide, he thought. "I was just saying," he said.

"Mmm," said Zoë, clearly not paying attention. "Listen, are we close to town now? I'm just thinking that I'm going to need a little time to shop."

"I'll head on over there now." Mack realized she was thinking about the time, because she was paying him by the hour. He'd never had this kind of business arrangement with someone before, and he could see how it complicated things. Previously, Moroney had handled all the money, and Mack had felt that there was something almost pure about his relationship with his students, since he got paid the same no matter whether he taught them well or not. In fact, Moroney hadn't wanted him to teach too much in the first lesson. But now that he was selling his own services, Mack could see that you had to make sure getting chummy didn't cross the line into pimping yourself.

Mack turned off Mountain View and onto the main road again, pointing out the Stewart's shop and gas station and liquor store on the outskirts of town. "Everything else you need is on Main Street," he said, pulling into the parking lot.

Zoë stood up, adjusting the long fringed scarf at her neck. Like her coloring, it had something foreign about it. "You're not coming in?"

"My ex-girlfriend works there," he said, indicating the shop. "I just had a little run-in with her new boyfriend, so I'm thinking better to just stay put."

Zoë pointed to the Band-Aid over his right eye. "When you say run-in, do you mean literally?"

"I pissed him off and he sucker punched me in the diner."

"Ah." Zoë readjusted her enormous shoulder bag. "That explains a lot. Okay, I'll be back in about ten minutes." She took about two steps, then turned around. "You'll be here when I come back? No mothers-in-law needing ambulance service?"

"I'll be here." Mack watched her ass as she walked away, then turned on the radio and drummed his fingers in time to the Dixie Chicks. The sky was clear and bright and there was a good woodsmoke smell in the air. He was feeling good enough to start singing along about poisoning Earl when he saw the person he least wanted to meet striding toward him, beer belly leading the way.

"Mack," said Jim Moroney, in a voice that promised a shitstorm of trouble. "We have to talk."

Eleven

he liquor store was not what Zoë had been expecting. One of Bach's Brandenburg concertos was playing in the background, there were framed Hudson River Valley School landscapes on the putty-colored walls, and there were *Wine Spectator* reviews on display in front of the bottles. A small, black dog with a porcine face and a red gingham collar waddled up to her, wagging its stump of a tail.

"Sit down, Vita," said a woman from behind the desk. The dog ignored her, grunting excitedly and darting between Zoë's legs. "I'm sorry," said the woman, walking over. As she approached, Zoë saw that the woman was about her own age but had prematurely white hair worn in an elegant short cut. She was wearing dark red lipstick, jade earrings, and a black turtleneck sweater with an asymmetrical hem, and for a moment, Zoë felt as if she were back in Manhattan, somewhere below Fourteenth Street. "I hope she's not bothering you. Vita's still a puppy and gets a little too friendly sometimes."

"I don't mind at all," said Zoë, bending down to pet the dog's short coat. "Large dogs make me nervous, but I like Vita here. What breed is she?"

"She's a French bulldog," said the woman, as if this were an accomplishment.

"Of course," said another woman's voice, "if you deliberately bred a person with stumpy legs, a bulging forehead, and a squashed-in nose, you'd be considered some kind of amoral monster." This second woman, who must have been in a back room, was tall and slender and nervy-looking, with high cheekbones and bright, naturally blond hair worn in an unflattering Dutch boy's bowl cut. In contrast to her colleague's elegantly bohemian style, she was wearing an enormous flannel shirt and dark, baggy jeans. If she were trying to disguise the fact that she was a natural beauty, she had failed miserably. "These dogs are so impractically designed, they pretty much all have to be delivered by C-section," she continued, reaching into a tin and handing the dog a treat. "You're a freak of nature, Vita, that's right, you are."

The first woman's dark eyes twinkled. "Gretchen rescues greyhounds, which is far more noble than spending wads of cash on a purebred puppy. But I suppose you could say I have a weakness for the freaky." The two women smiled at each other with the kind of tolerant affection that marks people as intimates.

Zoë felt like doing a jig. Lesbians! She had found a pair of lesbians! If the town was hospitable to wine-savvy same-sex couples, there was hope for other unexpected delights—Indian take-out, for example, or an internet café. Wanting to convey the extent of her approval, Zoë said, "Is this your store? I've just moved to the area from Manhattan, and I was prepared for a lot of tequila and zinfandel. But this is wonderful."

"You've just moved here? Welcome," said the elegant woman with the short white hair. "I'm Frances, and this is Gretchen. I used to live in the city, too."

"What part?"

"Downtown. I used to own a store in SoHo—Womanly Wines."

"What made you leave?"

"Well," said Frances, with a sidelong look at Gretchen. "It was a number of different things. I had a weekend cottage here for a while, and then I decided to move someplace quieter to work on my art." Zoë took a second look at the pictures hanging on the walls.

"Oh, not those. This is mine." She indicated a ceramic sculpture of a woman's torso. For some reason, Frances had stuck a taxidermy crow on the shoulder, which seemed a little kitschy.

"Very nice," she said, automatically.

"Do you think so? I'm still not happy with the eyes," said Frances. "I think this wild turkey really turned out much more successfully." She pointed to a large stuffed tom turkey that was standing in one corner, holding a frozen TV dinner in its beak. "Nowadays, though, I'm really into amphibians and reptiles."

"She's done an amazing snapping turtle," interjected Gretchen. "When she picked the body up from the road, it looked totally destroyed, and now the thing looks like it's about to take a bite out of you. Did she tell you she only uses bodies she finds on the road? Much harder artistically, but Frances feels it's also a political statement." She gave the other woman a fond look. "Anyway, I need to take Vita to the vet. You need anything from town?"

Frances fussed over the little dog as Gretchen lifted her into her arms, and then returned her attention to Zoë.

"Sorry about that," she said.

"Not at all. So, are there a lot of expat city folks here?"

"Look around you. Do you think this shop could survive without a sizable population of Manhattanites?" Frances went on to explain that her clientele was mainly made up of weekenders who drove in from the Upper East Side and SoHo on Friday evenings. "You may think this is just a sleepy little town," she concluded, "but we have our share of local celebrities."

"You have celebrities?" Zoë glanced away from a display of St. Emilion reds that had caught her eye.

"Oh, God, this place is crawling with famous folks now. There's a bestselling English mystery writer not far from the village, and a movie actress, the one who played a pregnant woman in that movie, and of course we have that newscaster fellow."

"Really. I'd never have known. I thought I was pretty isolated."

"I thought so, too, when I first moved here. Now I can barely get enough quiet time to do my art." Frances patted her hand. "Oh, it's an adjustment, I know, but you give it a little time. You'll wind up loving it. Here." She handed Zoë a card. "That's my number. Why don't you call me when you're free? I'll invite you over."

A little surprised by the use of the singular pronoun, Zoë decided not to press things. Maybe being a lesbian wasn't all that comfortable in Arcadia, and the two women had adopted a "don't ask, don't tell" policy. In any case, she hoped Frances really meant it. In the city, the exchange of numbers was often a symbolic act, but perhaps here people actually followed through and called new acquaintances.

Feeling cheered, she'd headed out to Mack's truck before she remembered that she had no way to get to Frances's house unless Mack drove her. Preoccupied with this problem, she was only six feet from the pickup before she realized that Mack was having a serious discussion with another man.

Slowing down, Zoë observed that the other man was doing most of the speaking. Muscular, barrel-chested, and in his mid-to-late forties, the man had a graying crew cut and was dressed in a navy blazer and khakis. Lawyer, she thought. As she got closer, she could see that he was lecturing Mack.

"Let me ask you something, Mack. Have you really considered what you're getting yourself into? I mean, you're going to have what, one car to teach in? What if it breaks down?"

"I can fix it," said Mack. "That's the nice thing about being a former gearhead. I actually know how cars work."

"What about insurance? Did you find out whether your personal insurance is going to cover your students?"

Mack smiled. "As you kept reminding me, Jim, I'm a vet. Turns out there's all kinds of help available for a wartime vet trying to start up his own business."

The crew cut took a deep breath, which seemed to inflate him for a moment. "All right," he said slowly. "All right. Let's look at this another way. I have operated a driving school in this town for the past twenty years. I have a reputation. I have folks I taught to drive sending me their kids. What the hell do you think you have that's going to compete with that?"

Mack cocked his head to one side. "I do believe you once mentioned the charm of having a former Special Forces medic teaching you how to parallel park. But what's the problem? You think this town's not big enough for both of us, Hoss?"

Even from where she was standing, Zoë could tell the other man was now seriously pissed off. "Nothing you do could have any real impact on my business, but you are turning yourself into a nuisance. Having two driving schools in one small town is going to confuse things, and you know it."

"Town's got two garages," Mack pointed out. "Nobody's gotten them mixed up."

"This is about Jess, isn't it?"

"Actually, it has to do with me trying to make a living," he said, very quietly.

"She was always too good for you." The older man paused, but Mack didn't say anything. "And if you think I'm going to recommend you as a safe driving instructor . . ."

Fascinated, Zoë started to walk closer to the men and accidentally swung the bag she was carrying, clanging the bottles of wine together. Mack and the other man both turned to her. The other man looked annoyed.

"I'm sorry," she said, self-consciously pushing her glasses up on her nose. "I didn't mean to interrupt."

"She's with me," said Mack. "Throw the things in the back, Zoë."

"Let me help you with those," said the crew-cut man, reaching out for her bottles of wine.

"That's all right," said Zoë, putting them carefully in the rear of the truck, propped up by a spare tire.

"She's a feminist," said Mack, sounding happy about it. "Zoë Goren, meet Jim Moroney. Jim runs a driving school, too, but at the moment he only has the one instructor, who's about to turn eighty."

Jim Moroney ignored Mack, addressing Zoë instead. "Listen, miss, I'm not the type to go sticking my nose in, but I hate to see any woman getting mixed up with John Mackenna. He tell you he just broke up with a girl? He tell you he just got fired?"

"No, but I'm piecing things together," said Zoë. She'd learned from interviewing people that when someone had to inform you that he or she was not nosy or cruel or vindictive, it was pretty safe to assume the opposite was true.

The man shook his head, as if she had disappointed him. "You may think you know him, but do you really? I don't like to mention it, but he came back from the war with some issues. As in post-traumatic stress." He shook his head, as if he were speaking out of sympathy, but Zoë could see the gleam of satisfaction in his eyes before he turned on his heel and walked away.

"Jesus Christ," Mack called after him, "is this the way you're going to play it, Jim? You're going to go around bad-mouthing me?"

Zoë climbed up into the passenger seat beside Mack. She could feel the tension coiled in his lean body, and she felt a moment's concern. "How much of what he's saying is true?"

Mack looked at her. "My name's really John Mackenna."

"Were you in Iraq?"

After a moment, he nodded. "I don't have any trouble with my temper, though. I just have a problem with him."

"In that case," said Zoë, "why don't we get out of here?"

Mack did something to the engine that made it growl, then pulled out in a squeal of tires. That was one thing car culture had going for it; you could make a quick getaway. As Mack left town and picked up speed, she gazed out the window, abruptly wishing for the easy anonymity of public transportation. It wasn't that she didn't like Mack, she did. And in a way, the whole parking lot incident had been diverting. But was she going to get sucked into some hillbilly soap opera every time she wanted to go out? She glanced at Mack through her peripheral vision. He seemed to understand that she was not entirely happy with what had transpired, but he didn't try to explain the whole story or argue his side. She couldn't decide if he was unusually sensitive to other people's moods, or if he just didn't care what she thought.

When he deposited her at her house, he hesitated, one hand braced against the open window of his truck.

"You want to call me when you know when you need me again?"

Zoë nodded. "I just need to check my schedule. I'm thinking probably Sunday or Monday, if you're available."

"All right then," said Mack, starting the engine. "By the way, by the end of next week, I'll have a car ready for you to start lessons. So you can be independent." The way he stressed the last word made her wonder if he had intuited what she'd been thinking.

"Mack, listen, I'm not sure . . ."

But with a growl of his engine, he was already halfway down her driveway and out of earshot.

*   *   *

The following day was the longest of Zoë Goren's adult life. A quiet day in the country with no interruptions was supposed to be conducive to work, but Zoë sat in front of her computer, feeling as restless as her cat.

The fifth time Claudius yowled and leaped up onto her bookshelf, toppling reference sheets everywhere, Zoë locked him downstairs in the basement. Then she looked around the kitchen, wishing that the mailman delivered her three subscription newspapers earlier in the day. Zoë sighed. This was, she knew, a fine opportunity to finish her article. She could also use the time to unpack and organize her many boxes of books, which were currently lined up against the wall in the living room. She could clean the kitchen. She could cook something interesting for dinner. Except, of course, that she didn't know how to make anything more complicated than a meatloaf.

Exercise. That was what she needed. If she'd been in the city, she could have gone for a walk, or taken a dance class. Or she might have walked to the dance class, and then to the store, and then home. Who would have guessed that moving to the country meant giving up walking as a means of transportation?

Zoë turned on the radio and sat down on the living room floor with her legs extended on either side of her. God, she felt stiff. She realized she hadn't been to a class since last month, when she'd canceled her gym membership.

Zoë reached her arms forward, intensifying the stretch of her inner thighs, and then found herself putting her elbows down on the floor and resting her chin on her palms. "Okay," she said out loud, "so I am not motivated to do this on my own." Maybe what she really needed was to talk to a friend. As she got up, her knees gave an audible click as she went to find the phone.

Claudius howled from the basement as she dialed Bronwyn's number from memory. She wondered if the move had driven him mad. "Bronwyn, it's me," she said. "My cat has gone insane and I'm right behind him. Listen? Can you hear that? That's him, howling."

"This is the same cat I used to think was stuffed because all he did was sleep?"

"No, this is some other cat inhabiting his body. The demon inhabiting my body, on the other hand, has sapped all my energy. I don't want to work, I don't want to clean, I don't want to work out." Zoë walked to the kitchen window and looked out at the mountain, which only served to make her feel more isolated. "I'm just staring out the window, the way Claudius used to. Bron, I think I'm depressed, and it's lovely weather outside. What the hell am I going to do when the weather turns bad?"

"Does this mean you're coming back? Please say you are."

"Tomorrow's Saturday," said Zoë, as Claudius howled and scrabbled at the other side of the basement door. "Maybe Maya and I can come and stay overnight."

"Oh! My gosh, that would be wonderful, but I meant, come back for good," said Bronwyn, sounding uncomfortable.

"Seeing as how we've only just gotten here, I can't do anything about moving back just yet. But I can spend the weekend."

Bronwyn made an unhappy sound. "The thing is," she said slowly, "we can't this weekend. I've got two frigging different birthday parties to attend."

"Oh, that's too bad. How about next weekend?"

"This is so lame, but I think Brian's mom is coming."

"I don't know whom I feel sorrier for, me or you."

Bronwyn laughed. "How about the weekend after that?"

Zoë checked her calendar. They were talking about November, when the picture of a pretty maple tree ablaze in color was replaced by the picture of an oak with one leaf clinging to its highest branch. "I guess that'll have to do," she said, penciling the date in. She turned back to October, and realized that she'd forgotten about Halloween. It fell on a school day this year.

"Crap," she said. "Bronwyn, do you have any idea what country people do for Halloween? There are no people on my road."

"Don't ask me, I grew up in the burbs. We couldn't escape our neighbors."

Zoë sighed, then felt the short hairs on the back of her neck prickle. "I think I hear something." She listened harder, and then there was a loud knock on the door that made her jump. "Oh my God, there's someone here!"

"Jesus, Zoë, try not to scream in my ear. So there's someone there. Why don't you go see who it is and call me back later."

Her heart pounding at the unexpected interruption, Zoë walked to the door. "Who is it?" In the back of her mind, she was half expecting Mack. She ran her hands over her hair, which was gathered into a bushy ponytail on top of her head.

"Satellite company. You order a dish?"

"Yes! Yes, yes, I did." She glanced down at herself. Her breasts were spilling out of a tank top with a built-in shelf bra. "Hang on a moment, and I'll let you in." Zoë ran to the closet, threw a sweater on over her tank top, and then came back to open the door.

The satellite dish guy stood in her doorway, a large, hulking shape in a beige uniform, checking something off on an order form.

"You know, I usually don't watch much TV, but I can't tell you how relieved I am to see you. I feel so cut off without CNN." A brief paranoid thought struck her: What if he's really an ax murderer? He looked a little like an ax murderer.

"Uh-huh. Sign here." He handed her the form.

She signed. "I was expecting someone earlier in the week, but I guess you're pretty busy around here." In the city, people complained that you could scream and your neighbors wouldn't even call the cops. But out here, thought Zoë, there was no one to even hear you scream.

But if the satellite guy really was a serial killer, he wasn't the charming kind. Barely glancing at her, he took the order form back and ripped off the bottom sheet. "Okay, I'll go set up the dish." He spoke in a low grumble, and Zoë was reminded of Lurch, the zombified butler from the old *Addams Family* TV show.

"Oh. Great," said Zoë. "I'll just get back to work, then. My editor at the *New York Times* is waiting to speak with me."

The satellite man barely nodded and walked away. Zoë walked over to her computer and turned it on.

In order to fully understand the plight of women in restrictive Middle Eastern societies, she wrote, you'd have to imagine yourself stuck in the middle of the country without a car, or the ability to drive a car if you had one. In that situation, you wouldn't just be isolated, you would be dependent on others, and therefore vulnerable.

On a roll at last, she'd just finished a thousand words when the satellite man walked into the kitchen and told her he was done.

"Just in time for the weekend. My daughter will be thrilled," said Zoë as Claudius began howling again from the basement.

The man's eyes widened, the first sign of human expression he'd shown. "Jeez, what's that?"

"Oh, shoot, I forgot my cat." Zoë opened the door and Claudius darted out, then sat down to clean his paw with an air of injured dignity. "He's been acting very strangely."

"Probably just wants to get out and go hunting," said the man, bending over to scratch Claudius's massive orange head. "You don't like being cooped up inside, do you, puss? Poor old feller." He straightened up. "Well, ma'am, you enjoy your satellite TV." He opened the back door, then paused. "And if you have any questions, feel free to call us."

"Thanks again," said Zoë, just as Claudius, seeing his chance, shot through the small gap and vanished into the wooded area behind the house.

"Whoops," said the satellite man, but Zoë had the feeling he'd done it on purpose.

* * *

The next day Claudius was still missing. Maya, exhausted from her first week of school, had gotten extremely upset when Zoë had told her that Claudius was out in the yard somewhere.

"Did you call his name? Did you try cat food?"

"I did, Maya. I'm sure he'll come back soon."

Tears glistened in Maya's eyes. "But why did you even let him out, Mom? It's dangerous out there!" Her voice, rising in panic, ended on a wail.

"It wasn't me, Maya, it was the satellite guy. You want to call him up and yell at him?"

Maya folded her arms in front of her chest. "*You* call him up."

"I already yelled at him in person. Come on, let's go have a look for the emperor. I can't imagine he'll want to rough it for long."

"Fine," said Maya, clearly not placated. "But if we don't find him we're never watching TV again!"

"Aw, please, that's not fair."

Maya narrowed her eyes. "Stop kidding around, Mom, we have a cat to find."

But in the end, even though they were still catless after much searching of the dilapidated chicken coop and the rattling of Claudius's food dish, they did settle down in the living room to watch one of the satellite stations. Some obscure programmer had decided to show *Born Free*, a film Zoë had last seen in 1971, when she'd been in first grade.

"Mommy."

"Yes?" Zoë stroked her daughter's head, which was in her lap. Onscreen, the slender blond British actress playing Joy Adamson watched Elsa the lion cub play across a faded African plain.

"But why does she want to release Elsa into the wild, Mommy?"

Zoë remembered wondering the same thing. Why would you give up a lioness that adored you? It had been incomprehensible, one of those crazy grown-up things, like putting on makeup that didn't look like you were wearing makeup.

"She can't keep Elsa as a pet anymore, and she doesn't want to have her lioness go into a zoo."

Maya, who had been listening, put her head back down on Zoë's legs. "I want to work with lions in Africa when I grow up."

Zoë smiled. "Do you know, that's just what I said the first time I saw this movie." For years she'd imagined herself as a kind of combination Hollywood Joy Adamson and young Jane Goodall, cool and composed in neat khaki shorts, her hair magically transformed into a smooth ponytail, her voice vaguely British as she described herd migrations. It was never clear to Zoë whom exactly she was describing the herds to—an invisible TV audience? Tarzan?

In any case, that dream had died when she was about twelve and went on a camping trip. Unable to sleep with the open sky above her, Zoë discovered that she was not at home in the great outdoors. But she'd passed the fantasy of working with animals on to Maya, talking about the way Jane Goodall's empathy and open-mindedness had made her a better scientist than other, more academically qualified candidates.

"So Maya," she said now, "don't you think you'd get a little lonely, living out there in the bush?" It was an old joke between them: Zoë always tempted Maya with civilization, and Maya always remained steadfast in her love of the wild.

"No, I'd be surrounded by animals."

"With no pizza parlors. No movie theaters."

"We don't have those things here either, and I love it." Maya watched the faded sixties African landscape on the TV set. "I want to live close to nature," Maya said. "I don't ever want to go back to the city."

Uh-oh. Their little routine had never ended with that punchline before. "Well," Zoë said, "you may find you'll change your mind about that."

"I won't. The city is too crowded."

"But there's so much to do there. Museums, restaurants, parks." Zoë realized that they were playing out their prescribed parts again, but this time there was a note of underlying seriousness in her own voice and, God help her, in Maya's.

"Who needs parks when you have a forest in your backyard?"

Zoë, deciding it was better to change the subject, tucked the knitted afghan more tightly around her daughter's narrow shoulders. "You cold?" No use convincing her daughter that the city had more to offer when they still had the whole school year to get through.

"No, I feel all right." Now that the sun was going down, there was a nip in the air, but they had agreed to leave a window open in case Claudius decided to come back. "But I am hungry."

"Me, too. What do you feel like? Roast wildebeest? Gazelle chops?"

"Something we can eat on a tray. Oh, Mommy, look, they're abandoning her!" On the television screen, the young lioness was galloping full tilt after Adamson's open jeep. Zoë didn't think she'd ever heard Maya say the word "abandon" before. The school was already having a positive effect. "Do you feel like a grilled cheese sandwich?"

"Okay, but no tomato. I hate warm tomato."

Zoë propped an extra cushion under her daughter's head.

"What do you mean, 'okay'? Do you mean, 'You are a wonderful mother to go fix me food and feed me on a tray like a princess'?"

Maya looked up, dimpling. "Indeed, Mother," she drawled in a fair imitation of 1940s BBC upper-class English, "that is exactly what I wished to say." Then, in a normal voice, she added, "Come quick before something happens. I don't want to be alone if something sad's going to happen."

"I won't be five minutes." Zoë hummed the theme song to *Born Free* as she grilled their sandwiches, feeling better than she had all week. This was the way things were supposed to be, mother and daughter curled up together, bound not just by love and common history but by the similarities in their tastes, their preferences, their personalities. Romances with men might come and go, but the romance you had with a child could be trusted to sustain you.

Zoë had just arranged the food on a tray when she heard a faint scrabbling sound, and a thump. "Maya?" She walked into the living room, where Maya was still lying on the couch while Elsa the lioness approached a male lion. "Strange."

Zoë took the tray and was carefully maneuvering her way back into the living room when her bare foot connected with something warm and furry. Shocked, she took a step backward, then slid on a patch of something wet and sticky.

She screamed and landed hard on her tailbone, the cheese sandwiches flying off the tray.

"Mom, what is it?" Maya stood in the doorway, her eyes wide. "Oh my God, Claudius!" For a terrible second, Zoë thought her daughter was saying that she had just tripped over the corpse of their cat. But then she saw that Claudius was ecstatically rubbing himself against Maya's ankles, his purr as loud as an outboard motor.

And then Zoë glanced down at the mound of matted fur at her feet, saw what it was, and screamed.

Twelve

"I am so sorry to bother you on a Saturday night," said Zoë, before she'd even opened the door completely. "It's just . . . it was still hopping. And bleeding. I think I could have handled one, but not both."

"Don't worry about it. My sister's lived in the country her whole life and she still freaks out about mice." Mack could smell a slightly foul smell in the air, which probably meant a ruptured large intestine. "In the living room, you said?"

"Well, there's a big part of it there."

"So we're talking search and recovery."

"It was search and rescue, but between the time I called you and when you got here, the rabbit died." She gave a wry smile. "Words to strike a man dumb."

"Excuse me?"

"The old pregnancy tests involved killing a rabbit," Zoë said over her shoulder as he followed her into the kitchen. "So 'the rabbit died' used to mean 'I'm pregnant.' Anyway, here are the cleaning supplies." She handed him rubber gloves, a plastic bag, a bottle of spray disinfectant, and a roll of paper towels.

Mack stared at the gloves, still a little befuddled by the rabbit-pregnancy connection. "Do we suspect this particular bunny of having Ebola? All I need is a paper towel."

"This isn't a bunny. This is a head, a puddle of viscous black stuff, a foot, and something that looks like an eel."

"You didn't consider taking the cat and putting him in another room?"

"He was rather insistent about staying. Here. Take the gloves. I'm sure you don't want to head out for your Saturday night frolics smelling like viscera."

"Actually," Mack said, "this is my big activity tonight." The minute the words were out, he wanted to hit himself. What the hell did he have to go and say that for? Why not just announce: I don't have much of a life?

"Well, let me tell you, you still want the gloves. I slipped in what's left of Bugs over there, and it wasn't pretty. I may never wear those clothes again." She pointed to something soaking in a bucket that smelled strongly of disinfectant.

As Zoë turned, Mack realized that the shapeless, tie-dyed cotton dress she was wearing was backlit and he could see the silhouette of her voluptuous body with embarrassing clarity. He dragged his eyes up, noticing that she'd twisted her thick, dark hair into a loose knot on the top of her head. It was still damp, he realized; she must have showered. In a way, this all reminded Mack of ambulance calls, where you showed up and found people half naked or in their pajamas, their dinner half eaten on the table. Except in those sorts of situations, he tended not to notice things like breasts. "Okay," he said, "I'd better get to it."

"I only spotted one foot, by the way. If you could look for the other three . . ." She was standing against the light again, and he turned abruptly toward the living room, only to find himself face to face with the little blond girl, who was wearing a pair of silky pink Cinderella pajamas the exact shade of liquid amoxicillin.

"I threw up," she said, sounding very matter-of-fact.

"Sorry to hear it."

"I'm worried that I'm not going to be much good helping animals in the wild if I throw up when I see a dead rabbit."

"It just takes a little getting used to. Why don't you go brush the bad taste from your teeth and I'll take care of the mess."

The girl tilted her blond head to one side, considering. "But how do you get used to it, if you never do it?" She paused. "I think I'd better watch you. Is it okay if I watch you?"

"As long as you don't throw up again."

"I wonder," said the girl slowly, "if that's really the kind of promise you can keep. I mean, it's not like promising not to steal or lie, is it?"

Mack was struggling to come up with a response when he saw that the girl's eyes were sparkling with mischief. "Hang on, are you having fun with me?"

She giggled and opened her mouth to reply, but before she could speak they both heard a bang from the other room. A moment later, Zoë shouted, "No!"

Walking back into the kitchen, Mack was greeted by the sight of the enormous, fluffy cat batting the rabbit head across the floor. Zoë looked as though she were about to pitch a fit. "There now, puss, what a good hunter." Trying not to laugh, he held the cat by its scruff and got the head away.

A sharp, feminine squeal made Mack glance up. Mother and daughter were both clutching each other, identical expressions of horror on their faces. "City girls," he said. "Honestly." And then he felt a sharp pain in his right hand, and looked down to find that the fucking cat had sunk its fangs into the fleshy pad of his thumb.

*   *   *

"You sure you're okay driving back if you have another glass of wine?"

"I'll be fine." Zoë refilled his wineglass and Mack settled back onto her couch. Something about her living room reminded him of houses he'd seen in Iraq—the big, tasseled pillows, the low brass coffee table, the Persian rug.

"How's the hand feeling?"

"Stop fussing, it's fine." She'd already put some antiseptic cream and some tape on his hand, which was really more than he would have bothered to do for himself. Cat bites were nasty, but Mack trusted his immune system.

"You didn't need to clean up the rabbit, you know," Zoë said, heading back into the kitchen. "I mean, after you got bitten. I could have handled it."

"Don't make a big deal out of it," he called after her. The kid, Maya, was sitting on the rug, cross-legged. "He's never done that to anyone before," she said. It took Mack a moment to understand that she was talking about the cat, now transformed back into a fat, lazy cushion of orange-and-white fur, asleep next to the hot-air vent by the window.

He turned back to the girl. Pretty child. Her eyes were the same shade as her mother's, but other than that, you'd never have guessed the two were related. "Guess he never had someone try to take his bunny head away before."

Maya laughed, revealing new front teeth, still too large for her face. "You seem to know a lot about animals. Have any?"

Mack shook his head. "Not at the moment. My sister works with horses, though," he added, since Maya was still looking at him expectantly.

"You're kidding," said Maya. "What does she do?"

"Trains them. Rides them."

"Can I meet her?"

"Okay," said Zoë, coming back into the room with a tray of food. Her tie-dyed dress billowed around her as she walked, reminding him of something. "It's not elegant, but it's hot." She passed him a plate with a piece of pita bread and a dollop of something that looked like wet cement. "Can you manage that left-handed?"

"Sure." Their eyes met, and Mack felt the twist of sexual attraction for the second time that night. *You're working for her, moron.* He gestured to his plate. "What is this, anyway?"

"Hummus." Zoë handed a second plate to her daughter. "Hope you don't mind, but it's pretty much all I have. I used up all the cheese on the grilled cheese sandwiches I dropped when I saw the rabbit."

"Mom, Mack's sister works with horses."

"That's nice."

Mack looked down and thought he'd been wrong; what this stuff really looked like was cat vomit. "I don't have a spoon," he said, not entirely sure that he wanted one.

"You use the pita to scoop it up," said Maya, tearing off a corner of the flat circle of bread to demonstrate. "Haven't you ever had hummus before?"

"Not that I recall." He tried a small taste and was surprised to find it wasn't bad—sort of salty, starchy, and lemony all at the same time. He ate another bite, awkwardly. "I think I like it." He looked up to see Zoë watching him. "Where do you buy this stuff, back in the city?"

"Actually I saw some back in your local supermarket, but I made this with a can of chickpeas and some tehina I had around."

Mack ate another bite. "Always wondered what to do with my spare tahooha."

Zoë smiled. "Tehina," she said, swallowing the *h* in a way that sounded like Arabic. "Here, I'll bring some back to show you." As she left the room, it finally occurred to him that Zoë might not be Italian. Of course, there were tons of Arab Americans, he thought, feeling stupid. He tried to remember if she knew that he'd been in Iraq. Yes, he thought he'd said something.

Mack turned to the kid, who had almost polished off all her bread. "You eat this stuff a lot?"

Maya nodded. "Sometimes my mom uses it to make a kind of hamburger thing, too. She calls it her specialty." She gave him a mischievous look. "That means it's one of the few things she can cook that turns out okay." She paused. "Does your sister live around here? Do you think she needs any help? The horses are my favorite thing at school, but I don't get to ride more than an hour a week."

"Moira lives right outside of town. I can ask her if she could use a little help, so long as you don't throw up at the smell of manure." Maya giggled and Mack wondered where the father was. Divorced, probably, but you never knew, maybe he was dead. Mack didn't want to blunder into anything by asking the girl, so he just let his eyes roam around the room. There were cartons of unpacked books, along with boxes marked "toys" and "living room." He crammed the last of the pita in his mouth and stood up to examine the handful of books that had made it onto the shelf: *The End of Faith, Reading Lolita in Tehran, Leaves of Grass.*

Mack glanced over his shoulder at the kid. "Still got a lot of unpacking to do, huh?"

"Mom says she needs help hanging those." Maya pointed to something around the level of his knees, and Mack looked down and saw that there were a few framed pictures propped up against the wall. The one in front was a black-and-white photograph of a voluptuous nude, her long, thick hair hanging down and obscuring her face. He did a quick mental comparison of the length of the legs, the shape of the breasts.

"Yeah, that's my mom," said Maya, standing up with her plate. "If you look closely, you can see that she's pregnant with me."

Sure enough, there was a definite curve to the naked stomach.

And a slight shadow underneath the raised arm. Jeez, was that what he thought it was? Mack leaned closer, fascinated. Up until this minute, he'd thought women with body hair were top on his list of turn-offs, but there was something shockingly earthy about the small dark blur against the paleness of her skin. He looked at the bulge of Zoë's stomach again, the shape of her hand resting against it.

"Maya, honey," said Zoë's voice from behind him. "Time to get ready for bed."

"Okay. But can I come down again after I brush my teeth?"

"No, I'll come up to say good night." Zoë pointed to the picture, which Mack was now studiously ignoring. "Five months along."

Mack glanced back over his shoulder at her. "That so? You don't— You didn't look it." He wasn't sure what was stranger: the fact that he was half-aroused by the photographic image of her naked, pregnant body, or the fact that she felt comfortable displaying the picture and discussing it. "Maya said you could use some help with these," he said, indicating the pictures.

"I'm not very domestic, am I?" Zoë didn't sound particularly troubled by this, and Mack thought about Jess, who'd been desperate to decorate his apartment over the barn. He hadn't been entirely sure what she meant by decorate, but had been pretty sure it was the human female equivalent of a dog marking the boundaries of his territory. "To tell you the truth, the only thing I really care about is getting the books sorted. The thing is, there are so many of them, I get a bit overwhelmed so I just sort of keep putting it off."

"I can relate to that." He removed a small book from one of the cartons. *The Gashlycrumb Tinies*. There was a cartoon of death on the cover, holding an umbrella over the heads of a number of small, blank-faced children. He opened it and discovered what appeared to be an alphabet primer for ghouls or ghoulish children. A, for example, was for Amy, who had the misfortune to fall down a flight of stairs. The accompanying illustration showed an old-fashioned little blond girl, tumbling down a staircase. Intrigued, Mack flipped to the next page, only to learn that B for Basil wasn't any luckier. When Mack reached the letter T, he gave a choked laugh. The ink drawing was of a small boy in an empty room, about to unwrap a package. The text, in its nursery rhyme sing-song, described the boy's explosive fate.

Strangely, this page aroused the same feeling as the poetry he'd been reading. As if someone had just come out and said the thing he was thinking, only he hadn't known he was thinking it until someone else said it. Mack looked at the picture again. "This for kids?"

"Not exactly. The writer and artist was a guy called Edward Gorey. He wrote things in the style of children's books, but as you can see, his sensibility tended toward the macabre." Zoë took the book from his hand and flipped to another page. "This one was always my favorite. I've always suspected you could die from ennui."

Mack considered whether or not to say something, then thought, What the hell. "At the risk of sounding stupid, what's on-we?"

For some reason, Zoë flushed as if she were the one revealing ignorance. "It's from the French, meaning profound boredom. Killing boredom."

"Good word." Mack nodded, filing it away. "And you said another word a minute ago, mickab?"

"'Macabre'?" She spelled it. "Another French word. Ghoulish, gruesome."

"Huh." He examined the book again. "There was this guy I knew in Iraq," he said. "He had a sense of humor like that. Macabre." Mack started to laugh. "I can just imagine him saying, 'D is for dog that lies dead in the road. E is for what the dog does—explode.'" Mack looked over at Zoë. "Well, okay, that wasn't good, but you get the idea."

She didn't smile, and Mack realized that she had, in fact, gotten the idea. "Did he die, your friend?"

"Yeah." Mack took a breath, but the weird thing was, it wasn't awful, talking about it. "About a year ago."

"I'm sorry." It was the standard line, but she delivered it well.

"Not exactly unusual, in a war."

"That doesn't matter. Your story is your story. It doesn't have to be original."

"Guess not." He hesitated. "He got blown up."

"I kind of figured that."

"We were in the front of a convoy and there was this dead dog in the road, and Adam was joking around. 'You can never just assume things are what they seem in a time of war,' he was saying, like he was lecturing a bunch of new recruits. 'Take that dead dog. He might actually be an important member of the new Iraqi government. He might not really be dead. He might be a spy.'" Mack looked at Zoë, surprised he was telling her all this. "Not too PC, I know, but at the time, it was funny. And then the dog exploded. And the other guy in the armored vehicle with us just kept saying, 'That was a bomb. That was a bomb.' As if we hadn't figured it out." Mack hesitated, remembering. "And the thing was, we knew better. We all knew better. But the driver didn't veer away and Adam didn't tell him to turn the damn wheel and I just sat there laughing until the dog blew up."

Zoë rested her chin on her hands. "I bet that happens to your driving students," she said. "For a while, in the beginning, they're very careful, but they're also nervous. And then they gain a little experience, and they learn to relax. Which ought to make them better drivers, except they get too relaxed. Which is probably when they have their first accident."

"Yeah," Mack said, amazed that he hadn't ever made the connection before. "They have to learn how to relax and still be alert. You can't really teach them that, you can just describe it—the sweet spot, where you're paying attention but you're not tense." He looked at Zoë. "Christ, you're sharp. How the hell does a woman like you wind up not knowing how to drive a car?"

Zoë narrowed her eyes, clearly annoyed. "I told you about what happened. My accident."

"I've been in car accidents, back when I was a teenager. My parents died in one. It didn't convince me not to drive."

"Everyone's different. Some people are more comfortable taking control, some are more comfortable giving it up. And frankly, I haven't needed to drive in my life. I've lived forty-one years as a nondriver without any problem."

Mack held her gaze, which was hard to do behind those spectacles. "You mean you arranged your life up till now so you didn't need to drive. But why limit yourself like that?"

Zoë shook her head. "It's not like I made a conscious choice. I didn't think of it as limiting myself." She hesitated. "Maybe it's what we all do. Arrange our lives so we don't have to do certain kinds of things that don't come naturally. I don't know. Why don't you live in a city? Why don't you go to work in a suit and tie? Is it fear? Avoidance?"

Mack watched her dance around, and then shook his head. "You haven't answered the question. You told me why you got scared. But why did you hold on to it for so long?"

Zoë raked her hands through her thick hair, causing it to tumble down from its sloppy knot. "Jesus. I don't know. My mother doesn't drive. I just never really thought of myself as a driver. I lived in cities. It just didn't seem like something . . ." She stopped. "It didn't seem like something I could do. I don't know why."

Feeling he was on to something, Mack opened his mouth, but before he could say anything, Maya called from the top of the stairs.

"Mommy, what's taking so long?"

They both looked up to see Maya gazing at them over the banister. "Aren't you coming to bed yet? I don't like being all alone up here."

"Oh, honey, there's nothing to be afraid of. I'll be up in a little while."

"How long is a little while?"

"Half an hour, say. Just go to sleep, sweetheart. I'll kiss you when I come up."

"I keep hearing noises. Can I sleep in your bed?"

Zoë looked a little tired. "Maya, you've been coming into my bed every night since we got here."

"But I want to start out there."

Mack watched all this, bemused. At that age, he would no more have thought of sleeping in his parents' bed than of wearing some kind of Disney pajamas. Either he'd grown up too fast or Maya was taking the scenic route.

"Okay," Zoë was saying, "you can sleep in my bed."

"Tuck me in."

Zoë turned to Mack. "I guess it's all still pretty new to her." She stood up, and Mack stretched, trying to gather himself together.

"I should go." God, he was wiped.

Zoë was standing now, looking down at him. "If you feel too tired to drive, you can stay here."

Mack rolled his head around, getting the kinks out of his neck. The girl was watching him, and he could feel her impatience to have him gone so she could reclaim her mother. Besides, he wasn't quite clear what kind of invitation she was making. "No, that's all right. I need to get back."

"I'll get your jacket," said Zoë. "Do you need any coffee?"

"Nah, I'm awake now." He waved to Maya. "Good night."

"Good night," she replied, waving enthusiastically in return. She sounded much happier as she added, "I'll be waiting for you upstairs, Mommy."

Thirteen

*H*appily cocooned in a heap of covers in Zoë's bed, Maya slept until nearly nine, then rolled downstairs yawning dramatically and announced that she intended to have a perfectly lazy day. Zoë, heartily sick of hanging around the house, tried to tempt her daughter with a drive to a pumpkin festival or a children's movie, but all Maya wanted to do was watch her DVD of *The Young Black Stallion* in her pajamas.

"But Maya, don't you think we should call Mack up and have a little outing? It's beautiful outside."

"I know," said Maya, spooning some cold cereal into her mouth, "but school is so active, Mom. I'm exhausted. And there's gym tomorrow, so I'll get exercise."

Good for you, thought Zoë, but what about me? She knew the answer, of course—she would either do some work, or think about doing some work. That was the problem with working at home: you did nonwork things when you were supposed to be working, and then worked when you were supposed to be having time off, so that all of life and work became garbled together. When she talked on the phone, sometimes Zoë herself wasn't sure whether she was being friendly or doing research.

And there were other drawbacks to not having an office. Right now, with her life so changed as to feel as though it belonged to someone else, Zoë would have liked to take refuge in work. The only problem was, her work wasn't a noun she could head off to, it was a verb she had to accomplish, and the piece about women living in purdah was pretty much ready to go out to her editor. Since the article was actually part of a book that Zoë was writing about invisible women, she knew that she could start researching her next section. Amish women? Mormon wives? Polygamy was a hot topic at the moment. But the book was a long-term project, and Zoë's bank account needed bumping up sooner rather than later. If she didn't turn around a quick features article, then it was going to be an extremely frugal Hanukkah this year.

The problem was that Zoë had no idea what her next big project would be. Usually, by the time she was at the end of one feature, she already had a few different story ideas that had been forming in the back of her mind. She might take Maya to the Tenement Museum on the Lower East Side and wonder whether life for a new immigrant from Congo in 2006 was easier, harder, or basically identical to life for a new immigrant from eastern Europe or Ireland a century earlier. Or she might visit a friend for dinner and discover that the Manhattan housing boom had created a mini civil war in many co-op buildings, the richer, newer tenants pitting their financial might against the poorer but more entrenched old-guard residents.

Once she had two or three possibilities, Zoë would call her editors at *Vanity Fair* or the *New York Chronicle.* Sometimes she met the editors in their offices, and if she was lucky and her last piece had been well-received, she got taken out to lunch. But meal or no meal, one of her ideas was always picked up, and presto, she had a new assignment.

But with all the distractions of finding Maya a new school and moving out of the city, Zoë hadn't managed to come up with anything promising to run past her editors. And since she was living in the middle of nowhere, it was unlikely that she was going to draw any inspiration from taking a walk.

Zoë glanced at the time on her computer. Almost eleven in the morning. Exactly five minutes after she'd sat down in the first place. If time continued to move this slowly in the country, she'd still be forty-two while all of her city friends were turning fifty.

At the moment, this did not seem like sufficient consolation. The cat jumped up and walked across her keyboard, and Zoë shooed him off and returned to staring at the computer. *Z is for Zoë who died of ennui.*

Crap. Zoë got up from the computer and looked in the refrigerator for inspiration. She shoved the frozen bagel into the toaster, feeling disgusted. Which was ridiculous. So Arcadia didn't have decent bagels. Back in the eighties, she'd been forced to eat dog at an Indonesian feast day so as not to offend her hosts.

The toaster pinged, but the fake bagel seemed to have dissolved into the hot metal. Zoë extracted it in pieces, staring out her window at the pretty, empty landscape of grass and trees. She could hear the persistent percussive sound of a woodpecker, and the honking of migrating geese, and all Zoë could think was, I miss hydraulic drills and cops shouting through megaphones and I want to go home. She dialed Bronwyn's number.

"I can't stand it," she said, in lieu of a greeting. "I've lost my life and my mind."

"I'm guessing you finished your article."

"I have no ideas anymore."

"You always say that right before you get the next idea. Hey, guess what I was doing when you called?"

Zoë opened a box of Maya's Cocoa Krispies. "Checking Petfinder?"

"There are these two dogs advertised, Dwaine and Eddie, that were found tied to a gate with their mouths taped shut. One's blind, he needs the other to lead him around."

Zoë shoved a handful of cereal into her mouth. "Yeah, just what you need, a dog with a Seeing Eye dog. What's really going on?"

"I don't think the twins are getting into preschool. The school we thought was our safety said that Byron displayed signs of emotional immaturity."

Zoë wondered how they'd figured out which twin was Byron. "He's not even two yet, what else would he display?"

Bronwyn gave a broken hiccup of a laugh. "It's just gotten so ridiculously competitive. You have to have some kind of precocious wonder child, and be the kind of mother who spends all her free time chairing fund-raisers and volunteering to help the teacher grade papers. I hate to say it, but you were smart to get out when you did. I bet your school doesn't expect all the moms to jump through hoops."

"You know what the real problem is? It's all this staying at home that's killing us," said Zoë, closing up the box of cereal before she was tempted to eat more.

"*Us* as in women of our generation, or *us* as in you and me?"

"Both. If women went back to work earlier, they wouldn't keep turning preschools into mini–corporate takeovers. But on a personal level, back when you were practicing law and I was on staff at *Newsweek*, we were too busy to notice when we were depressed."

"Bullshit," said Bronwyn. "I was miserable because Feingold and Bright was like a dysfunctional family, and you spent all your time fretting that you were missing out on being with Maya. Which was why you quit, remember?"

Of course, that was back in the good old days, when she'd been exhausted and guilty because Maya had wanted to play with her all day long. Zoë reopened the box of Cocoa Krispies. "So I didn't appreciate it then. But looking back at it now, it was a bit like college. Everyone indulging in a little intellectual competition, a little free-floating flirtation, and a lot of frenzied collaboration." Zoë ate another handful of crispy, overly sweetened rice.

"So what are you saying—there's no flirtation in the country? What happened, did the Republicans ban it?"

"Well, there's a little flirtation. A hint of it. But only of the non-viable, pro-gun-younger-man-with-a-ponytail variety. But the real problem is, my mind has died. I have no more ideas for stories because I'm out of the loop." Zoë began to eat a stray Cocoa Krispy that had clung to her wrist, than realized with horror that it had legs.

"Zoë? What's wrong?"

"I have a tick on my arm. A bloodsucking, disease-spreading tick. Have I mentioned that I hate the country?" She pinched the tick between two nails, hoping it wouldn't slip out and attach itself somewhere else.

"If you're going to whine, I'm heading back to Petfinder," Bronwyn warned her. "What about local stories? I bet there's something going on right under your nose that you can use. You know small towns—somebody's always shtupping the mayor's wife or building a shopping mall on a sacred tribal burying ground. Hey, are you peeing?"

"No, I'm washing tick off my hands." Zoë turned off the kitchen tap. "Anyway, it's a nice idea, but the best I can come up with here is a lesbian liquor store owner who likes taxidermy and a controversial proposal to build some shops on a completely empty field."

"Zoë Goren," said Bronwyn in a stern voice, "you know very well that until you've gone digging for bodies, everything looks like an empty field."

Zoë was suddenly reminded that before her friend had become a frazzled stay-at-home mother of twins, she'd been a damn fine lawyer. "You're probably right," she said. "There's bound to be something rotten there somewhere. But I can't get excited about it. Maybe there's a rare species of skunk that's going to lose its breeding ground. Maybe old Farmer Johnson is the last of a dying breed, and when he moves to Miami, a vital part of rural America dies. But what's that got to do with me?"

"You cared a lot when those nesting red-tailed hawks were getting evicted from their perch by the building's co-op board. And I remember you writing a hell of an article when that old Jewish deli went out of business."

"It's not the same. I don't have an emotional stake in the local flora and fauna. I'm just passing through here. This isn't my beat. These aren't my stories."

Bronwyn sighed. "I don't know what to tell you, then. Oh, shoot, that's the twins waking up. Listen, I'll call you back later."

Zoë hung up the phone, felt something tickling the back of her neck, and pulled off another tick. Ugh. Cursing the country, Zoë scratched her head, checking for any other unwanted visitors. Maybe Bronwyn was right. Maybe there was a story buried in the field development proposal, no pun intended. Mack had said his sister was fielding an offer for her horse farm. Should she call Mack and ask him for more background? She didn't want to always be bothering him. Maybe she should she try Frances and Gretchen from the liquor store. Just as Zoë was about to pick up the phone, however, it rang.

"Mrs. Goren?"

"Ms."

The woman on the other line paused. "Is this the mother of Maya Goren?" She had a distinct New York accent, and Zoë wondered if she were the school receptionist.

"Yes, is everything all right?"

"Everything's just fine," she said, giving the last word two syllables. "I'm Kiki Armstrong, calling on behalf of the PTA. We hadn't heard back from you about the new parents' cocktail party tonight, and wanted to know if you'd be attending."

"There's a cocktail party tonight?"

"Yes," said Kiki, still speaking at Brooklyn volume. "It's at my house at seven-thirty tonight. Didn't you get the invitation we mailed you?"

Belatedly, it occurred to Zoë that she hadn't checked the mailbox at the end of the driveway. She'd seen mailboxes used in the movies and on TV, but she'd never actually had one herself—in the city, her mail had been delivered to her door.

"I guess it didn't get here yet," she said, embarrassed to admit that she hadn't even looked.

"Well, we do hope you can make it," said Kiki, warmly. "We think it's important for the parents of new students to feel like they're part of the school community."

"Well, I'll do whatever I can to make it," said Zoë, thinking that this was exactly what she needed. She'd been very involved with Maya's old school, working on the school newspaper and talking to various classes about her experiences in developing countries and going along on school trips. If she got busy volunteering with the Mackinley PTA, she'd feel less isolated from her daughter and her surroundings. "Can you give me the address and directions?"

"Of course," said Kiki. "It's Twenty-nine Foxfield Lane. Just take Route Eighty-two North past the Morningdale Highland Cattle Farm. We're up the dirt path to your right."

Zoë wrote this down on a scrap of paper. This was perfect. She'd been feeling left out now that Maya did all her homework at school, and the truth was, she probably had too much free time on her hands, always a disincentive to working well. Here was a chance to meet some people who might actually be in her idiom. According to the head of admissions, a lot of the school parents had originally come from Manhattan, and like her, a lot of them had moved only because they'd wanted their children to attend the Mackinley School. "This sounds great," Zoë said. "Anything I can bring?"

"Oh, no." Kiki gave a little gurgle of a laugh. "Just come and mingle."

Zoë hung up the phone, already wondering what she should wear. A moment later, she realized that she needed a ride and a babysitter. And once again, the only person she could think of to ask was Mack.

*   *   *

"I'm sorry, Zoë, but I can't."

"Any way I can get you to change your plans?" Transferring the phone to her other ear, Zoë scooped her cat up in her arms and cradled him like a baby. As Mack paused on the other end of the line, she resisted the urge to beg and wheedle. The problem was, she'd done a damn good job of convincing herself that she had to attend this party, both for Maya's sake and her own. She needed to have a network of friends here, or wind up one of those crazy ladies who talk to their cats. As soon as she thought this, Claudius narrowed his eyes and rubbed his cheek against her chin.

"I would if I could, but the fire chief had to go to his daughter's wedding. I promised I'd be around in case we had an emergency."

"Damn." Zoë pushed her glasses up her nose. "Well, it's not like I had a babysitter, anyway." Ugh, that really sounded like whining. Very attractive. Mack was on standby to save lives and she was whining about missing a cocktail party.

"Let me think," said Mack. "My sister could probably sit for Maya, if we can figure out someone else to drive you." He seemed to hesitate, then added, "Want me to ask Rudy?"

"Not if he's going to leave me stranded there."

"Maybe I'd better not. I think you might have upset him with that whole 'we are apes' argument," Mack admitted. "Say, here's an idea. How about old Pete Grell? He's the other driving instructor I used to work with, and he'd be happy to earn a little extra. Not so sure about his night vision, though. You have to take a lot of back roads?"

"No, according to my directions, it's a main road, then a dirt driveway."

"Pete should be fine, then. Just don't let him fall asleep at the wheel."

"You're not exactly filling me with confidence in his abilities, Mack."

"So learn to drive already."

"I didn't say I was gaining any confidence in *my* abilities."

Mack didn't laugh. "I can fix that," he said, as if she were a car with a faulty transmission.

"I'm not looking to be fixed," she replied.

Fourteen

When the call came in, Mack had just been explaining to the new EMT something they didn't teach in school—that in a small town, you often wound up treating folks who were your friends and neighbors, which meant you had to cultivate excellent tunnel vision. You might get a 911 call and discover that big Bert down on Main Street had come within inches of opening up his femoral artery while shaving off all his pubic hair. You might find out that your old high school history professor hadn't gotten the lesson that it's a bad idea to mix pills and alcohol. Or, saddest of all, you might learn that whatever you did to treat the youngest Andersen child, she was still going to die before spring. Whatever you discovered in the course of treating folks, you treated them with dignity and compassion while you were providing medical care, and you never told a living soul what you knew.

But there were times, Mack thought, when you really ought to get a medal for service above and beyond the call of duty: the Acting-as-If-This-Weren't-the-Asshole-Screwing-Your-Ex badge of honor.

"I'm fine, I tell you," said Jim Moroney, struggling to get up from Jess's lap. His fat stomach bulged up over his Devil Dog boxer shorts. Mack knelt beside him, trying to take his pulse.

"Well? Nothing's wrong, right?"

"It's a little fast," said Mack, "but not abnormally so."

"I told you it was a false alarm. Heartburn, not heart attack."

"But Jim," Jess said, "you said your chest hurt."

"I said it felt funny," Moroney countered. "I didn't ask you to call for a fucking ambulance. And he's the last guy on earth I trust to take care of me in a crisis. I mean, Jesus, Jess."

She looked at Mack entreatingly over Moroney's head. "He said his chest hurt," she insisted. "And he was out of breath." She was wearing a man's T-shirt, and her blond hair was disheveled.

Mack focused on Moroney again, trying not to think of what they'd been doing immediately before the onset of symptoms. "Can you describe what you're feeling right now? Any discomfort in or around the chest area?"

"I got a little short of breath," Moroney replied, sounding irritated. His graying crew cut, grown about an inch too long, was sticking up in a way that made him look as if he'd had a shock. "Which was pretty damn normal, under the circumstances. And my stomach was upset. We'd just had a big steak at O'Flannigan's in Poughkeepsie."

"Nausea can sometimes be a symptom of a heart problem," Mack said. "So let's just check this out a little further. Are you experiencing any sensation of pressure? Pain in either arm?"

"I'm not having a goddamn heart attack," bellowed Moroney, but of course, this was what many heart attack patients insisted, right up until they keeled over. Moroney was flushed but not sweating, and despite all his protests, he was no longer trying to get up from Jess's lap. Mack concentrated on taking his former boss's blood pressure. He glanced around Moroney's room—the immense bed, the massive flat-screen television, the state-of-the-art exercise bike—trying to figure out the easiest path to the front door. He nodded at the junior EMT, an earnest young cop named Danny Boyle. "Go get the stretcher," he instructed Danny.

"I'm not going to the hospital," Moroney said, and then, as if to punctuate his decision, he barked, "Ow."

Mack looked at him sharply. "What?"

Jim's ruddy face had gone pale, and his eyes were wide. "Hah," he said, sounding surprised. "I . . . uh . . . " he sounded winded. "Pain."

"Oh, God, Jim, I knew you shouldn't have taken that Viagra," wailed Jess.

Okay, so there was a possibility of a cardiac event brought on by a drug. Removing the oxygen from his kit, Mack made his voice very even and sure. "Don't worry, Jim, I'm going to make you more comfortable," he said, fitting the nonrebreather mask over the older man's face. "That's oxygen, it'll help. Jim, do you have a history of cardiac problems? You got nitroglycerin?"

"No," said Jim, sounding thoroughly frightened now. Right on time, Danny arrived with the stretcher, and Mack stopped thinking anything that didn't have to do with getting his patient to the ER, because this was real now, an emergency, and the clock was ticking down the moments of the golden hour, that precious optimal period between onset of medical crisis and surgical treatment.

"All right, Danny, you get in the back and I'll drive."

Danny cleared his throat. "Mack, maybe you ought to sit with him. Driving fast I can do, but this other stuff . . ." He shrugged, his classically Irish face wearing an almost comical expression of dismay. Mack stifled a groan and went into the back of the ambulance with Jim while Jess, still semi-hysterical, drove behind.

"You," Moroney panted behind the oxygen mask, "must love this."

"Just lie back and take it easy," said Mack, wrapping the blood pressure cuff around Moroney's thick arm. "Deep, slow breaths. Try not to talk."

"Ha," said Moroney, the word coming out in a dry wheeze. "You will."

Not really paying attention, Mack said, "Let me get your pressure, Jim," and checked the older man's numbers. Too high, Mack thought as he removed the cuff, and one look at Moroney's red face and clenched jaw said his attitude wasn't helping matters. What was the man so wound up about? After a moment, he put it together: Moroney thought he was going to be spreading funny Viagra stories around town. "Jim, you have to try to relax. If you're worried about me telling someone about this call, then forget about it. I signed an oath of confidentiality, Jim. It comes with the job."

"Ha. You tell on me," Moroney grunted, then paused, "I tell on you."

"There you go, then, no need to fret," Mack said composedly, having absolutely no idea what the man was going on about. He called the hospital and briefed them about his patient's condition, then walked back over to the stretcher, where Moroney was still busy converting fear into anger. "You doing okay, Jim? We're almost there."

Moroney gritted his teeth. "Your file. Read it."

Mack looked out the front window and was relieved to see the lights of the hospital. "Oh yeah?" He was so busy humoring Moroney that it took him a moment to process what had been said. The bastard had read his army file.

Moroney winced, and Mack came over to him. "Are you experiencing any discomfort?"

"I know." Moroney sucked in a hard breath. "About you." He reached out and grabbed hold of Mack's latex-gloved hand. For some reason, the pressure was painful.

Mack removed the other man's fingers, wondering if he was

going to need restraints. On the one hand, Moroney was exhibiting clear signs of irrational aggression. On the other hand, the last thing Mack wanted to do was agitate his patient further. Mack patted Moroney's hand, then held it.

"Listen to me, Jim. I know you're scared, but it's going to be all right. Okay, that's it, we're here." He positioned himself near Moroney's feet at the back doors as Danny pulled up in front of the emergency room, and after that everything went smoothly as they transferred Moroney into the hospital's care.

"Wow," said Danny when they were back in the ambulance. "You think he's going to be all right?"

Still writing up the report, Mack grunted. "That horny old bastard? He'll probably live to be a hundred." In the back of his mind, he half understood Moroney's problem. Since Jim used information to manipulate people, he figured Mack would do the same. Kind of like that quote of Zoë's about the confidence you have in yourself. "Come on, Danny boy, let's get out of here."

Danny put them into reverse and then pulled out onto a side street. As they passed the tidy town houses immediately surrounding the hospital, Danny turned right, taking them down into the center of Poughkeepsie.

"Wrong way, Danny. We need to turn around."

"Yeah, I know, but I'm hungry. I know a great Mexican place around here."

"We can get a bite on the way back to Arcadia."

"Yeah, but not good Mexican. It's just around the corner." Mack thought about protesting, but then remembered Moroney saying, *I know about you.* So he let Danny make a left turn onto a street filled with squat, rectangular buildings, the lone streetlight only revealing the multitude of shadowy areas and blind corners. A number of cars were parked in a lot outside the largest building, which had huge plate-glass windows and a neon sign that read "Mama Mexico."

"I used to come here all the time when I was in the Academy," Danny was saying as they walked in the front door. Mack absently rubbed the sore pad of his thumb where Moroney had squeezed, then pressed again, deliberately concentrating on the slight pain. Problem was, thinking about the panic attacks always seemed to bring them on, and worrying about other people noticing made it worse. Trying to distract himself, Mack looked around. The restaurant was a dark maze of tables, with potted plants placed at angles that obscured a clear line of vision. If that wasn't bad enough, there were also balloons and streamers hanging from the ceiling, and piñatas dangling low enough to catch on people's heads.

Danny turned back to him. "You want take-out, or we could sit at the bar?"

Mack managed to mumble, "Take-out." He followed Danny into a knot of people gathered by a high desk and looked out at the dinner crowd. Despite the late hour, there were small children seated at high chairs, clearly entranced by all the noise and bright colors.

A woman in tight jeans gave him a look. Next to her, Mack spotted a teenager wearing a heavy jacket, despite the heat from all the packed bodies. *Stay alert to your surroundings.* Mack's palms began to sweat; any appetite he might have had disappeared. The distinctive, overpowering odor of refried beans and chili powder was beginning to make him feel sick.

"I'm trying to decide," said Danny, showing him the take-out menu. "Should I go for a taco, or try one of the enchiladas?"

You have to adopt a different mentality. Assess and evaluate in terms of potential threat.

"This looks good—the steak and chicken combo. And you have to try the red beans, dude."

Mack nodded, hoping he looked like he was holding it together. He could feel the hum of conversation setting up a sympathetic buzz in his ribs and sternum. He felt as if he was shrinking inside himself, away from the noise and vibration. Mack tried to focus on the ordinariness of the situation. Teenagers giving each other secret, lustful glances. Mothers telling off their kids. Waiters bumping each other as they maneuvered laden trays. *Do not make assumptions about what you see. Describe only what things appear to be. Just because an object appears to be a cow doesn't mean it's a fucking cow.*

Mack blinked his eyes. "Hot in here," he said, scraping his fingers through his hair.

"You're not kidding."

As always, he was amazed that no one noticed what was happening to him. His voice felt like it was coming from the bottom of a well. For all he knew about the body, he'd never figured out why he'd begin to see things as if lit by a strobe light. *Retrain your brain, boys.* The hostess turned to them, and to Mack's eyes she appeared to move in the speedy, jerky motions of an actress from a silent film.

She smiled at them. "You ready to order?"

"Yeah," said Danny, but Mack interrupted him.

"Danny, I got to go."

"What? Are you kidding?"

Mack pressed the sore pad of his hand, allowing him to ignore the illusion that Danny's freckled face was flickering from black to white. "Meet you outside."

He pushed blindly through the crowd, feeling like he couldn't breathe. His heart was racing so fast he had a moment of wondering if he would need oxygen, and then he was outside, sucking in the cool night air. He leaned against the ambulance, head between his knees, as the humming in his body grew fainter and his vision cleared.

"Hey, you okay, dude?" Danny had apparently decided to leave without placing an order.

"Yeah, yeah, I just needed some air." Mack straightened up.

Danny frowned, clearly suspicious. "I thought you were going to pass out."

"It's just the smell. Chili powder. I think I'm allergic." And then, because he was embarrassed, he added, "Jesus, Danny, how can you eat that shit, anyway?"

Danny gave him a sharp look as he climbed back into the driver's seat. "Before you say anything else, you should know that my best friend on the force is Mexican American."

"No offense meant," said Mack, staring out the window as they left the lights of the city behind. He thought about explaining himself, but decided against it. Maybe the army doctors were right, and there was nothing unusual about him freaking out in crowds, but Mack thought he'd rather Danny pegged him as an asshole than as a mental case.

Fifteen

*O*ld Pete Grell was not exactly a bundle of charm. He drove in complete silence, maneuvering his sturdy old Chevrolet down the dark road with a kind of studied deliberation that was somehow more unnerving than recklessness. Every two seconds he moved his head an inch to the right, then an inch to the left, like an animatronic figure on a Disney ride. On the bright side, Zoë thought, he was certainly patient, waiting placidly while she dropped Maya off at Mack's sister's house, giving her plenty of time to exchange a few pleasantries and get a sense that Maya liked the horsewoman and vice versa. Moira reminded Zoë of Mack a bit: both had dark blond hair, wiry builds, and similar strong-boned jaws and watchful eyes, and both gave an impression of being laid-back and easygoing. But while Mack still possessed more than a hint of youthful curiosity and recklessness, his sister exuded an air of centered calm that made Zoë feel immature by comparison. In any case, she seemed more than willing to show Maya all her horses, and Maya was thrilled. Her one request: see if her classmate Allegra's mother would agree to a playdate.

Back in the car, however, Zoë began to wonder if Pete really knew where he was going. It seemed as though hours had passed since they'd turned onto the dirt road, which wound up and around the mountain at a very steep angle.

"Crazy rich people," muttered Pete. "How they're going to plow all this in winter, I'd like to know."

The answer, it became clear as they turned the corner, was that Kiki Armstrong had enough money to buy her own highway department. Zoë had been expecting a standard McMansion, but what she saw as they approached the top of the hill was a bona fide castle, built of stone, complete with wrought-iron gates, turrets, mullioned windows, and liveried servants who stood ready to greet them.

"Huh," said Pete, scratching his head. "Would you get a load of that? You'd never even know it was there from the main road." He sounded a little bewildered, as might be expected of a man who'd lived in a place his whole life but had no idea there was a castle in the neighborhood.

It made Zoë wonder what other country fantasies might lay at the end of other nondescript dirt driveways. She might have neighbors who had constructed a miniature racetrack for their vintage Model T Fords. A Moorish pleasure palace might be hidden behind the scrubby viburnum bushes in the back of her house. Hell, there could be an entire pack of tigers stashed in someone's private zoo not a mile from her front door. In the city, there are rules about whether or not you can own a llama, and in the suburbs, committees decide whether or not you can add a gargoyle to your roof. Only in the country, Zoë thought, are you limited only by your bankbook.

There could well be a story in that, she thought, wishing she'd brought a pen to write the idea down.

"May I park your car, sir?" The valet, a young man in an emerald green jacket, gave no outward sign that she and Pete weren't usual guests at the castle.

"Not going to hand over my car," said Pete. "I'm just going to wait for the young lady over here."

Aw, crud. Somehow, Zoë hadn't thought about Pete sitting out all alone in his car while she mingled with other parents. "Are you sure you don't want to come in?" Under the circumstances, she assumed it would be all right to invite a nonparent.

"Not my kind of party," said Pete.

Not mine, either, Zoë suspected. "Well then," she offered. "Why not just go home and then swing back in an hour or two?"

"Go out four times instead of two," said Pete, raising his grizzled eyebrows as if she were crazy. "Not on your nelly."

"You won't be cold out here?" Zoë had dressed in her most conservative dress, a fitted black 1950s shift with matching cap sleeve bolero jacket, and her arms were already prickling in the chill night air.

Pete sniffed. "This ain't cold," he said, with a dismissive wave of his hand. "Go on, you have yourself a good time. I'll be right here."

"I won't be long, then." Crunching over the gravel path in her chunky 1940s heels, Zoë wondered how long she had to stay without giving offense. She couldn't imagine keeping old Pete waiting for more than an hour, but could she stay less than that without giving offense to her hostess?

Zoë walked through the heavy, Tudor-style front door and realized that she didn't have to worry. She'd been to a couple of snazzy Fifth Avenue apartments for cocktail parties, and she'd seen her share of gorgeous SoHo lofts and swank Brooklyn brownstones. But this wasn't garden-variety Manhattan wealth. This was vast, palatial, country wealth, complete with timbered ceilings and marble busts displayed alongside antique oil paintings of oddly proportioned horses and weak-chinned ladies.

Zoë wondered whether Kiki Armstrong was aware that decking your home out like a period film set was proof positive that yours was not bona fide old WASP wealth. A real Daughter of the Revolution wouldn't have built herself a citadel in the middle of horse country, no matter how many acres she had to play with.

As she approached the main room, Zoë could hear the animated murmuring of a large crowd, accompanied by the clinking of glasses. She followed the sound to a room done up to look like a British gentlemen's club and began pushing her glasses up her nose before recalling that she was wearing contact lenses.

"Caviar, madame?" A waitress, the only woman besides herself dressed all in black, paused to offer Zoë her choice from a platter.

"Thanks." Zoë took a tiny blini and a napkin. "Now all I need is a drink."

"The bar's over there," said the waitress with a small smile of amusement, "and there's someone walking around with champagne."

"Excellent," said Zoë. She went straight to the bar and ordered a scotch and soda.

"Single malt?"

"God, yes. Make it a double." A woman of about her own age came up beside her. She was wearing a headband and an expensive, frumpy dress that, on close inspection, bore a pattern of maroon horse's heads. Zoë gave her a friendly smile. "Some party, huh?"

"Oh yes," the woman agreed. "The Armstrongs always make an effort." She turned to order a gin and tonic, then said, "Are you new to the school?"

"My daughter, Maya, started fourth grade this fall."

"Ah. My son, Amory, is in the second grade. It's been so good for him. Did you move from Manhattan?"

"Yes, I'm still adjusting to this country life. I feel a little like Eva Gabor in *Green Acres,* only without the negligee and the chickens."

The woman smiled politely. "Give it a month, you'll love it. Lots of the other parents are from the city, and after a year or two, hardly anybody uses their Manhattan apartments anymore."

"I'd use mine," said Zoë, "but the new owners might object."

"You sold? Very wise," said the woman. "The market's probably peaking, and a hotel is so much easier. Although I do find it convenient to have a little pied-à-terre when I go in to see a Broadway show. Tell me," she went on, "does your husband still work in the city?"

Zoë took a fortifying sip of her scotch. "No husband, just my daughter and myself. I'm a freelance journalist." She waited for a follow-up question, but instead the woman smiled politely again.

"That's convenient," she said. "You can work from home. And which town are you in?"

"Arcadia," said Zoë.

"Oh, land is so reasonable out there," the woman enthused. "I've been telling my husband we ought to move out of Milton, we really need more room for the horses."

Zoë was beginning to suspect that her Manhattan repertoire of small talk—indie films, new nonfiction, *The Daily Show*—was not going to serve her here. After a beat too long, she came up with a suitable question. "How many horses do you have?"

"Twelve," said the woman. "Do you ride?"

"I tried it once, but then decided I'd better quit while I still had some nerve endings left down there."

The woman's smile flickered for a second before vanishing. "Oh, gosh," she said, scanning the room, "please excuse me, I see someone I've been searching for all evening."

The woman vanished into the crowd, and Zoë took her scotch and wandered around the room, catching various fragments of conversations: "The vet said to wait a good month before I jumped him again." ". . . came up to me at the charity dinner, and I said there was a three-year waiting list for my stone mason." "She left you all alone with the two kids for the last week of August? I'd complain to the au pair service."

The men, whose voices didn't carry so well, seemed to be discussing golf and finance, but Zoë did overhear one political debate.

"What people don't understand about the war," said a short, chubby man with bright blue eyes, "is that if we withdraw our troops from Iraq, we're just rolling over and letting Iran take over the region."

"And no one can argue that they don't have weapons of mass destruction," added a tall, thin man in a bowtie.

"Well, they certainly don't have them at the moment," said Zoë, joining the circle of men. "But you're right, they do have the capability. On the other hand, it could be argued that President Khatami was making diplomatic overtures to the States before Bush made his big Axis of Evil speech. Maybe removing our military presence will convince some of the moderates that we don't just want to control oil production around the Caspian Sea."

There was a moment of silence, and then the chubby man recovered enough to say, "What do you call a moderate? The Iranians are living in the Middle Ages."

"Yeah, well, we have no problem making deals with the Saudis, and their women don't have as many rights as Iranian women do. At least in Iran, a woman can drive a car, cast a vote, and sit in parliament. Not to mention show her face."

The new silence went on a little longer than the last. The chubby man cleared his throat. "Are you certain of your facts? Because I'm pretty sure that Iranian women aren't allowed to drive."

"Absolutely certain," said Zoë. "I've just finished researching and writing an article about it. So I think the question really is, What are the criteria for being a member of the Axis of Evil? Totalitarian regime? Repression of minorities? Fostering intolerance of other religions? The Saudis qualify on all counts." Zoë smiled, waiting for the riposte. Her blood was up, and she felt more alive than she had in weeks.

"Well," said the man in the bowtie. Zoë began to feel like a Major League player who had struck out a bunch of Little Leaguers. Before she could think of something else to say, the chubby man turned back to his friends. "Now, not to change the subject, but have any of you been playing any golf recently?"

The men eagerly pounced on this new topic, and Zoë drifted toward another group of women. Two were pretty ponytailed blondes in pastel cashmere twinsets, one was a plump redhead bursting out of a tight red suit, and one was a poised brunette in a navy silk dress.

"As a friend, I'm telling you not to buy it," the brunette was saying to one of the blondes. Unlike the other women present, her long, silky hair was worn loose, and occasionally she flicked some of it over her shoulder, making it ripple. "They're going to go ahead with that development behind the post office."

"What a shame, Renata," said a blonde to the brunette. "It's an incredible price for forty acres with a view of the mountain."

"You're going to wind up with a strip mall in your backyard," Renata insisted, with a definite hint of upper-class British in her accent. "And that's not all. They're also going to subdivide the whole area near the base of the mountain. A year from now, there will be ticky-tacky houses as far as the eye can see."

"Are you sure?" This from the second ponytailed blonde. "My husband does a lot of work for Audubon and I thought he said that area was some sort of designated wetland thingy. Breeding ground for some rare bird or turtle or something."

Renata shrugged, then leaned closer to her coterie of listeners. "Well, maybe it is. But Arcadia doesn't have any proper zoning, which means it's all up to the discretion of the planning board. And the big man on Arcadia's town planning board just got a clean million for a tract of land that's worth maybe half that. Three guesses who paid him the big bucks." She looked at the women knowingly; they stared back blankly.

"You're saying the developers paid him off," said Zoë, becoming interested. Maybe Bronwyn was right about doing a local story.

The women looked startled, except for Renata, who narrowed her eyes. "I didn't say that."

"Don't worry," Zoë reassured her. "I'm not going to tell anyone else. It's just that I've been hearing about this developer a lot lately, and I'm getting curious."

"I'm sorry," said Renata, flicking her long, dark hair over her shoulder. "Have we met?"

"Oh, I'm Zoë Goren. My daughter, Maya, and I just moved here from the city, and we've been renting this amazing colonial just outside of Arcadia. I was actually thinking of buying, but given what you just said . . ." She let her voice trail off, something she often did when interviewing reluctant subjects. But Renata was more than reluctant. She was recalcitrant.

"Well, Zoë," she said with a practiced smile, "I'm sure you shouldn't pay any attention to what I say. After all, you hardly know me. How do you know you can trust my opinion?"

"Oh, I don't trust anyone's opinion," said Zoë lightly. "Not even my own. That's why I always like to gather as much information as possible before making any kind of judgment." You rebuke me, she thought, and I correct you. Move and countermove.

Renata raised her eyebrows. "And you say you're a new parent?"

"Yes. My name is Zoë Goren, mother of Maya, fourth grade."

"Oh, Zoë, hello," said the redhead in a strong Brooklyn accent, offering her a plump hand with a wedding ring ablaze with diamonds. "I'm Kiki Armstrong. So glad you could come. And Renata has a fourth-grader, too. Allegra's in the fourth grade now, right?"

"Yes." Renata looked a little rueful as she added, "I can hardly believe how grown up she is."

"It's funny I should bump into you like this," said Zoë, feeling encouraged. "My daughter asked me to try to arrange a playdate. Has Allegra mentioned Maya?"

Renata looked pensive. "You know, I believe she has."

"So we should get them together."

Renata smiled, but didn't respond with an invitation.

"And is your daughter enjoying her first year at the school?" This from Kiki, filling in the awkward gap.

"Very much so," Zoë replied. It struck her that Renata might be assuming that this talk of a playdate was merely a ploy to get the development story. "But it's still a bit of an adjustment for her, getting used to a new environment and group of kids." She nodded at Renata. "That's why I mentioned the possibility of our girls getting together sometime outside of school."

"That would be nice." Renata sounded almost sincere, but added instantly, "Allegra gets quite busy on the weekends, though."

"That's too bad. Well, I'd better be getting back to relieve the sitter, I promised Maya I wouldn't be out long." She smiled at all the women and turned, using all her years of dance training to make a graceful and dignified exit. But when she got to Pete's car, she crumpled into the backseat, feeling as though someone had pulled out her plug. "Let's get the hell out of this place, Pete," she said, and then, when he didn't respond, she added, "Pete?"

For one terrible moment she thought he was dead. "Pete?" She opened the car door so the ceiling light went on. "Pete, are you asleep?" To her relief, Pete finally lifted his gray head. His hair was sticking up in the back. "Who lef' the lightsh on," he asked thickly.

Okay, good that he was still alive, not good that he was having trouble talking. "Pete, do you know where we are?"

"Coursh I do," he said. "Now, lesh go to bed."

Crap, crap, crap, he'd gone and gotten himself toasted. "Pete, did you have something to drink while you were waiting? Pete?" She leaned forward, making an effort to keep her voice very calm and clear. "Pete, look at me. Did you have any alcohol?"

Pete tried to look at her, but there was something wrong with the left side of his face. He squinted at her, suddenly looking like Popeye. "I'll jush have a Bud," he said, "and the meatloaf."

"Oh, Pete," she said, finally comprehending.

Sixteen

*B*ack at the firehouse, a pepperoni pizza had restored Danny's good humor. "Dude," he said, rolling his shoulders till they popped. "I'm beat. Spent all day on patrol, and now this." In the background, the radio was playing a soft rock song from the seventies, and Mack wondered if the room they were in had changed at all since "Billy, Don't Be a Hero" had topped the charts. The dark orange fabric on the couches and chairs looked like they would have fit in just fine in Archie Bunker's living room, and the old photographs of Arcadia on the wall had probably been yellow back when Mack was still in diapers. He supposed a few of the paperbacks in the bookcase might be new, and there had to be a few new interdepartmental softball trophies behind the glass case. Mack hadn't attended any of the games, or the picnics and awards dinners, or the annual pig roast. In general, the firehouse volunteers were a tightly knit clique of men and women, and Mack couldn't quite shake the feeling that he didn't belong. Growing up, the garage had been his home away from home, and then he'd had the Rangers. He wasn't sure what he had now, besides a newfound fondness for poetry.

Put like that, it sounded ridiculous and fluffy, even in his own head. But in the high school textbook he'd found strange combinations of words, like spells, that captured the feeling of the familiar suddenly become unfamiliar. Not all poems, of course. A lot of it was pure shit. But still, Mack got the feeling that some of these guys knew what it was like to feel like you were floating up inside your head, unable to remember how to operate your eyes and hands and feet.

"Hey, Mack, we done here? 'Cause I'm about ready to see my girl." Mack glanced at Danny, who was finishing off a can of soda. He had some kind of Chinese writing tattooed on the inside of his right biceps. Mack wondered whether it said what Danny thought it did.

"We still need to clean out and restock," Mack replied, taking another bite of pizza. It was almost cold, but that was all right. At least Danny had stopped treating him like a suspected racist.

"Shoot, I forgot about that." Danny opened the pizza box and peered inside. "Hey, did you eat the pepperoni off that last piece?"

The radio bleeped, shocking them both upright. "Dutchess 911 to Arcadia 5627, respond for a seventy-eight-year-old Caucasian male, possible stroke at 29 Foxfield Lane off Route 82."

Mack pressed the button to respond. "Dutchess 911, this is Arcadia 5627. We are just finishing another run and low on equipment. Can you also notify Northern Dutchess paramedics?"

"Affirmative," said the female voice at the other end. "But their ETA is twenty-five minutes."

Mack turned to Danny. "We didn't have time to restock after the last run, so we'll have to take the basic ambulance. And make some noise, kid."

Danny looked confused.

"Siren, Danny, and let's move it."

It took them nine minutes to get to the location. Danny pulled up at what appeared to be Dracula's castle, behind a knot of anxious dressed-up people.

"He's over there," said a brunette in a mink coat, leading Mack and Danny over to the one car that wasn't a Mercedes or a BMW. There were a lot of well-dressed folks dithering about in the cool evening air, most of them still holding drinks as if this were a part of the evening's entertainment.

"Danny, get these folks to move back."

In an eager, carrying voice, Danny yelled out, "All right, everyone, let's make some space so we can work."

Mack approached his former coworker, wondering whether the stars were in some strange, unlucky alignment tonight. "Hey, Pete," he said in a strong voice, "it's Mack. How are you?"

Still sitting in the driver's seat of his car, Pete turned a little toward the sound of his voice. "Get out of my way," he said, slurring his words. "Can't you shee I'm driving?" The left side of his face was slack, the corner of his mouth drooping.

"Let's pull over for a sec," Mack suggested, shining a small penlight into his friend's eyes to check his pupils. The left one was dilated and fixed, and much larger than the right. "You know who I am?"

Pete moved his head, as if trying to focus his right eye. "Mm," he said. Mack patted his hand, then reached around to take a pulse. Breathing normal, awake but not oriented to person, place, or time.

"He was like this when I found him fifteen minutes ago," said Zoë, startling Mack. He hadn't noticed her sitting in the passenger-side seat next to Pete. "He's been sitting out here for almost an hour, though." She sounded surprisingly calm, but when she looked at Mack, her face looked strangely naked. "I shouldn't have left him out here in the cold, but he didn't want to come in."

"Well, that was not a contributing factor, and everything's under control now." Except that he'd used up his oxygen, which Pete needed now. Damn. Where were the paramedics? He checked Pete's arms and neck for any tags. "Pete, do you ever take insulin? Are you a diabetic, Pete?"

Pete looked past him, clearly not understanding. Mack opened a patch to County. "Dutchess 911, this is Arcadia 5627 on the scene. What's the paramedics' ETA? Subject needs oxygen, and our supplies are depleted."

"Arcadia 5627, this is County. Paramedics should be pulling up there momentarily. Do you see them?"

Mack turned; to his relief he spotted their ambulance coming up the drive.

"Affirmative," he said, getting off the radio. He recognized both professional paramedics and approved of the way they had Pete masked up and ready for transport in less than three minutes. Mack gave them his wife's number from memory, but said he'd call her and see if she needed a lift to the hospital.

"I don't understand why you want to run around pretending to be a basic EMT," said Mario as he started Pete's IV. "How come you don't come ride with us?"

"I've done enough twelve-hour days back to back in the army," Mack said. "I like my easy life." He was suddenly aware of Zoë, listening in the background.

"Yeah, well, then take it easy," said Mario, and then he flicked on the ambulance's siren and they were off.

"Is he going to recover?"

Mack started to reply and then realized that Zoë was shivering in her short-sleeved dress.

"Hang on a sec." He reached into the back of the ambulance and found a clean wool blanket to drape over her shoulders. "Better?"

Zoë nodded, looking miserable. "I thought he was drunk at first."

"You figured it out faster than most."

She gave him a rueful smile. "I was mad because I just wanted to get home."

"You did fine by Pete." He looked at her, still shivering slightly under the thin blanket, and had to fight the urge to put an arm around her shoulders.

"Excuse me," said a pretty, plump redhead in a fur coat. "Is the old fellow going to be all right? Is there anything I can do? I feel responsible, this happening right in front of my house."

"Careful, Kiki," said the sharp-faced brunette beside her. "You don't want to say something that leaves the impression that you hold yourself responsible for this unfortunate event."

Mack tried not to show what he was thinking about the brunette. "No one's to blame, miss," he said, speaking to the red-head. "He had a stroke."

She gave him a warm, slightly cynical smile that reminded him of Deanna from the diner. "Renata can't help thinking like a lawyer. Zoë, do you need someone to give you a ride home?"

"That's all right," Mack said. "We can take her."

"Are you sure? Because I can easily arrange for someone else . . ."

"No, thanks, I'd rather go with Mack. Besides, my daughter's staying at his sister's house."

Mack thought Zoë didn't quite notice the brunette's reaction. Yes, lady, he thought, she's choosing the local yokel.

"Well, if there's nothing else I can do . . ." Kiki gave them both a gracious smile.

"No, we're all set." Partially because the fur coat crowd was watching, he put his arm loosely around Zoë's shoulders as he walked her back to the ambulance.

* * *

It hummed between them throughout the drive. Mack tried to ignore the undercurrent of desire as he dropped Danny off at the fire station with the ambulance. He told the younger man he owed him one, but Danny said he didn't mind having to clean up and restock by himself, he understood the situation.

But how much did he really understand? Sure, Mack had a good excuse: he had to swing by Moira's and pick up Zoë's daughter, and then he had to bring them both back home. But how obvious was it that the moment he'd put his arm around Zoë's shoulders, he'd felt every nerve in his body prickle with awareness? He'd tightened his hand on her shoulders, almost involuntarily, and she'd looked up at him. That was all that had happened, but now they were sitting alone in his pickup truck and there was something else in the air that hadn't been there before. He thought of the way she'd looked at him, and then about the naked picture of Zoë pregnant, and his mouth went dry. He didn't think he was wrong about this, but now that they were sitting with a gearshift between them, he wasn't completely sure. Reaching out his hand, Mack tested the waters. "You okay?"

"Yeah." She took his hand, and he threaded his fingers between hers. Her eyes met his, and she caught her breath.

No, he wasn't wrong about this. Impulsively, he raised her hand to his mouth and kissed the back of her knuckles. "You were good with Pete," he said. He wondered if she would feel guilty about doing anything enjoyable after what happened, and hoped not. Maybe he'd become callous, but the way he looked at it, you never knew what the next hour was going to bring. Maybe you'd agree to hire yourself out as a taxi and have a stroke. Maybe you'd go out for a date and get totaled by a drunk driver. Maybe you'd decide to do a little extra work in the garden and drop dead of a heart attack. Why, right this very minute, terrible things were happening to people just like him and Zoë. So if you brushed up against someone who suddenly made you feel twice as alive, the real crime was not taking hold of pleasure with both hands.

"Mack? Are you okay?" She stroked her thumb against his palm.

"Yeah." He cleared his throat. "Fine. I'm just . . . I like holding your hand." He figured that was more polite than saying, *I haven't had a hard-on from this kind of contact since seventh grade.*

"I like holding your hand, too." There was a small, knowing smile on her lips. She brushed her thumb against his palm again, and he felt a wave of heat. "But maybe we should get out of here before Danny comes back out."

"All right," he said, letting go of her hand to turn the key in the ignition, his heart suddenly slamming in his chest. If just touching her fingers could affect him like this, he wondered what the rest of the night was going to be like. He cleared his throat, hoping his voice sounded normal. "Off to Moira's." And then, the minute he said it out loud, he realized that nothing was going to happen tonight. She might want him as much as he wanted her, but when it came right down to it, logistics was going to trump lust. They'd get Maya, bring her home, and she'd be unsettled and they'd go through that whole can-I-sleep-in-your-bed routine. There were banks of fog on the back roads now, forcing him to drive slowly.

"So. Zoë. I was wondering, does Maya ever sleep in her own bed?" The moment the words were out, he wished he hadn't been quite so blunt. It was just, Jesus, what a night, first Jess and Moroney and the fucking Mexican place, and then Pete. He felt like he'd been awake and strung out for days, and for a moment he'd thought he was going to get a chance to feel good.

Zoë glanced at him, and he could see she was only a little surprised by the change in subject. "Of course. It's just that since we moved to the country, she's a little unsettled."

"She has to learn to handle being frightened."

"I know that." Their eyes met, but only for a moment. He had to keep watching the road.

"Put your hand on the wheel."

"What?"

"I said, put your hand on the wheel."

"I don't think this is such a good idea."

"Do it anyway. I won't let anything bad happen."

"Maybe we should try this in the daylight?"

"Put your hand on the wheel, Zoë."

She put her hand on the wheel.

"Hold it steady."

"Mack, this is crazy."

"If you let go, I'll let go, and we'll crash."

"I'm holding on." They drove together, very slowly, as the mist drifted across the path of their head beams. Then they saw head-lights coming from the opposite direction.

"There's a car coming," she said.

"Don't let go."

"Don't you let go." They drove past the other vehicle, Zoë's arm vibrating with tension. "Are we through yet? Can I let go?"

He curled his right hand over hers, touching her for the second time that evening. "Not yet." He waited until they had pulled up into Moira's driveway, and then he killed the engine. They sat there for a moment in the dark, his hand still covering hers.

"She has to learn to sleep in her own bed again," he said.

"I know." She met his look with perfect frankness. For a moment, he wished he'd suggested taking a longer drive, parking somewhere. But he couldn't imagine that was her style, and besides, he probably stank from the residue of fear and sweat.

"Hey, Mack?"

"Yeah?"

She leaned over, cupping his face in her hands, and kissed him, hard, on the lips. "I just thought it needed to be done," she said, pulling back with a little smile. "What? Did I shock you?"

"Not yet," Mack said, reaching over to pull her back. "Try again."

This time, she slid her arms around his neck and kissed him openmouthed as he tangled his hands in the thick, curling mass of her hair. For the first time in the whole, long night, he felt himself relax, and then she made a little sound in the back of her throat and he felt a new, pleasurable tension in his stomach and thighs. They were both panting a little when she looked up. "Maya has to learn to sleep in her own bed again," she said as he nuzzled her neck. "Oh, my God, that feels good." She had a warm, musky smell, womanly and wonderful. He put his nose to her hair and inhaled her into his lungs.

"Come sit on my lap," he suggested, all his earlier anger dissolved.

"I can't."

"Am I moving too quick?"

"No, this dress is too tight."

"Pull it up."

She glanced at him, then started to pull her dress up until he could see that she was wearing lacy black panties. "You know, I'm not entirely sure this is such a . . ."

He silenced her by pulling her onto his lap, making sure to lift her over the gearshift. She looked startled to find herself straddling him. "You're stronger than you look," she said.

"Uh-huh. Used to be helpful in bar fights," he said, tangling his hands in her hair and pulling her down for another kiss. And brother, could she ever kiss. He'd never been the kind of guy who went straight from one girlfriend to another, figuring that you needed a bit of time to clear your head in between women, and he wouldn't permit himself to compare her with Jess. But it surprised him to find that touching Zoë didn't just feel good, it felt right. In some hard-to-define way, her body felt right, the way some cars felt right, as if the controls had been custom made to your specifications. He liked the sheer size of her, the uninhibited way she unzipped the front of his blue medical coveralls, shoving up the T-shirt underneath so she could slip her cool hands inside. When she touched the muscles of his stomach, he said, "Hang on, I need to rearrange things."

"Oh, no, I must be crushing you," she said, but he ran his hands down her hips, discovering the firm muscle underneath the generous curves as he prevented her from wriggling off.

"You are not crushing me," he said, "but if you were, I'd die a happy man."

"Very funny. I probably weigh twenty pounds more than you do." She felt his stomach again. "Maybe thirty."

He deliberately lifted her again, then brought her back down. "I may look weedy, but I promise you, I'm not some ninety-eight-pound weakling."

"No, you're well-muscled, unlike me." She made a little face, and he thought how ridiculous it was that this fabulous Amazon of a woman shouldn't know how incredible she was.

"You," he said, looking up into her face, "are gorgeous."

"'Without your glasses, Miss Jones,'" she added. At his quizzical look, she added, "That's the classic line, isn't it? You know, when the librarian takes off her glasses?"

Mack reached out and touched the tip of her nose. "I like you with your glasses, too." He traced her ear with his finger and she closed her eyes and arched her back. One of her breasts had almost come out the top of her dress and he stared at it, mesmerized. "I like all of you." He leaned down and pressed a kiss to the top slope of her breast, then darted his tongue down beneath the fabric of the dress, reaching her nipple. When he looked up at her unguarded face, he found her watching him as if mesmerized. Something hushed and sharpened between them.

"I want to be inside you," he said softly.

She gave a shaky laugh, and it felt as if someone had turned the lights on. "Me, too," she said, the words a gentle withdrawal. "But I'm not sure that we should continue this in your sister's driveway."

He nodded, sliding his hands back down to the delectable curve of her hips, unable to prevent himself from squeezing. "We could go somewhere else." Hopeless, he knew, even as he suggested it. Where were they going to go? A cheap motel? A field? The moment had passed, but he was still hard and she was still sitting on top of him, and one head wasn't yet in agreement with the other.

Zoë squirmed off his lap, pulling the hem of her dress back down. "I have a better idea. How about tomorrow, when Maya's in school, we can arrange to have you drive me . . . crazy."

And just like that, Mack felt himself begin to deflate. Of course they needed to arrange things, but their current location and Maya's penchant for climbing into her mother's bed weren't the only obstacles to overcome. Belatedly, he recalled another compelling reason why they couldn't just tear off their clothes and have tomorrow-we-might-die sex.

Zoë was paying him by the hour.

Seventeen

*I*t was ridiculous. It was a power game. It was blackmail.

"What exactly are you saying?"

"You heard me."

Zoë moved the phone to her other ear. "So what you're saying is, you don't want to see me anymore unless I take driving lessons?"

"Zoë, you're paying me to drive you around." He sounded pained when he said it, which made no sense.

"So?" She stared down at her toenails, which were half painted with gold polish. After getting Maya off to school, Zoë had shaved her legs, moisturized her elbows, applied a mud mask to her face, and attempted to use a do-it-yourself wax kit on her bikini area and upper lip. She'd also decided to remove the tiny tufts of hair under her arms, because she had no idea whether Mack would find them bohemian and sexy or downright appalling. Boy, did she ever wish she were back in the city where she could just walk around the corner and pay to get all this done. But then again, if she were back in the city, she wouldn't be seeing Mack. Just thinking his name made her recall the feel of his hands and mouth on her skin. Dear God, he had the touch, she hadn't felt anything like that since 1989, with Ian the radical Scots newspaperman. She'd always wondered if it had been the intellectual sparring or the physical chemistry that had made the affair so powerful, and now she was guessing the latter. After all, she was clearly not going to have a great meeting of the minds with Mack, but boy, did she want to get naked with him. "Mack? Are you still there?"

"I don't know what else to say. You're paying me."

"So quit."

Mack didn't respond right away, and it slowly dawned on Zoë that he was having second thoughts.

"The thing is, Zoë, you still need a driver, and I . . ." his voice trailed off.

"And you aren't that into it. Let's cut the b.s., Mack, I get it. Last night, you were in the mood, but now that you've had some sleep, it just doesn't seem right." And here was where being forty-one really did make things better. Zoë knew better than to take this too much to heart. Maybe he usually went for pretty, little blondes. Maybe she intimidated him. Whatever it was, she wasn't about to do what she'd have done at twenty-one or even thirty-one: become plagued by self-doubt as to her own attractiveness. So he didn't want her. She could live with it. She'd have to find a new driver, of course, but until she did, she'd have to put up with the minor humiliation of unreciprocated desire. She capped the bottle of nail polish and yanked off her best lacy underwear.

"Zoë, please don't be angry at me. It's not that I don't want you, you know that."

She snorted, rummaging in her underwear drawer for an old cotton pair. "Oh, please."

"I got turned on when you held my hand! I nearly bit your head off when I realized that I couldn't just take you home and jump into bed with you!"

Zoë paused in the act of pulling out a dingy gray brassiere. "You did seem a little testy." Maybe, she thought, I'm going to need lace after all.

"I was mad because I wanted to go home with you, and it sounds like Maya keeps getting into your bed. To be frank, that's all I was thinking about at first—how to get between the sheets with you. But then I had to stop and think, How's this going to work? I come over, drive you around, you pay me fifteen dollars an hour, and then we have sex?"

Zoë pulled on an ancient pair of sweatpants, now fully prepared to give up on the man. "What is this, some kind of old-fashioned hang-up about a woman who makes more money than you? I was kind of assuming the sex would be off the clock."

"I'd still feel like a kept man." He waited. "Zoë, right now you are the only paying job I have. With Moroney and Pete out of commission, I figure I'm about to get some more work, but until then, I can't even afford to just not work for you." He sounded less certain of himself than usual.

It was Zoë's turn to sigh. "All right. So what's your solution? You give me driving lessons and what, my big reward for passing the road test is I get to have sex with you?"

Mack cleared his throat. "I was thinking more that it was *my* big reward for your passing the test. And it usually takes about twenty lessons; if we do two a week, that's less than three months."

"This seems like a lot of time and effort for what I was assuming was going to be a fairly casual, physical relationship." Zoë stared at her newly shaved and moisturized leg, suddenly aware of all its imperfections, the cellulite padding her thighs, the places where she had discovered spider veins, tiny red or blue starbursts that she didn't recall seeing at the start of summer.

"Maybe we can fool around a little after you pass your written test," he suggested.

"Was that meant to be a joke?"

"More of a short-term goal."

"Forget it." For a moment, last night, she'd felt the kind of incontrovertible, impractical lust she'd felt in adolescence, and the thought of it had been making her ignore the obvious: Mack wasn't bitten by the same bug.

"What do you mean? Listen, three months isn't that long to wait, and wouldn't it be good to have something to look forward to?" He sounded perfectly reasonable, without any hint of the desperation that always goes with a strong desire.

"Spoken like a true salesman. But as the saying goes, if you can resist passion, it's because the passion's weak, not because you're strong."

"What saying is that?"

"La Rochefoucauld. I'm paraphrasing." She waited. "Mack? Are you still there?"

"How do you spell that?"

She expelled her breath. "That's it. I'm hanging up now."

"No, Zoë, wait. I've already said, it's not that I'm not attracted ..."

She hung up. What an idiot she was. Mack probably went around feeling attracted to all kinds of women. He was a physical person. He didn't go around complicating things by trying to find some intellectual fit with a woman. And what was an intellectual fit for him, anyway—love of NASCAR racing? She deliberately squelched the memory of him in her living room, clearly delighted in the discovery of the concept of the macabre. For him, she was far more important as a client than as a lover.

Well, too bad, because he'd just lost her as both. There had to be someone else who could drive her to the store, for God's sake. Preferably, a woman. *Three months. Nice to have a goal.* Yeah, he was really hot for her. For a moment, Zoë allowed herself to consider just how bleak the country was going to feel in November, when the days grew short and cold. And then she realized that she did have a goal. She picked up the phone again.

"Zoë? Did you change your mind? Because let me assure you ..."

"No, Mack. This is about something else entirely." Zoë turned on her computer. "I want to speak to your sister about the developers who've made her that offer on the farm."

* * *

One of the few things that could have distracted Zoë from the blighted prospect of good sex was the ongoing promise of a good story. And the Amimi Mountain development project was starting to look like a very good story.

First of all, there was the distinct whiff of corruption, always appealing to a journalist. The main source of the smell seemed to be Jim Moroney, who did far more than run the local driving school. For all intents and purposes, Moroney was the town's mayor, so it had interested Zoë a great deal to learn that he had accepted an incredibly inflated payment for a five-acre plot and a gingerbread Victorian from the developers. The local paper carried a quote from Moroney, stating that "This deal had nothing to do with my decision to approve the development project, which I've judged by its own merits." She'd found this out from Mack's sister, who had been surprisingly forthcoming, considering that she was still contemplating the sale of her farm.

"I don't mind filling you in, so long as you don't stick me in the middle of some fight," Moira had told her. "Personally, I can see both sides of the issue. On the one hand, I hate to see the land get built up, but on the other hand, the local economy could use a boost."

Moira had added that "Your daughter is free to come over and help out with the horses any time she likes." When Zoë had explained that she didn't drive and didn't want to take up too much of Mack's time, Moira had said "Oh, I know he won't mind" in a way that made Zoë think she knew more than she was letting on.

"He's been very helpful," Zoë responded in a carefully neutral tone, "but I don't think it's good to depend too much on any one person."

"You two ought to get along just fine," Moira had responded. "That's what he always says."

But Zoë really didn't want to keep calling Mack or his sister. In retrospect, she realized that when he'd said that he didn't want to feel like a gigolo, it was because he was, in fact, vying for that position. And it made sense that a man who was younger and had less social status than she did would conflate sex with power. This understanding, however, did not reconcile Zoë to Mack. Quite the opposite; it made her feel mildly repulsed by the very thought of him.

Not that she spent too much time thinking about him. She had continued to research the proposed development on the internet, discovering that Arcadia was one of the few remaining towns that had absolutely no zoning. If you wanted to open a carwash or a dog-racing track or a strip mall smack dab in the middle of Arcadia's quiet, tree-lined residential streets, there was no law preventing it.

So who could blame a bunch of developers from taking advantage of this freedom by snatching up nearly one hundred acres of untouched wilderness at the edge of town and pursuing their version of the American dream?

Well, there were at least two people actively casting blame— Frances and Gretchen, whose liquor store had a perfect view of Amimi Mountain and Starling Pond. The two women were so eager to tell their side of the story to a bona fide national journalist that they came over to Zoë's house, bringing two excellent bottles of retsina, a homemade spanakopita, and most delicious of all, the real dish on Moroney. According to Frances, Moroney was strong-arming the town board and telling them to avoid any delay that might derail the proposed project. This meant that the board was ignoring the Arcadia Wetlands Foundation's pleas that an environmental impact assessment be done. "We need to determine whether any rare wildlife would be adversely affected by this development," said Frances. "But so far, we can't get anyone in Albany to step in and demand a state environmental review."

As far as Zoë could tell, Frances and Gretchen *were* the Arcadia Wetlands Foundation, although they claimed that most of their clientele were already outspoken in their opposition to the development.

City folks, it transpired, did not relish the prospect of their quiet weekend retreat becoming a bustling strip mall. Manhattanites had all the convenience and Starbucks and health clubs they needed during the workweek. On holidays, they wanted quaint little country shops filled with bric-a-brac, and charming cafés that sold homemade jam. And even if they didn't actually get out and hike into the wilderness areas, city folk liked knowing they existed, and that wild things roamed there.

"The locals aren't particularly moved by the plight of snapping turtles and timber rattlers, and they actively hunt the bear and coyote," said Gretchen. "They'll work to protect the bald eagles, though. But weekenders understand that once we lose this habitat, these species aren't going to be coming back."

Privately, Zoë thought there was something more than a little ironic about these ecologically minded city people, who gobbled up resources by owning two homes and didn't count the cost in burned fossil fuels as they traveled back and forth between town and country. And, of course, part of what the weekenders were protecting so vehemently was their property value. This, in truth, was the other angle she was considering for her article—the vainglorious hypocrisy of weekend environmentalists, fighting the development that might improve the lives of the full-time locals.

But as she continued to dig, Zoë learned that things were not so simple. Not all the townies were in favor of the proposed development. In fact, according to Rudy the evangelical cabdriver, a lot of folks were strongly opposed.

"We're worried that this will change the whole character of the town. Don't see why they can't build their stores on Main Street," said Rudy, who had called Zoë and announced himself available whenever she needed a taxi service. Zoë had been surprised by this change of heart, and even more surprised by his explanation.

"Frankly, I thought you were one of those Godless city people," he clarified, presenting her with a gift of freshly butchered venison. "But Moira told me that your little girl told her that you belong to the People of the Book. I totally respect that." According to the Book of Revelations, he explained, Jesus would return to earth when all the Jews were gathered together in the Land of Israel.

Logically, this meant that Zoë herself was standing in the way of Rudy's salvation by living in Arcadia, but she decided not to point this out. Especially since Rudy was now willing to be her driver, which meant she didn't have to deal with Mack. And unlike old Pete, whom she'd heard was recovering from his stroke at home, Rudy wasn't likely to keel over on the way to the supermarket.

All in all, Zoë admitted to Bronwyn, she'd been almost content lately.

"And I thought you said this wasn't your kind of story," Bronwyn needled her over the phone one Saturday morning, an unmistakable hint of smugness in her voice.

"Well, I'm still not even sure what my angle is," Zoë replied, looking out her window just as a red-tailed hawk swooped down and scooped up another bird. Thanks to Gretchen and Frances, she could now tell a hawk from a buzzard.

"But you sound like you do when you're working well."

"I am working well," Zoë admitted. "It's interesting, finding out how everyone has such different fantasies about the same bit of swamp." She stepped out the door, and for the first time, the grass was cold beneath her bare feet. It was nearly the end of October, and a strong breeze was whipping the leaves off the trees, adding to the sense of urgency in the air. Overhead, a V-shaped formation of brown and beige Canada geese urged one another to hurry it along.

"Who's honking like that? It sounds like rush hour."

"It is, for geese." Zoë went back into the house just as Claudius appeared with a mouse in his mouth. "Oh, no you don't. Drop it right there. Sorry, cat has a mouse," she explained, using her foot to keep Claudius out of the kitchen.

"This you say to me calmly? Zoë, you're not turning into a country girl, are you?"

"That's like asking Solzhenitsyn if he was starting to love Siberia." Zoë took an onion out of a straw basket on the counter and began chopping. "Right now I am missing Starbucks, Gourmet Garage pre-prepared dinners, and you. Not necessarily in that order. But I'm holding it together because I'm coming next weekend, remember?" With a large sniff, she wiped her streaming eyes with a paper towel.

"Zoë, sweetheart, what's wrong? Are you crying?"

"From onions."

"Oh, good, you scared me. Why are you messing with onions?"

"I'm making a quiche."

"Since when? You make hummus and meatloaf and microwaved veggies. And maybe a scrambled egg. You're like one of those 1950s bachelor guys who can cook exactly one dinner and one breakfast. You don't make quiche." Bronwyn's voice was a shade too sharp for irony, which, Zoë knew, was what she intended.

Zoë rinsed off the cutting board. "What can I say? There's no take-out here. I've had to adjust." She checked her cookbook.

"You're never coming back," wailed Bronwyn. "I'm getting a dog. Look, I see a papillon-rottweiler mix here, only six months old. Housebroken."

"That's not a dog, that's a crime against nature," said Zoë, searching the fridge a second time. Had Maya really finished the entire carton of milk this morning? "Hey, why don't you get a French bulldog? This woman Frances here has one, and it's rather cute." She took the milk out of the fridge and discovered that she was almost out of butter and eggs. Rudy was due in half an hour to drive her to Maya's school for an all-day parents' visiting program. She wondered if they'd have time to stop off at the supermarket.

"You're cheating on me with other women," said Bronwyn.

"She's just a passing friend fling," Zoë assured her. "You're the one I'm coming home to. Hey, I forgot to ask about the hunt for a preschool. How's it going?"

"I think we've found one really nice Unitarian church nursery that might accept us. The problem is, they were hoping for more diversity, so they won't give us an answer till they hear back from this Korean-Irish family. Hang on, the boys are hitting each other, let me do the bad mommy thing and turn on the TV to distract them."

Zoë heard the sounds of the boys' shouting diminish as the TV went on. She was more than a little alarmed to see that her store-bought crust seemed to be crumbling as she poured the cream and eggs in.

"Okay," said Bronwyn, "I'm back." In between each word, Zoë heard a loud clicking noise.

"What's that? I can't hear you too well."

"Where the hell are you living, the Antarctic," said Bronwyn in a loud voice, but now there was a buzzing sound on the line. "I get better reception to Europe."

Zoë looked out the window and saw that the wind had really picked up, bending some of the younger trees almost double. "Shoot, Bron, I think there's something wrong with the line."

Bronwyn said, "You have got to move someplace civilized," and then the phone went dead. Zoë was about to try back on her cell phone when she glanced at the clock and realized that she was still wearing the T-shirt she'd slept in and Rudy was going to be there in less than fifteen minutes. She had just shoved the makings of her quiche in the fridge and hung up the phone when she heard a knock at the door. "Hey, Rudy, I'll need a few more minutes," Zoë said, opening the door a crack and admitting the spicy woodsmoke smell of some unseen neighbor's bonfire. But it wasn't Rudy standing there.

"I can wait," said Mack, slouched against the doorjamb with his hands in his back jean pockets, the wind blowing thick strands of his dark blond hair into his eyes. His smile hit the perfect note; both wry and rueful, as if the two of them were sharing a private joke.

Without hesitation, Zoë slammed the door in his face.

Eighteen

*O*kay, so she was still pissed off at him. Mack turned the key in the ignition as Zoë sat beside him in the passenger seat, looking remote and distrustful in a smart black suit. He'd expected a cool reception, but she seemed to have demoted him straight back to stranger, or to something that ranked even lower—the kind of annoying acquaintance who does not understand that any previous offer of intimacy has been canceled and revoked. Mack saw that he was going to have to revise his original strategy, which had been to act as though their disagreement hadn't happened.

"You haven't mentioned the new car," he said, thinking he might as well plunge in with a neutral topic. "I mean, it's not new, it's restored, but you know what I mean." This was the car's first official outing, and he thought it was handling great. A bang-up job, if he had to say so himself. "Notice anything unusual about it?"

Zoë took a magazine out of her enormous bag. "There's a small steering wheel on the wrong side," she said, indicating the object with her chin, as if she found it offensive.

"Dual passenger-side steering, added security for student and teacher," he corrected her. "Moroney's cars never had that."

"Hmm," Zoë said, flipping through her magazine.

"Bet you can't guess what it started out as?" Silence. "Two

weeks ago, this was a battered old Crown Royal. Some cop rode that sucker into a tree. Now we're talking perfect alignment, the dual passenger-side steering, which I pointed out to you already, and of course dual passenger-side brakes. Plus we had a little fun with the bodywork." He chuckled, remembering that first day in the garage. "In the beginning," he said, "I objected to Skeeter's plan to raise the wheels. I mean, a driving school needs something that looks like a sedan, not a muscle car. But Skeeter—that's my old gearhead friend—he was really insistent about the popeye headlights, and adding that ridge to the front, and then I said, What the hell, let's go all out and paint red stripes on the black. And you have to admit, the end result is pretty cool. And who's to say that there isn't an added incentive to students in learning to drive on a car that looks cool?"

Zoë lowered her magazine. "I'm sorry," she said, "I wasn't really listening. Did you just ask me a question?"

Okay, Mack thought, she was more than just a little pissed off. For the first time in two weeks, Mack wondered whether the night they'd made out was going to be a one-night stand, minus the payoff. Up until now, he'd just pushed the whole Zoë thing off to one side, concentrating on working in the garage with Skeeter. Moroney had called him twice from the hospital, to see if he wanted to have his old job back, but Mack had apologized, explaining that he'd already made another commitment and was too busy.

Mack hadn't mentioned that the commitment was to establishing his own driving school. And even though she hadn't spoken to him, he'd remained convinced that Zoë was going to be his first student, and that eventually, the two of them were going to wind up shifting gears into a different kind of relationship. He'd figured he might as well let her get over being mad at him while he focused on getting the car ready.

He'd wondered if Skeet had a girl, but hadn't asked. Besides

himself, Skeet was the only one of the old high school class who
hadn't been married at least once, and that included fat Max Bill-
son and twitchy Gene. It had occurred to Mack that there might
be a story there, but he hadn't wanted to blow their renewed
friendship by sticking his nose where it didn't belong. Instead,
they'd talked about cars, and the dumb things people did with
them. The guy who didn't notice that he'd been riding around on
a flat for two days. The woman who turned straight into a house
because her car's GPS told her to. The rich kid who asked if he
could pay Skeeter to clean up the vomit that had gotten into the
dashboard vents. The past two weeks had been comfortable and
busy, and Mack hadn't wasted much time mulling over Skeeter's
apparent lack of interest in women, or his own short-term failure
in that department. At the end of the day, he'd known that when
a man and a woman are both interested and relatively unencum-
bered, it doesn't take a lot of maneuvering to hook up. Once the
car was ready for her, he'd thought, he'd make his move. And
then Rudy had called, asking Mack if he could fill in. Perfect tim-
ing, Mack had said.

Only now Mack thought he might have misjudged things.
Maybe he'd made a mistake by letting things sit as they were, since
instead of cooling down, Zoë seemed to have festered like an ulcer-
ated wound. Maybe he should have called her, tried to explain himself better. Maybe he should have just come over and said, To hell
with everything else, let's go for it.

Glancing sideways, Mack saw that Zoë was still reading her
magazine with a slightly ostentatious display of interest. The print,
he noticed, was very small. There was a small black-and-white cartoon on one page showing two leashed dogs going for a walk.
Underneath, the caption read: "Frankly, I'm disappointed in his
leadership."

"I don't get it," said Mack. "Why is that funny?"

"What?"

"That cartoon."

Zoë looked down at it. He could now see that she'd been reading an article called "The Building That Ate the Upper West Side." "Typical *New Yorker* joke," she said, after a moment. "It's not very funny."

"Ah." He drove on, admiring her confidence: I don't like it, it's not funny. Last week, he'd bought a collection of Edward Gorey's cartoons called *Amphigorey,* which he suspected was a pun that he didn't quite get. Then, because he'd gotten to talking to the bookseller about poetry, he'd let himself be talked into buying a book by Frank O'Hara, who had been Gorey's roommate. O'Hara, it turned out, was a fag, and some of the poems were pretty faggy, but Mack kept reading because he liked the man's attitude. According to the intro, O'Hara believed poetry should be immediate and spontaneous, and scribbled most of his poems down on bits of paper, shoving them into his pockets. He also seemed to be saying that it didn't matter how much or how little you understood, it mattered only if you felt something from the words. If people didn't feel the need to read poetry, O'Hara said, bully for them. Still, there were bits that Mack wished he could talk over with someone. What did it mean, "to shatter the supercilious peace of these barked mammals"? He wasn't sure, but when he looked up the word "supercilious" he thought that maybe the poet was describing what he sometimes felt when he saw a bunch of fat, happy families munching away at their picnic table on the beach while their kiddies played, all of them acting as though disaster wasn't lurking all around them, in the grass, in the lake, hell, even inside their arteries.

Mack stole another look at the article Zoë was reading. There were words in bold that he didn't recognize. Weltanschauung.

Embourgeoisement. Dystopia. He felt a stirring of something like desire, but it was as much a wish to inhale those words as it was a longing to press his mouth to hers.

"Listen, I wanted to tell you something," he said, swerving to avoid a tree limb lying in the road.

"If it's about the other night, I don't feel we need to discuss it further."

"Actually, what I was going to say was, Rudy asked me to tell you what happened to him." Outside, a strong gust of wind pushed against the car, and Mack paid attention to his steering for a moment.

"Don't tell me, his great-aunt's poodle has gout," said Zoë, still looking down at her magazine. "His Bible group had an emergency prayer meeting."

"His kid is sick."

Zoë turned back to face him. "I'm sorry."

Glad to see her looking a little less mad at him, Mack nearly drove by the sign for the Mackinley School. He hit the brakes a little harder than he'd intended, and Zoë gave him the fishy eyeball, like he'd done it on purpose. Maybe he needed to apologize. Women always liked you to say you were sorry about something. But what to apologize for, not nailing her? That wouldn't fly.

"Listen," he said slowly, casting about for something else he might have done wrong, "I know I got on your case earlier, about the driving and all. Truth is, you were right when you said we all have things we kind of avoid doing."

Zoë shook her head, making her earrings dance. "Don't tell me you're still banging on about driving lessons? Please, do us both a favor and forget it."

"I don't want to forget it," he said.

She looked exasperated. "Why is it so important to you?"

"Because," he said, "you're different from the other women I've known. You're . . . you know things I have no idea about." Feeling embarrassed, but somehow compelled to finish, Mack added, "You're so smart. And it's sexy to me, the way that you're smart."

"If you're impressed by the fact that I have a large vocabulary . . ."

"Please, give me more credit than that."

He thought Zoë might have said something else, but by then they had driven right up to the school, where they were greeted by a great white hand-painted banner. The cloth was rippling so hard in the wind that it read ELCOM PARENTS.

"Listen," said Zoë, "I have to go find my daughter." She pushed her glasses up on her nose. "We can talk later if you want."

"I don't mind staying with you. Let me just figure out where to park."

She sighed. "Mack, I can't deal with you right now."

Knowing when he was beaten, Mack put the car in park. "Hey." He gestured at her magazine. "You done with that?"

"Not quite, but you can borrow it."

"Thanks." For a moment, their fingers brushed as she handed him the *New Yorker,* and then she was walking away, forcing him to call after her. "When and where do I meet you again?"

Zoë paused. "Can you come get us around four? I was wondering if you wouldn't mind heading over to the riding ring. The program ends with a horse show, and I think it'll be over by then, but I don't want to walk out too early."

"I'll find you," he promised. Then, because he had time to kill but no money, he decided to just park the car and hang around. It struck him that the Crown Royal looked a little out of place among all the vintage sports cars and gleaming SUVs, like a beer-drinking NASCAR fan who had taken a wrong turn and wound up at the Kentucky Derby.

Ah, well. The old convertibles spent most of their lives in a body shop, and SUVs were trucks for people who didn't need to haul things.

Mack found himself a big spreading oak tree and sat down with his back against the wind. He knew that the Mackinley School was some kind of special-ed deal, but the kids all looked normal to him. He'd been surprised to find out that Zoë's daughter was going here, because in his day, special ed meant you were basically a drooler and a bed-wetter. But Maya seemed like a bright kid, and nobody else he could see here today was visibly impaired.

Of course, these days, everyone treated everything as if it were a disease. Kid can't throw a ball well? Must be a spastic-at-sports disorder. Kid tunes out in history class while the teacher drones on about the Revolutionary War? Clear sign of brain malfunction. And God forbid you blew a spitball at someone, they doped you up like an old boxer.

Hell, using today's standards, Mack thought, I'd probably have been diagnosed as five different kinds of misfit. If only my old teachers could see me now, he thought, sticking a stalk of grass in the corner of his mouth and folding Zoë's magazine so it wouldn't blow away. They'd never even believe that John Mackenna was reading some literary rag, considering how much he used to hate the books they assigned.

But it's not easy to love something you're not good at, and Mack had stunk at English, or at least, he'd stunk at the kind of English they used to teach at Arcadia Grammar School.

Mack sat straight up, the blade of grass falling out of his mouth. Jeez, what was the matter with him? Here he was, at a school that specialized in the hard-to-teach, on a day when you could just walk into their classes and see how they did it. Maybe they could show him something that would help him reach the really hard cases, the ones like Zoë who were too freaked out to even want to learn to drive.

Mack stood up and started walking toward the WELCOME PARENTS banner, where a woman with enormous calves appeared to be directing people to one building or another. Of course, he wasn't a parent. But unless school had changed completely from the days he'd attended, nobody ever noticed you in the back of a classroom.

Nineteen

M ommy," Maya whispered in Zoë's ear, "what's Mack doing here?"

Zoë turned and spotted him, slouched in the back row, the only man not wearing a polo shirt or a tie. "I have no idea," she whispered back. He met her gaze and gave a little half shrug. Probably got bored trying to read the *New Yorker,* she thought. Don't let him distract you.

Zoë turned her attention to the large, brightly lit classroom, which still bore some of the hallmarks of the gracious family dining room it had once been. There were a number of different projects on display, canoes and wigwams and terrariums, an assortment of essential oils with note cards that said things like "Tearful" and "Heady" as well as a multitude of cave dioramas. On closer inspection, these seemed to all have little figures making their way up out of the darkness—a reference to Orpheus and Eurydice? There were certainly some creepy figures at the bottom of Maya's sculpture.

Strangely enough, there was no sign of a book in the room.

"Welcome, everybody," said the teacher, a blocky, stern-faced woman with a determinedly frilly dress and haircut. Somebody, somewhere must have told Ms. Weyr that she had a hard look and should soften the effect with ruffles and curls, but the effect was simply disconcerting, like finding lace doilies on a tank. "I'm Ms. Weyr, and this is fourth-grade English. If you look around the room, you might be able to guess that we've been talking about lots of different myths and legends, and how you can find elements of these old stories in so many of the books we read, from *Charlotte's Web* to *Harry Potter*."

Zoë's mind drifted a little as Ms. Weyr went on talking about stories. As always, the distinctive chalkboard and wood-polish smell of a classroom made her feel as if she'd been transported back in time and was once again Zoë-Knowy, the best and least popular student in her grade. And had she changed much since the days when her teacher had to ask her to limit herself to two questions an hour? Perhaps the Jesuits were right in focusing on the very early years. How much did anyone really change after the age of seven?

Zoë watched her daughter's face for a moment, noticing Maya's rapt expression as she absentmindedly twisted a strand of her blond hair around her pencil. She was so pretty, Zoë thought, so contained. Nobody would ever complain that Maya was being a show-off, or snap their hands like little yapping mouths behind her back. If we were both the same age, she wondered, would my daughter even want to be my friend? Yes, Zoë decided, she would, but only because she was kind. Maybe she would even give me a few pointers on how to make friends. Maya might not be able to read at grade level, but she could see social signals that Zoë had been blind to until college.

Looking around the room, Zoë noticed that her daughter was smiling at another girl, who was dressed in a similar combination of bright blue shirt and embroidered jeans. This must be her friend Allegra, who had the same shining, dark hair as her mother, but had clearly inherited all her other features from the squat, beetle-browed man sitting beside her. Allegra's mother, Renata, did not acknowledge knowing Zoë from the cocktail party, but sat with perfect posture in her chic navy suit, while her husband kept making silly faces at Allegra when the teacher's back was turned.

Zoë surreptitiously observed the other, equally fascinating combinations of parents and children in the room. To her left was a tall, horse-faced woman with a genial smile sitting next to a boy who looked like her twin. To her right was a thin, nervous, balding man in a rumpled suit and tie and his lumpish, bespectacled daughter, unfortunately dressed in formfitting lavender. One couple, who looked old enough to be grandparents, wore velour tracksuits and so much heavy gold jewelry that they actually rattled when they moved. Their son, a small, handsome, sullen child in a leather bomber jacket, glanced back at them reprovingly.

"Now," said Ms. Weyr, "I'd like to go around the room for a moment and have each of the parents introduce themselves. If you can, sum up in a few sentences what kind of English students you were."

The man in the velour tracksuit raised one hand, rattling the bracelet of his gold Rolex. "Do we have to?"

Ms. Weyr leaned back against her desk and gave a smile that transformed her face. "Will it help if I admit that I hated the books I had to read for class, but loved the paperback mysteries my mother brought home?"

There was a little ripple of appreciative laughter, and then the parents began. The horsey woman agreed that she hadn't much liked English, but had enjoyed reading Nancy Drew books at home. The man who looked like an accountant said that he had only liked reading science fiction. As the parents spoke, Zoë tried to imagine them as children: the horsey woman as an earnest, plain girl with careful handwriting and neat lists of "things to do"; the nervous, balding man as a shy, nerdy boy, turning out messy, brilliant science papers; the elderly couple in their matching velour tracksuits as friendly, popular kids, not leaders but joiners who were quick to volunteer for clubs.

Some of the other parents took longer to figure out. The Indian woman, for example, was so neatly groomed and polite that it took Zoë a while to see the mischievous girl underneath the silk dress.

One parent, however, was impossible to imagine as a child. After five minutes of listening to Renata going on and on about Pinocchio, specifying that she meant the original classic tale by Collodi and not the cheap Disney version, Zoë decided that the woman was a replicant and had, in fact, been designed in some upscale Italian factory.

When the teacher turned to her, Zoë didn't want to sound as arrogant as Renata, so she admitted that she'd loved English and done well in it, but didn't relate the fact that by the middle of third grade she'd already raced through the book the class was supposed to read, along with the complete works of Roald Dahl, *Alice in Wonderland*, Anne Frank's diary, and T. H. White's *The Once and Future King*. She didn't mention that at the end of the year she'd received a special English prize, a big, hardcover edition of Dickens's *Oliver Twist*, which her parents made her return because he'd been the author of *A Christmas Carol* and they thought he was too Christian a writer.

"I've always loved books," Zoë said instead, "and I've been trying to find a way to help Maya love them, too. Hopefully this class will do the trick."

Ms. Weyr paused for a moment, looking as though she were about to say something, but then just nodded her head and turned to the back corner where Zoë knew Mack was sitting. "And what about you?" When he spoke, Zoë turned around to look at him, along with everyone else in the room.

"I'm not really a parent," Mack said, sitting up straighter in his chair and drawing in his long, jean-clad legs as if he'd been caught out doing something improper. "I'm sort of here as a guest." He was the only man in the room wearing heavy-soled work boots, and while the fathers sat in various attitudes of mature stiffness, Mack slouched with the easy, slender muscularity of youth.

"That's all right," said Ms. Weyr. "You can still answer the question, even if you're not a parent."

Mack ran his fingers through his shaggy, sun-streaked hair, revealing his sharp, surprisingly delicate features. "Well, back in school, I pretty much ignored the reading assignments. Or else I picked up the Classic Comic and read that instead." He smiled boyishly, and it was all too easy to imagine him as a kid. He was a type, Zoë thought; the bad boy who distrusted all forms of authority until the moment he joined the army. "I guess I read a couple of Stephen King books for fun, but most of the time, I can't really say I read much of anything."

Ms. Weyr looked pleased as she turned back to the other parents. "You know, this gentleman . . . what's your name?"

"Mack. John Mackenna." Zoë thought he looked a little flustered.

"Mr. Mackenna here makes a good point. Not all of us love books." Ms. Weyr smiled at Zoë and the Indian woman. "I know that this may be a shocking thing to hear from an English teacher, but just as not all kids love sports, not all kids are going to love books. It's hard to love something that doesn't come easy."

Zoë was dumbfounded. She felt her heart beating faster with agitation. Wasn't this why she'd moved to the goddamn country in the first place? What had all that sacrifice been for, if not so that the world of books would finally open for her child?

She raised her hand, ignoring the fact that her daughter now wore a strangely pinched, anguished expression, as though she were trying not to complain while being devoured by army ants. "Excuse me," Zoë said, her voice suddenly sounding overly loud in the quiet room, "but isn't that why we've sent our children to this school? To help them read better so that they can experience the thrill and joy of books?"

Ms. Weyr smiled again with infuriating calm and walked around the classroom, her old-fashioned leather boots squeaking with each step. "Your children are here to learn," she said simply. "They are here to learn to read more efficiently, yes, but they are also here to learn in other, equally important ways. Some of us learn best by hearing things spoken out loud. Some of us learn best by working something out with our hands. Some of us learn best by a combination of hearing and doing. But for those of us who have to work hard at the mechanics of reading, it can be very hard to concentrate on the content of books while we're decoding words."

"Like a new driver trying to figure out directions at the same time as he's trying to remember all the rules of the road," said Mack, sounding excited.

"Exactly like that." Ms. Weyr beamed at him, despite the fact that he'd called out. "I don't know how many of you know this, but at our school, we don't ask our students to do any reading from books in the classroom. I mean, there is reading, but I do it out loud."

"They're not going to read any books in English class?" Jeez, thought Zoë, why am I the only one speaking up? Maya looked as though she wanted to ask the same question, though Zoë thought her daughter would probably have used a different inflection.

"Because," said the teacher, "we've learned that when you feel vulnerable about doing something, you're better off tackling it one on one, in a private tutorial. We also put a great deal of value on restoring our students' confidence and sense of mastery, which is why we're so proud to show you what your children have learned at our horseback riding show later this afternoon. I always say, 'If you can tackle your fear of an animal that weighs over a thousand pounds, well, heck, you can tackle an irregular verb.'"

Dear God, thought Zoë, that joke I made about caring more about horseback riding than academics is coming back to haunt me. "But the end goal is for these kids to be able to read their own books in school, right? For them to become good readers and go back to join mainstream schools." Out of the corner of her eye, she could see Renata looking at her approvingly.

"That's what I've assumed," she said, and Zoë wasn't sure whether or not it was a good thing to have Renata on her side.

"Yes, that is our goal, but speaking honestly, not all of us are going to grow up to be avid readers. May I ask what you do for a living?"

"I'm a journalist."

"So for you, for your work, reading is very important, but so is questioning things deeply. Which you do very well," she added, and the class laughed. "Now, let's take a look at someone else. Mr. Mackenna, what do you do?"

Everyone turned in their seats to look at Mack. "Um, teach driving," he said. "Work on cars. I mean, I used to work in a garage, and I've been doing that again for the past two weeks. And I'm a volunteer EMT."

"So am I right in thinking that in your work, you don't need to do much reading? In the garage, you probably spend more time looking to see how things work, yes, or running trial-and-error experiments to see what's wrong?"

"Well, yeah," said Mack.

"And when you teach, and when you work as a medic, you need people skills—much like Maya's mother here."

Zoë narrowed her eyes, thinking that this was getting a little irritating. She didn't mean to be elitist, but she wasn't taking a year out of her life so that Maya could grow up to be a car mechanic or a driving instructor or even an emergency medical technician. Since that was not an acceptable thing to admit out loud, she decided to equivocate a little. "I'm sorry if I seem argumentative here, but I'm sure that I'm not the only parent who wants her child to succeed to the fullest extent of her potential. And to me, it's great if Maya can use her hands and has great people skills, but I also want her to be exposed to all the great things that books can offer."

"Of course you do," said Ms. Weyr, and there was a firmness in her voice now that suggested that she really did understand, perhaps more than Zoë herself did. "And as an English teacher, I share your love of books, and I try to show my students what excites me about books. But I also need to accept that we are all built along different lines. I'm sure your parents wanted some things for you that you didn't want for yourself." She walked back to her desk. "My point is, we are exposing your children not only to books here but to the building blocks of older forms of storytelling. Because telling stories is a much older tradition than reading and writing," she went on, "and even if all of us aren't going to become big readers, we all do respond to stories."

There was more, but Zoë wasn't paying attention. Instead, she was thinking of her parents, and how she had never been able to please them, because in their world, she was a failure. She was remembering how she had brought home her senior high school thesis, which had received the highest marks in her class, only to find her father enraged that a boy with the non-Jewish last name of Smith had called for her.

But Zoë had long ago resigned herself to being the black sheep of her family. She had resigned herself to being single, to the moderate level of her career success, even to being unhappy for the next eight months. Was it really too much to expect her own child, her only child, to be in her idiom?

Maya's hand stole out from underneath her desk, finding her

mother's fingers and squeezing them. She looked anxious, and Zoë smiled, hoping to reassure her. At least she's not mad at me for speaking out to her teacher, she thought.

But out of the corner of her eye, she could see Mack, and he was not smiling.

* * *

The last event of parents' visiting day was the horse show. The wind had not died down and as the crowd of parents approached the bleachers, more than a few people commented on the storm clouds darkening the sky. Zoë would have been just as happy to lose Mack in the crowd, but Maya grabbed him by the hand and pushed them both onto a bench together. "I have to go change," she said, grabbing the schedule of events that had nearly blown out of her hand. "Mack, can you make sure my mother doesn't do anything embarrassing, like yell out my name or ask my riding instructor something in the middle of the show?"

"Maya," Zoë said, wanting to explain, but Mack took her arm and yanked her down beside him on the bench.

"I'll watch her," he said. His voice and expression were warm, until Maya was out of sight, whereupon he opened up the *New Yorker* and read it as if he were about to be tested on its contents. I should just ignore him, Zoë thought, so she sat there, a hum of people around her, as a bad feeling congealed in her stomach. The bad feeling was a combination of too much black coffee, no toast, and the sense that she might have behaved badly in front of her daughter's teacher. Adding to her indigestion was the growing realization that she had not, after all, really understood the implications of Maya's being diagnosed with dyslexia. Up until now, she'd figured that a learning disability was something you dove into, researched, ontts on...

dealt with, and ultimately overcame, like being pigeon-toed or frightened of the dark. But now it struck her that this might be the kind of thing you learned to live with, like a clubfoot. Or a phobia about driving.

Out of the corner of her eye, she watched Mack's impassive profile as he flipped the page. He was looking at an article about literary responses to war.

"Oh," she said, recognizing a name. "You'd probably enjoy Tim O'Brien. He wrote about Vietnam," she added.

"Here," he said. "You can have it back." He thrust the magazine into her hand.

She sat there for a moment, feeling completely bewildered. *Mack* was mad at *her*? When did this happen? As of this morning, he'd been completely friendly, even apologetic. Zoë tried to read the magazine, but the mystery of Mack's sudden displeasure with her, along with her residual feeling of having behaved badly in Ms. Weyr's class, made it impossible for her to concentrate.

"All right," she said, "spit it out. What's your problem? You're doing that loudly quiet disgruntled-guy thing."

He raised one eyebrow, something she used to try doing in the mirror. "Guy thing? Seems to me that you were the one giving me the silent treatment this morning."

"Ah, so this is tit for tat."

"No, I figured you had a right to be ticked off at me." His tone had a slight but unmistakable hint of a sneer. "I figured I'd hurt your feelings or your pride or both. But now I understand that isn't possible."

"And why is that?"

"Because you're a snob."

"Mack, look," Zoë began, but he turned and interrupted her.

"'Fullest potential,'" he mimicked her. "As in, God forbid my kid should grow up to be some kind of blue-collar bumpkin."

Zoë felt a hot wave of embarrassment rush up her neck. "I didn't say that."

Mack gave her a thin smile. "You implied it."

"I don't think you're a bumpkin."

He shook his head. "But you think you can sum me up in about two sentences, right?"

Now Zoë felt her chagrin giving way to irritation. "And I'm sure you think the same about me. Come on, what am I, book-smart city lady who doesn't even know how to drive? Or am I missing some crucial nuance?"

"Yeah," said Mack, gazing at her steadily, "you are."

"And what is that?"

"I think you know."

Zoë smacked her hands down on her lap. "Oh, wait, I get it. Now I'm supposed to remember that you were overcome with slow-burning desire for my person?"

Mack gave her a knowing look. "Aha. So that's it. You're lacking in self-confidence."

"I'm perfectly confident."

"Not in this area. You made jokes when I called you beautiful."

"Spare me the five-cent analysis, Mack. I may not be beautiful, but I am confident. I am an attractive woman and I am extremely comfortable with my sexuality."

Mack leaned forward, putting his face about an inch from hers. "Yeah? So how come you backed off so damn quick?"

She mimicked his posture, fist under her chin. "I didn't back off. You did."

"I wasn't backing off, Zoë." His breath warmed her face. Nice breath. But his neck smelled faintly of some aftershave, a light, masculine, spicy smell that she disapproved of on principle. Real men didn't wear perfume. None of the men she'd ever dated had worn aftershave.

"Oh, please, that's bullshit and you know it." On the other hand, Mack actually smelled good, slightly woodsy. She inhaled. Maybe it wasn't aftershave. Maybe it was just soap and him.

"Fine, then. I'm not going to argue the point. But I'm not backing off now." His lips were inches from hers. Jeez, she hoped her breath was as sweet as his.

"Didn't you just call me a snob? Seems to me you don't know what the hell you want." She had her glasses on, and she was afraid they'd get in the way if he kissed her. Not that she wanted him to kiss her in public. But if he did, she didn't want her glasses to be crammed up against his face.

He dipped his head closer, the tip of his nose brushing the top of her ear. "I know I want you."

She pushed him away, very conscious of the feel of his firm chest underneath his T-shirt. "I don't like playing games, Mack."

"I'm not playing." He glanced at all the parents gathered around them. "If my choice is now or never, I'll choose now." His eyes focused on her mouth, and Zoë felt her stomach twist with excitement and anxiety. How long since she'd flirted with someone who'd quickened her pulse? It had taken her history professor fifteen minutes in bed to get her to the state Mack induced just by sitting too close.

"Don't be stupid." She didn't want to be making any more of a spectacle of herself than she already had. But just in case he did lean forward and kiss her, should she take her glasses off?

"I double dare you."

"What are we, thirteen?"

"Why," he said mockingly, "was that the last time you did something a little reckless, Zoë?"

"Fine." Zoë whipped off her glasses, but before she could even touch her mouth to his, a loudspeaker gave a roar of feedback, and then a woman's voice said, "Welcome, everybody, to the Mackinley

School Autumn Horse Show." There was a roar of applause, and Mack gave Zoë's waist a light pinch.

"Think you got out of it, don't you," he murmured, making Zoë feel a little less foolish as she replaced her glasses.

"Shh, it's starting." Very much aware of Mack watching her, she kept her own eyes trained on the arena below, where three dun and chestnut horses now trotted around, ridden by upper-graders in white button-down shirts and black velvet helmets. But she was very much aware of the man beside her, who was no longer sullen or aggrieved.

It took a full hour before Maya's group emerged, and by then, the wind had really picked up, and a few fat drops of rain had fallen. "I don't know about this," Zoë said. "Don't you think they should call things off?"

"Maybe it'll stop," said Mack, as the sky darkened and the tree-tops swayed. The girls on the horses were trotting in patterns, their slim bodies rising effortlessly out of the saddles as they posted, the heels of their black ankle boots down, their backs supple and straight. After a few more minutes, these girls left, and another group came in, mostly younger boys dressed in tricolor silk tunics, their riding helmets covered in tinfoil. Some of the horses were also wearing silk blankets, and it was clear that this was a class of beginners. Their horses walked the patterns, one of the knights' mounts led by a girl rider from the earlier demonstration.

"Look," Mack said, pointing at one of the boys, "isn't that Maya?"

Zoë squinted, and sure enough, it was her daughter, her face half-hidden underneath a foil-covered helmet. It seemed to Zoë that her daughter looked more graceful and right on the horse than any of the other kids. Suddenly, she remembered her father telling her about the old laws in many parts of the Middle East that prohibited Jews from riding horses or camels in the old days. Would he be proud or simply dumbfounded to see his own flesh and blood mastering this alien sport?

Mack leaned over. "She looks great. Did you bring a camera?"

"Oh, Christ," Zoë said, rummaging in her bag. "Of course, I did."

And then it began to rain, and there was a sort of mass grumble from the parents in the audience.

"Crap," said Mack, and for a moment Zoë thought he was talking about the weather. Then she followed the line of his vision and saw something that made her throat close up: one of the horses, a small gray, was panicking, its hindquarters bunched as it backed away from some imagined menace, its ears pinned to its head as it suddenly reared up on its hind legs. She didn't see the gray's rider fall off, so it took her a moment to realize what had happened. Oh, God, Zoë thought, the horse is going to trample that child. Mack was already in motion, leaping over the bleachers, but he couldn't possibly get down there in time, and then another rider slid down to the ground and grabbed hold of the gray horse's reins. Her eyes on the drama unfolding below, Zoë charged after Mack, bruising her shin on a bench but not slowing down until she reached the riding arena.

Through the sheets of rain, she could see the other horses reacting to the gray's anxiety, stamping their feet and sidling nervously away as their young riders struggled to stay in their saddles. An older woman in jeans and a riding jacket had appeared and taken hold of the gray, and other adults were in the arena, soothing both the novice riders and their mounts. Mack was already crouched on the dirt ground, examining the fallen child.

For a long, terrible moment, Zoë stood in the driving rain, immobilized by the fear that the injured student was Maya, or how badly hurt she might be. Then Mack removed the child's helmet and Zoë put her hand to her chest.

And that was when she realized where her own child was: standing beside the gray horse, holding its reins and patting it on the neck.

"Maya, my God, get away from that animal."

"Oh, he's fine now, Mom." Maya stroked the horse's nose, looking like a medieval page in her silk tunic. "Did you see me grab him right when he was freaking out? Mrs. Fletcher, the riding instructor, was about to take him but I said I had him under control. What made you lose it, Cloud?"

"I told you to let go of him. What if he starts panicking again? He could kick you."

"I can't just let go of him," said Maya with a note of exaggerated patience, as if explaining something basic to a young child. "I've got to bring him into his stall."

"Don't you go anywhere with him, Maya!"

"I can take him back," said an older woman with a leathery face and frizzy gray hair. "Your daughter has a way with horses," she added, smiling at Zoë. "He calmed down right away when she took hold of him."

"That's fine for the horse," said Zoë, "but what about my daughter? There could have been two children hurt today."

"This was a very unusual occurrence," said the woman. "Usually, these horses are calm, even in the midst of a storm. But they are living creatures, so there's always some degree of unpredictability."

"I don't know how I feel about that."

The woman gave Zoë a level look. "To my mind, the small risks involved with riding are well worth the gains. The girls and boys who train with me learn to be empathic to someone else's emotions without losing sight of their own objectives, and they learn to be brave without being impulsive. You did very, very well today, Maya." And then the woman walked off, leading the now-placid gray.

Zoë grabbed her daughter and held her in a tight embrace.

"Did you hear her, Mom? She said I did very, very well!"

"Yes," said Zoë, reluctantly letting Maya pull back. "You were great, but after today, I don't want you riding any more horses."

"Mo-om," said Maya, as if Zoë had said something silly. "Everyone rides here. I can't be the only one not allowed to do it."

"But Maya, honey, I thought they said the horses here were safe. I don't want you taking any unnecessary chances."

"But I won't. And you saw yourself how good I am with them. And on the very first lesson, everyone thought I'd be scared because I was a city girl, but I was less scared than anyone."

"Honey, we'll talk about this later."

"I'm good with horses, Mom. It's something I'm good at."

"Later, Maya."

As the rain slowed to a drizzle, Zoë watched as Allegra's father said something to Mack, a relieved smile on his face. A woman Zoë recognized as Mrs. Benning, the head of the lower school, had also arrived on the scene, and she and Renata were both listening to Mack talking to his patient as a third parent handed him a first-aid kit.

It was a little strange to see how everyone suddenly deferred to Mack, and Zoë felt a burst of pride in him, which was ridiculous. It's not as if he were her partner or boyfriend. And worse still, less than an hour ago she had been thinking that his accomplishments were nice, but somehow less valuable than intellectual achievements.

Mack searched the crowd and then met her gaze, and Zoë nodded at him, feeling again that absurd sense of satisfaction that he had singled her out. This is what was missing from my last relationship, she realized. She had respected Jeremy but had not admired him. His strengths had been too similar to her own, his failings equally familiar. Watching Mack splinting Allegra's arm, Zoë felt the sense of wonder that comes from watching someone accomplish with ease what you could not. It struck her that admiration, for all its Austenian overtones, was actually a crucial element of desire. Combined with lust, it worked a subtle alchemy, turning attraction into something more complicated.

But Zoë's daughter was in the grip of a different drama. After determining that her injured friend was going to be all right, Maya spent the next twenty minutes pleading to be allowed to ride horses.

"You can't do this to me, Mommy! I'll be the only kid who can't ride horses!"

"We can go now," said Mack. "Sorry to keep you waiting."

"That's all right," said Zoë. They fell into step side by side, while Maya shuffled her shoes along the gravel path. "You were great, by the way."

"I didn't do anything but apply a splint," Mack demurred. "The nurse could have done that just fine. But Maya here, now that was some fine riding for a beginner, kid."

This was a perfect opening for Maya, who instantly wailed, "But now she says I'm not allowed to ride! Talk to her, Mack. Tell her she's going too far. She'll listen to you."

"Honey, it's not my place," Mack began.

"I know you think I'm overreacting," Zoë said, "but today was a real wake-up call. I don't know much about riding, and now I see that it's a lot riskier than I had realized."

"But you just said that you don't know about riding, Mom! It is safe. I mean, not totally safe, but like bike-riding safe. Everyone rides here, Mom. You might as well live in the city and say you can't ever ride the subways. Or you can't go into a tall building because terrorists might fly a plane into it."

"Maya," Zoë said, "it's not the same."

"Yes it is! It's exactly the same! You tell me how it's not the same."

"Because riding horses is risky, a fact I didn't completely take in until I saw a well-schooled horse rear up and toss a child."

"But she wasn't even hurt badly, and it was the wind and the rain. I wouldn't ride in bad weather. I'd be extra careful."

Zoë started to speak, then stopped, suddenly overwhelmed. She had never given into her daughter's wheedling before, had always explained her views and stuck to her position. As a result, Maya seldom nagged at her to change a "no" to a "yes." But today seemed to be a day for self-doubt. Zoë had given up her apartment and her life in the city to send her child to this school, and now she wasn't sure that she agreed with everything the school was doing. No books in the classroom. Horseback riding every day, with all its attendant dangers. Zoë turned to Mack. "What do I say to her?"

Mack shrugged. They had reached the car, and he opened the back door for Maya. "I can't tell you what's an acceptable risk. But most of the kids around here do ride at some point in their lives. Way I see it, if you really love doing it, it's worth doing."

"You see, Mom?"

"Oh, God, please. Maya, I just don't want you to get hurt."

"Neither do I, but I can't live my life in a glass bubble. And remember what you always said about the monster under the bed? How he gets bigger when you give into the fear?"

"I was talking about irrational fears, honey. The monsters under the bed aren't real. We're talking about real danger, here."

"There are real dangers everywhere, Mom. Are you saying we should never fly in a plane or drive a car?"

"She has a point," said Mack, looking as if he were fighting back a grin.

"Stay out of this," Zoë told him.

"That's not fair," said Maya. "You just asked his opinion. Just because you're too scared to do something doesn't mean I should be!"

"Everybody leave me alone!"

"But Mom . . ."

"Give her a minute, honey," said Mack.

Zoë buried her face in her hands. "I don't know what to do. I can't figure this out." She turned to Mack. "I hate it here," she said. She'd intended for it to come out as a joke, but her voice cracked. "I am not built for this life."

"Shh," Mack said, and drew her into his arms.

"Mom? Are you okay?"

"I'm sorry, Maya," said Zoë. "I just— When that horse reared, I got so scared it was you. And all of this still feels so strange." Mack's hands were on her back, patting her as if she were a child, and she was upset that her daughter was seeing her falling apart like this. "I don't feel like I know anything out here in the country." She sniffed and wiped her eyes, noticing that she'd dampened a patch on Mack's jean jacket. Oh, God, she hadn't snotted him, had she? Zoë tried to pull back, to show Maya that she wasn't really that upset, but Mack tightened his arms around her fractionally. With a ragged sigh, Zoë relaxed, giving in to the wonderful feeling of being held.

"It's going to be okay," Mack said. "You're just a little over-whelmed."

"Mom, it's okay, I won't ride anymore, just don't cry."

Zoë turned to her daughter, speaking over Mack's shoulder. "I don't want either of us to make a decision right now. I'm upset, like Mack said, and I'm a little overwhelmed with all the changes in our lives this past month. I need a little time to figure out the horseback riding, that's all. Don't worry. We'll figure it out." She reached for her daughter and for a moment, all three of them embraced.

After agonizing over her choices for what seemed like a very long time, Zoë felt that the end of indecision came with surprising abruptness. This is who I used to be, she thought: someone who can make rapid changes in direction, someone who knows when to start following a new lead. The next day, she decided to speak to Maya's riding instructor and reassure herself that her daughter was going to be as safe as possible during her lessons. And, acutely aware of the example she was setting, Zoë told Mack that she would take driving lessons with him.

"I was thinking about what you said about the monster under the bed," she explained to Maya over dinner. "And how you have to keep fighting the fear so it doesn't take over the whole room."

"But that was you," said Maya, smiling at her mother's mistake. "You taught me that."

"And then you taught it back to me."

That night, and for the rest of the week, Maya slept the whole night in her own bed.

Twenty

Zoë put off calling her mother until the last minute, and then realized she was being ridiculous. What was the worst thing that could happen when she told her mother that she was coming into the city? Her mother would say it wasn't a convenient time to see the grandchild she hadn't visited in more than five months. Well, Zoë was used to that sort of rejection. She dialed the familiar number.

"Hello, Ema?"

"Hello, Zehava," her mother said in funereal tones. Either she wanted Zoë to know this was an inconvenient time to talk, or somebody's great-aunt had died. Zoë decided to forge ahead with the point of her call.

"I just wanted to let you know that Maya and I are going to be in town this weekend."

"That's nice, but it's not a good time, honey." More portentous flatness of tone. Clearly, Zoë was not going to be allowed to escape from asking what the matter was.

"What's wrong, Ema?"

"I can't talk now."

"You mean my father's home."

A pause. "Yes." A longer pause. "He's been very sick. A stroke."

"Oh, my God. Ema, is he okay?"

Zoë remembered Pete and tried to imagine her stern father loosened, weakened, possibly softened.

"He's recovering. Slowly. But it was touch and go for a couple of weeks."

"And nobody called me?"

"Zehava, what do you expect," her mother said in a furious whisper. "We should aggravate your father when he's at death's door?"

"You don't think he might want to make his peace with me before he dies?"

"I don't want to send him to an early grave."

"And now that he's recovering?"

An uncomfortable silence. "You know I've tried to talk to him. And maybe in the future, your sister and I can try again to convince him . . ."

"Is Aviva there now? Is she visiting from Israel?"

"Yes, she came right away when she heard what happened."

Zoë hesitated, then hung up the phone. It didn't matter. Nothing had changed, not really. Except that it was finally, conclusively clear to her that the estrangement from her family was not going to be resolved with some melodramatic deathbed reversal. She was never going to see her father again, or sit with him at the Passover table. He had abandoned her, and to some extent, her mother had, too. And her sister, who hadn't called to tell her any of this was going on.

It really didn't change anything. She'd already accepted that Maya was her only family now. She'd known for years that the city was the only home she had to go back to.

But it still hurt.

* * *

The train trip to Manhattan took exactly one hour and fifty-eight minutes, which wasn't long for a journey that seemed to span worlds. At one end, there was Mack and trees suddenly bare of leaves, stubbled fields and tractors chugging deliberately down the road, slowing their car down and making Zoë frantic that they'd miss the train.

At the other end, there was the city, so dear that even the vacant buildings and knots of barbed wire they passed on the way to the station looked like art to her. When they reached 125th Street, Zoë emerged grinning onto the platform, inhaling the fragrance of exhaust and rain-dampened concrete, and absorbing the delicious stimulus of noise and bustle and variety and people. Everywhere she looked, little dramas were being played out as Chinese tourists debated their next move and helmeted construction workers shouted at each other to mind the winch and raucous teenage girls informed their friends exactly what they had told their other friends.

"I don't remember it being so busy," said Maya, sounding a little worried as Zoë led her down the stairs from the elevated platform.

"I know, isn't it wonderful?" Zoë was wearing her good black leather jacket and heeled boots, which she had begun to think of as city clothes. "I feel like Persephone, out from the underworld and back in the land of the living."

As they reached the street, Zoë heard a Connecticut matron in a navy blazer turn to her dreadlocked son and say, "But isn't this Harlem? Are you sure it's safe at this time in the evening?" It was six o'clock.

Zoë maneuvered in front of them and hailed a gypsy cab. "We're going to a Hundred and Tenth and Riverside," she told the driver.

"So, bubby," she said to Maya, "what do you want to do tomorrow? I figure this first trip back is really for you, and as long as I get an hour to shop for food at Zabar's, you set the schedule. Feel like the Museum of Natural History? We could call one of your old friends, if you like. Or would you rather go to a playground? Just walk around?"

"That all sounds nice," said Maya.

"You sound a little preoccupied. Something wrong?"

"Oh, I was just thinking about horseback riding," said Maya, fingering a rip in the cab's fake leather upholstery. "You did speak to my teacher, right? I am allowed to continue?"

"I already agreed that you were, so long as you took it very slowly and wore the special safety vest I bought."

"But no one else is wearing the vest, Mom."

"Maya, I've agreed to the riding. You should be happy. And we're in the city this weekend. Can we try to focus on enjoying that?"

"Oh, absolutely," said Maya, with a gambler's instinct for when to fold. "I'm very glad to be back," she added. "I missed the city, too."

Zoë tried not to frown, recognizing that tone of voice. It was the one her daughter used when she assured Zoë that she did, in fact, like books.

* * *

"So, how is it, being back?" Bronwyn was bringing down clean sheets from the top of the linen closet, which, like the rest of the apartment, was organized to take maximum advantage of every square inch of space. Bronwyn and her husband had bought their apartment at the peak of the market, and had unwisely chosen to value light and charm and a quiet residential block over square footage. As a result, they had to devise ingenious arrangements of built-in shelves and oddly shaped hampers to fit their family of four into an apartment better suited for a young couple.

"Well, you know all those movies where the big-city girl moves out to the sticks and she starts out hating it but winds up discovering the real allure of small-town life?"

"Uh-huh." Bronwyn handed down the sheets, causing the step stool to wobble.

"Not happening to me," said Zoë, steadying the stool. "I mean, I'm not as abjectly miserable as I was the first couple of weeks, I have a story idea and this flirtation with the driving instructor is certainly diverting, but when I stepped off the train, my first thought was, I'm home."

"Flirtation? Hang on." Bronwyn passed a towel to Zoë and stepped off the stool. "As I recall, after the big make-out session that went nowhere, you said you were a big girl and could accept it if a man didn't find you as attractive as you found him. As I recall, you told me this at least four or five times, and each time you sounded a little more pissed off. So what's going on now?"

"Well, I'm not completely certain." Zoë peered into her friend's bedroom, where Maya was happily engrossed in some Animal Planet program about hedgehogs. "I told you about Mack driving me to Maya's parents' weekend last week."

"Uh-huh." Bronwyn folded the stool and carried it to the kitchen. "You said that you two had come to some sort of understanding. He was going to drive you again, you were going to take lessons. Which I think is great, by the way."

"Well, there's a little more to it than that." Zoë followed Bronwyn as she placed the stool against the wall in the service stairway, where it lived illegally alongside the twins' stroller, Brian's racing bicycle, and a shopping cart.

"What kind of more? More as in unlawful carnal knowledge more?"

"That's the weird thing. He keeps flirting with me, and I keep flirting back, but so far, he hasn't made a move."

"What do you think's going on? Another woman? An STD? A deep-seated psychological problem?"

"Actually, I think he's stringing me along until I get my learner's permit. That, or he's terrified of the way he feels when he touches me, which is so much more intense than what he's felt for any other woman."

Bronwyn looked almost hungry at this description. "You think?"

Zoë rolled her eyes. "Please, Bronwyn, what are we, fourteen? I was being sarcastic."

"Well, all I can say is, at least you still have some libido. I can't remember the last time I wanted any. Which is convenient, since my husband seems to want me no more than I do him." Bronwyn took a deep breath, as if preparing herself for battle. "Let's go into the living room and get your bed ready before I keel over."

"I can do it myself."

"Don't be silly," said Bronwyn, bending over to remove one of the heavy cushions from the convertible couch.

"I'm not being silly, you're being compulsive," said Zoë, grabbing for the second cushion. "Sit down and let someone else work for a change."

"You know me, I can't just sit around."

"Which is why you look shattered." The two women tussled over the third cushion for a moment, and then moved it together. Even though they were both laughing, Zoë was worried. Bronwyn was not looking well, had not, in fact, looked well since the birth of the twins. Her face had the drawn, slightly haggard look she'd acquired in the last month of pregnancy, her dark auburn hair, once lit by red highlights, had become a muddy brown, and there was something a little spongy about the look of her pale, freckled skin.

"Stop a moment," said Zoë, as Bronwyn reached for the handle to pull the bottom of the couch out into a bed. "Wait, Bron, let me do that with you."

"I'd rather finish everything and then relax." Bronwyn pulled again, and the bed sprang out, hitting her in the shin. "Son of a bitch," she shouted, and from the other room, one of the twins gave a feeble cry, followed by a second, stronger, squall.

"You're not a bitch," said Zoë.

Bronwyn didn't laugh. "I've been up since six this morning and neither one of them napped. I can't take it, Zoë."

Zoë put her arms around her friend. "Tell me what's going on."

Bronwyn leaned back against Zoë's embrace, trying to break free. "What do you mean, what's going on? The twins have taken to biting each other, I had to fire the last babysitter after she yelled at me for not giving her two weeks' paid vacation one month after I hired her, and the church preschool is saying that they think the boys might have a speech delay. Oh, and my husband is working twelve-hour days." Bronwyn shrugged. "The usual."

In the background, the toddler's howls were growing stronger.

"I have to get up," said Bronwyn, not moving.

"No, you don't." Zoë stood up. "You sit, and let someone else take charge."

Bronwyn cocked her head to one side, listening. "Shit, Zoë. Now both boys are crying." With an enormous sigh, Bronwyn pulled herself upright. "We might as well both go, you can't handle two at once."

The twins' crying had kicked into a new, angrier rhythm, like a heavy metal rock song hitting its bridge. Zoë picked up the closest screaming child as Bronwyn reached for his brother. "What happened, huh? Dirty diaper? Hungry? Difficulty making transitions?" The boy stopped yelling and blinked his bright blue eyes at her, clearly nonplussed. "Never mind, little boy, Aunt Zoë's going to fix you up."

She checked his diaper as Bronwyn wearily tended to her second son, then they switched places so she could change the other boy's diaper. Maya came into the room and watched, fascinated, as the second twin urinated straight up in the air the moment his diaper was removed. Twenty minutes later, when peace had been momentarily restored, Zoë picked up the phone and dialed Brian at work. "Brian? Zoë. Whatever you're doing, drop it. Come home immediately, you're watching the boys, and Maya and your wife and I are going out." She paused, very aware of Bronwyn and Maya watching her. "No, Brian, I don't know what's on your to-do list, but I do know that your wife is about to go under. She needs a break, and she needs it now. And it's seven o'clock on a Friday, so you are absolutely allowed to close up your computer and come home."

She hung up before he could reply.

"He won't do it," said Bronwyn.

"I think he will."

She shook her head. "He won't."

An hour later, they bundled the boys up and took them out to the diner, along with Maya and enough plastic toys to start a nursery.

That night, she heard furious whispering. "You don't." "Not fair." "Realistic sense of things." At one point, it sounded almost like the hissing of cats, and at another, Zoë thought Bronwyn was going to start shouting.

When she woke up the next morning, Brian was already gone.

Zoë took one of the twins out of his high chair. "But where is he? He can't be at work, it's eight o'clock on a Saturday."

Bronwyn handed one of the boys a plastic bowl of oatmeal, which he instantly dashed against the opposite wall. "No, Brian's gone to the gym. Then he's off to Home Depot, to get a bookcase, which he will spend the rest of the day assembling."

"But he can't keep running away like this. It's like you're a single mother of twins. You need help."

"He has to work, doesn't he? And when can he do chores, if not on the weekend? And can I really be begrudging him an hour at the gym twice a week?" Bronwyn's voice was dull, as if she were reciting an old lesson. "He loves his kids and spends as much time as he can with them. He's not good with small children, but this phase won't last forever. Why don't I get a babysitter to spell me?"

"Why don't you?"

"The teenagers can't handle it and the full-time nannies want to work full time. Brian says I don't know how to delegate. He complains that whenever he does try to help with the boys, I criticize him."

Zoë came up behind her friend and put her arms around her. "Listen, everything seems hopeless when you're depressed. Let's concentrate on cheering you up right now. I'll finish giving the boys breakfast, you go get showered and put on your game face. We're going out on the town."

"I don't have the energy."

"Then go nap. And then we'll go."

It was not the weekend that Zoë had planned on having in the city, as she wound up enlisting Maya's help with the twins and spending two hours in a playground and four in the Children's Museum, where the boys took turns sliding down a six-foot tongue and crawling through a bright-red artery. On Sunday morning, while Maya still slept beside her, Zoë tried not to listen as Brian and Bronwyn argued again. She feigned sleep herself as Brian slipped out the door a few minutes later.

"Since I have you here, he figured he might as well go into the office to catch up on work," Bronwyn explained later in a flat voice.

"I see. And is he different when I'm not around?"

"Not really. Well, he usually waits till noon on Sunday to head into the office." Bronwyn knelt down on the rug and started picking up brightly colored Duplo blocks and tossing them into a big plastic bucket. "You know what's funny? When Brian and I first got together, I loved how responsible he was. All my boyfriends before him had still been focused on sports and vacations and the bar scene. But Brian seemed really ready to settle down."

One of the twins woke up with a fever and it was raining outside, so Zoë brought back bagels and lox from around the corner and they spent the rest of the day at home reading the Sunday *Times* while Maya watched cartoons on TV. Making sure that Maya wasn't in earshot, Zoë finally told her friend about her father's stroke and her mother's decision to keep her in the dark. Bronwyn's indignant anger on her behalf had made Zoë feel a bit better. And then it was time to leave.

"I'm sorry it wasn't more fun," Bronwyn apologized as Zoë finished packing her bag. "You didn't get to go shopping, or see a foreign film, or eat anywhere ethnic."

"I loved it," she said. "For me, the wonderful thing is just being back in the city, walking around, feeling all the possibility. I don't need to do special things like a tourist." In a way, it was true. It was also true, however, that it had been stressful and difficult being a guest in Bronwyn's house. Zoë almost wondered if it would have been better to rent a hotel room, although the thought of spending over $200 a night for a view of an alleyway was depressing. She suspected that paying for a hotel room would make it official—she no longer really belonged in Manhattan. And yet it had not been easy to be right there, in her city, with her best friend, without really feeling connected to either.

Bronwyn must have sensed some of what Zoë was thinking. "You'll come back soon, won't you? I haven't put you off with all my problems?"

"As if." She hugged her friend, and whispered in her ear, "Don't let him get away with this, Bron." It struck her that her friend, who lived in the midst of the most vital city in the world, was just as trapped and isolated as she was.

When Mack picked her up at the train station, she was surprised to see how young and scruffy he looked in his flannel shirt and work boots. He didn't seem like anyone who belonged in her life, and she was both relieved and regretful that he no longer struck her as particularly attractive. Mack smiled, holding eye contact a fraction too long, and Zoë thought, I'm going to have to let him down easily.

Which was why, when Mack asked her how her trip had been, Zoë said, "I'm actually kind of glad to be back."

"That so?" Mack took Maya's bag and loaded it into the trunk. Maya, engrossed in a new handheld electronic game, said thanks without looking up and got into the back of the car. "So what's changed your mind?" Mack reached out for Zoë's overnight case. Up close, his flannel shirt smelled pleasantly of hay, and there was a growth of dark blond stubble on his chin.

"After a weekend spent wedged between toddler toys in a too-small Manhattan apartment, I need some space." Zoë slid into the front passenger seat.

"That's too bad."

"Why?"

Mack's eyes met hers. "Because I was thinking about crowding you."

Just then, Maya's game gave a little electronic burble from the backseat, reminding Zoë that her daughter could hear every flirtatious word Mack had said. She must have looked slightly perturbed, because Mack took her hand and gave it a reassuring squeeze before starting the car. As the engine kicked on, so did the radio. Garrison Keillor's sonorous voice filled the car, concluding the day's writer's almanac with the words ". . . and do good work."

"Shoot, I missed it," said Mack. Then, after a moment, he glanced at her sideways. "Okay, what are you looking at?"

"I'm just surprised that you listen to National Public Radio."

"Course I do. I've been addicted to *Car Talk* for years, and I like their news analysis better than . . . what?" He turned his head to look at her this time. "Why are you grinning at me like that?"

"Watch the road, please. What's car talk, anyway?"

"You never heard it? Two guys taking all kinds of calls about cars. 'Why does my engine make this sound, how come my car seems to lose power at thirty-five miles an hour, what kind of car do I get to replace my eighty-five Pontiac Firebird.'"

"Interesting."

"No, no, you don't get it. See, Click and Clack, these two brothers, they're really talking about people, about why we do the things we do. Like, how most of us tend to ignore the early-warning signs of a problem, or how we pay attention to the wrong details, or how we get locked into one way of thinking that holds us back."

"In other words, the poetics of engine trouble."

"Yeah. Yeah, I like that. That's what I like about you, Zoë. You make these connections between things that aren't obvious."

"You made the connection, Mack. I just recognized it."

Without looking at her, he took her left hand in his right and held it, steering the car one-handed while Zoë gazed blindly ahead, listening as her internal engine made a new and startling noise.

Part Three

Zoë Goren

Mustang Zoë

After my previous essay ("A Gas Guzzler's Manifesto"), I've received a few rather snide letters saying that I must be ignorant of the visceral, almost carnal thrills that motor vehicles can provide. Since one of those letters was from an ex-boyfriend, I thought I should respond in my own defense. Now, while it's true that I have remained a confirmed non-driver up until this, the autumn of my forty-second year, I am not entirely ignorant of automotive bliss. There are times when, in the words of the female country group SHeDAISY, "Life's so sweet in the passenger seat," especially when the sun is shining, the wind is blowing your hair back, and the driver's suntanned hands are exactly where you want them to be, whether that's on the wheel or your left thigh. (Of course, it helps if there aren't too many dead skunks on the road.)

But because I have a deep-seated fear of driving, I've never even considered motoring along on my own for the sheer solitary pleasure of the journey. Driving, it seems to me, is rather like parenting in that it requires the coordination of many different complex skills and abilities in order to do it properly. And frankly, considering the current number of American parenting and driving casualties, I think more people should be discouraged from participating in either activity. But now that I live in a place where only the very old, the very young, the infirm, and the indigent are carless, I have started to take driving lessons. And since my driving instructor is teaching me in a souped-up muscle car, I may yet learn what it's like to be Mustang Sally or that girl who took off in her daddy's T-bird, with no particular place to go, and no need for any man to help me get there.

Or better yet, I'll move back to the city and hail a cab.

New York Chronicle **Op-Ed**

Twenty-one

$\mathcal{J}$n the country, November was a month that moved people inside, away from public spaces like parks and trails and flea markets. It wasn't a pretty month, since there wasn't any snow on the ground to hide the dead grass or decorate the bare trees, and the days were getting shorter As Zoë was fond of pointing out, most calendars pretended that the country went straight from foliage to snow. False advertising, she said.

Mack himself didn't mind. As a rule, there were fewer medical emergencies in November, because you were well past the drownings of summer and the "thought it was a deer" accidental shootings of early hunting season. Best of all, the roads were mostly clear of ice and snow, making it easier for a novice driver to drive.

At least, it would be easier, if you could get the novice driver behind the wheel. So far, one week after she'd come back from Manhattan, Zoë was still refusing to make a trip to the local DMV to take her test and get her permit.

"I'm still studying," she insisted, holding up the driver's manual.

"We have to take advantage of the weather," he reminded her. "Come December, we'll have to contend with the snow."

"But I'm not ready."

"Yes you are. And I'm ready. More than ready."

Zoë raised her eyebrows. "Now, that was your choice."

They were sitting in the Crown Royal, having finished grocery shopping, and Zoë was looking particularly pretty in a navy blue pullover, her hair pulled up in a messy bun, her face clean and glowing with the knowledge that she was desired. "Listen to this," she said, reading from the local paper she'd picked up at the store. "'Wild turkeys cause minor accident on Route Sixty-five. Could be a case of bird rage, according to local business owner Jim Moroney.'" Her lip curled in disgust. "Don't they ever cover a real news story? What about that development, that doesn't warrant coverage?"

"Hmm," said Mack absently, not really paying attention. Zoë's face was hidden behind the front-page photo of a large tom turkey.

"Wait, there is something on the development, but it's on an inside page, hidden under a piece about Boy Scouts." She gave a little grunt of irritation, and Mack wondered what else might make her produce that guttural noise.

Christ, he was losing it. He ought to turn to her right now and say, You're right, fuck this waiting, we have four hours before Maya comes home from school, let's go back to your place and get naked. The money problem no longer bothered him: he'd gotten a few other students from the high school, and besides, it looked as though Moira was going to be selling the farm and giving him a share of the profits, whether he liked it or not. So why not go for the gold? What was he afraid would happen?

You know what, said a voice in his head. First you'd screw each other's brains out, and then it would all be over. Because, let's face it, she's used to interesting, sophisticated people, and how long do you think you're going to hold her interest once the shiny new wears off the sex?

Of course, she might be forced to hold on to him until the end of the school year, or whenever it was she was planning on moving back to Manhattan. But Mack didn't relish the idea of being a mercy fuck.

"This isn't news," Zoë said, her voice heavy with contempt. "This is propaganda for the developers. And it's not even very good propaganda."

That caught Mack's attention. "Why not?"

"Because according to the paper, everyone's doing a fabulous job and all the approved development projects are exciting opportunities. No dissenting opinion, no attempt at balance. The paper probably published a press release from one of the interested parties." She closed the paper, crumpling it up. "And even if your aim is to manipulate public opinion, the more objective a story appears, the more effective it is at convincing its audience."

Mack remembered the army news, with its self-congratulatory reports. "So isn't all news propaganda? I mean, everyone has a point of view."

Zoë glanced at him. "I don't know. I've always believed that even if you can't be completely impartial, real journalists attempt to be objective. Maybe it's the intention that counts."

Mack considered this as they passed a house with a sign that said "Grow Smart Not Big." "You know what I like about you?"

"What?"

"You may know a hell of a lot more than I do, but you never cut me down when I offer an opinion."

"As the old Jewish saying goes, I'm not so small that I have to make myself out to be so big."

Mack grinned. "I never heard that one before. Is it Iraqi Jewish?"

"No, actually, I borrowed it from a Russian Jewish friend." When Zoë had told him her family was originally from Iraq, but Jewish, his mouth had pretty much dropped open. He hadn't even thought Iraq had Jews. But remembering Adam, Mack thought he could see some family resemblance, or tribal resemblance, whatever. Not a physical resemblance, more of a quality of being, cynical and yet warm, clever and yet kind. Except that he'd always heard that Jews were close with their families, and that clearly wasn't the case with Zoë.

She didn't talk much about her father, except to say that he had never even seen Maya, and that her mother would meet up with them only when the father was away. There was a sister in Israel, but Mack got the feeling that she was in more contact with the folks than Zoë was.

So in a weird way, Maya was growing up the same way he had, with just one strong female. Except that Zoë was really a mother, not just a substitute who'd been drafted into duty, as Moira had been. Plus she was older and a lot wiser than his sister had been, and was clearly enjoying her responsibilities. No wonder the kid was a little too dependent on her mother. But he liked her, the truth was that she was an easy kid to like, funny and smart and surprisingly determined. In some ways, it was easier to imagine life with a kid like Maya than trying to wrap his head around the idea of some mystery baby. What if it turned out that you didn't actually like your own kid? Everyone laughed when you said that, but it was clear that a lot of folks didn't like at least one of their offspring.

But Mack knew he liked Maya, liked the way she thought things through, liked the way she was willing to take chances. And he thought that Maya might be beginning to warm to him. He'd given her a harmonica and in the evenings they attempted "On Top of Old Smokey" and "Oh, Susanna." He wondered if she and Zoë could ski, or if they'd be willing to learn this winter. He'd already started looking at catalogs and circling the kind of sleds he wanted to get them, one a disk, the other a three-person toboggan.

So, yeah, Mack wanted to go to bed with Zoë, but not just that, and not just once or twice. And if waiting a little meant that he could keep this thing going a while longer, then he wanted to wait. And as far as he could see, the only way he could get Zoë to stay in the country would be to teach her to drive, and the only way to do that would be to seduce her into it.

If only she'd grown up thinking about cars like everyone else, as something basic and necessary, if only she had grown up sitting on her daddy's lap and steering the last half mile home.

Mack looked at Zoë. "Okay," he said, "I have an idea."

"Watch it," she said sharply, staring at something at the side of the road. Mack swerved just in time to avoid hitting a wild turkey that took off, wings beating wildly against the windshield.

"Jesus," Zoë said. "I guess that turkey story was news. Hey, where are we going?"

"To do a little remedial driving work."

*   *   *

"Okay, that's a ridiculous idea. And also not so safe." Zoë looked at Mack, who was sitting in the driver's seat, which he had moved farther back to provide extra room.

"We're in an empty parking lot. Trust me, it's safe." He gestured at the squat brick town hall and its large, vacant lot, ringed by a few scraggly pines and bare locust trees. "What can you hit here? Nothing."

Zoë put her hands on her hips. He had gotten her to stand outside the car on the driver's side, but once he had told her what he had in mind, she had buttoned her black leather jacket and refused to cooperate. "But I haven't even passed my written test yet, or gotten my learner's permit."

"We'll do that next. First I want to show you that this isn't so scary."

"And you actually want me to sit on your lap?"

"You bet." Her cheeks had turned pink, possibly from the cold.

"You're insane."

"Come on, quit stalling. It's not as if you haven't done it before."

"Yeah, but that was fooling around, not a driving lesson."

"Your point being?"

"I must be crazy, too." She climbed on top of Mack's lap, and a small grunting sound escaped him which she misinterpreted as discomfort.

"That does it, let me go," she said, trying to squirm off. "I'm crushing you!"

"You're not." He spread his thighs so she was essentially sitting between his legs instead of on them. Still, there was a certain amount of contact. Mack did his best to ignore it.

"Even if I'm not crushing you, what's the point of this? We can't drive like this."

"Right now, we're just going to get you comfortable the way a kid gets comfortable. The first lesson most people have is sitting on Daddy's lap, steering around the parking lot."

"Mack, that's ridiculous."

"I got the idea from that teacher at Maya's school. We have to make this really fun and simple. This way, I can work the gas and brake, and all you have to do is steer."

"Do you plan on doing this with all your nervous students? Because I'm sure there's some sort of federal guideline against it."

"Most of my students are teenagers. Besides, you're different."

"In what way?"

"We're already involved."

Zoë sighed. "What if someone sees us?"

"Trust me, nobody goes to the town hall parking lot on a Monday morning. There aren't any meetings until noon, which is why I picked this place."

"What if I crash the car?"

"You can't. I'm controlling the gas and the brake, and my hands are right here. Are you ready?"

"No."

"I'm going to start anyway." Mack turned the ignition and stepped lightly on the gas. Zoë squealed and began to hold the wheel with shaking hands.

"Which way do I go?"

"Anywhere you want. The parking lot is empty."

"I think I'll go straight." They drove very slowly to the end of the paved lot, then Mack stepped on the brake.

"What now?"

"Right?"

"First you need to reverse."

"I can't reverse!"

"Sure you can. Just turn and look over your right shoulder and . . . ah."

"What's wrong?"

"Nothing?"

"What is it? You just got a funny look on your face."

"You're not supposed to be looking at my face, Zoë. Look over your right shoulder, you always look in the direction you're going, and . . ." They reversed a few feet.

"I did it!" She looked back at him, grinning broadly.

"Excellent. Now, if you want to reverse and turn the wheel, look and see what happens."

They reversed as Zoë turned the wheel to the right. "Oh, that's weird," she said. "I remember reading about reversing direction in the driver's manual and it didn't make sense, but now I . . . Mack, what's wrong?" A horrified look crossed her face. "I'm hurting you, aren't I?"

"Not hurting. Not in a bad way."

"Oh, I . . . oh. What do you want me to do?"

"Nothing, I can just ignore it till we finish the lesson."

"Oh, good, because I'm really starting to enjoy this. Let's try going forward again."

It took Mack five minutes to realize that Zoë was torturing him on purpose by shifting ever so slightly in her seat every time she turned the wheel.

"Okay," he said, "I think that's enough." He turned off the engine.

"Aw, I was really getting into it. Couldn't we just go for ten more min . . . oh!"

Mack had bitten her, gently, on the fleshy pad of muscle where shoulder met neck. He slid his hands up under her sweater, cupping her breasts through the silky material of her brassiere, plucking her nipples until they were hard.

"Is this part of the lesson?"

Mack made an odd growling noise, and if he hadn't heard the sound of a car pulling up he thought he might have just gone ahead and pulled down their jeans and taken her right there in the car.

"Someone's coming," he said, and Zoë banged into the gearshift as she wriggled over him and into the passenger seat.

"Who is it?"

Mack checked in his side mirror. A white pickup truck, its wheels caked with mud, was pulling into the front of town hall. For a second, Mack thought the truck looked like Moroney's, although Mack couldn't imagine what his former boss might be doing with a chainsaw. His former boss wouldn't be risking another heart attack when there were Mexicans around to hire for inadequate wages.

Mack checked his side mirror again, and saw that the truck was continuing on around to the back parking lot.

"Shit." Mack didn't want to imagine what Moroney would do if he figured out that Mack was mixing business with pleasure. Refastening his seat belt, Mack threw the car into drive so fast he nearly stalled it. For a moment, as the two cars passed each other, Mack and Moroney locked eyes. Was it his imagination, Mack wondered, or did Moroney look sheepish? He tried to imagine what was giving his former boss a guilty conscience. Maybe's he's killed someone and chopped the body up, he thought, but when he turned, all he could see in the back of the truck was some chopped-up firewood. And why the hell was Moroney keeping the chainsaw in the front seat? There was something fishy going on.

"Wow," said Zoë. "That was interesting."

"Well," he said, when they were back on the road, "sorry about that."

"Don't be," said Zoë, casually pushing her glasses farther up on her nose. "You just accomplished something I thought was impossible. I'm looking forward to our next lesson."

Mack was so pleased he forgot about Moroney.

* * *

"Okay," said Mack, lighting a small twig and placing it under a heavier log in the fireplace. "Let's talk about the driver's test. Have you been studying your manual?"

"I have," said Zoë, sitting down on her couch, "but I'm never going to be able to remember all of it. What color and shape are warning signs and what does a double solid line mean and turn in the direction of the skid."

Mack brushed off his hands on his jeans and moved to sit at Zoë's feet. "Sounds like you remember a lot already." He pulled one wool sock off Zoë's foot, and she tried to tuck it under her.

"No, they might be stinky."

"They're not." He grabbed hold of the bare foot and began manipulating it, using his knuckles in the arch, kneading with his thumbs.

"Oh."

"And I bet what you're really worried about is, how will you remember it all when you're driving?" He pulled the sock off her other foot. "But you don't need to worry about that, because when you start driving, it's all going to start to make sense." He massaged up toward her calf. "Okay?"

"Mmm."

"Okay, let's start with something basic. What color and shape are most warning signs?"

"Can't remember."

He stopped rubbing and removed his hands. "You can do better than that."

"Yellow and diamond?"

"Very good." He worked the taut muscle of her calf. "You have strong calves. Smooth, too. I bet you didn't shave for me, either."

"I didn't."

"All right, then. What does a double yellow line in the middle of the road mean?"

"Do not pass or change lanes."

"Except when?"

Zoë frowned. "There's an animal in the road?"

"Well, yes, but only if you're not going to hit anyone head-on. Still, the answer they'll be looking for is to turn left in order to enter or leave the highway." He looked at her foot. "Did you just paint your toenails?"

"Yes, why?"

"Because that means you thought I might be seeing your feet."

"No, I do it for myself all the time. Because I have ugly feet."

"No, you don't."

"I do. See? I have a bunion and arthritis in my big toe. Comes from dancing."

"You dance?"

"Used to."

"What kind of dancing?"

"Stripping."

"You're shitting me!"

"Yes, I am. I danced with an Israeli folk troupe in high school, and I've taught ballet and tap. And I used to belly dance."

"Okay, now I know you're joking."

"No, that was serious."

"Would you ever do that for me? No, wait, don't answer that right now. We need to focus. Now, tell me what do you need to do before making a left turn?"

"Look right?"

Mack kept a perfectly straight face, which he thought was quite an accomplishment. "Why would you want to look right, Zoë?"

"I don't know. I thought it was one of those counterintuitive things, like speeding up when you're entering a highway and you're scared someone's going to wham into you and all you really want to do is stop and get your bearings. Oh, stop laughing at me, I'm never going to remember all this shit."

"You know, I felt like that when I was trying to learn how the engine works. The instructor kept talking about how the Otto cycle had four phases: induction, compression, combustion, and exhaust. And I couldn't even remember the name Otto."

"So what did you do?"

"I asked the instructor if he could break it down any easier, and he said, 'Sure. It's like really good sex. You just remember: suck, squeeze, bang, blow.'" He grinned at her, anticipating her response.

But Zoë just raised her eyebrows. "That's great, and if I ever decide to become a mechanic, I'm sure that'll come in handy. But do you have a salacious mnemonic for making left turns?"

Mack considered. "Approach your turn with your left wheels as close as possible to the center line" did not lend itself to any sexy shorthand. "How about, if you get it right, I'll suck your toe."

"You'd better hope I get it wrong, then. I haven't washed my feet since this morning."

"What are you, a neat freak? That's only two hours ago. They're perfectly clean."

"I still don't want you shrimping me." The fire crackled, as if punctuating her remark.

"Oh, fine." Ignoring her protests, he picked her up and carried her over to the bathroom, where he deposited her on the edge of the bathtub.

"What are you doing?"

"Washing your feet, you prude." He rolled her jeans up, then turned on the taps. He could feel her watching him as he soaped her toes and rinsed them. "There," he said, pulling the towel down from its hook.

"That tickles," she said as he dried between her toes.

He picked her up again, which was easier when she didn't struggle. "What is a solid line?"

"You may pass other vehicles or change lanes," she said, burying her face in his neck.

He sat her down on the couch, then placed her feet over the bulge in his jeans. "But only if . . ."

"Only if you need to . . . ah."

Mack bit her big toe, then suckled it.

"Are you a foot fetishist?"

"No. Are you?"

"I think I might become one."

Mack deliberately put her feet down. "Back to business. What does it mean if a cyclist stops in front of you and sticks his arm straight out?"

"He's going to make a left turn. Aren't we going to do any more with the feet?"

"Not right now. You need to focus."

"I want more feet."

"First answer the question. What does it mean if his arm is up at a right angle, like this?"

"He's saying, Screw you, gas guzzler, get on a bike."

"Try again."

"Why, what are you going to do, spank me?"

"Do you want me to?"

"I was just joking, Mack."

"Because I would spank you if you wanted me to."

"Oh, I don't know, I was just saying that to be, you know, provocative."

Mack looked at Zoë's flushed face, thinking that it had been more than fifteen years since he'd spent this long touching a woman before actually having sex with her. Back then, of course, he'd been entirely focused on himself, and how far he could get. Now he was learning that you could find out quite a lot about a person by taking things slow. For example, he was learning that however sophisticated Zoë might be about art and politics, she was not as experienced as he was in bed.

"Tell me what you like," he said, indicating that she should lie down next to him. Mack put his arm around Zoë as she lay across him, resting her head on his shoulder.

"Oh, I don't know. The usual."

"There's a pretty wide range of usual, Zoë. Do you want me to be gentle? Slow? Do you want to be in control? Or do you want me to be on top? Overpower you? Hold your wrists down?"

Zoë buried her face in his chest. "Yes."

He stroked her hair, loving this feeling of being excited and yet holding off, filled with lust and tenderness and a teacher's pleasure in having something to impart. "Yes to being held down?"

"Yes to all of it."

* * *

The next day, Maya stayed home sick from school with a cold, and Mack came over with cans of chicken soup and lotion-coated tissues from the drugstore. Zoë sent him out again for cold remedies, and then he built up the fire and they made popcorn and watched Animal Planet.

The day after that, he came by at eight to drive Maya to school. The school bus came a full half hour earlier, and he'd wanted to give the kid a break. Zoë asked to come along, putting a jacket on over her nightgown. After they dropped Maya off, he drove to the entrance of the Oakdale Nature Preserve, slipped his hands under Zoë's jacket, and started kissing her.

"You're not wearing a brassiere." Still a little intimidated by her, he sometimes found himself slipping into an incongruous formality.

"Of course not, I'm in my nightgown. Listen, Mack, maybe you shouldn't kiss me, I think I might be getting Maya's cold."

"I know. I can taste it. No, don't pull back. I don't care. If you get sick, I'll take care of you."

"And what about when you get sick—oh." She leaned her head back as he exposed her bare flesh to the cold air. "Oh, my God, Mack, what are you doing, why are we doing this here?"

"Because if we go back to your house I'm going to fuck you."

"Oh," she said, and then, as his kisses dropped from her breasts to her belly, "Oh." Hunched over her in the car, uncomfortable beyond belief, Mack tasted her intimately, smiling as her fingers tangled in his hair. "Please, please, please."

He kept going until he did please her three times, and then he held Zoë in his arms while she said, "It's not enough. I want you to make love to me."

"When you pass the written test."

Zoë punched him, then gave him a hard look. "Fine," she said.

"Fine? You'll take it?"

"I think I'd better get dressed first. And take a shower."

* * *

Zoë passed the written exam on her first try, surprising herself but not Mack, who said she'd probably never failed a test in her life.

"Academic tests, no," Zoë replied. "Practical, real-life ones, I don't always do so well at."

Mack grinned at her, his hands shoved down into the back pockets of his jeans. "Guess you just need the right motivation."

"Speaking of which . . ." Zoë pushed Mack up the stairs and into her bedroom, where she knocked him down on her bed and started pulling off her sweater. Mack propped himself up on his elbows, enjoying the view. "Easy, Mama. I plan on taking my time."

"We only have twenty minutes till Maya's school bus is due back."

"Maybe we should wait until . . ." The words died in his throat as Zoë pulled up her ankle-length denim skirt, revealing thigh-high black-and-rose-patterned socks that extended six inches over the tops of her motorcycle boots, and nothing else. It was a memorable sight.

"You're not wearing any underwear."

"Do you have a condom?"

Mack thought about the past few hours, standing in line at the

Department of Motor Vehicles in Milltown, making conversation with some folks he knew. He tried to swallow. "You were walking around like that all day?"

Zoë straddled him, still wearing her boots. "You've got a problem with that, soldier?" Her breasts were nearly spilling out of her black brassiere, her cheeks were flushed, and she'd just spent the whole day with him bare-assed under her skirt.

Mack grabbed her by the back of her head and kissed her like he was about to head off to battle, and they grappled with the foil packaging for a moment, and then he sank into her, his hands on her hips, and she moaned his name as if she found it unbearably exciting that it was him and not someone else sliding into her. Feeling as though the top of his head might explode, Mack thrust three times, and it was over.

"I'm sorry," he said, panting as she looked down at him with a gentle smile. He was too embarrassed to meet her eyes. After all the buildup, a two-second race to the finish. She must think he was the worst lover she'd ever had.

"I love you," said Zoë, wrapping her arms around his neck and half choking him.

"What did you say?" He pulled back, startled, and then they both heard the distinctive noise of the school bus reversing into the drive. "Oh my God," said Zoë, pulling herself free.

"I'd better go," he said. "Unless you'd rather . . ."

"No! Go! Go!" She pushed him out the door.

*　*　*

He thought about writing her a note, quoting Rilke:

A woman so loved that from one lyre there came
More lament than from all lamenting women

But instead, Mack called her up after he knew Maya was in bed that night and said, "I want to do that again. Better."

"I'll have to think about my conditions."

"Conditions?"

"You know, some test you might need to pass."

Mack groaned, then laughed. Then he said, "Was it just sex talk?"

"What?"

"What you said."

"You mean, the kind of thing you say when the sex is so good you don't know what you're saying?"

Mack put his head under his pillow. "I can do better."

"Why don't you say what you really want to say, Mack?"

"What do you mean?"

Zoë sighed. "Why don't you tell me not to get too involved, or not to get too serious, or whatever it is you're building up to. But let me assure you, I didn't mean it like that, I was just sort of overcome with . . . feeling good and tender and silly and warm to you. But I'm not planning any wedding here. I said something intimate. We did something intimate. That's all it meant."

Mack was silent. And then he said, "I love you, too."

"Mack, you don't need to . . ."

"No, it's true. I just didn't . . . I just didn't understand what it meant before."

*   *   *

In the end, he got Maya's cold while Zoë remained healthy. He came over to her house, feverish and sleepy, so that she could heat him cans of Campbell's chicken noodle soup and put cool washcloths on his head. He remembered Jess complaining that he never let her take care of him, and realized that this was a different kind of chemistry, because when Zoë touched his uncomfortable skin, he felt comforted. She let him spend the night downstairs, covered with an old quilt that smelled like the back of her neck. Maya gave him a teddy bear to hold and he went to sleep thinking about Thanksgiving, and how they would spend it together, and after that came Christmas, if they celebrated Christmas, and this year he would need to really think about presents.

Twenty-two

*I*n all the books and movies and TV shows that Zoë could recall, the big emphasis was always on the first time a couple made love. Sexual tension ratcheted higher and higher, and then came the big payoff.

Except that after all the delicious buildup with Mack, the first time had been awkward and rushed. And even though Zoë had felt quite tender toward him afterward, it hadn't exactly portended carnal bliss to come.

The second time had been better, but not perfect. Mack had been tense, and Zoë had felt more than a little self-conscious about her body, and the way her breasts spilled to the side when she was supine. She hadn't been able to forget that she was ten years older than him, probably more than ten years older than his last girlfriend.

"You didn't come," Mack had said, clearly disappointed.

"Sometimes it's not about that," she said, curled around his side, his wiry arm around her shoulders. She wasn't the only one who was a little shy about being seen naked. Mack had an army tattoo on his chest, American flag and frowning eagle, and a dagger high on his right biceps that he liked to keep covered. She didn't blame him; they weren't even particularly well drawn pieces. Otherwise, his body was almost too perfect, arms roped with muscle, belly taut and lean, his thighs so hard she felt like he was a member of a different species. Her own thighs were sticking together, and Zoë absent-mindedly thought about how she'd have to change the sheets before Maya came home.

"Zoë, what's this?" Mack held up a book he'd taken from her bedside table. The cover displayed a woman's stiletto-clad foot and a man's fanged profile. She'd hidden it under Thomas L. Friedman's *Longitudes and Attitudes,* Robert Kagan's *Of Paradise and Power,* and Maureen Dowd's *Are Men Necessary?*

"Oh, that's just . . . you know, bedtime reading."

Mack looked at the back cover. "'A hardened warrior from another time, Varek has not known a woman's softness or a moment's peace since the fateful day when he was cursed to be an immortal mercenary. But professor of archaeology Felicia Evans might just hold the keys to Varek's release . . . in more ways than one.'" He raised an eyebrow.

"I'm not apologizing for my fantasies."

Mack flipped open to where she'd left her bookmark. "'Pinning her wrists, Varek snarled, a white hot fury lancing through his veins. Yet Felicia continued to defy him, seemingly oblivious to the danger she faced. Did she not understand that for him, to unleash his passion was to unleash his beast? "You would do better not to tempt me, Human," he growled.'" Mack stopped reading out loud, his eyes flickering across the page as he scanned the scene. When he looked up at Zoë, there was a strange look on his face. "So this is what you like? I'm a soldier with a dark side, careful or I might fuck you to death?"

Zoë pulled the sheet higher over her breasts. "I'm sorry if you feel insulted, Mack, but there has always been a link between Eros and Thanatos, the urge for sex and the urge for death, and it's hard to be politically correct in your . . . what are you doing?"

Mack grinned as he yanked the sheet down and moved over her, pinning her wrists. "I didn't say I was insulted."

"Oh, sorry. It's just, my last boyfriend . . ." She let her voice trail off, not wanting to compare them. She was also more than a little distracted by the fact that Mack was pressing up against her, and it was now abundantly clear that what he was feeling wasn't insulted.

"Yeah, well, maybe your last boyfriend was a wuss. I can do soldier with a dark side." He put his knee between her thighs, parting them. "But be careful, Zoë. Because I've been holding myself in check. But if you're saying I can really let go with you . . ."

"Okay, now, when you say really let go, are we implying pain or subjugation?"

"I don't know," Mack said, nipping at her neck. "I didn't read that far yet." He winked, and Zoë realized that he could, indeed, do soldier with a dark side extremely well. And when he stopped smiling, and tightened his grip on her wrists, she felt a measure of trepidation mingle with her desire, intensifying it. But Zoë noticed that Mack continued to watch her carefully, his eyes more green than blue as he entered her with one strong thrust. His gaze never left her face, so she closed her eyes, experimentally twisting her wrists, to see how hard it would be to free them.

"Look at me," he said, and she opened her eyes again. Apparently reassured by what he saw, Mack tightened his grip, and rocked his narrow hips into her. She said, "Oh," and then it all changed. Mack did let something out, something wilder, more intense, more rough-edged and raw. It wasn't dark, exactly, but it wasn't gentle, and for the first time, Zoë really was aware that he was a soldier. She moaned, and he said, "Tell me and I'll stop," she wrapped her legs around his lean waist and said, "Don't stop, don't stop," and impossibly, Mack kicked into a higher gear.

The bed went away. So did all thought of the sheets, and laundry, and what might come after. Gone also was any lingering self-consciousness about her body or the wet, fleshy sounds they were making. All consciousness was now bound up in the feeling of Mack's sinewy body as he moved powerfully inside her, churning her up, conjuring her up out of her flesh. Zoë wrenched her hands free, clutched his back, dug her heels into his muscular buttocks, and cried out.

Afterward she couldn't look at him. She buried her head in his chest as he patted her comfortingly, stroking her hair. He didn't ask her what was wrong. Maybe he was used to making women fall apart.

Now the sex was all she could think about. The more she touched him, the more she wanted to touch him, the more he seemed to take up residence in her imagination. All through their driving lessons, as she checked her mirrors and signaled before moving out, or reduced speed to navigate a turn, or practiced her three-point turns, she was distracted by what they had done last time, and by what they would do afterward. In bed, her legs over his shoulders. In a chair in the living room, straddling him. Standing in the kitchen, fully dressed, her cheek resting on the counter as he took her from behind. They did it tinged with roughness, shaded with tenderness, broken up with laughter. She had never experienced so many moods of sex with one person before.

"I have to get some work done," she said now, unbuttoning her jeans. "It's almost Thanksgiving, and then Maya will be out of school and I won't get anything done."

"Me, too," Mack said, pulling off his shirt.

"Just once, just a quickie today, and then I have to work."

"Okay."

They fell to the floor together, wrestling like puppies.

"Ouch."

Mack raised himself up on his arms. "What's wrong?"

"I'm just—don't stop. Just a little sore."

"Let me see what I can do about that." He moved down between her thighs.

"You don't have to . . . I . . . "

There was a knock on the door. "Hello?"

"Mack, someone's there." He popped up, glazed and guilty.

"One moment please," she said, straightening her clothes. "Yes," she said, coming to the door.

"You have a UPS package," said the man, peering into the kitchen. He was wearing a brown uniform that matched the truck Zoë could see out the window, parked next to Mack's Crown Royal. "Oh, hello, Mack."

"Hello, Ed." Mack was standing against the kitchen counter, partially turned away. She wondered how much Ed was taking in.

Zoë signed for the package, which was from Bronwyn. She wondered if the kitchen smelled of sex. Surely not.

"Ed used to go to school with me," said Mack.

"Pleased to meet you," said Ed, openly curious. He had a weak chin, a thin brown mustache, and a faint smell of nicotine about his person. "So," he said to Mack, "what's new?"

"Well," Mack said. He looked at Zoë, as if for permission. She looked away. "You know I'm starting my own driving school."

"Yeah, Moroney's sure burned up about that."

Zoë ripped open the box and found that Bronwyn had sent her a bunch of articles. There was a *New York Times Magazine* essay about a couple who had left Manhattan to open their own goat farm in Dutchess County, and a magazine piece entitled "Beyond Suburbia: The Commutable Wilderness." There was also a *West Side Spirit* cover story about the many New Yorkers buying up second homes in the area. "It used to be that middle-class Manhattanites moved out of the city after they had children," the reporter wrote, "but now many choose to have their city and leave it, too."

"Thought you would find this useful for research," Bronwyn had written. "Seems as if you're part of a big trend, moving out there. Property values are going way up. The magazine is Brian's, so don't throw it out. Miss you terribly. Wish we could spend Thanksgiving together, but am being forced to see the dreaded mother-in-law." Zoë felt a rush of guilt: she had hardly called Bronwyn in the past three weeks, embarrassed to talk about her affair with Mack while her friend was so miserable.

"So," Mack was saying, and his voice sounded tighter than she was used to, "what's he saying?"

Ed looked profoundly uncomfortable. He glanced at Zoë, and she thought his little brown button eyes looked shifty. "You know, stupid stuff."

"Like what?"

"Mack, I'm not sure this is the place . . ." This time, the glance at Zoë was telling.

"He means that your old boss is talking about me," said Zoë. "What's he saying?"

"Oh, now, I didn't mean that anyone was talking about you, ma'am."

Zoë snorted and watched Ed's face. "Let me see . . . he's bad-mouthing Mack by impugning his professionalism, saying that Mack is taking advantage of me . . . no, wait, that I'm taking advantage of Mack?"

"Now, look, I don't know where all this is coming from," said Ed, who had clearly never been interviewed by a hostile reporter.

Mack moved a step closer. "What's he saying, Ed?"

"What he's saying," said Zoë, "is that I'm paying you for more than just your expertise behind the wheel." The whole thing seemed so amusing to her that the words were out before she remembered that this had been the subject of their first fight. Funny how that happens, how the place where you're most sensitive always gets reinjured.

"I never said that," said Ed, almost spluttering. "Besides, everyone knows Moroney is full of shit." He shrugged at Zoë. "Pardon my language, ma'am."

"I'm going to kill him," said Mack.

"Calm down."

"I'm going to kill him!"

"Look," said Zoë, "if I'm not that upset, you don't need to be, either."

"It's me he's insulting."

"Don't be silly. His point is that the only reason you'd be interested in someone ten years older and not conventionally beautiful was because she was paying you."

Mack stared at her as if she'd gone mad. "No way. I think the point is, the only reason an attractive, sophisticated woman with a high-powered career would hang around with a poor, dumb, blue-collar slob was because she was hiring him for services rendered."

Zoë laughed. "As in, you're only good for one thing?"

"Exactly. And I don't think it's funny."

"Think about what we both just said."

Now Mack laughed. "You're right," he said. "It is funny." He put his arm around her shoulders. "What makes you think you're not conventionally beautiful?"

"What makes you think you're dumb?"

"Aha, so you do think I'm a poor blue-collar slob."

"Yes, but not dumb."

Ed, who was clearly sorry he hadn't just left the package on the porch, cleared his throat. "I'll just be leaving now," he said.

"Yeah, well. You tell that son of a bitch Moroney that if I hear one more word about this rumor, I'm going to forget I ever signed a confidentiality oath."

"I don't even talk to him, Mack."

"You just tell him that I don't care what he says about me, but I don't appreciate his bad-mouthing my girlfriend."

Ed left and Zoë stood there, feeling bemused. "So, I'm your girlfriend, huh?"

"Well, yeah." Mack took a deep breath and rolled his shoulders. "Of course. What else would you be?"

"I don't know." She smiled. "It just sounds kind of young." She tried to remember the last time she'd been called someone's girlfriend. Ten years ago? More? It sounded like something that belonged to another phase of life, along with ID bracelets and prom dates.

"So what do I call you, my womanfriend?" Mack wrapped his arms around her. "Hey."

"What?"

"Want to come over to my sister's for Thanksgiving dinner?"

She looked at him. "Shouldn't you ask her first?"

"Nah, it's fine. She'd just get bored with old Bill and me." Although, if he were being completely honest, "boring" wasn't the right term for the carefully maintained monotony of his sister's marriage.

"All right then. Thanks."

"What do you want to do now?" Mack looked at the clock. "We only have another half hour before Maya gets home."

"I don't know. I guess we kind of ran out of time."

"I guess so." Mack kissed her, cupping her face in his hands. "Never mind."

"We won't be able to do this when Maya's home over vacation, you know. Even though she's sleeping in her own bed more, I just wouldn't feel comfortable."

"That's all right. We can still hang out, can't we? I mean, you'll want some time alone, but we can also do some stuff together, right?"

"Of course we can." And Zoë, who had never felt such a fierce sexual pull toward any man, was amazed by how much sex didn't matter to Mack. It was as if, with all the other men she'd known, there was life, and then there was sex, a thing apart, something you did and then finished, like a meal. With Mack, sex seemed interwoven with everything else, seemed to matter both less and more.

"I love you, Zoë," he said, sounding somber.

She touched the side of his face, amused. "Try not to look so upset about it."

* * *

It was a good thing they had decided not to wait to have sex until she passed her road test, thought Zoë, because she was beginning to think it wasn't just a matter of being phobic about driving. Perhaps some people weren't really meant to operate motor vehicles. It could be a kind of learning disability, directional dyslexia and vehicular gross motor dysfunction. Mack said that was ridiculous, anyone could learn.

But driving, Zoë decided, was the most unnatural activity she had ever attempted. How the hell did anyone ever remember everything? All of a sudden, after a lifetime of moving your legs to get from one place to another, you had to learn how much pressure to apply to a pedal with the pad of your right foot. Meanwhile, you had to get used to your left foot sitting off to one side, useless as a vestigial nipple. And then there was the steering. None of the chapters in the driver's manual seemed to cover how far you were supposed to turn the wheel, and Mack kept saying, until the car is pointing where you want it to go. But there was a time factor involved, a coordination of hand and foot that was completely unlike the coordination of dance. And while you were struggling to get the combination of foot push and hand turn synchronized, you still had to pay attention to all the road signs and other cars and miscellaneous unexpected hazards, such as deer and road crews and cyclists who appeared not to realize that a little plastic helmet really didn't provide all that much protection.

"Zoë, watch out!" Mack gave a sharp tug on the passenger-side steering wheel, swerving around the cyclist.

"Oh, my God. Oh, my God." Zoë turned back. The cyclist was pedaling obliviously along the road leading out of town, his face half-hidden by the hood of his black sweatshirt. "I could have killed him."

"You were only going twenty. That's a trip to the hospital, not the morgue. But you do have to remember to look out for people as well as cars. Now, come on, remember you're still driving."

"Oh, my God. Why isn't he wearing something bright and reflective?"

"Because he's not from Manhattan. Come on, remember to signal before you turn." Mack guided her into the parking lot behind the liquor store.

"I nearly hit him!"

"Nothing happened, that's why we use dual steering wheels," said Mack. "Now take a deep breath. Are you okay?"

"No." Zoë was shaking, sweat running between her breasts, staining the armpits of her shirt. He reached out his arms and she pushed him away. "I don't want to do this anymore."

"You did fine until we saw the cyclist."

"You mean, the one I nearly ran over."

"Okay, let's talk about that. Remember what I said about the car going where your eyes go? So when you saw the cyclist . . ."

"I was looking at him because I didn't want to hit him!"

"And it's good to look. Once. But after looking at him, Zoë, you need to think about giving him enough room . . ."

"You said never to cross the double yellow line unless I was pulling off the road!"

"Well, yes, but this was an exception to that rule. That's why we take lessons, because you can't learn everything from the rule book."

Zoë got out, slamming the car door. "I'll say." The driver's manual didn't tell you that if you were going the wrong way, you couldn't just stop when you wanted to stop, or turn when you wanted to turn. It didn't spell out that you had to look, check, indicate, turn off the windshield wipers, which you kept turning on by mistake when you meant to signal a turn, and then check again because you'd let more than two seconds elapse. By the time you were through with all that, you'd probably missed your turnoff. And could you just turn around? No more than you could reverse the earth's orbit.

She walked into the liquor store, wondering if she should just down a quick vodka so Mack wouldn't expect her to drive back.

"So," said Frances, who was dusting a large taxidermy turkey. "How are the driving lessons going?"

"I don't think I was meant to drive."

"That's what I always used to say."

"No, but I really don't think I was meant to drive. Before I sit down at the wheel, I feel as though somebody's tied my intestines into a knot."

"At least you don't throw up," said Mack, closing the door carefully behind him. "I had one boy who was always puking when he got tense."

"At least he didn't almost kill someone. Nice turkey, Frances. Did you just do that one?"

"Yeah, he got hit by a horse trailer near my house. I thought he was very appropriate for the season. Speaking of which, do you have somewhere to go for Thanksgiving? Because Gretchen and I would love to have you over."

"Oh, thanks, Fran," said Zoë, feeling a little uncomfortable. "I would have loved to, but I'm already eating with Mack and his sister."

"Oh, of course," said Frances, looking bemused.

Zoë felt as if she should just post an ad in the local paper: "I'm screwing my driver." She could feel Gretchen's speculative look from behind the counter, and knew that she was going to be discussed at length as soon as she left the store.

Mack, however, seemed not to notice any undercurrents. "You and Gretchen are welcome to join us," he suggested, bending down to pet the little French bulldog.

"Oh, we wouldn't want to intrude," said Frances, beaming down at her dog.

"You sure? Might be the perfect opportunity to convince my sister about the evils of development."

"Oh, we couldn't do that, could we, Gretchen?"

But Gretchen looked as if someone had electrified her. "Of course, if the subject naturally came up after dinner . . . why don't you just pick out the wine you want and let it be on us? We'd love to come."

"Don't forget," said Mack as they left, "the best propaganda sounds almost completely objective." He winked, and both women waved, looking happy.

"That was a nice thing to do," said Zoë as they walked back to the car. "What made you invite them?"

"I want you to have your friends around you." Besides, he figured Bill and Moira could use a little more liveliness at the dinner table.

Were Gretchen and Frances her friends, Zoë wondered. And if not, what would it take for them to become friends? "What about your friends," she asked. "That guy you work with at the garage."

Mack looked surprised. "You're right. I never thought of him, but I should invite Skeeter."

Mack had his hand at the small of her back as they reached the car, and a pretty, blond woman stiffened as she saw them. She was standing outside of the Stewart's shop, wearing the maroon uniform and smoking a cigarette.

"Hello, Jess," Mack said, raising his hand.

She raised her own hand. "Happy Turkey Day," she said, sounding miserable.

"You, too. And hey, cut that out." He indicated the cigarette. "I thought you'd quit."

"I did, but you know how it is."

Mack waved again, then got into the car.

"So that was Jess," Zoë said. "She's pretty."

"So are you."

"I'm not angling for a compliment, Mack."

"Never said you were." He drove in silence for a moment. "I'm in deeper with you than I was with her. Just so you know."

"Mack, I'm not asking for reassurances or promises. I'm not jealous of your ex-girlfriend. I'm only going to be here until the spring, when the school year ends."

"I know that."

"You know, if you were to drive back instead of me, we would have a little spare time."

"Are you trying to seduce me into cutting your lesson short?"

"Of course I am. Is it working?"

"Of course it's working."

* * *

He took her in the house and made love to her in the kitchen, from behind. But at the last moment, Mack turned her around and took her into the living room, where they sank down on the rug. He paused, then rearranged her so that she was on top of him. Even though Zoë could feel he was still hard inside her, she knew something was wrong.

"Zoë."

"Yes."

"Did you love him? Maya's father."

"Not exactly."

"Who was he?"

"A photojournalist."

"Did he ever see her?"

"No. He didn't want to. He was angry. He said he felt forced into something he hadn't agreed to."

Mack stared up at her. "Are you sorry?"

Zoë shook her head, gently disengaging herself. "I wasn't sure I was ever going to have a baby, but then, when I was pregnant, it felt right. I was sorry for him, it wasn't his choice, but I didn't want to get an abortion again."

"Again?"

"When I was eighteen, I had one. I don't regret that, either."

Mack stroked the side of her face. Just as Zoë was beginning to think about getting up, he asked, "Do you ever want another baby?"

"I don't know. I haven't really thought about it recently. I don't know that I could go back to diapers and sleeplessness again." She looked at him carefully. "Why?"

"Because you're so good at it. Being a mother."

"Thanks, Mack. But you're not having baby fantasies that involve me, right?"

"No, I'm not having baby fantasies." He paused. "Do you think Maya misses having a father?"

Zoë sighed. "I think maybe she used to. I think it can be a little intense, being raised by one parent, because there's no system of checks and balances. And I wish she had more positive male role models in her life. But we do okay."

"Maybe I could, you know, do some of that guy stuff with her. Teach her how to build a birdhouse. Take her camping."

"Show her how to swing a bat?"

"I hate baseball, but yeah, if she wants to learn . . ."

"I was teasing. Yes, Mack, that would be wonderful." She had assumed that sex had pretty much been derailed, but then Mack covered her with his body, entering her again. He started to move, straining inside her with a controlled intensity that brought her along with him as he collapsed. Zoë's hair was damp on the side where his face rested. She stroked his back. "Are you okay?"

He pulled out so that he could dispose of the condom. Then he returned to her, letting his hair hide his face as he held her close. Zoë's heart melted a little, the way it did when her daughter was sick or sad or needy. How strange to feel so much for a man with whom she had so little in common, with whom there was no chance for a future.

Twenty-three

Mack leaned against the kitchen wall, trying to avoid being run down by his sister. She was in the throes of some kind of manic cooking meltdown, and he wondered out loud what could have caused it.

"You caused it," snapped Moira. "Now get out of my way."

"But what's the point of buying a bird that weighs as much as a toddler if you're not going to have guests, Moira?"

"The point," said Moira, opening the oven door, "is that you're not the one cooking it."

"But I said I'd do whatever you asked me to. You want me to stick my hand up the bird's ass and shove breadcrumbs inside? Done. You want me to peel yams, or, I don't know, wash dishes, I'm doing it."

Moira closed the oven door again and straightened up, her face glistening with sweat. "By the time I get through explaining to you how to do something, I might as well have done it myself."

"But it's all done now, right? You can go and get changed. And don't you think it might be nice, having a few people over this year? You always complain that Bill just watches the game and nobody talks to each other."

"Five people, Mack. You invited five people to my house on Thanksgiving without even consulting me first."

"They're all contributing a dish, though," said Mack. "So how much more work can it really be?"

Mack's sister flashed him a look that promised great, heaping mounds of horseshit, which he would be shoveling. "Shut up and wash the lettuce leaves. Oh, God, was that a knock at the door?"

It was a knock. "Calm down, Sis. Honestly, you deal with panicking horses without batting an eyelash, and all of a sudden a little dinner throws you into a tizzy."

"Get the goddamn door!"

He greeted the women from the liquor store at the door. The one with short gray hair was wearing lipstick, a red sweater, and earrings. The blonde with the Dutch-boy haircut was wearing jeans, work boots, and a fisherman's sweater. Guess he could figure out their deal. "Hey, guys," he said, then flushed, worried that you didn't say that to lesbians. He gestured at the straw hamper in the blonde's arms. "You gave us all that wine. You didn't have to bring anything."

"It's not food," said the blonde, whom he now remembered was named Gretchen, flipping the top. "It's Vita." The French bulldog stuck out her bulbous little head, and Mack thought, great. If there was one thing his brother-in-law disliked, it was small dogs. And of course, there was more than one thing that Bill disliked. Like a lot of men Mack knew, much of Bill's limited conversation revolved around things that bugged him, like laws against smoking indoors and cops who gave you a ticket for driving without a seat belt and the fact that the school wasn't allowed to display a crèche. According to Bill, being an American meant being free to do pretty much what you wanted, when you wanted, in your own home, car, or business. Sometimes Mack wondered what Bill would have done in the army.

"Why don't you come on in," he told the women. "I have to go fetch Zoë and Maya."

The gray-haired one, Frances, cocked her head to one side like a bird. "Do you want us to do that?"

"Nah," said Mack, eager to get away from the tense atmosphere in the kitchen. "You go meet my sister, Moira."

He returned, not twenty minutes later, to find that his sister was now incandescent with fury. She was bustling around the kitchen like a mare about to foal, banging pots and clanging glasses while Frances and Gretchen sat, cradling their ugly little dog and sipping very large glasses of wine.

"I wish I'd known she was a vegetarian," Moira snapped at Mack. Her brown hair was frizzing out of its long braid, and her face was red. She was still wearing the old flannel shirt she'd been cooking in all morning.

"I already told you, I'll be fine just eating the potatoes and greens," said Frances.

"Are you sure? I could fix a lasagna. I think I have the noodles here."

Mack put his hands on Moira's shoulders. "Relax," he said. "Go shower and change. I'll take over here."

"You can't cook!" Moira looked over Mack's shoulder and saw Zoë, who was saying hello to Gretchen and Frances. "Oh, thank God, Zoë. Can you keep an eye on the turkey and the yams? And the gravy's just thickening, it needs frequent stirring."

She left the room, and Zoë stared at Mack. "I have never once in my entire life attempted to roast a bird, let alone coordinate said bird with side dishes."

"I have, back when I was married," said Frances, opening the oven.

"Back when you ate sausage, you mean."

Frances laughed, shaking a wooden spoon at Gretchen, then

frowned as she stirred a pot. "Oh, hell, it looks like there are bacon bits in the green beans. And she's already put marshmallows on the yams."

Maya stopped petting Vita for a moment. "What's wrong with marshmallows?"

"They have gelatin in them. From animals' hooves."

"Ew, yuck. Mommy, I want to be a vegetarian, too."

"Not today, you don't."

"Who wants to be a vegetarian," asked Skeeter, bringing in a crisp smell of the outside with him, along with a tray of something that smelled deliciously smoky. He took one look at Gretchen and his husky blue eyes widened.

"My daughter does," said Zoë, coming forward. "But I think she wants to be the kind that doesn't actually eat vegetables. As for me, I'm a dedicated omnivore, and whatever wonderful meaty thing you're carrying, it's making my mouth water."

"Venison sausages," said Skeeter, his eyes returning to Gretchen.

"Ooh," she said, winking at Frances. "Sausages."

"You like 'em? These are from a buck I shot myself."

"Mmm," said Gretchen, looking deeply amused. "Nice tats," she said, as he pulled off his jeans jacket. As usual, he was wearing a black T-shirt to show off his permanently inked shirtsleeves.

"Thanks. I have a great guy I go to in Woodstock."

"Jimmy? He did these," said Gretchen, pulling up the hem of her baggy jeans to reveal a leopard, some vines, and a redheaded woman in a fur bikini.

"I love Jimmy," said Skeeter, almost dropping his tray of sausages.

"Let me take that, man." Mack wondered how to make the introductions so that his friend would get the picture. "Skeeter here's the owner of the Big Dog Garage. Gretchen and Frances own the liquor store. And this is Zoë, and her daughter, Maya."

"This is Vita," said Maya, waving one of the little dog's paws.

Skeeter's eyes kept returning to Gretchen. Mack looked at her, trying to see what she would look like if he didn't know she was batting for the other team. Or rather, for the same team that he did. Shit, she was actually very pretty, in a boyish way.

"You from around here," Skeeter was asking.

"I am. Frances moved from the city."

"You didn't go to Starling High, though."

"Of course I did. Class of Ninety-three."

"So I was a junior when you started. Now that I think of it, you look familiar."

"I think we were in shop together."

"No way!" Skeeter looked astonished. "There weren't any girls in shop."

"I used to go by my last name, Jones. I think some people assumed I was a boy."

"No way," said Skeeter. "I can't believe a pretty girl like you could ever be mistaken for a boy. Those guys must have been blind."

It was going to be a strange meal, thought Mack, meeting Zoë's eyes.

"Nice scarf," said Frances, fingering the turquoise silk wrapped around Zoë's throat.

"Mommy's using it to hide a big tick bite," said Maya.

"Really? They don't usually bite on the neck. Let me see if there's a bull's-eye, because a double dose of doxycycline taken right away prevents Lyme disease."

"There isn't," said Zoë, moving away.

"Better to check."

Zoë looked at Mack, who said, "I, er, already checked it." Everyone looked at him.

"It doesn't look like a bull's-eye," offered Maya. "It looks more like lips."

There was a silence in the kitchen, broken by the sound of Moira's voice yelling from upstairs. "Bill, you have to."

"I don't know any of them, and I'll come down when there's food," came Bill's reply. A moment later, Moira reappeared, wearing a clean flannel shirt and a forced grin.

"Well, Bill's coming right down so we might as well all head on into the dining room," she said. "How's my turkey doing?"

"Ready to come out," said Frances. "Although it's probably a good thing I don't eat meat."

"What do you mean?"

She removed the bird from the oven, and Maya said, "Wow, I didn't know they made them that small."

"It must have shrunk," said Moira, as Bill came down the stairs, radiating a silent hostility that made the little bulldog growl from her basket. "Maybe because it's free range and organic?"

Bill shambled past the turkey, giving it the same dirty look that he spared for the dog.

"Hush, Vita, stop it," said Frances, without conviction. The dog kept growling.

"Why don't you all go into the other room," Mack said, "and I'll help Moira bring in the food."

"We'll all help," said Zoë, so that everyone wound up carrying something to the long dining room table where Bill sat, looking disgruntled in his work-stained blue sweatshirt and torn Carhartt overalls. Apparently, his brother-in-law intended to make it very clear that he made no concessions to dining with company, as he had not bothered to shave, comb what remained of his hair, or clean his fingernails very well.

Mack cleared his throat. "You want me to carve, Bill?"

Bill shrugged. "Do what you like." In an undertone, he added, "No one seems to care what I want."

Mack started carving. "I guess I'd better aim for thin slices," he said, then wished he hadn't when he saw his sister's face.

"I should have just bought the regular kind, like last year. But this was supposed to be better."

"It is better," said Frances. "Not only is buying organic healthier but it promotes the farmers who are acting most responsibly toward the environment. Oh, thanks, Moira, but no yams for me."

"But there's no meat in there," protested Moira, serving spoon in hand.

"The marshmallows have hooves in them," said Maya. "But not horse hooves, right, Moira? Because you wouldn't eat horse hooves."

"So," Skeeter was saying to Gretchen, "where else do you have tattoos?"

"It's not going badly," Mack whispered to Zoë. "At least everyone's talking."

"I think your sister's a little upset."

Mack turned to Moira, and therefore had the chance to see her face as Bill said, "Not more crap about the environment. You know who talks about the environment? City people who build some big honking eyesore up on some mountaintop, and then want to stop everyone else from building anything."

"Mom, he said 'crap,' " said Maya.

"Shh."

"But you wouldn't want people building up all the wetlands and destroying the rural nature of Arcadia," said Frances. Unlike the others at the table, she was undistracted by the food, since she had nothing but a few lettuce leaves on her plate.

"That's the argument outsiders use when what they really want is to price out the working-class people who've been living here their whole lives."

"That's not true, and some careful zoning laws would ensure that Arcadia does develop."

"Zoning," said Bill, as if it were a dirty word. "You put in a law that no house can be on a plot that's smaller than five acres, and you know what happens? Most of the kids growing up here can't afford to stay."

From her basket by the table, Vita began to make little unhappy grunting noises, as if she were trying to clear her squashed nose.

"I think she wants some turkey," said Maya, craning her head. "Or maybe I can sit with her on the floor to keep her company."

Mack wouldn't have minded sitting with the dog himself. God knows he was in the doghouse for arranging this dinner.

Zoë put a restraining hand on her daughter's shoulder. "No, Maya, you let Frances take care of her."

"It's okay, plumpkin, it's all right," Frances said, attempting to soothe her. The dog, picking up on her owner's tension, began whining.

"Jesus Christ, make her stop that noise," said Bill.

"Does that count as a curse?" Maya looked at her mother. "I mean, I know it's not a bad word, exactly, but when you use it instead of one?"

Frances half stood up. "Maybe I should go."

"Oh, no, please don't." Moira turned to Bill. "Let's talk about something else."

"Like what? The fact that we might be moving to Virginia?" Bill put down his fork and knife. "Next she's going to lecture us and say we don't have the right to sell our property to the highest bidder."

Frances stared at Bill. "Are you telling me you're thinking of selling this place to the developers? Because I'm sure you are aware that our town's lack of zoning means that all this could be completely destroyed." She waved her hand in the direction of the window, with its view of the mountain.

Bill turned to Mack. "If I want to hear about goddamn zoning,

I'll ask somebody who's grown up around here and is entitled to an opinion."

"'Goddamn' is definitely a curse," said Maya in a loud whisper.

"Maya, that's enough."

Mack forced himself to swallow the bite of turkey he'd been chewing. "Well," he said, "I suppose no zoning's better than bad zoning."

"You see," said Bill, slightly mollified.

"On the other hand, you don't want corrupt idiots like Moroney free to do whatever suits him, so maybe it would be good to have a few rules in place."

"Spoken like a diplomat," said Zoë.

Bill snorted. "Spoken like a guy who's banging a weekender."

"Bill," said Moira. "There is a child at the table."

Maya stopped scraping the marshmallow off her yams and turned to her mother. "Mommy, what's a weekender, and who's banging on one?"

Mack caught the hint of mischief in Maya's face. She might not know what she was asking, but she sure as hell knew it was something fresh. "That's just car repair talk," he said, trying not to show how pissed off he was at his brother-in-law.

Skeeter reached over and speared a sausage. "Personally, I don't hold with this idea that there's us and there's them. Weekenders make up a good sixty to seventy percent of my business, and I'm not the only local guy who couldn't survive if city people weren't coming and spending their money in this town." He nodded at Gretchen and Frances. "Fact is, a lot of the guys I grew up with take their business to Poughkeepsie and Kingston. And Frances may not have grown up here, but she sure is helping the town's economy."

Frances raised her glass to him. "Thank you, Skeeter."

"Jesus, man," said Mack, shaking his head. "And here I thought all you knew about was cars."

Skeeter looked embarrassed by all the attention. "Yeah, well, sometimes you got to have an opinion." He shoved a spoonful of mashed potatoes in his mouth.

"You know," said Gretchen, "you ought to stand up at the next town board meeting and say some of this."

"It's too late," said Bill, sounding smug. "The town board already approved the developer's plan."

Gretchen choked, and Skeeter pounded her on the back. When she recovered, she said, "That's impossible. We just reported seeing a bald eagle nest in an old oak tree not half a mile from our store, which would be directly in the path of the bulldozers. By law, Moroney has to get an environmental impact assessment done before he can even hold a vote."

Bill helped himself to a heaping forkful of turkey. "Yeah, well, you might go take another look. Remember, nests can fall down." He took a heaping mouthful of potato. "And so can trees."

Mack suddenly felt a sick feeling in the pit of his stomach, remembering the day he'd seen Moroney's pickup truck pulling into the town hall parking lot, interrupting his driving lesson with Zoë. No wonder Moroney had looked so guilty. He had used that chainsaw to commit a crime, although killing trees and birds might not count as murder.

Mack stared at his brother-in-law. "Did you help him do it?"

"Did I help who do what?" Bill served himself another spoonful of mashed potatoes.

"Don't play games with me. Did you help Moroney cut down that tree?" You had to know just what you were doing to take down an oak with a single chainsaw, working with the weight of the tree, cutting to take advantage of the slight asymmetry of the growth. Mack didn't know if Moroney knew that much about trees, but Bill sure did.

"Mack, I don't have time to cut down trees for other people. But the highway boys do make their rounds, and if they hear an old tree might be about to drop some limbs on the road, they have to do something about it."

Frances dropped her fork with a clatter. "That tree wasn't near any road! Gretchen and I found it on a hike!"

"Yeah, well, the highway department takes their orders from the town supervisor," said Mack, not bothering to disguise the bitterness in his voice. "Maybe they decided to define the dirt path going up Amimi Mountain as a road." He pushed his plate away, his appetite gone. "You know, Moroney's going too far. He can't just run this town like it's his own personal kingdom."

"Oh, come off it," said Bill. "Your beef with Moroney is personal, not political. And if you really cared so much about how this town is run, you wouldn't spend all your time teaching Manhattan here how to drive. Assuming that's what you're doing for five hours a day, every day, for the past month. Slow learner, isn't she?"

"You know, for the entire twenty years you've been married to my sister, I thought you were a quiet, cranky guy. Maybe a little old before your time, but I kind of liked you. At least, I liked that you stuck by my sister. Now, all of a sudden, you're a bundle of venom. What's going on?"

"How the hell would you know what I was like," snarled Bill. "You were off in the army the whole time. This is me, Mack, take it or leave it."

"If this is the real you, I don't think anyone should take it."

There was an ominous silence at the table. No one was even pretending to eat anymore. The little dog was making strange, low, huffing noises, as if she wanted to bark but couldn't quite work up the nerve.

"Get the hell out of my house."

"Bill, you're not kicking my brother out in the middle of Thanksgiving dinner."

"Oh, shit, you defending your baby brother again? I'm telling you, Moira, I've had enough. He's over thirty, and there's no reason for us to have to make our decisions about selling or not based on the fact that he's living over our barn."

Moira banged her fist down on the table. "Bill, we are not discussing this here and now."

Bill snorted. "Yeah, right. Of course she needs to worry. You live your whole damn life as if you were about to go back to the army, only you aren't going back."

"Bill."

He turned to Mack, his lip curled in a sneer. "Moira says you've seen so much death, you're still living like anyone that gets next to you might die at any minute. I say you're still looking for someone to mommy you."

"Come on, Maya," said Zoë, getting up. "Let's go to the bathroom for a moment."

"But I don't have to go," protested the child, refusing to leave the table.

"Bill, you have no right to do this!" Moira was standing now, her face scarlet.

"Yeah, well, he didn't have the right to invite a bunch of strangers into my home."

"It's his home, too, and it's also mine and . . . get out."

Bill remained in his seat. "Don't say it unless you mean it, Moira. You really want to throw away twenty years of marriage because I don't want strangers offering me opinions about my land?"

"But it's not your land, Bill." Mack stared at his sister. As far as he knew, she and Bill had never fought before. He'd always assumed that was a good thing, but now he was having second thoughts.

"Or are you just mad because I don't want to spend the next eighteen years of my life raising some stranger's kid."

"I didn't turn this into a fight."

"Yeah, you did. You know how I feel, and you won't stop nagging me about it." Bill stood up, scraping his chair back from the table, and walked out the front door.

There was silence at the table, as Mack and everyone else took in the fact that his sister's marriage had apparently just disintegrated before they'd finished the first course.

"Is she pregnant, Mommy?" whispered Maya.

"No, honey, I think he meant . . . something else."

Moira's face crumpled. "If you'll excuse me." She left, and Mack looked around at Gretchen and Frances and Skeeter before he finally met Zoë's eyes.

"Well," Skeeter said to Gretchen, "that's strange. Usually turkey makes everyone sleepy."

Zoë leaned closer to Mack. "Did you know she wanted to adopt a baby?"

Mack shook his head. "I didn't even know I was living like I expected everyone to die."

"Look, everyone, look," said Maya, and Mack turned to look out the window, where a pair of wild turkeys were ambling across the lawn, as if protesting the consumption of their brethren.

"Happy Thanksgiving," said Gretchen, raising her glass of wine. "God bless all of us turkeys."

Frances stood up and walked over to the other woman, then bent down and kissed her warmly on the lips. "Well put." Then, glancing back at Skeeter's expression, she added, "I think it's time to open another bottle of wine."

Twenty-four

The weeks between Thanksgiving and Christmas passed in a blur. Mack had joined Gretchen and Frances in actively challenging the development, and the three had taken to holding their planning sessions in Zoë's kitchen, so that she could take notes for her article. Sometimes Skeeter dropped by after work with a six-pack of Budweiser, a look of almost painful longing on his face whenever he turned in Gretchen's direction. Yet despite his unrequited crush, Skeeter was the most clearheaded of the group when it came to articulating what was at stake.

"The thing is," he said one night, after Frances launched into an impassioned attack on Moroney, "you don't want to go around saying that you're antidevelopment. This town is going to change in the next few years," he said. "The question is, what kind of change? If we let Moroney and his crew convince people it's us versus them, working-class country against rich city folks, then Moroney's going to be the one deciding how the town gets developed."

"He's right," said Mack. "And maybe we need to change our name from Arcadia Wetlands Foundation to something . . . broader. So it doesn't sound like all we care about is endangered turtles."

"How about Arcadia Progressive," suggested Zoë, looking up from her notes. "Nobody can accuse you of being antiprogress when it's right in your name, but you can argue that it's more forward-thinking to preserve the attributes that make the town so attractive."

"I didn't think you found the town particularly attractive," said Mack.

"I think it needs a bagel shop, a bookstore, and a couple of cute boutiques, not a bunch of big box stores with parking lots large enough to house a fleet of RVs for a week."

"And that can be our slogan," said Mack. "We'll need to print up bumper stickers."

Zoë whacked him lightly over the head with the local newspaper. "Listen, Truck Boy, you want pithy? I'll give you pithy." She unfolded the newspaper and read, "'Town Board of Arcadia votes against proposed zoning ordinance. "Way I see it, no zoning is better than bad zoning," says Bill Gunnison, a local horse farmer.' Which, by the way, was what you said at the dinner table—your lovely brother-in-law stole your quote. And that is the end of the article. No dates given for the meeting, no discussion of the issue, no comment from the opposing camp." She flipped the paper open, checking the byline. "Who is this reporter? And who edits this crap?"

"That's a dollar," said Maya, who was sitting in a corner, studying a book on horse anatomy.

Mack took the paper from Zoë's hand, letting his fingers brush hers. "As far as I know, Pete Grell's wife was editing the paper, but she's been busy taking care of him after his stroke. And she was always looking for reporters—all you need is a high school diploma and a car, and you're hired."

"Would she let me submit an article?"

Mack grinned. "She'd let you take over the paper if you wanted it. She's been looking to retire for about five years now."

And despite the fact that Zoë had no intention of remaining in

Arcadia past the spring, she felt a sudden burst of excitement at the thought of turning the local rag into a real paper. She looked down at the patchily laid-out front page and had a flash of understanding as to why Bronwyn was so pulled to adopting stray and abandoned dogs. There was this newspaper, neglected and ugly and incomplete, all but gazing up at her with big, sad eyes and pleading to be made right. Most seductive of all was the thought that if she didn't do it, no one would. That was perhaps the biggest difference between the city and the country: in the city, there was the electricity of competition. In the country, there was the surprisingly powerful charge of knowing that your skills were needed.

Mack touched her shoulder. "What are you thinking?"

"To tell you the truth, I was thinking about what you just said about the paper needing people."

"All you need to do is get your driver's license." Zoë laughed. "Shoot, I forgot that part. Guess I'm missing the really crucial skill."

"But you're learning." Zoë found herself unable to look away from Mack's steady, warm blue gaze, and for the first time in her life, she had a fantasy of what life might be like living permanently in the country, with a loving man and a job that brought her into contact with living human beings once in a while.

"So, what do you think, Zoë?"

"What?" Zoë turned back to Frances, who'd been poring over the agreement between the town board and the Amimi Mountain Development Project. "Oh, sorry, Frances, I was thinking about something else."

"I was asking if you knew any lawyers."

"Especially lawyers who want to donate some free time," amended Gretchen. "And there's so many of those."

"Actually, I might be able to help you there," said Zoë. She had not been talking to Bronwyn as often as she used to, and she felt faintly guilty calling her up. On the other hand, Zoë thought that doing some work that did not have to do with toddlers would be very good for her friend.

"Come on, Bron," she said, carrying the phone into the other room, away from the others. "It's only for two days. All you have to do is hop on the train, and we can help you with the twins," said Zoë. "And Mack says the boys would love the town's parade of lights this weekend."

"I don't know," said Bronwyn. "It's so close to Christmas, and I'm just so tired."

"The fact is, we need your legal expertise."

"My what?"

"You know the article you talked me into doing? Well, the group that's trying to get responsible zoning for the town needs a lawyer."

"I'm a zombie mom of two. Surely they can do better than hire a person so sleep-deprived she can barely remember where she puts her keys."

"This is the country, Bron. It's you or nobody. And if this development goes through, a lot of baby turtles and innocent wood ducks are going to be flattened by progress."

"Zoë, this is blackmail. And unlike you, I am nominally Christian, and therefore expected to actually celebrate the birth of the Christ child. Which means that I need to find a way to buy and wrap things, which I still haven't done because I never have a break from the boys."

"That's what the internet is for. Meanwhile, without your legal expertise, little baby foxes will be steamrollered flat. Possums paved into speed bumps. And besides," Zoë said more softly, "I miss you. I'm having the best sex of my life and I don't have anyone to tell about it."

"You're having the best . . . this driving instructor is the best?"

"You know what my feet are like, right?"

"I try not to think about them, but yes."

"Well, he sucks my toes."

There was a momentary silence, and then Bronwyn let out a long-suffering sigh. "Okay, so how the hell am I going to pack enough to keep the twins entertained for two hours on the train?"

Zoë gave out an exultant whoop. "You're coming!"

"I'm coming."

Despite Mack's inspired attempts to convince her to drive to the train station, Zoë refused to take the wheel after five PM, when the sky began to grow dark.

"I don't care if you do spank me," she said. "I'm not doing it."

"What if I promise never to spank you again unless you drive?"

"Sorry, Mack. First of all, I can barely force myself to drive when the sun is shining and the sky is clear. Second of all, I have terrible night vision." She tapped her glasses. "I can barely see where I'm walking at night."

"That's why you have headlights. And you'll drive more slowly. But you're going to have to learn sometime," he said. "The world doesn't stop after the sun goes down."

"Around here it does." Zoë slid into the front passenger seat, suddenly filled with a fierce longing for the city, with all its lights and noise and activity. She had learned that in Arcadia and all the surrounding towns, stores closed at five, leaving only the occasional porch light or flickering television to offset the early darkness.

Of course, it wasn't all bad. She quite enjoyed the evenings, sitting with Mack and Maya around the roaring fireplace, listening to music or watching a movie together. The small video shop in town, which hadn't even switched to renting out DVDs yet, had a quirky collection of eighties action-adventure films, Sundance Film Festival selections, and classic Hollywood comedies. Zoë usually wound up renting the latter, so that Maya had finally gotten a chance to see Carole Lombard as a charmingly deranged heiress. Zoë thought her daughter might have given her a speculative look after seeing Carole and her butler winding up in an embrace, but didn't think Maya really knew that she and Mack were a couple. They had been extremely discreet, never touching each other when Maya was home from school.

On this particular evening, however, Maya was over at Moira's house, helping her get the horses' manes braided with ribbon for the town parade. Bill had made good on his threat, and had not come back after the debacle of Thanksgiving dinner.

Moira, who no longer wanted to sell the farm, did not seem as upset as Mack would have expected, given the duration of the marriage.

"Tell me something," Mack said, as he put the car into gear. "Do you think Moira's doing all right on her own?"

"I think so," said Zoë. "Sometimes anticipating a change can be worse than the change itself."

Mack shot her a sideways glance. "Is that the way it was with you?"

"I was never married."

"I'm talking about leaving the city."

Zoë thought about it, remembering the emptiness and despair of her early days. Looking back on it, she realized how unhappy she had been. "Yes," she said at last. "I don't mind being here so much anymore." She paused. "Well, parts of being in the country I more than just don't mind. Parts of it I like. A lot."

"Just like?"

"Maybe more than just like."

And for some reason, even though they had already invoked the word "love," this use of the word "like" lingered in the air between them as if it were the expression of some deeper commitment.

Breaking all his own rules about safety, Mack took her hand in his and held it, driving one-handed the rest of the way to the station.

* * *

Bronwyn's reaction to the house was completely unexpected. "My God," she kept saying as she went from room to room, "it's incredible. Look at all this space. Look at your backyard! Oh, God, imagine it in spring, the twins could run around outside and . . . Zoë, I may just have to move out here with you."

"Don't tease me."

"I'm not sure I'm teasing. Oh," she said as they reached the bathroom. "A clawfoot bathtub." Bronwyn turned on Zoë, eyes narrowed. "How could you not have mentioned this? And the faucets?"

"What about them?"

"They're vintage. Look, one for cold and one for hot. I love it!"

Bronwyn also loved the octagonal window on the upper floor, the chenille bedspread, and the tin-top table. "This is what replaces sex in women's fantasies, you know. One day, you look at all the magazines that promise to help you flatten your tummy, please him in bed, and choose the right pair of jeans, and you think, I don't care if I'm flabby or how my jeans fit and I really don't care whether or not I'm pleasing him in bed, because he's sure as hell not pleasing me out of it. So you start looking at the magazines that promise to help you make your kitchen look like it belongs in an old farmhouse, complete with recipes for zucchini bread and an easy-to-plant herb garden. You dream about what it would be like to sit somewhere beautiful, with something delicious to eat and a few good friends to share it with."

"You never told me I was living your fantasy when you were begging me to come back to the city."

"Well, I'm coming around to thinking that maybe it's me who should leave." Bronwyn pointed to Zoë's favorite painting of a Cyclops and his mod girlfriend, which Mack had hung over her bed. "That just doesn't go here." She gestured at the picture of a heavily pregnant Zoë, which Mack had also hung in the bedroom, confessing that it had turned him on the first time he'd seen it. "And neither does that."

"What are you saying, that I should change my tastes to suit the house?"

"Oh, I don't know. It's just . . . this is so peaceful. So comforting. You want a nice landscape or a portrait . . . but on the other hand, you're right, you have to be you." Bronwyn took a deep breath. "Oh, listen to that."

"Listen to what?" Mack had driven home an hour earlier, Maya and the boys had gone to sleep, and aside from the faint sounds that old houses always make, sighing as they settle themselves for the night, everything was quiet.

"Exactly." Bronwyn curled up on Zoë's bed. "You know what? I could move here. The boys could go to a normal, stress-free pre-school, I could hang here with you—we could even get a dog!"

"It's a nice fantasy, but I don't intend to stay here next year." Zoë turned her back on her friend as she pulled off her shirt and unhooked her brassiere. "The plan was always for us to give Maya a kick-start and then return to Manhattan."

Bronwyn looked bemused. "You know, for some reason I always assumed that even though you said you were coming back, you'd wind up loving it here."

Zoë shook her head. "There are things I love about it, but I'm a city girl."

"And I suppose I am, too. But maybe we could share the place for the summer?"

Zoë pulled on the black silk underwear she'd been wearing since the weather changed. "That's a nice idea, but how would your husband feel?"

Bronwyn gave a contemptuous little laugh. "He might not even notice. I mean, how often does Brian see the boys and me, anyhow? And he could always commute on weekends."

"You don't think he'd miss you not living in the same city during the week?"

"I doubt it. He'd probably be relieved." Bronwyn looked out the window, with its pretty gingham curtains that clashed with Zoë's embroidered Middle Eastern pillows and her postmodern artwork. "Hey, look, it's starting to snow."

They both peered as the first flakes began to tumble down, silvered by moonlight. "Maybe it's a mistake to expect men to be real partners. Our brains are different. Our way of processing information is different. What do they say, men compartmentalize, women synthesize? I know I could raise children with you and not feel like I'm sharing a home with a complete stranger. I wouldn't have to explain to you what intimacy is. We could work side by side, raising children together, cooking meals and then watching old movies in the evenings. Who needs men?"

Zoë dragged a brush through her hair, temporarily smoothing out the thick waves. "Well, they do have their uses. And Mack actually does some of that stuff with me. Hey, want a late-night cookie?"

"You bet." Bronwyn followed her down the stairs. "You know, it stands to reason that the completely inappropriate guy likes to cook and cuddle on the couch. He cuddles, right? Besides being a sex god?"

Zoë opened up the kitchen cabinet and pulled out a box of chocolate chip cookies.

"He's a cuddler." She bit into her cookie. "And he's also . . . I don't know about sex god, but let's just say that when it comes to physical intimacy, he has a lot of range."

"I think I'm jealous." Bronwyn took a cookie from the box. "I want a boy toy, too."

Zoë laughed. "He's not exactly a boy. Or a toy."

"So what is he, your soulmate? You get into long, heartfelt talks about carburetors and fan belts?"

"He's a little deeper than that. Besides, what do you and Brian spend your time talking about, the meaning of life?"

"We used to, back in the day. Look, I'm not saying I have a great relationship at the moment. But if you don't start out with a common frame of reference, then what's going to happen when the shiny new rubs off?" Bronwyn gazed out the window, where the lawn was now covered by a thin veil of snow. "I say, enjoy the sex, but don't lose sight of what this is, and what it isn't."

"You're making it sound like this is just about sex."

"Isn't it?"

"Look, Mack and I may not be built for the long haul, and he may not know who's being skewered in the pseuds page of *Private Eye*, but he's not some stupid redneck I'm screwing for fun."

"Zoë, I may not have had it in a long time, but I do remember that good sex is never just about sex, any more than a great restaurant experience is just about the food. But you're a forty-one-year-old international journalist, and he's a twenty-something car buff who probably hasn't read a novel since high school."

"Thirty-something. And not everyone's a reader, Bron. There are different kinds of intelligence."

"Oh, please." Bronwyn closed the box of cookies. "He's a fling, Zoë. And if you start believing there's more to it than that, you're going to be pretty damn disappointed when he leaves you for some blond checkout girl at the local Stop and Shop."

As if this were the cue for some unseen stage director, the lights went out, the refrigerator giving a long, last whine before subsiding into silence.

"Jesus Christ, what happened?"

"It must be the snow. I think Mack left a flashlight in a drawer somewhere." Fumbling around, Zoë banged her knee. "Ow!"

"What is it?"

"Nothing. Okay, found it." Zoë turned on the flashlight, illuminating her friend's worried face.

"How long before the lights come back on?"

"I don't know, Mack said it can take anywhere from five minutes to overnight. It used to take longer, but I think they've been working on the lines."

"So what do we do now?"

"I guess we go to sleep."

"I can't just go to sleep. It's too early. Besides, I always need to watch some TV or read something before I nod off."

"I don't think that's an option."

"What if the twins wake up? How will I ever find my way to them upstairs? What if they need something from the kitchen?"

"I think we'll all just have to make like the pioneers and sleep until it's light," said Zoë, who had gotten used to the fact that the country didn't always provide one with a multitude of alternatives.

"Jesus. How often does this happen?"

"I think Mack said it's gotten better in the past few years."

"No wonder your car boy's so good in the sack. There's nothing else to do around here during a power failure."

Zoë didn't say anything for a moment, thinking, The reason Mack's so good in bed is because he pays attention to everything that isn't said out loud. She felt a flash of intense irritation with Bronwyn, knowing that all that talk about moving to the country had been just that—talk. But she refrained from saying anything, not wanting to start an argument in the dark. There was a faint scuffling sound, and Bronwyn gave a sharp squeal of alarm.

"What was that?"

"Probably just the cat."

"Are you sure there wasn't just someone at the door?"

Zoë wasn't sure. Funny how you never noticed how much

sound even a quiet house made, she thought, until the electricity died and you became aware of the stillness. It must have been much harder to sneak up on people in the old days, before you had all the distractions of modern life. Zoë felt her way to the door and opened it, letting in a rush of cold air. "Hello?" It was still snowing outside, the brickwork now a shimmering blanket of white. The moonlight made it easier to see outside than in.

"Any ax murderers out there?" asked Bronwyn, coming up behind her.

There was a thump as Claudius jumped from a low stone wall and streaked into the house.

"I think maybe I will be able to sleep." Bronwyn yawned. "All this tension is making me tired. You?"

"I'll be up in a minute." Zoë remained by the open door, wondering how much of what she'd been feeling with Mack was due to the isolation of her current circumstances, and not quite convinced that someone besides the cat had been standing by the door, listening to the end of their conversation.

Twenty-five

The problem with romantic relationships, Mack decided as he drove to Zoë's house, was that you were never in the same one as the person you happened to be sleeping with. With Jess, he'd been in a comfortable, friends-with-benefits situation, while she'd been in a frustrating dead-end affair with someone who wouldn't commit. With Zoë, he'd been in a serious, mind and body connection that had left him thinking about taking the next step, while she'd been entertaining herself with the hired help. There are different kinds of intelligence, she'd said to that pissed-off friend of hers, and then the friend had said, "Oh, please," and Mack had waited, knowing he should announce himself and walk in, but needing to know what Zoë would say when she didn't know he was listening.

And she'd said nothing. Her friend had dismissed him as a meaningless fling, and Zoë hadn't denied it. Sure, he could pretend that she would have defended him if the lights hadn't gone out, but she'd already taken two beats too long to respond. And then the friend had summed it all up perfectly: *No wonder your car boy's so good in the sack. There's nothing else to do around here.* Making it perfectly clear that Zoë had explained what he was good at.

It was what Adam used to call a reality disconnect. "It's not just that we don't share the same view of the world as these guys," he'd said one night. "We don't share the same world."

"Bullshit," Mack had replied. They'd been crammed up together in the rear of a Humvee, pretending they weren't lying ass to ass in search of a little warmth. Outside, the wind was whipping and wailing, filling the armored vehicle with the surprising nighttime chill of the desert. "Reality is reality. If a dead body is lying on the ground, it's a dead body, no matter what I think it is."

"Yeah, right. So if you go and burn that dead body, because it's just a bunch of meat that's going to rot and spread germs, then you've taken a reasonable action—in your reality. But in someone else's reality, you've just desecrated the corpse of their brother, and you've broken a serious taboo."

"So we have different customs, we see things differently. But there's only one reality."

"Because reality is created out of actions, and not perceptions? But who is perceiving the actions, and interpreting them?"

Impressed, and feeling a little outclassed, Mack had tried to make a joke out of it. "Jesus, man, you're a fucking philosopher."

"Yeah, well, what else are you going to think about when you're facing the distinct possibility of being blown up every day?"

"I don't know about you big-city intellectual types," Mack had said, adhering to the script their friendship had been using for more than a year, "but thinking about sex works fine for me." He'd waited for Adam to say something back about ignorant rednecks, but his friend had remained silent for so long that Mack had assumed he'd gone to sleep. And then, out of the blue, Adam had asked, "You ever get scared?"

"Sometimes, sure."

"Lately, I got this feeling, like my luck's run out."

"Don't be stupid."

"I keep thinking, What if this is it? The last night. The last day."

Adam had rolled over, his face inches from Mack's. "You never feel like that? You never think, So many things I haven't done?"

"Sure I do. Everyone does. But you have to shake it off."

Adam had paused. "What if I can't?"

The silence stretched on, changing the meaning of their last spoken words. Mack had felt a clench of excitement in his stomach, mingled with repulsion. And, somewhere mixed in with it, curiosity. For a moment, he had thought he might actually do it, might close that small, crucial distance, just to find out what lay on the other side.

What had stopped him, in the end, had been the fear that what they had, their strange friendship that was unlike any friendship he'd ever had before in his life, might change into one of those godawful things where the other person feels something for you that you can't reciprocate.

"I have to take a piss," he'd said, rolling away, and when he'd come back, Adam had been faking sleep. The shit of it was, it had been ruined anyway. Something had shifted between the two of them, because they both knew that there was a reality disconnect. What Adam had felt for him was not what he had felt for Adam. And if his friend hadn't died, they probably would have wound up drifting further and further apart.

If he'd known that Adam was going to die, he wouldn't have left the Humvee, of course. It was funny, thinking back about what Bill had said at Thanksgiving. Maybe he was right about Mack. Everyone thought that when you knew you could die at any moment, everything had so much more meaning. And it did, but it also had so much less. So what if your last meal was beef stew? So what if you let a friend touch you? When you dealt with death all the time, you could feel how easy it would be to let the things that defined you just fall away.

Mack looked to his right and suddenly realized that he'd arrived at Zoë's house without being conscious of the past few miles. *Great.* If your body's driving and your mind's not engaged, that's a recipe for disaster, he always told his students. Mack slammed the car door, zipping up his down vest. It felt like it might snow again, although none had fallen yet.

He knocked on the door. "You ready?"

"That we are." Zoë came out, wearing a woolly white hat and a big fringed scarf, and it occurred to him that she wouldn't notice that he hadn't kissed her, because Maya was around, and he couldn't have kissed her anyway. "Did you have any problem with your power? Because our lights went out last night." He wondered if she was testing him.

"We didn't have any trouble. Your power back on now?"

"Everything's fine now," she said. He made no comment.

"How are we going to fit everyone in one car," asked the friend, who was carrying one twin and holding the other by the mittened hand. "I need help with the car seats."

"It's only a two-minute drive into town," said Mack. "Can the boys sit on your laps in the back?"

The friend gave him a hard look. "No, we could not. There is snow on the ground."

"No problem."

"Excuse me, but when I say there is a problem, there is a problem."

"No, I meant, I'll take care of it. Look." Mack took the two car seats from the porch and wrestled them into place. "If Maya can sit on a grown-up's lap in the back, then we should be fine. Do you mind being a little squashed for a few minutes, Maya?"

"Nope."

It took a few more minutes of searching underneath thighs for seat-belt buckles, and then they were ready to roll, Mack acutely aware of Zoë beside him, and of her friend in the back. Her best friend. Maya touched the back of his hair. "It's so long now. You going to cut it, or would that make you lose your strength?"

"I don't think it was the hair cutting that sapped Samson," Mack said, keeping his eyes on the road. "I think he was just upset because Delilah let him down."

"Maya, don't distract him," said the friend.

Mack wondered if she even knew she was jealous. Not that she had any reason to be. Clearly, she was the person Zoë felt she could talk to, the one she dreamed about moving in with. He wondered if he would still want to screw around with Zoë after her friend had gone back to the city and Maya had returned to school. Would it feel better or worse to be physically close, now that he knew that was all it was? Maybe it was better to make a clean break.

They parked at the edge of town and walked to the grassy park below the clock tower, where a crowd had already gathered. Yesterday's snow hadn't melted away, and Arcadia looked like an old picture postcard, the doors of its Victorian gingerbread houses hung with winter wreaths, living room fires visible inside a few Colonials. A few people waved at him, and he saw Deanna from the diner and waved back. Despite the frigid air, Mack felt a prickle of nervous sweat on his upper lip as they moved closer into the press of bodies. *Not a bunch of strangers here, no potential terrorists, these are your neighbors so fucking hold it together.* Mack forced himself to keep inching forward, ashamed of the way his heart was pounding. When he glanced back at their group, he saw that Bronwyn was struggling to get one of the boy's mittens on his hand while balancing the other boy on her hip.

"You want me to take one of them?" Not that she deserved help, but if he was taking care of someone else, he knew the panic would subside.

"Thanks," she said, giving him a genuine smile for once. Mack propped the kid on his side and pointed to the fire engines idling around the corner.

He turned to the boy, who was all huge eyes. "You like parades?"

"Yeah!" The little boy bounced up and down, and Mack said, "Steady, now," tightening his grip. He could feel his own pulse slowing down as he scanned the crowd.

"I didn't know the town had this many people," Zoë said, putting a hand on his arm.

Mack flinched, then tried to hide his reaction by readjusting the kid. Zoë's hand fell away; she thought he was rejecting her. Maybe he was. "Some of them are weekenders."

"Okay, everybody, move back," said a hearty voice, amplified by a handheld loudspeaker. Mack scowled, recognizing Jim Moroney's lying face under the big fake white Santa beard. He'd stuffed a pillow under his red-and-white tunic, not that he needed to, and was having a swell time telling everyone where to go. "That's it, folks, we need to clear the road now."

"Santa," said the little boy in Mack's arms.

"Satan," Mack corrected him.

"Satan! Satan!"

Luckily, someone chose that moment to blast out a recording of "Jingle Bells," drowning out the kid's squeals.

"We're going to need your cooperation," Moroney boomed into his loudspeaker. "Everyone move to the sides and we can begin!"

It was a pretty standard small-town parade, with the fire trucks blasting their horns, and the tractors pulling hay wagons filled with waving Boy Scouts, and Sam Dickenson of Dickenson Tractor Supply waving from his flagship vehicle, which was decorated with fairy lights. Moira rode alongside one of her clients down Main Street, doing something that made the horses raise their hooves up as if they were marching. Mack waved at her, glad that she hadn't canceled because of Bill.

Zoë grabbed his arm. "Tell me that's not what I think it is," she said, pointing at one of the last floats.

"What do you think it is?"

"A Porta-Potty on wheels, lit up with Christmas lights and—oh, my God—is that supposed to be Santa in there?"

"It's a little free advertising for Jerry Bix, who rents the units out."

"Nobody objects to having a portable toilet on parade?"

"Even small-town folks understand irony, Zoë." A little embarrassed by his own harshness, Mack turned away from her, watching the tractor pulling the Arcadia Preschool float as it chugged down the street. A few elf-hatted parents and teachers threw hard candies into the crowd.

The toddler on his hip struggled to be put down, so he could scramble for Tootsie Rolls and sucking candies along with the older kids.

"Go," he said, "go!"

"Sorry, little guy, I don't want you to get run over."

"No!" The boy's face screwed up as if he were about to explode.

"Hey, now, no crying. Look, the parade's just about over." Two girls walked in the rear, twirling batons. One of them waved at Mack. "Mr. Mackenna, you still giving lessons? You weren't at the school when I went back."

It was the plump blond girl, the one whose poetry book he'd swiped. "I started my own driving school."

"Good, because I don't like that Jim Moroney at all," the girl said, nearly dropping her baton. Her friend said something that made her duck her head and giggle, and then they were gone, moving on ahead with the rest of the parade.

"More," said the toddler in his arms, craning his neck. "More fire truck."

Mack gave the kid a squeeze. His cheek smelled like curds. "I know, but those fire trucks got to go fight some fires."

"Fight," agreed the kid, pumping his fist in the air.

Moroney was back, shouting at everyone to come around town hall for some hot chocolate and Christmas cookies. "And don't forget to look at the exciting new plans for the development behind the post office!"

Just then, someone grabbed the loudspeaker. "Don't forget to tell them about the paybacks you took to approve those plans."

"What the . . ." Moroney turned around, startled, as Frances continued addressing the crowd.

"Not to mention the laws you broke in order to pander to these big developers."

"Somebody get this crazy lady off of me," Moroney bellowed.

"Look," said a child in the crowd, "Santa's hurting that lady."

"Get off, Frances," shrieked Maya, breaking away from her mother.

"Oh, shit, Mack, she's going to get hurt."

Mack looked around but couldn't see Bronwyn. Still carrying the little boy, he joined Zoë, who was looking furious as two police officers tried to pull Frances away. They were hampered by Gretchen, who had joined in the tussle and was shouting, "Ask Moroney what happened to the bald eagle nest off of Route Eighty-two! Ask him about the impact the development is going to have on the town's school system!"

Moroney tried to twist away from Gretchen. "Get off me, you lesbo freak!"

"You're the freak," shouted Maya, and then Skeeter was there, trying to get in between Gretchen and Moroney. Mack felt useless, but he couldn't help anyone without endangering the kid in his arms. "Hang on," he said. "You're not scared, are you?"

"No," squealed the boy, bouncing with excitement. "This is fun!"

An off-duty state trooper, not recognizing Skeeter as a townie, took one look at his black leather jacket and brought out his billy club.

"Police brutality," shouted Frances.

"Maya, get over here," yelled Zoë, but the fight had spread, as might have been expected in a crowd with so many present and former police officers and firefighters. "Mack, I need help!"

Finally spotting a frantic Bronwyn in the crowd, Mack handed the little boy over to her and shouldered his way into the melee, but he couldn't find Maya. He did see Moroney, who was pointing a finger at Frances as a cop Mack didn't recognize closed in on her.

"You son of a bitch," said Mack, closing in on Moroney. Miraculously, marvelously, all his fear was gone, replaced with a clear, sharp fury. Then he spotted Maya. "Jesus, your mother's going mental, get over here and let me . . ." Moroney clocked him when he wasn't looking, and Mack stumbled back, falling into someone's arms.

"You okay?" It was Zoë.

Mack shook his head. "No, I am not fucking okay. He sucker punched me. Again!"

"That's not fair," yelled Maya. "Get him back, Mack!"

"I can't," said Mack, standing up and spitting on the sidewalk. "He has a weak heart."

"Oh, I do, do I?" Moroney punched him again, knocking Mack to the ground this time. The crowd drew silent, and suddenly Mack found himself next to his ex-boss, in the middle of a circle.

"Punch him back," someone shouted—it sounded a lot like Deanna from the diner.

"He doesn't have the guts," taunted another female voice. Jess.

Moroney circled him, slowly rotating his fists. "Come on, Mack," he said. "You want to prove something? Go on and prove it." He'd pulled down his Santa beard.

"You want to hurt? Fine." Mack gave him a short, fast jab that sank into the pillow strapped to Moroney's stomach.

"Ha," said Moroney. "You call that a punch?"

And then Mack lost it, and did what he hadn't done in years and years. Fought like a Ranger, deflecting Moroney's punch with his left hand, simultaneously punching out with his right, then dropping to kick out with both his legs, knocking the older man to the ground.

He circled the man, ready, and as Moroney struggled to his feet, Mack moved in again, chopping near the windpipe with his right, sending his opponent crashing back down the the street.

"Jesus, Mack, stop, I think he's really hurt!"

Mack knelt down. Moroney was lying with his eyes closed, his breathing fast and shallow. For a moment, Mack thought, Good. And then, right behind the satisfaction came another feeling: fear. And he remembered why he'd made the switch to being a medic. Not because it was hard to kill but because it wasn't. Because he'd been afraid that if he kept on soldiering in a war zone, he might not be able to make the transition back to civilian life. He'd be like the assholes who came off the interstate doing ninety miles an hour and didn't apply the brakes until they plowed someone down on Main Street.

"Shit," he said. *Assess the patient's condition.* "Jim, can you open your eyes? Tell me where it hurts."

"Don't you dare touch me," said Moroney, his voice a hoarse croak. "My chest . . . ah, Jesus, I need a doctor." A thin snow had begun to fall on his ruddy face, making the scene even more heartrending.

Mack looked up at the surrounding crowd. "Is there a doctor here?" No reply. Shit. He searched the faces staring down at them until he saw her. "Zoë, can you get my medical bag from the back of the car?" He threw her the keys.

"On my way," she said.

"You're going to be okay," he reassured Moroney, who was lying with eyes closed and jaw clenched. "Where does it hurt?"

"It's going to hurt you, Mack," Moroney promised, and when he opened his eyes, there was no pain in them, only a sharp, calculating look, coupled with a gleam of malicious satisfaction. "You think you're going to have a driving school after this? I'm going to press charges, asshole. I'm talking assault and battery on a government official, and considering the fact that you've had Special Forces training and knew that I had a potential heart condition, maybe we can even argue for aggravated assault."

It was such a perfect revenge, Mack wondered if Moroney had planned it. A criminal record would mean he couldn't teach driving. Jesus, it might even mean he couldn't work as an EMT. Aggravated assault on the town supervisor was going to get him banned from the town squad, and beating up a former patient wasn't exactly going to thrill any other potential employers. And the hell of it was that Moroney probably hadn't planned anything, Mack had just dived headfirst into this cluster fuck. Shit. There was a reason he didn't like crowds. Whenever you had a large group of people gathered together, you could never fully anticipate the repercussions of your actions, and you sure as hell couldn't control them. Keeping his face carefully blank, Mack watched as Zoë returned with his medical bag.

"Thanks," he said. "Listen, I think you'd better let Skeeter take you all home."

"Sure," said Zoë, looking so calm and practical that he felt a misguided wave of affection. "Are you going to take him to the hospital?"

"No," Mack said, as the ambulance pulled up. He glanced sideways at the off-duty state troopers, who were muttering something about assault and battery. Either the troopers hadn't seen Moroney hit him first, or else they didn't care. Maybe they just liked Moroney. Maybe he was paying them off with favors. On the other hand, Mack reasoned, it could just be that cops take a dim view of a guy with serious hand-to-hand combat training whaling on a fat bastard in a Santa suit. Mack thought about arguing his case and felt a sudden wash of bone-deep fatigue. He became aware of a throbbing pain in his right knee where he'd landed badly on the pavement. "I think I'm headed for another state-operated facility."

Zoë turned in the direction of his gaze, taking in the huddle of confabbing state troopers, Moroney's malignant glare, and the general aura of impending doom. "Maybe I should remain behind," she said.

"That's all right. I think I know a way to placate the authorities."

She hesitated, and Mack had the urge to kiss her good-bye. He resisted it. "Go on, Maya is probably freezing."

"You'll call me later and tell me what happened?"

"Sure," he lied. He figured that Zoë would find out eventually, either from Skeeter or Moira. And although he was pretty numbed out at the moment, he wasn't above feeling a mean stab of pleasure at the thought of her remorse when she learned he'd reenlisted.

Twenty-six

Throughout the next week, Zoë found herself unable to fall asleep. She would stand in the doorway of Maya's bedroom, watching her daughter's slender form sprawled atop the covers, and fight the urge to curl up beside her. She hadn't heard from Mack since the night of the parade. At first she'd waited for his call, and then, when the time had arrived to take Bronwyn back to the train station, she'd run outside without her coat, anxious to hear what had happened.

But it had been Rudy who had pulled up in her driveway, scratching the back of his neck and looking like he knew more than he was saying. At first Zoë had worried that something terrible had happened to Mack—a ruptured appendix, or some unexpected injury from the fight with Moroney. But then Rudy had said, No, Mack wasn't sick, he'd just said he couldn't come.

With no explanation.

Zoë changed the channel on the TV set. Infomercial. Cop show rerun. Reality show rerun. She watched for a moment, trying to figure out whether these were people who had been famous, wanted to be famous, or simply found it entertaining to air their dating, dressing, or child-rearing problems in public. Zoë had never understood why reality TV shows were so popular. Dishing out servings of reality was what journalists did, as they attempted to relate the story of an event with as much objectivity, accuracy, and relevant detail as possible. But there was nothing particularly real or instructive about stage-managing confrontations between prim has-beens and promiscuous wannabes. It catered to the worst, voyeuristic tendencies of an audience. I'm going to turn this program off, thought Zoë. In a minute. As soon as the drunk ex-starlet finishes having her tantrum.

The program broke to a commercial, and Zoë changed the channel and found a news program recorded earlier in the day. "Can your cat give you an incurable disease? You and your family might already be infected and not even know it. That story and the tragic tale of the hit-and-run granny in just a moment, but first, here's a look at a new trend—video therapy sessions for people in remote, rural areas."

Oh, yeah, that would work, thought Zoë. *I feel so lonely and isolated, Doctor. Why do you think you feel this way, Zoë? Wait a minute, you're not in focus.*

She changed the channel yet again, and found herself watching a Spanish soap opera. As far as she could tell, the man in the pirate shirt had been kidnapped by the woman in the leather pants, who either wanted to force the man to confess or have sex with her, or possibly both.

Too bad she couldn't try that with Mack. Because as cheesy as *Amor de mi vida* was, Zoë felt fairly certain that the show wouldn't disappear a major, recurring character without providing at least some kind of lame cover story to explain the sudden absence. And Mack had become a major, recurring character in her life, something she hadn't fully grasped until he'd dropped out of contact. I have an abandonment theme going, thought Zoë, surprised to find that Mack had secured himself a place alongside her father and

Maya's biological dad, forming an unholy trinity of men who had profoundly disappointed her.

Zoë overslept the next morning, and Maya shook her awake. "Mommy, we have to get ready for parent-teacher conferences."

"Oh, God, what time is it?"

"Almost nine."

Zoë surged out of bed. That was another thing she disliked about the country; there weren't any garbage trucks to wake you up on time. Fifteen minutes later, she was dressed and ready, if still not quite as wide awake as she would have liked.

"Is Mack taking us, Mommy?"

Zoë stared at her coffeepot, willing it to brew faster. "No, honey. I called him but he didn't answer."

"And you left a message?"

"Yes, I did."

"Did you speak to Moira, Mommy? Because she said I could come over and help as soon as school let out."

"I left a message for Moira and for Mack, but neither of them has called me yet. Which is why Rudy is going to drive us to your school today."

"I just don't understand it," said Maya, sounding miserable. "Why would they both just not call us? Maybe their phone's not working."

"Maybe. We'll try them again later."

"Because it's probably the phone. You know what the country is like."

Zoë gave her daughter what she hoped was a reassuring smile. Maya was wearing Moira's usual outfit, a brown turtleneck, flannel shirt, Wrangler jeans, and waterproof hiking boots—all purchased at the local Tractor Supply Company for so little cash that Zoë had bought herself a pair of jeans and a cowgirl shirt as well. "Now, you look like a local," Mack had told her. That had been less than two weeks ago. What the hell could have happened in the interim?

Zoë smoothed her daughter's blond hair back from her face, noticing that the shade was beginning to darken, from age or lack of sunlight, or both. "Sometimes things change, and people come into your life, and sometimes things change, and people fall out of your life." Not a lesson she'd wanted Maya to have to learn more than once.

"I just don't like changes that I don't even know are coming."

"Neither do I, baby."

Rudy arrived in a pickup truck filled with seasonal lawn decorations. Zoë wasn't sure if they were all destined for his own house or whether he was intending to sell them for additional income. He surveyed their lawn, which was still covered with a foot of snow, except for the path Zoë and Maya had inexpertly shoveled to the back door. "You don't have any holiday decorations up," Rudy noted.

"Not our holiday," Zoë pointed out.

"Don't you have something Jewish you can stick on the lawn? Or a light-up reindeer with moving head. That's not Christian."

"Oh, can we have one, Mommy?"

"We'll talk about it another time." On the drive to the school, Zoë ripped open the envelope she had retrieved this morning from the mailbox, belatedly remembering that she had to check it. Zoë shook the envelope and out tumbled her daughter's report card. Taking a deep breath, Zoë glanced at Maya, reassuring herself that the girl was engrossed in reading her book before opening the report. Zoë did not want Maya asking her to read it out loud, as experience had taught her to expect a lot of phrases such as "not making enough of an effort" and "continues to have trouble in decoding and recognizing core words," all of it sweetened by a closing assertion that Maya was charming, gregarious, and had a great sense of humor.

"Hey, Mommy," said Maya, "what are you reading?"

"Just some work papers," said Zoë, unable to believe her eyes.

English

Maya is making remarkable progress in her ability to analyze stories. She shows real insight and thoughtfulness as well as a solid grasp of the literature we are covering in class. Her reading is also improving by leaps and bounds, and given her enthusiasm, and interest, by the end of the year Maya may be at or near grade level.

"Mommy," said Maya, "what's wrong? Why are you crying?"

"Because I'm so happy," said Zoë. "Because I'm reading your report card." And because, although she didn't say it out loud, her big gamble had paid off. Maya was catching up, and they would be able to go back home to Manhattan. She didn't need to learn to drive, she didn't need to figure out how to fill the empty hours when Maya was gone and she wasn't working. Maya was going to be all right, and so was she. They were going back to the city. They could start looking for a new apartment immediately, maybe something closer to Bronwyn, maybe a two-bedroom in a brownstone for a change, with a little garden out back.

Zoë was so relieved and elated that she arrived at the school in a kind of haze, kissing Rudy's cheek as he parked the car, then absently waving to Maya as she went off to the library to play board games.

"Ms. Goren?" The reading specialist opened the classroom door. She was a large, soft woman with warm, slightly protruding eyes, and Zoë could see at first glance that she was a hot-water bottle of a teacher, all comfort and reassurance. "We're ready for you now."

Zoë settled herself into a small chair opposite the bovine reading instructor, the austere Ms. Weyr (who had dressed for the occasion in a pink ruffled blouse), and the head of the lower school,

Mrs. Benning, who resembled the beaming, active grandmothers who were always gardening, painting, and playing concert piano in arthritis medication commercials. Zoë listened to these three women as the golden words from the report card were repeated: remarkable progress, solid grasp, enthusiasm and interest, and the last four words that rang in her ears like a blessing from on high— reading approaching grade level.

"I can't tell you what this means to me," Zoë said, her eyes welling up with tears. "Maya has been so happy here, and she was actually reading a book in the car. And enjoying it! I am just so very grateful."

"We feel lucky to have Maya in our school," said Ms. Weyr, her square jaw softened by a genuine smile.

"I can't wait to see what she accomplishes next year," added the reading specialist.

"God, yes, I keep forgetting how close we are to January." Zoë took a deep breath, a little uncomfortable at bringing up the subject of changing schools. She didn't want to sound ungrateful, or as though she were anxious to leave the school because there was something wrong with it. But that was ridiculous. There was no reason for these women to feel insulted because she wanted to get Maya back into a mainstream school. After all, that was the whole idea, wasn't it? And she could be honest with them, explain how hard it had been for her to adjust to living in the country. Zoë straightened her shoulders.

"Speaking of next year, I realize that I'd better get going on the admissions process for next fall. I know Maya could always go back to her old school in Manhattan, but I've begun to think that a more structured class would be better for her."

"Excuse me," said the head of the lower school, tilting her graying blond head to one side. "But are you thinking of taking Maya out of the school?"

For some reason, Zoë felt her cheeks heat in a guilty blush. "Don't get me wrong, it's not that I don't love the Mackinley School, but the country isn't really my place, and now that Maya's doing so well . . ." She let her voice trail off.

"Oh, dear," said Mrs. Benning, exchanging looks with Ms. Weyr and the fluffy reading specialist. "I see we should have made ourselves a little bit clearer."

"When I said next year, I meant the next school year, in fifth grade," the reading specialist explained. "And I was assuming that Maya would be staying on. Because while it's true that she's reading at near grade level, a child of her intelligence should be reading well above."

"And since fourth grade is an important, transitional year, we never recommend removing a child from Mackinley at this point," added Mrs. Benning. "We've seen time and time again what happens when a student leaves us too early."

"They lose confidence, they feel pressured," offered Mrs. Weyr. Like the other women, she was gazing at Zoë with a combination of compassion and concern. "They go from feeling that they are doing well to feeling that they can't keep up. Especially in fourth grade. Up until that point, children learn to read, but afterward they are expected to read to learn."

Zoë looked from woman to woman. "But I thought her case was mild. A year, you said, would make a huge difference."

"And it has," said the lower school head, putting her rawboned, ringless hand over Zoë's limp fingers. "But we never said that she would spend only one year with us, Ms. Goren. We always recommend a minimum of two years for each child, and some stay far longer. I know you moved from Manhattan just for your daughter, and I know how hard that must have been. Believe me, you're not the first parent to feel like a fish out of water. But I really think we should give Maya at least two years to really consolidate her gains before mainstreaming her." She paused. "And as you just said, it would have to be the right school, one that doesn't make her feel like there's something wrong with the way her mind works."

For a long moment, Zoë clung to the fantasy of the brownstone. I don't have to listen to this, she thought. I have options. I can transfer Maya to another good school for dyslexics in Manhattan. Or else I can teach Maya at home, get her tutors. After all, this is my life, too. Surely it still matters whether or not I'm happy living here?

And then she flashed on the memory of sitting in her living room with Frances and Gretchen and Skeeter and Mack, thinking of alternative names for the Arcadia Wetlands Foundation. She remembered Mack saying the local newspaper needed an editor, and the seductive pull of that word: "needed." She remembered Mack, soaping her legs in the bathtub, asking her a question about journalism and listening intently to her response.

"Ms. Goren? Are you all right?"

"Yes," she said slowly, "I am. I'm just . . . readjusting myself mentally." Or having an epiphany, if that was the right word for a sudden realization that came not with a leap but with a thud. Because it was clear to her now that she had, in fact, been happy here in the country these past six weeks or more. She had been busy working on a story, she had made friends, she had found a lover who made her feel safe enough to play a little at danger.

She still longed for Manhattan the way Jews had traditionally yearned for the Promised Land, but Zoë could not lie to herself and say that she was buying her daughter's education at the price of her own misery.

"So are you rethinking your decision to take Maya out of school?"

"Yes, I . . . I guess I wasn't really thinking things through," Zoë said.

"You mustn't be hard on yourself. The main thing to remember is that Maya is doing wonderfully well," said the reading specialist. "And not just in the mechanics of reading, but also in analyzing content. Now, when something doesn't make sense to her, she knows how to go about figuring it out."

Zoë shrugged and smiled, trying not to show how close she was to crying. "I think I need to do more of that myself."

Because it was now painfully apparent to Zoë that she'd made two rather crucial mistakes. The first was pretending to herself that she could fix her daughter in the space of one year. She might not love the country or have cottage-and-garden fantasies, she might not want to spend the rest of her life here, but she had made the decision to move out here, and by God, she and Maya were going to get everything they could out of this experience. And if that meant two years, or three or four, then she would find a way to make that work. She'd learn to drive, so she wouldn't be housebound or dependent. She'd plan a way to spend more weekends in Manhattan. And she'd take advantage of the good things that the country did offer. Friends. Work. The challenge and rewards of moving out of her comfort zone.

The second mistake was a direct corollary of the first: treating Mack like a temporary lover, and believing for even one second that he would do the same to her.

Twenty-seven

M ack, this is ridiculous."

Mack kept his eyes on the television, which was showing an old repeat of *Monster Garage*. "I don't know what you're talking about."

"I'm talking about you, hiding out in your apartment, living on beer and Slim Jims." Moira began clearing empty bottles and plastic wrappers from the glass-covered NASCAR tire that he used as a coffee table. "How many damn car shows can you stand?"

Mack raised the longneck and took a long swallow of Bud. "Sounds like you're awfully eager to have me on that plane to Fallujah."

"Now, that's ridiculous, too. Why have you convinced yourself that you need to reenlist in the damn army just because of Jim Moroney? You've never cared what he thought before?" She looked at him more closely. "Or is this about Zoë? You know, if you don't answer her calls soon, I'm going to."

"I told you before, you talk to her. I'm heading to Kingston to reup."

"Well, if you made up your mind, why wait? No need to extend this little vacation in self-pityville for my sake."

Mack finally turned to look at his sister, who was standing with her hands full of his garbage. Well, he hadn't asked her to clean up after him, and he sure as hell wasn't thanking her for it. "I just figured I'd hole up till Christmas was over so you wouldn't be all alone. But seeing as how you feel so negatively about my presence..."

"Oh, yeah, like you're staying for me. Mack, let's face it, you don't want to go back to the army. You have a life here now, or at least you were beginning to, and that's where you want to be."

"Jesus, Moira, will you give it a rest? I already told you, I don't have a choice. If I stay here, Moroney's going to press charges."

"So fight him! Fight it!"

"I tried to fight him, Sis, and this is the happy result."

"Not with your fists, moron. Talk to Zoë, I'm sure she'll have an idea how to deal with his lies."

Mack snorted. "She's a journalist, not a lawyer. Besides, I don't think she's going to want to get in too deep here."

"Don't be stupid. She's... I mean, you're... I mean, you two are a couple. Of course she'd want to help."

"She's screwing me to amuse herself while she's stuck out here. That's not exactly a pledge of eternal devotion."

"It's more than that. Believe me, I know when a relationship is fake, and you and Zoë are the real deal."

"Yeah, you're a real expert."

Moira narrowed her eyes, then, without warning, opened her arms, showering him with empty cans and plastic wrappers. "You want to go back to war? Fine. Go. But don't pretend it's because you don't have any other choice."

"This is how it works," said Mack. "You either get to throw stuff, or you get the last word. Not both." He was paraphrasing the brilliant asshole doctor from some TV medical drama, but it still sounded good. His sister slammed the door, and Mack sat up, looking around at the mess. "Fuck," he said, to no one in particular. The truth was, he really didn't want to go. He wanted someone to stop him, just like in the movies, a big chase scene and Zoë telling him she loved him and they'd make it work. The whole town turning up in front of the local jail and showing its support. We love you, you're not just a stressed-out grunt with a bunch of issues, you're a hero, oh, and yeah, you're smart, too. And deep. Don't forget deep. And sensitive.

He reached under his couch and fished out his borrowed copy of the *Ardsley Anthology of Poetry*. Bunch of bullshit, really. Bunch of limp-wristed old assholes writing about death like they knew something about it. He ought to give the damn book back to that high school girl, or else throw it out. After all, what was the point of reading a lot of fancy words that didn't even tell a proper story? Opening the book at random, he found something he hadn't noticed before: "Lessons of the War."

And there it was again, the feeling that someone had just given him the coordinates for the terrain he was stuck in, the sense that someone else had noticed that the old maps just didn't describe what he was seeing anymore. Mack glanced at the date, and saw that Henry Reed had been writing about World War I. Fuck it, Mack thought. Taking a deep breath, he began to put on his boots.

The strange thing was, no one he'd ever met read poetry over there. The soldiers he knew all read porn and thrillers if they read anything. Well, maybe you didn't need poetry in a war zone. Maybe war was a kind of poetry, in the sense that it made ordinary things mean more, and mean different, and it mixed up death and life in ways that made you uncomfortable until it changed you. And honestly, he had to admit that he'd made a hash of civilian life. He hadn't even turned out to be a very good driving instructor, because when it came to the student he'd most wanted to reach, he'd failed miserably. Zoë might have passed her written test and gotten behind the wheel a few times, but she was as nervous and resistant as ever. He thought about Maya's school, and how they separated out all the components of reading, and how when you weren't naturally good at something you needed all the rules made explicit. How they took the fear and embarrassment out of the process. There had to be a way for him to use all that, he thought. Come up with a whole new system, make a difference. Or maybe you needed to approach things from the opposite end, and think about the design of the control panel. Was there a way to change the arrangement of the gauges and dials, or the shape of the wheel, so that it made more sense? For a moment, Mack felt a thrill of excitement, thinking about what he and Skeeter could do in the Big Dog Garage. There was probably a whole business to be made, redesigning cars so they were easier to learn on.

And then Mack felt the air go out of him. Who was he kidding? The minute he showed his face in town, Moroney was going to slam his ass in jail. And then the best he could hope for was a career cleaning toilets at the high school.

Mack stood up, swayed for a moment, then lurched toward his bed, where his old army rucksack was already packed. Shoot, maybe he should eat something besides little smoked jerky sausages to soak up some of that beer.

No, better keep moving. He could always stop by a McDonald's. On his way out the door, Mack remembered to turn off the television set. ". . . chance of snowstorms," said the blond meteorologist. He hesitated, thinking about turning it back on to hear the rest of the report, then decided not to bother. Instead, he opened the *Ardsley Anthology,* turning back to Henry Reed's poem about war and warring realities. As he read the opening lines, Mack found himself lulled by the steady rhythm of the poet's words, taken to a garden during weapons practice, distracted by the bees fumbling for honey as he fumbled to assemble his gun.

Yeah, and that's all the poem was—a distraction, not a goddamn set of instructions. He snapped the book shut and threw it on the bed, then shouldered his rucksack and headed out the door.

Twenty-eight

Zoë raced up the stairs to Moira's house, and knocked loudly. No response.

"I'll try the barn," said Maya, not bothering to hide her pleasure. "And say hi to the horses." Glad someone's having fun here, thought Zoë. She knocked again, then tried the door.

"Don't tell Mack," Rudy called from the car, "but you can try his apartment. The stairs go up the back of the barn." He pointed, and Zoë headed for the little apartment over the barn, realizing that she'd never even seen where Mack lived. She felt a moment of doubt.

Maybe this wasn't the relationship she'd thought it was. Maybe it had been a casual, physical thing, and he'd just gotten tired of her and hadn't had the maturity to end things in person.

Well, then, that's what I'm here to find out, Zoë thought, trying for composure. Here is your intrepid reporter, finding out. She knocked. "Mack? I know you don't want to talk with me, but I want to talk with you. And I think you owe me that." Silence. "Plus, I owe you money." More silence. "Not that I'm saying that you're in it for the money." God, this was awkward. "Mack, let me in."

"He's not there. You missed him by minutes."

Zoë turned to see Moira standing at the bottom of the stairs, wearing a dingy green coverall and looking older than she ever had before. "Where is he?"

"Going to kill himself."

"What?"

"He's off to reenlist."

"You've got to be joking. Without saying a word to me? What the hell happened?" The look on Moira's face made her add, "Does it have something to do with our relationship?"

"According to Mack, you're just screwing him for fun, and Moroney's going to have him arrested for assault if he stays."

"That's ridiculous!"

A hint of curiosity replaced the stoic blankness in Moira's expression. "Which part?"

"Both parts! Moroney can't arrest Mack for assault when he started the fight, and there are witnesses. Not to mention a lot of incriminating evidence that Moroney is five different kinds of corrupt. Which I intend to expose in an article. Or a series."

"And Mack's not just a way to pass the time while you're stuck in the boondocks?"

"No," said Zoë, slowly. "He's my lifeline here."

"Well," said Moira, "in that case, you'd better hightail it over to Kingston before your lifeline gets himself shipped to a war zone."

Zoë raced back to Rudy. "Do you know where the recruitment office in Kingston is?"

"Yeah, but Zoë, look at the sky. If we head out now, we stand a good chance of getting caught in a major storm."

"Rudy, Mack's going to reenlist!"

"I feel awful, Zoë, but I can't be stuck in Kingston all day. I promised my wife we'd visit her mother in hospice after I took you back home. The old lady doesn't have too long."

Zoë had a very uncharitable thought about Rudy and his never-ending supply of ailing relatives. Zoë ran back to Moira, who was now talking with Maya. "I need you to take me."

"Rudy can't?"

"Rudy won't. Moira, we have to hurry."

"I can't." Moira held up her right hand, and for the first time, Zoë could see that three of the fingers were splinted. "Not to mention a sprained ankle and bruised ribs."

Zoë looked at Maya. "I told you horses were dangerous."

"He was green. Look, Zoë, if you drive I can direct you."

"You've got to be kidding." A thought struck her. "Can't we just call him on his cell phone?"

"Of course!" Zoë fished her own phone out of her pocket and pressed his number. "Goddamn it, it went to voice mail."

"Maybe he's not getting reception because of the snow." They looked up at the sky, which was the unsettling, blank white that presages a storm. "Zoë, we have to do this."

"All right." Zoë took a deep breath. "Maya, I hate to break this to you, but you're going to stay with Rudy and visit his sick something or other."

"But Mom!"

"I'm not even sure I can drive, it's about to snow, and I don't want you in the backseat. Now go!"

"You'll be careful?"

Moira had hobbled into the barn and was now bringing an armful of blankets and a flashlight to her four-wheel-drive truck. "I'll take good care of your mommy. Remember, I'm the one who taught Mack to drive."

Maya gave Zoë one last beseeching look. "But now I'll miss the big smoochy bit."

"I'll miss it, too, if you don't run over to Rudy and tell him he's babysitting you."

"Good luck, Mommy," Maya said, giving her mother a quick

kiss. "I know you can do it." Then she was running toward Rudy, singing the dun-dun-dun chase music from *Mission: Impossible* at the top of her lungs.

* * *

"Okay, Zoë," said Moira, much more bracingly than Mack would have done, "you're doing fine, but try not to grip the wheel so tightly. Your knuckles are white. Now check both ways before pulling out into the road. Good."

"What now?" Zoë was too frightened to look at the other woman. She kept her eyes on the road, which looked narrower with snow banked on either side of it.

"Go straight until I tell you different."

Zoë hesitantly held the car to a straight line, all too aware that there were no driver-side brakes, let alone dual steering. "How am I doing?"

"About twenty miles an hour. Zoë, we're trying to catch him, not get there in time to wave good-bye to his carrier plane. Speed it up."

Zoë forced herself to step on the gas. "How's that?"

"The speed limit's forty-five here. Most people do sixty. You are traveling at a mind-boggling thirty miles per hour."

"Okay." Zoë stepped a fraction more on the gas pedal. "There."

"At this rate, we'll get there in time to congratulate him on his new deployment."

"I don't want to die!"

"We'll compromise. Forty miles, all right? That's slower than a funeral procession."

Zoë watched as the gauge moved up to forty. She tried not to imagine what a tree would feel like if encountered at this speed. "I'm doing it," she breathed.

"Now don't forget to turn with the road, that's it . . . you need to brake a little, Zoë, brake!"

Zoë recovered the turn, but only barely. Shaking with nerves, she tried to keep going, albeit a little more slowly.

"Mack did teach you to slow down before taking sharp turns, I assume?"

Miserably, Zoë nodded.

"Okay, no harm, no foul, bet next time you'll remember. Okay, now you're going ten miles an hour. Zoë, you need to speed it up!" Moira glanced behind them. "Shoot, there's a line of cars behind us. Pull over a little and let them pass."

Zoë watched as four cars whipped past them, each looking as irritated as a car can look. "Oh, God, there's no way we're going to catch him."

"Nonsense. Pull back onto the road and step it up to forty again. We have to make it, Zoë. And I don't think Mack's all that anxious to get to Kingston, anyway. Bet he's not taking the short way. If we cut across the back roads we can make up time."

"But it's starting to snow."

Moira reached over and flicked on the windshield wipers, then turned a knob at the end of the signal indicator. "There."

"What's that?"

"Just your headlights."

"I haven't learned headlights yet! Why the hell do they put them there?"

"Just concentrate on the road, Zoë."

"You keep trying to reach Mack on the phone." She saw what she thought was a squirrel, began to brake, and then realized it was a black plastic bag fluttering in the breeze.

"Jesus," Moira moaned, "she brakes for trash."

"Your brother is much more encouraging."

"Which is why you want him back. Okay, indicate right, we're going to take Starling Road over to . . . get over, Zoë, it's a blind corner and you have to keep to your side of the road. Yes. All right. Good."

"I'm doing it," said Zoë, amazed that she was still operating the vehicle. "I'm driving." She tapped on the gas, speeding up without being told as the road straightened out.

"Yes, you are. Now just keep an eye out for hidden drives, there are a lot of them on this road. You don't want someone charging out of their driveway and slamming right into you."

And then the snow began to fall in fast, steady flurries that obscured the road. Just as Zoë was about to ask what they should do, another car came barreling out from the left, smashing right into them.

Something hissed and then the world went white as the air bag deployed with a force that knocked all thought out of Zoë's mind.

A moment later, Zoë opened her eyes. "Oh my God, Moira," she said. "Are you all right?"

"Yeah," said Moira, sounding miserable as she gingerly examined her face with her hands. "Except my ribs ache, my fingers hurt, I've probably got two black eyes now, and we just lost any chance of getting to Mack in time."

Zoë touched her own face, which felt as though it had been slapped. "What do we do now?"

"Make sure the other guy is fine, too."

"I'm sorry, Moira." She put her hand on the other woman's arm.

Moira closed her eyes. "Me, too."

They walked over to the second car, a black Ford pickup, and Moira said, "I don't believe it." They both peered in the window of the pickup to see Mack, pinching the bridge of his bloody nose. As always, he kept his window open, and a fair amount of snow had gusted in, dusting his shoulders and hair. Moira gestured that Zoë should have the pleasure of interrogation.

"Mack, my God, what are you doing here?"

"Bleeding."

"Is your nose broken?"

"Probably." He looked thinner and younger and more miserable than just two weeks earlier, and his shirt looked as if he'd slept in it at least once. He smelled faintly musty, too, and Zoë was torn between relief and irritation and some other emotion that was slowly bubbling up from deeper inside.

"I thought you were going to Kingston to reenlist. Why won't you look me in the eye?"

"Because there are two of you, and I can barely handle one at the moment."

"Oh, Jesus, Moira, we have to call for EMTs."

"Don't you dare."

"Don't be stupid, of course I dare. Moira, call. Mack, how about I start by telling you the reason I was driving into a goddamn snowstorm was to stop you from throwing your life away."

Now Mack did look at her. "You were driving?"

"You were throwing your life away!"

He turned to his sister. "How'd she do?"

"Let me put it this way, she still needs your services." His sister leaned in closer and said, "Also, she loves you."

"The way you said that almost sounded Jewish," said Zoë.

Mack looked back at Zoë, his eyes slightly crossed. "Well, this is a hit in the head."

"That definitely sounded Jewish." Zoë opened the driver-side door and stroked the snow off his hair. "Mack, how could you just leave like that?"

"Had a little crisis of faith. But I was coming back. That's why I smashed into you. I was turning around in the driveway."

"But what took you so long? I thought you would have been way ahead?"

Mack shrugged, looking sheepish. "I stopped for a sandwich. And while I ate, I was rereading this." He held up a school anthology of poetry, and then indicated which page: Rilke's poem about Hermes, Orpheus, and Eurydice. "I got to the part where it says, 'She was already root,' and then I figured it out."

"Figured what?"

"She was already dead. At least, in her mind." Mack stopped pinching his nose, checked to make sure that no blood was still coming out, then looked at Zoë directly, his eyes now focused and clear. "It wasn't Orpheus's fault that Eurydice was lost. Even if he'd never looked back, even if he'd already brought her out and gotten her home and spent the next fifty years with her, she was already lost."

Zoë tried to understand what Mack was saying. She had an idea, and didn't think it boded well for their relationship. "Do you mean she already belonged someplace else?"

Mack shook his head, then winced. "No, I mean, she'd already signed off on life. She wasn't yearning for hubby anymore, she was longing to go back to deathsville. And that's what I've been doing, more or less." He smiled at his sister. "You nailed it, back at Thanksgiving. I mean, Bill did, when he repeated what you'd said about the way I was acting."

Moira gave a little huff of embarrassed laughter.

Zoë gave them a moment before asking her question. "What made you realize that you wanted to come back to the world of the living?"

"Fear."

Zoë tried not to show her surprise. She'd half been expecting some big romantic declaration, half been expecting to hear something that would spell the end of their affair. "What do you mean, fear?"

"For the first time, I was scared shitless to go back over there. And you know what? Fear's not always such a bad thing. I mean, some kinds of fear you have to fight to overcome, just like you said to Maya. But other kinds of fear, like the fear of getting blown up in a war that seems to be making less sense every day, well, maybe that's not the monster under the bed."

"Or maybe the monster isn't always a bad monster."

They paused for a moment, staring into each other's eyes. "So, you drove, huh?"

"I did. And you came back. Were you going to call me?"

"No." He reached for her hand. "I was going to come for you."

"That's good, because it looks like I'm stuck here for at least another year."

"Stuck, huh?"

She leaned in and kissed him, blood and all. "Maybe that's not exactly the right word."

Epilogue

W hen I said I missed walking, Mack, I meant to stores and people's homes. Not up a mountain."

"Quit complaining," said Mack, who was already two yards ahead of her. When she wasn't scrabbling for handholds, she was admiring her lover's rear view.

"Come on, Mommy," Maya yelled from farther up the trail. "We want to get to the top before noon."

"Couldn't we have waited until it was actually spring before attempting a vertical climb? There are still pockets of ice and snow."

"Are you kidding? It's a gorgeous April day, nearly sixty degrees." Mack held out his hand and helped Zoë over an icy patch. "All this is melting. And you've made it. We're almost at the top."

"Are we?" Zoë paused, opening her canteen and taking a drink. The truth was, it was a lovely day, and despite the fact that the ground was still crusted with frost in places, it was thick with mud in others, and almost all the trees were budded with green. Because the trees hadn't actually leafed up yet, she could see the town of Arcadia below, spread out in a patchwork of fields and houses, picturesque even in the soggy early spring, doubtless breathtaking in full flower. If only the developers could see this, she thought. So far, their little group had been successful in stopping any actual bulldozing, and there was a moratorium on any real decision making until the new town board, headed by Pete Grell's wife, had agreed on a zoning plan.

As editor of the *Register Herald*, Zoë had plenty of opportunity to speak with the new town supervisor, who was, in typical incestuous country fashion, also the former editor. As for Pete, Edna said he was doing much better after his stroke, and although he no longer drove, he did sit with his old boss in the driving school, complaining about Mack and weekenders and how city folks were changing the way things were done in the old town. Neither Moroney nor Mack had seen the inside of a jail, which was half fair, thought Zoë. And half fair was a lot better than you often got in this life.

"Nice view, huh?" Mack had come up behind her, resting his hands on her waist.

"Yeah." Zoë glanced up at Mack, and he leaned in to kiss her.

"Salty," he said.

"Sweaty."

"Will you guys get a move on?" Maya was standing atop a log, looking a little like Robin Hood with her hands on her hips. "As I recall, folks, we have a ton of people coming over for a Passover dinner tonight."

"Don't remind me," said Zoë, starting to climb again. Once she'd accepted that they were, in fact, going to be living in Arcadia for a while, she'd found herself gradually warming to the idea of making the ritual spring feast. In the past, she and Maya had gone to friends' houses for the holiday, and Zoë had grumbled about how she would rather just ignore the whole thing. But this year she realized that she wanted to celebrate the ancient festival of freedom and spring.

"Need a hand?" Mack was crouched on a rock, watching her with an amused glint in his eyes.

"No, I do not need any assistance. Just turn around and leave me alone or I will stop right here."

"You'll have a lot of hungry guests."

"I said, Turn around, Laughing Boy." With a salute, he obeyed.

Of course, she and Maya would be the only two actual Jews at the seder, but that was all right. The way Zoë interpreted it, they were all celebrating some form of emancipation.

Moira was looking forward to finalizing her divorce from Bill and getting ready to adopt a baby from China. Gretchen and Frances, who were now openly calling themselves a couple, were also considering having a child, and Skeeter had surprised everyone by falling in love with a Manhattan lawyer named Ursula who rode a vintage Harley. Bronwyn, on the other hand, had been unable to come to the seder. Brian, it seemed, was still working long hours and one of the twins had an ear infection.

As for Maya, she was loving school, enjoying books, and dreaming of a career training horses.

"Hurry up! You're almost there, Mom!"

Too out of breath to speak, Zoë just concentrated on not losing her footing on the loose stones. She reached up, grabbing the limb of a small sapling as a handhold, and then cursed as it broke off. She cursed again when she scraped her knee, but Mack and Maya were already at the top, out of earshot.

Brushing herself off, Zoë scrambled up the last rise and there she was, at the top of Amimi Mountain. She reached her arms over her head to stretch out her shoulders, and thought about how the spring was different in the country. In Manhattan, April was an occasion for light fabrics and alfresco lunches, and there was a gentle sense of general happiness at the change in the weather. But here, Zoë felt as though she had emerged from the long, dark tunnel of winter into light and warmth and the surging possibility of new things growing up all around.

Of course, she still wanted to get back to Manhattan. And Mack had sworn he would come with her next time, despite his uneasiness with crowds.

"So," said Maya, slipping beside her mother. "What do you think? Are you ready to climb the fire tower?" She indicated the rickety structure of open stairs that culminated in a tiny lookout.

"I'm not sure about that."

"Of course you are," said Mack. "You're going first. I have to write our names up there, remember?"

Zoë put her foot on the first step. "It doesn't look terribly safe."

"It is unless you plan on flinging yourself over the side."

"I don't like seeing that much air between my feet and the ground. What's my incentive for doing this again?"

Mack slipped something metallic into her hand. "Why, you get to drive home, of course."

Zoë didn't know whether or not she wanted to live in Arcadia forever, and even if Mack hinted at wanting to get married, she was too much of a cynic to trust that what they had would last for a lifetime. Still, learning to take pleasure in something that had previously been a source of frustration and anxiety made her a bit more optimistic.

Trying not to think about falling, she kept going up.

Acknowledgments

I owe a debt of gratitude (and a preemptive apology for any mistakes I made) to my research sources: Dominic Calabro of Factory Lane Automotive for helping me understand the finer parts (and some of the rusty ones) of automobilia; April Brown of Stanfordville Fire and Rescue for walking me through all the things a country medic needs to know; Sandy Charlap and Francine Borden of the Kildonan School for teaching me a new way of looking at reading, writing, and learning; and John Henry and Constanza Low for financial information. I am grateful to be working with the hard-working Atria team—Judith Curr, Isolde Sauer, Hannah Morrill, and special thanks to Greer Hendricks, my editor, for all her wisdom and support. Holly Harrison, I owe you big for catching my mistakes when you had fires of your own to put out. Jennifer Crusie, thanks for all the many kindnesses, and for the really good chocolate. As always, I am beholden to my husband, Mark, my kids, Matthew and Elinor, and my mother, Ziva, for putting up with the weirdness of a writer on deadline. And last but not least, a huge thanks to my agent, Meg Ruley, for all the tangible reasons, and the intangibles, too.